ALL *the* CHILDREN *are* HOME

ALSO BY PATRY FRANCIS

The Orphans of Race Point
The Liar's Diary

ALL *the* CHILDREN *are* HOME

a novel

Patry Francis

HARPER PERENNIAL

NEW YORK • LONDON • TORONTO • SYDNEY • NEW DELHI • AUCKLAND

HARPER ● PERENNIAL

HarperCollins books may be purchased for educational, business, or sales promotional use. For information, please email the Special Markets Department at SPsales@harpercollins.com.

FIRST EDITION

Designed by Jamie Lynn Kerner

Library of Congress Cataloging-in-Publication Data has been applied for.

ISBN 978-0-06-304545-3 (pbk.)
ISBN 978-0-06-306507-9 (library edition)

21 22 23 24 25 LSC 10 9 8 7 6 5 4 3 2 1

In memory of my granddaughter
Emma Drew Francis
forever loved and missed

ALL *the* CHILDREN *are* HOME

DAHLIA

I USED TO THINK THAT IF I JUST STAYED HOME I WOULD BE SAFE. SO WHEN the chance come, I struck a deal with a boy so homely and tongue-tied no one else would have him: I'd put some kind of supper on the table and sleep in his bed every night and he'd bring me jigsaws, and teetering stacks of books from the library and never ask me to leave the house again. Louie was just nineteen. And me—I was even younger, though I hadn't felt like a girl in a long time.

Then one night I woke up to a particular kind of lonesome, one that couldn't be answered by him or the people who kept company with me on the TV, or the ones that moved between my books and my head and sometimes deeper. It was the ache that wants a child, and no matter how I tried to shoo it out, it wouldn't leave.

That's when I found out there was no safe place. That even locked up in my six rooms, I'd never stopped traveling. And what's more, there was some kind of unseen direction to it all. What it was—and why—well, I wouldn't begin to understand that till the kids were practically grown. And most I don't expect to know in this lifetime.

But once I got a glimpse, everyone looked different. Louie and the boy my loneliness drug to the door and all the rest that followed. It was like there was a radiance to them. I only wish I'd seen it sooner. I only wish everyone could see it.

PART I

1959

CHAPTER ONE

A Place Called the Moscatellis

Agnes

THE DAY SHE CAME TO TAKE ME AWAY THE SKY WAS PURE WHITE. I sat on my crate by the window, wishing for snow so I could watch the kids next door play in it. Every time they opened up their mouths to taste it, I opened mine, too. It made me forget the bad thing I had done. But the snow never came, and neither did the kids.

I took out the secret box I hid in a corner of the attic, and I touched my presents one by one: a glass stone so clear the blue showed through when I held it up to the window, a broke whistle, a wishbone, and a tiny doll with hair the color of mine. I tried to open her eyes to see if they looked like me, too, but they were sewed shut forever.

When I heard Mrs. Dean calling my name on the stairs, I snapped my box shut and put it back in its hiding place. The door flung open.

"You better come down. Someone's here for you."

Someone? Was it the one who used to bring me presents? I didn't dare ask.

Downstairs, a lady I'd never seen before sat on the edge of the couch. She patted the spot next to her and made a face like a smile. "Hello, Aggie."

I stood in the middle of the room, looking at the floor till she got up and crouched beside me—so close I could smell the stuff she sprayed on herself when she got out of the tub. She was talking, too, but all I heard was Mrs. Dean's voice inside my head. *You touched my Jean Naté, didn't you? Don't lie to me!*

The lady said something about the 'vestigation, that word Mr. and Mrs. Dean had been saying every day. It made my bad hand ache worse. "I'm here to take you to a new home. Just temporarily. Do you know what that means?"

I studied the pink swirls in the carpet, trying not to think of the day I lied about the Jean Naté or the other thing I did. The worser one that started up the 'vestigation. Did she really expect me to answer?

"You'll be staying with the Moscatellis until we can find you a more permanent family."

The color of her coat reminded me of the tree outside my window when the daddy next door came home from work and the light poured through. I wanted to touch it, but I knew better.

Mrs. Dean had folded my clothes into a pile and packed them neatly into a paper sack with a red lollipop on top. It was the first sweet she'd ever given me. When she held out the bag, I closed my eyes and dreamed the word *no*.

"See what she's like?" she told the lady in the summer-green coat, pressing the bag into her hands. "Good luck to the next family if they think they can do better."

The lady must have heard my secret *no* because when we were leaving, she set the brown bag on the floor just inside the door. "How about we leave all that right here, Aggie? What do you say?"

I squinted at the lollipop and her pink mouth talking to me and the white day outside and nodded. Then I stopped and pointed at the attic stairs until she understood.

"Is there something up there you want to bring with you? Something of yours?"

Mrs. Dean was still listening from the living room. "Everything she owns is in that bag. She's got nothing of her own."

But when I didn't move, she let me go upstairs to look. "Long as she doesn't try to steal something on the way out."

She made Nancy let her see my secret box after we came down.

"Where on earth did this junk come from?" Her face knotted up like it did when she was going to tell Mr. Dean on me. Only he wasn't home. Finally, she shrugged and handed it back. "Belongs in the trash if you ask me."

AT THAT POINT, everything I knew about myself came from the Deans:

Mr. Dean was the first one to tell me I was an Indian. "See those people getting their asses kicked?" he said, pointing at his TV when I came downstairs to pee. "Well, that's you." Since I didn't know anyone else who looked like that, I was pretty sure I was the last one left. Me and the one who gave me my presents. Only I hadn't seen her for so long I was pretty sure the people in Mr. Dean's TV got her, too.

Yourmother, they called her, like she was something bad and I was the one who did it. Yourmother was a whore who didn't care two shits about me and I was going to turn out just like her. A dope fiend, too. *You know what that is, Agnes?*

That's when I learned you don't have to know what words mean to understand them. I nodded at Mr. Dean. Yes, I knew.

I didn't grow right or talk right or look right, but it didn't matter because nobody would ever want to talk to me or look at me anyway.

My father was no one. No one didn't know I existed and if he ever found out, he'd either piss on me or strangle me. One or the other. If it was him, Mr. Dean said he'd choose door number two. That always made him laugh.

Something called the asthma lived in my chest. It slept for weeks, but if I caught a cold or tried to run or got scared, it squeezed until I couldn't breathe. I stopped running, and I gave up being scared, too—at least most of the time. But sometimes the asthma went right ahead and attacked anyway. Then they took me to the hospital where

I slept in a tent and ladies who thought my name was Honey gave me medicine. I learned my colors from their Jell-O. Green was the best. After I went back to the Deans, I tasted it in my mouth every night before I fell asleep. Green. It wasn't just the best color; it was the best anything.

I didn't tell anyone my name wasn't Honey and it wasn't Agnes, either. It was Agnés. When I spoke it to myself, it sounded like the whispery noise the trees make when they talk to each other. *Ahhhn-yess.*

Mine was never the story of all that, though. Not the room with the window where I lived at the Deans' house or the paper bag with the red lollipop on top I tried to leave behind or all the ways it found to follow me.

No, mine was the story of the river. I had never seen it or heard its name, but it was the only thing that never abandoned me. When I sat on my crate and watched the kids next door, it ran and leaped. When I kept quiet so I wouldn't wake Mr. Dean or scare the asthma, it sang in the dark; and when I thought I was all alone, it reached out and stroked my face.

Everything will be all right, the river said, and somehow I believed it. I always believed it.

CHAPTER TWO

The Dangling Button

ZAIDIE

I PEERED THROUGH THE CURTAIN AT THE PAIR COMING UP THE walkway. "They're here!" Ma kept her eyes on the TV as if she didn't hear me.

The first thing I noticed was the solitary button hanging by a thread from the kid's corduroy jacket. It was a boy's coat like the one Jon wore in the spring, though hers was at least two sizes too small. She was holding on to a cigar box as if she expected someone to take it away.

"It's a colored kid, Ma."

After rousing herself from what Jimmy called her headquarters, Ma snuck a look out the side window. "Dear Lord."

The last time we took in a colored, Jimmy had to beat the tar out of Mark Zarella for calling him a bad name. Not that Jimmy didn't use the word himself sometimes—just not about our kids.

Ma held the handle of the inside storm door and talked through the glass like she still hadn't decided whether she was going to let them in or not.

"Two weeks, Nancy," she said. "Tops."

"Good afternoon to you, too, Mrs. Moscatelli."

When the theme for *The Edge of Night* came on the TV, Ma's eyes

turned toward the sound. At that point, no one was paying any attention to the kid with the dangling button. Her expression was blank, as
if it didn't matter where she went. I'd seen that look before.

Ma gave her a once-over the way she might examine a roast in
Edward's Market and turned back to the case worker. "You said she
was six."

"It's freezing out here. You gonna let us in or what?" Nancy exaggerated a shiver.

"Damn right it's cold, and that sorry excuse for a jacket wouldn't
keep a doll warm. Where's her stuff?"

"Don't worry. I already requisitioned the department. In the
meantime, I thought you might have some of the kids' old clothes
around."

"Oh, that's what you thought, huh?" Reluctantly, Ma opened the
storm door and allowed the two to enter.

"You told me she was six," Ma repeated. "A six-year-old white
girl. Like I don't catch enough guff from the neighbors already?"

Nancy dropped the file she was carrying on the card table where
Ma did her jigsaws, disrupting the yellow sun she'd worked on all
morning, and helped Agnes out of her skimpy jacket.

"Look at that beautiful hair," Nancy said. "We're guessing her
father might be Italian."

"And he might be the Pope, too." Ma shook her head. "Louie's not
gonna like this."

By then, the boys were flanking Ma and me. They stared down
the Emergency like an opposing army.

Jimmy swept back a wing of brown hair with the flat of his hand.
At thirteen, he was beginning to suspect he might be handsome, but
he wasn't sure. "And you said we were done taking in Emergencies,
Ma." He smirked at me. "At least this one won't be sleeping in my
room."

"Louie's not gonna like this at all," Ma repeated. It wasn't clear whether she was speaking to Nancy, to the girl with the dangling button, or to herself.

Jon, who was in his mimicking phase, removed his thumb from his mouth and shook his head. "Louie not gonna like this."

Jimmy sauntered over to Ma's table and flipped open the folder. "Agnes Josephine Juniper," he read. "Sounds like someone's grandma. And look, she really is six, Ma. It says right here. Date of birth: April 4, 1953. Are you a midget, kid?"

Fortunately, the girl with the dangling button was as oblivious to my brother's insults as she was to everything else. Was she deaf?

Instead of punishing Jimmy like she would have done to me, Ma lifted her eyebrows in Nancy's direction. "Well?"

"There have been some growth issues, but she's not going to be here long enough for you to worry about it." The dismissive flip of Nancy's hand indicated that Agnes's size was the tip of the iceberg.

"Do you want to see my Ginny doll?" I said in a voice loud enough to drown out Ma's reluctance, my brothers' mockery, and the case worker's weariness. I attempted to take a hand the kid was holding behind her back, but she winced and pulled away. That's when I noticed the cast.

"Sorry," I stammered. And then to Ma: "I—I didn't know she was hurt."

"Another thing no one bothered to tell us." Ma glared at Nancy.

"We're looking at ten days here; I promise. Aggie here's had a rough time of it and you're the best home I've got."

Ma drew her mouth into a straight line, irritated by the obvious flattery. "So you're giving me a colored kid who doesn't have a coat or a pair of mittens to her name. Now I hear she's got stunted growth and a broken hand—and God knows what else."

"Not colored. Indian."

"In this neighborhood, she's colored. And even if I had the time to run back and forth to doctors, we've only got the one car."

Nancy's eyes flickered over the room, taking in the toys that were scattered everywhere, a bowl of unfinished Cheerios Jon had left on the coffee table that morning, and the rug that hadn't been vacuumed in weeks, as if to ask what exactly kept my mother so busy. Finally the case worker's gaze settled on Ma's headquarters: a ratty armchair, a card table for her jigsaws, the small TV with foil-lined rabbit ears, and a staggering pile of books on the floor. Reader's Digest Condensed books mixed with the ones she made Jimmy bring home from the library. *Raise Your Child's IQ with Classical Music, How to Stop Thumb Sucking,* and the dog-eared *Start Planning for College Now.*

Research for a doctor degree in useless information, Dad called them.

Ma opened her eyes wide the way she did when anyone implied she was a less than perfect housekeeper: *Go ahead and say it.*

Like everyone else who was the recipient of that look, Nancy thought the better of it. "By the time her next appointment comes up, she'll be with her new family—speaking of which, I'm due for the home visit in about—" She consulted a rhinestone watch I had been envying since her last visit. "Gosh! Fifteen minutes ago. How about I give you a buzz tomorrow and see how she's settling in?"

Again, Ma glanced wistfully at the TV set where two of her favorite characters were kissing on the screen. I always thought the only reason she allowed Agnes to stay was because she didn't want to miss her soap.

Almost as a second thought, Nancy turned to the child. "You be a good girl, okay, Aggie? Don't give Mrs. Moscatelli any trouble." She didn't appear to expect an answer.

"Agnés," the kid corrected her matter-of-factly. It was the first word she'd spoken since she arrived. Everyone, including Nancy, was stunned.

"At least she's not mute," Ma said.

"No, just retarded. Kid can't even say her own name right." Jimmy looked at the Emergency like a steer at the fair. "A retarded midget."

"A retarded midget," Jon parroted, nodding.

"And you told me her name was Agnes. A six-year-old Italian named Agnes," Ma said. "Hmph."

"Agnés is the French pronunciation. Maybe from her father's side," Nancy said hopefully. "*Parlez-vous Francais*, Agnés?"

Ma scowled. "If she stays here, she's going to be Agnes—and she damn well better speak English."

The girl skimmed our faces with her dark eyes but said nothing in either language. Finally, her gaze settled on me. "Agnes go pee."

No one seemed impressed that she knew enough to accommodate Ma. "It's down here." I cocked my head in the direction of the bathroom.

"The house doesn't usually look like this," I explained as she followed me through the rooms. "Ma hasn't been feeling too good lately so she hasn't been able to clean much." It was what I always said when I brought a friend home.

Agnes, however, seemed as unimpressed by my excuse as she was by the chaos. Maybe Jimmy was right about her intelligence. He should have said *slow*, though. That was only polite.

I tried to give her some privacy in the bathroom, but she reached for me with her good hand and pulled me inside. Then she insisted on leaving the door open.

While she sat on the toilet, I stood in front of the mirror, pretending to readjust my barrettes. She kept her box on her lap even while she peed.

I could hear Ma talking in a voice somewhere between serious and angry. "Two weeks better not turn into three months like it did last time. Louie won't have it."

Agnes looked at me quizzically as she pulled up her pants. Apparently, no one had ever taught her to wipe herself.

"Louie's our dad," I explained. "He might look mad when he first sees you, but he's really not. He just acts that way."

While the negotiations continued in the foyer, I opened the medicine chest, took out Dad's shaving cream, squirted a perfect ball of foam into my hand, and with one finger, wrote my name on the mirror. I stood up particularly straight as I pointed like Miss Robarge at the blackboard.

"That's me: Z-A-I-D-A. But you can call me Zaidie."

When it was obvious that she didn't recognize the letters, I erased my name with a face cloth, taking care to clear away every trace. "Don't you go to school?"

She gave me her opaque stare.

I looked down at her shoes, a faded pair of pink Keds with a hole in the big toe of each.

"When Dad gets paid, we'll go to downtown and buy you some new ones at Taymor's. And socks. A coat. And . . . and . . . do you have any barrettes?"

I unclasped the plastic shamrocks on each side of my head and attempted to clip them onto her hair, but it was too thick and tangled to hold. "Don't worry. We'll get you some bigger ones."

Agnes fastened one onto the top layer of her hair and returned the other one to me. "You have that one; Agnes have this one."

BY THE TIME we returned to the living room, Nancy was gone and Jimmy had taken off on his bike as he did every afternoon, even in the winter. Sometimes he rode to his friend Kevin's or Bruce's, but the days he liked best were the ones he just traveled.

"Like I own this town," he said. And when I saw him pedaling up the hill, the hair he spent far too much time combing loosed by the wind, an enraptured expression on his face, I understood.

In her own way, Ma was traveling, too, absorbed in the love scene on her show, still sipping that morning's cold coffee. At her feet, Jon played with his train, speaking in alternating voices as he imagined himself conductor, passenger, and crew. A Maxwell House commercial came on the TV. It was so familiar that I hardly heard it, but Agnes stopped and listened in wonderment to the tune played by the percolating coffee pot on the screen.

"Good to last drop," she said after the announcer.

Jon glanced up at her, seeing a potential playmate for the first time. "That coffee is good to the last drop," he repeated in his conductor voice.

"Why don't you show Agnes where she's going to sleep?" Ma suggested, without looking up from the jigsaw she worked on during the commercials.

Agnes, however, had wandered from the TV to the picture window, where all her attention was focused on the street.

She didn't hear me when I attempted to call her away. Nor was she aware when Jon again asked what was wrong with her. Only touch broke the spell, causing her to jump.

"Mr. Dean come there," she said, pointing into the deserted street.

Though I didn't know who Mr. Dean was, her fear surged through the room, a force so powerful that Jon looked up from his train and Ma even forgot the couple who were kissing on the screen.

I put my arm over Agnes's shoulder and led her away from the window. "No one's coming here, Agnes. And if they try . . . If they try—Dad will call the cops. And Jimmy . . ."

"Will beat him up like the Lone Ranger; that's what he'll do." Jon jumped up to shadowbox with Agnes's bogeyman. "Jimmy and me, too."

But Agnes heard nothing. Drawn back to the window, she repeated the dark litany we would all learn by heart in the next few weeks.

"Mr. Dean come. He come in his yellow car. That road. Mr. Dean drive his car right down there. Mr. Dean come for Agnes and he find her, too."

At this point, she pivoted in the direction of the foyer, pointing at something that terrified us all even though we couldn't see it.

"That door."

CHAPTER THREE

Franco-American Spaghetti

AGNES

THAT AFTERNOON THE GIRL WITH THE GREEN BARRETTE TOOK me to her room and pointed at the bed across from the window. "You sleep here, okay?"

I didn't know the answer so I kept quiet.

Then she looked at my box like she was wondering what was in it and why I wouldn't set it down so I shook it at her, making my secrets rattle. "These my presents. Only no one can see but me." I repeated her word: "Okay?"

"Okay."

After that, she stared at me the same way she had looked at the box before. Like maybe there was something secret inside me, too.

She swung open the closet door, where her clothes hung on hangers. "You can hide your, um, presents in the back under the shoe box if you want. No one will know they're there."

"You?"

"I won't look. I promise. Do you want to go outside?"

She started for the stairs while I hid my secret box in the closet.

Downstairs, the girl tied a knit hat under my chin and gave me a single mitten with a hole in the thumb for my good hand. "All our mittens have holes," the boy explained. "Cause of Princie. Right,

Zaidie?" The kids led me away from the window and toward the backyard, but the lady stopped me at the door, scowling at my pink Keds.

"Couldn't you find her any boots?" she said to everyone but me. "Well then, she'll have to stay in. Can't have her catching pneumonia on top of everything else."

"Please, Ma," the girl pleaded. "Just an hour. I promise to bring her in if she gets cold."

The lady turned back to her chair. "A half hour and not a minute longer."

"Once she starts working on her puzzle, she'll forget us till supper," the girl whispered as we headed into the frozen yard.

I had a lot of practice watching kids play from my window in the attic, but this time the kids watched back. They watched me and said my name, too. Especially the girl said it. Zaidie. I spoke hers inside my head at first, then I whispered it, and finally, I said it right out loud. "Zaidie!" A name as pretty as the color green.

"Look, Agnes." she laughed, exhaling a smoky plume of air. "I can see my breath!"

"That's cause it's really, really cold out," the boy whined. "I wanna go in."

"Agnes has holes in her shoes and you don't hear her crying about it, do you? Stop being a baby!"

I touched the skin of my face. Cold. Exhaling my own ghost breath, I walked across the yard. The ice crackled beneath my pneumonia shoes. "Cold." I repeated it the way I had Zaidie's name. Zaidie laughed again. "It's winter, Agnes. Of course it's cold."

"I wanna go in," the boy said.

When some other kids came into the yard to play, I went back to the steps and watched as they chased each other around the yard to keep warm. I had seen the kids next door play that game from the Deans' window.

"You got another new kid," one of them said.

"Yes, a midget—" the boy began before Zaidie stamped on his foot.

"Sorry," she told him sweetly when he began to howl.

"Maaa," he yelled in the direction of the house. Then he turned back to Zaidie. "What do you care anyway? It's not like she's staying."

Another boy about his size gaped at me. "Can she talk?"

"Just Martian words. Right, Agnes?"

Not knowing the answer, I folded my knees to my chest to warm myself inside the oversized jacket they had dug out of the closet. My toe, peeking through the hole in my sneaker, was numb, even though I was wearing Zaidie's socks.

"Shut up, Jon." From the yard, Zaidie narrated the action for me, announcing the important words by raising her voice. "This is freeze tag cause when someone tags you, you do this. See?"

"Now we're gonna play Red Light/Green Light. Watch," the boy chimed in. "Have you ever played that?"

I followed them with my eyes. As gray light began to seep through the trees and hedges, the neighborhood kids were called home one by one. *Jeffrey! Lucy and Joe! Theresa Marie! Su-pperr!*

My stomach lurched as I imagined Mr. Dean's voice coming through those trees.

Didn't I tell you I would find you? You can't hide from me, Agnes.

When the neighborhood kids were all gone, Zaidie picked up a stick and hurled it at the dog. The boy, who had already started inside, turned back and joined the game.

"That's Princie," he told me through blue lips. "If you want to pet her, you have to ask me first cause she's my dog."

"She's the family dog and you know it, Jon," Zaidie said.

"No, sir. We got her on my birthday so that makes her mine."

"Yeah, and he insisted on naming her Prince—even though she's a girl. Is that dumb or what?"

"Princie likes the name, right, girl?" When Princie barked, they laughed.

Both of them noticed the open gate the same time the dog did. "Stop her!" the boy cried.

"Princie! Don't even think—"

But it was too late. The dog surged toward freedom, tongue and tail flying joyfully, energized by their orders to stay.

Just then Ma stepped out onto the back porch wearing the same scowl that crossed her face when she had looked at my pink shoes. The kids immediately turned on one another.

"If Zaidie went inside when I told her I was cold, Princie never would have got out."

"Shut up, Jon. It was your stupid friend who—"

"My dog's gonna end up in the pound and get put asleep all cause of you."

But something else was on Ma's mind as she scanned the yard. "Jimmy's not back yet?"

Zaidie put a finger to her lips, but it was too late.

"Smoking cigarettes; that's where he is," the boy sang out, relieved that Ma was too preoccupied to notice the open gate. "Right there in the garage."

Hearing his name, Jimmy stepped into the gray light. "My bike got another flat in front of the O'Connors' house. I think Crazy Joe's dropping nails in the street on purpose." He held up his grease-stained hands in evidence.

"I told you to stay away from that street, didn't I? The kid's a menace," Ma said before turning to the small boy. "And what did I say about lying?"

I waited for the boy to give her a whiny *Shut up* like he did to everyone else, but he just folded his arms and clamped his jaw into a pout.

"Jimmy's the favorite," Zaidie whispered when Ma went to check the stove. "Because he came before all of us."

Jimmy opened his mouth and flaunted the piece of white candy between his teeth. "That means Ma always believes me. And even if she doesn't, I never get in trouble. Keep that in mind if you ever get the idea to rat me out."

He took out a roll of candy and handed a piece to Zaidie and me.

"Peppermint Life Savers," she explained. "So Ma and Dad won't smell the cigarettes. If you keep Jimmy's secrets, you get one. And if not—"

"Shut up, Zaidie. I didn't mean to tell." The small boy tripped over Princie's stick as he hurried to catch up with his brother. "Are you mad at me, Jimmy?"

"No one likes a squealer, pal—not even Ma."

The small boy's face turned deep red as if he was about to cry, which immediately softened the favorite.

"Aw, come on, buddy. You know I never get mad at you. But next time Ma asks about me when I'm in the garage, what are you gonna do?"

They both ran their finger over their lips like a zipper in what was obviously a well-rehearsed routine. Then Jimmy hoisted the small boy onto his back and carried him into the house.

Inside, the small boy led me into the bathroom. "You wash your hands like this, see?" He pointed at the two bars on the soap dish. "Just don't use the stinky green one. That's Dad's on account of his hands get really dirty at the garage. Right, Jimmy?" he called into the hallway.

"Stinky," I repeated, which made him laugh for some reason.

When I sat in my window at the Deans', I used to see the kids laughing like that in the yard next door, and sometimes I laughed with them even if I didn't know why. This time, I did the same.

I followed Zaidie and the boys through the kitchen into the dining room. The dishes didn't match and there were paper towels beside each plate instead of pretty blue napkins like Mrs. Dean used, but otherwise I recognized the way the table was set in my old house. I lowered my head and started toward the room Zaidie had shown me, pausing only to check for the yellow car in the picture window.

"Where are you going, Agnes?" she called, saying my name extra loud. In case I had forgotten it, I guess. "You sit here. Beside me."

I shook my head quickly. "Agnes go to room."

"In this house, you sit where you're told," a man said. I watched his Adam's apple move in and out as he gulped a glass of water. "And there's no food in the bedrooms."

I had been so determined to escape that my eyes had refused to see him sitting right there at the table. Now I was overwhelmed with his presence, the weight of it, the smell of the stinky soap—Fels-Naptha, Zaidie called it—and something else. It took a minute before I realized it was gasoline, like the kind Mr. Dean kept in a red can in his garage. *Stay away from that*, Mrs. Dean snapped when I stopped to inhale the odor before climbing into the car. I sat at the table beside Zaidie as I was told.

"Zaidie let the dog loose," Jon said, as he took his own seat.

When Dad ignored him, Zaidie stuck out her tongue triumphantly. "Remember what I told you?" she whispered to me. "Dad looks mean, but if you're going to the store, he'll give you a nickel."

The store? A nickel? I squinted at the new world I had entered.

"For candy. A nickel will get you this many pieces," the small boy added, holding up his fingers. "Zaidie let the dog loose," he repeated.

"I did not. It was Jon's friend Jeffrey."

As the man took another long drink of water, I studied his oversized hands. What was the difference between being mean and just pretending? I wanted to ask. But mostly, I just wanted to go to the room Zaidie had showed me. Even though I didn't have to pee, I had that feeling like I might do it anyway.

"Did you see the new kid, Dad? She's a midget from another planet," the small boy announced when he got no reaction about the dog. "Right, Jimmy?"

Dad grunted while Ma moved around the table, spooning a glob of orange-colored noodles onto each plate. To me, she was a shadow—always present, but less real than everything around her.

"Do you like Franco-American?" Zaidie asked, speaking louder when she said words she thought I might not know. She passed me a slice of bread and rolled a corner of her own piece into a little dough ball. "Sunbeam—my favorite."

After the shadow shot her a look, she opened her eyes wide. "I'm just showing Agnes how I like to eat bread; I swear, Ma."

It was too late, though. When the shadow returned to the kitchen, Jimmy pitched his own doughy ball across the table at Zaidie. A minute later, the small boy hit me between the eyes with a bread pellet.

"Jimmy!" the shadow hissed as she moved around the table, pouring milk into every glass but the man's. "For goodness sake; you're supposed to be setting an example around here."

"An example," the small boy repeated.

"Yeah, Jimmy's teaching us how to be juvenile delinquents," Zaidie said.

Ma looked at her sharply. "Zaida. For goodness sake."

In the course of the meal, the names looped around the table so often that I would recite them in my sleep that night the way I used to say the word *green*.

Jimmy.

Zaidie who was sometimes called Zaida. Jon who was also named *buddy* and *pal*. Ma.

There was Dad, too, but I was still afraid to look at him.

"All I can say is Nancy better come up with that placement in two weeks or she'll find a kid parked at her door," Ma said.

Mrs. Dean talked in that voice when she was trying to stop Mr. Dean from turning mad. But Louie pretended not to hear her just the way he had when Jon told him I was from outer space.

While they talked, the kids ate quickly—bread slathered in yellow grease and squishy noodles followed by large gulps of milk. They argued about whose turn it was to wash the dishes, who had thrown the first dough ball or forgotten to bring the dog in.

"I don't care who did it," the shadow interrupted. "You're all going out to look for her after supper. God knows what she's already dropped on the porch."

"Princie's the best thief in Claxton; right, Jimmy?" Jon said with obvious pride.

"The Robin Hood of dogs. Toys. Cat dishes. Shoes. You name it; she's brought it home. If you don't watch out, she'll snag the hat right off your head." Jimmy reached over and lifted an invisible cap from my head. I could still feel his touch when I put my hand on my hair.

"Her favorite thing is to rip down the clothes from people's clothesline," Zaidie added. "The nicer the better. Remember when she got Jeffrey's mother's white dress and dragged it down the street through the mud?"

"Man, was she proud of herself that day. Till Mrs. Beales pulled a switch from her tree and whooped her," Jimmy said. "Dad pretended to beat her, too—just to make the neighbors happy, but he mostly just hit the ground."

Dad grunted. Aside from the sound of his fork scraping the plate, it was the first I'd heard from him since he told me what we do in this house.

"You think that scared Princie? Never. Next day she did the same thing to the Correias' morning glories," the small boy added.

Zaidie giggled. "Tore 'em down and paraded through the street like it was the Olympic torch. Remember that, Jimmy?"

My eyes shifted from one face to the other as they passed stories back and forth the way they had hurled dough balls. "It's not funny," Ma insisted after each one, but they snickered anyway.

Jimmy was the first to notice I hadn't eaten anything. "What's the matter, kid? People don't need food on your planet?"

Dad, who had yet to look at me, shot a dark glance at my plate. "In this house, you eat what's in front of you. It ain't Howard Johnson's."

I wondered if he prefaced everything he said with the words *in this house* just like the small boy ended every sentence with *right, Jimmy?*

As all eyes focused on the uneaten noodles on my plate, Zaidie leaned in close and put her hand on my knee. "What's the matter? Aren't you hungry, Agnes?"

Jon waggled a finger at me. "No Chips Ahoy if you don't eat your spaghetti. All of it, right, Jimmy?"

Didn't Mr. Dean or the lady in the green coat tell them I wasn't supposed to sit at people's tables? And I wasn't supposed to touch their silver forks, either.

"Agnés go pee," I whispered, forgetting I wasn't supposed to call myself that. My mouth watered from the sweet smell of the food. When they all continued to watch me, I was sure I was going to pee right there. I shivered like the boy had when he was cold in the yard. Jon.

For the first time, Dad stopped eating and looked directly at me. "You sit right there till you finish. And why are you saying your name like that?"

"It's French," Ma put in. "Must be a little Canuck in her somewhere."

"Well, in this house, we talk American. You hear that, Agg-nes?" He turned to the shadow. "What the hell's a kid like that doing in Claxton anyway?"

Jon appraised me with four-year-old frankness. "What kind of kid is she, Jimmy?" No one answered, but I knew. I was the kind from TV.

The shadow cocked her head in the direction of the bandaged hand resting on the table for Dad's benefit, but the kids saw, too. "All I know, Lou, is they had to get her out of the last home fast."

"What's wrong with her?" Jon persisted.

"Be quiet, Jon." Zaidie kicked him under the table as she returned her hand to my knee.

I pushed her away. If I thought about the cast or the hand throbbing inside it, Mr. Dean's face would rise before me more clear than it already was. And I would remember the bad thing I did. Worser than touching Mrs. Dean's Jean Naté. His voice, too. *You wanna piss on the floor like a filthy animal? In my house? Answer me, Agnes!*

Inside, I had tried to say no as loud as I could. No, I didn't want to be a filthy animal. I didn't want to be a dirty whore like yourmother. No. Inside I wanted to tell him how I'd taken my stick and knocked on the floor of the attic the way I was supposed to when I needed to pee, but him and Mrs. Dean were yelling so loud no one heard me.

If I came down without permission, if I interrupted, Mr. Dean would get so mad he'd scare the asthma. But I had to pee. I had to pee and I couldn't wait anymore. I knocked a little harder and then harder than that. I banged my stick on the floor till my insides ached and I felt oily water oozing down my cheeks and then, with horror, but relief, too, a burning stream of yellow leaked down my legs onto the floor.

As soon as I saw Mr. Dean coming through the door, I knew he had been drinking from the glass with the gold letter on it the way he did before he yelled at Mrs. Dean. Long before I learned my blues and greens, I knew the color of mean and his face was dark with it.

Jesus Christ, Agnes, what's the racket up here? he said. Then he took in the stain on my pants, and he stopped in the middle of the room. His hands rested on his hips the way they did and his eyes were narrowed to a little black spark and the mean color got meaner. That's when he saw the hammer he'd left behind when he came up to fix a loosened floorboard. *You wanna piss on the floor like a filthy animal in my house? Is that what you wanna do?*

I squeezed my eyes hard to make Mr. Dean go away, and when I opened them, I was stunned by the messy table and the faces around it, a dog barking in the distance—Princie, the greatest thief in the world—but above all, by the smell of the canned spaghetti.

Dizzy with hunger, nauseous with it, I fisted the Franco-American and swallowed it in one clump. Then I shoved the Sunbeam into my mouth before anyone could take it away. I was licking grease and the color orange from my fingers when I realized that all the arguing and laughing and eating at the table had stopped; even the sounds outside the house stilled as the family stared at me.

The dog barked again, as if to restart the world, and they all spoke at the same time.

"Wow." Jimmy sounded as if I'd done something as impressive as tearing down the neighbor's morning glories and parading them through the street.

"Is that how people eat where she comes from?" Jon cast a quick glance at his brother before returning to me.

Zaidie's hand hovered protectively close, but she had already learned not to touch me. "Leave her alone, all of you. Just leave her alone."

But Ma's face rose above the others. It was as if she was seeing me for the first time. Or maybe it was the first time anyone had seen me. And I was seeing her, too. No longer a shadow. Her.

"Someone get her a cookie," Louie said.

CHAPTER FOUR

Shamrock Barrettes

ZAIDIE

THE TROUBLE WITH EMERGENCIES WAS THAT SOMETIMES THEY stayed so long we started to think they really belonged to us. A month, three weeks, and six days after Agnes arrived, we heard the ominous click of Nancy's heels coming up the walkway. I touched the shamrock barrette I'd been wearing ever since the day I'd pinned its match onto Agnes's hair and prayed to the man whose picture hung on the wall. *Please don't let her take my little sister away,* I told Nonna's Pope.

Since Agnes came, the most commonly used word in my vocabulary was *See?*

Every time I said it, I saw more myself.

This is hot cocoa. You stir it up and add marshmallows, and then you drink it.

See?

When the clock says seven on Sunday night, it's time for Lassie. *My favorite show. It's about a dog.*

Can you tell time? Do you know what a clock is?

Have you ever watched TV? With Agnes, I took nothing for granted.

Look, this is how you turn it on. Do you want to try? Like this. See?

Agnes watched silently, but the next day Ma caught her switching the knob on and off, her eyes opening wide every time the images on the screen appeared.

"Where Lassie? Agnes want to see Lassie," she said, which made everyone laugh—including Agnes herself.

"I. I want to see Lassie. When you're talking about yourself, that's what you say, see?" I thumped my chest.

Agnes, giggling, did the same. "I. I. *I!*"

"Jon's going to Jeffrey's birthday party today," I told her one Saturday. "This is the present. Ma wrapped it up to make it look pretty." (I grimaced as I looked at the lumpish gift.) "You're supposed to put a ribbon on it and a boy's present shouldn't have ballerina paper, but Ma ran out of money. See? When it's your birthday, you get a cake with candles and everyone sings to you."

"Candles?" she repeated.

"Yes. Um, little sticks with fire on them. You blow like this."

Agnes blinked as if she could see the tiny fires winking out one by one.

"Then your friends give you presents and everyone tries to pin the tail on a donkey."

"A donkey?" She shook her head vigorously. "Agnes not stick no donkey."

"Not a real donkey, silly," I said, laughing. "A paper one you tape on the wall. Like this. See?"

"You think we torture live donkeys for fun, kid?" Jimmy said, looking up from his comic book. "I told you she was from another planet."

But he, too, had gotten into the act. "This is bubble gum. Bazooka. First you look at the comic, then you chew. Like this. Don't swallow it, though, or they'll have to cut your stomach open with a knife." He picked up a stick and pretended to operate. "If you do that, I'm not responsible."

Agnes chewed her gum so solemnly we all laughed. "Agnes do it right like Jimmy say. See?"

"I. I do it right," I said. "I. I. *I*."

When she smiled, we all did, too. It was just that kind of smile.

WITHIN THE FIRST week, Jimmy had taught her to blow bubbles and throw a ball with her good hand. She chucked it so hard we didn't find that ball till spring. And with every new accomplishment, she laughed the way she had the first day she played in the snow. Like no one on earth had ever done it before.

Even Jon had picked up my new favorite word. "These are my toy men. The green ones are cowboys; they're good ones. And the red ones are Indians. They're bad. See?"

Jimmy was at the card table helping Ma put together Big Ben. "Jeez, Jonny, can't you see who you're talking to?" He inserted a piece of the clock Ma had been looking for all week. "She probably doesn't even know what an Indian is anyway; do you, kid?"

"Do too know," she said, leaping up from the couch the way she did when she was eager to demonstrate her knowledge. She picked up one of the red plastic figures. "These the bad ones. See?"

Ma removed her glasses the way she did when she wanted to see in a different way. "Who on earth told you that—Mr. Dean?"

Agnes glanced briefly toward the picture window and then plopped back down on the couch. "What time Lassie come on?" There was no mistaking the shadow that crossed her face.

Ma tried to return to Big Ben, but her eyes kept drifting to the picture window, as if she, too, were seeing the yellow station wagon that haunted Agnes. "I never met your Mr. Dean, but I know his type and let me tell you this. Every word they say is a lie, Agnes. Every single word."

"Every. Single. Word," Jon repeated, shaking one of his toy Indians. "See?"

AS THE WEEKS passed and Agnes settled in, Ma reminded her of her temporary status almost daily. Sometimes, to make the point, she pretended to dial the department. We knew she was faking because she always spoke in an extra-loud voice.

"Well, hello, Nancy. What? You've found a family for Agnes? A week, you say? Yes, I'll make sure she's ready. Did you hear that, Agnes?" she'd say cheerily, after she'd hung up the phone. "It's good news."

Agnes put her jacket on and went into the backyard to toss the stick to Princie.

Even though we'd been through it countless times, we were always stunned when the call really came. Nancy would be here to pick up Agnes Thursday morning at nine. "A nice family named the Dohertys," Ma gushed. "And they have a little girl right around your age so you'll have a friend—just like Zaidie. Isn't that wonderful, Agnes?"

"This Thursday?" My voice was so small I was surprised anyone could hear me.

"Don't make this any harder than it already is, Zaida," Ma warned as Agnes headed for the backyard again.

IT WASN'T UNTIL Wednesday night that Agnes acknowledged what she'd been told. "I not go to that house," she said, crawling into my bed when she thought I was asleep. "Not going," she corrected herself.

While I breathed quietly beside her, she allowed her claim to grow louder and more emphatic until it filled the room: "I staying here. This house. Miss Holdsman's class. Zaidie's bed. I staying right here."

I didn't even bother to remind her that she'd forgotten *am*.

THE NEXT MORNING she had been up and dressed for school as if it was an ordinary day. Ma had made Bisquick pancakes. It was supposed to be a treat, but Jimmy called it the "kiss of death breakfast" because she always served it to kids on their last morning.

When she saw that Agnes had dressed for school, she held the spatula aloft, as if poised for battle.

"This is the big day, Agnes! Did you see the bag I packed for you?"

Agnes poured more syrup on her pancakes. "Sorry, can't go today, Ma."

Ma turned around. Again, the spatula was in the air. This time, though, it looked like a shield. "What did you say? Of course—"

"Can't," she repeated, cutting her pancakes into neat squares the way I'd taught her to do.

"What do you mean you can't? Your case worker's coming whether—"

"Miss Holdsman teaching letter Z today," she said, as if it were obvious. "Z for Zaidie."

Ma returned to the stove and flipped the last batch of pancakes.

By then Agnes's determination had grown so fierce it was giving off sparks. It seemed to be fueling her hunger, too. I'd never seen her eat so ravenously.

"They teach the alphabet at the Grainer School, too," Ma said, still facing the skillet. "And they have such a nice playground. Jimmy rides his bike over there almost every day. Right, Jim?"

"Only reason I go over there is to see Debbie D'Olympio. Playground's a dump."

Dad, who had focused on the newspaper until that moment, stood up abruptly, leaving his plate of half-eaten pancakes. "Two brake jobs and a tranny," he said. "Don't expect me early."

After he'd put his work boots on, he looked back at the girl with the shimmering black braid, one shamrock barrette pinned optimistically to her hair, wondering if he should say something to her. Then he shook his head and left without another word. The first rule is don't get attached, he'd told me when I cried after one of the new-borns left.

"I hear the Dohertys have a nice backyard, and your new sister is named Kathy," Ma continued in her saleslady voice. "She can't wait to meet you."

Agnes slid her chair closer to mine, the metal legs grating against the linoleum. "Already have a sister." She looked to me for approval when she used the word I'd taught her the other day.

"Nancy says it's a very good family. It's not going to be like . . ." Her voice trailed off. "You got lucky this time, honey. I promise."

I winced. The only time Ma called kids *honey* was when they were leaving. It obviously grated on Jimmy, too.

He pushed his chair backward. "Why don't you tell her the god-damn truth for once?"

"James!"

"I don't care. People have been lying to this kid since the day she was born—if they bothered to talk to her at all."

"Enough, Jimmy. Please."

"Tell her the Grainer School playground has three swings and one's busted. In the spring you can't even play ball there cause it turns into a mud pit. Tell her the new family ain't gonna be any better than the five she was in before and most likely they won't want her neither. The kid hasn't got a chance of seeing happy till she's eighteen and busts out of the system for good, and by then, she'll be so messed up, it won't matter."

Agnes leaped up so abruptly she knocked her milk over. She ran into the bathroom and slammed the door.

Ma glared at Jimmy as she reached for a dish towel. "Now see what you've done. You can clean up the mess, too."

"I'm not the one who made the mess; you are. I thought you said you were done takin' in kids." He slammed out of the house, leaving his books on the table.

"You might as well go, too, Zaida," Ma said. "The last thing we need is another scene."

"But I want to say goodbye and my school doesn't start till—"

"Goodbyes only make it worse; you know that. Now, while she's in the bathroom. I don't care when school starts."

Unconsciously, I rubbed the top of my hand where Agnes had held it so tight her nails left marks the first day she went to school. Though they hadn't punctured my skin and the little red indentations disappeared in an hour, I could still feel them.

"But I've been trying to tell you I—I think I have a fever." I put the back of my hand to my forehead. "And I'm going to throw up. And—"

"And you're getting the bubonic plague, polio, and the mumps all at once," Ma muttered, clearly too overwhelmed to argue. "Take your brother and go up to his room, then. I don't want to see either of you until this is over; do you understand?"

After I shepherded Jon to his room, I sat at the top of the stairs and watched Ma retrieve her menthols from the shelf where she hid them.

YOU KNOW HOW *you can tell when things are really bad around here?* Jimmy had told me in my early weeks. *Ma gets out her old pack of Newports.*

"What's bad about that?" I wondered aloud. I had vague memories of my first mother and her friends, filling ashtrays and sipping drinks with cherries in them, as they giggled in the kitchen. That was a long time ago, before she got sick, but sometimes I could almost hear their laughter.

"Ma hasn't smoked for ten years. That's what's bad," he said as if it was obvious. "Doesn't even light 'em up. But every now and then she takes one out and sucks on it like her life depended on it." Eyes narrowed, cheeks drawn in, he demonstrated. "When you see her doing that, well—don't say I didn't warn you."

I retreated to Jon's room, where I found him rocking back and forth on his bed, eyes closed, a thumb jammed in his mouth, comforting himself as Ma did with her Newports. He was what they called my real brother, and sometimes when I saw him doing things like that, I could almost feel myself back in those rooms where we'd lived with our first mother. It was no good to think of that too much, though.

I slammed the door behind me. "Do you want me to set up the train for you?"

Dragging out the box, clicking the pieces of track together, and lining up the cars had a calming effect on me. But as soon as I plugged it in, all I could see was Agnes's face as she watched it spin around the track. What if Jimmy was right and this home was no better than the previous ones? Who would sit with her when she tried to run and fell into an asthma attack? Who would lead her back to bed when she got up in the middle of the night to watch for Mr. Dean?

I stood by the window, taking in the view of the street where Agnes had often kept watch. At ten thirty, with still no sign of the case worker, I felt myself puffing up with hope.

"Maybe the new family changed their minds," I told Jon.

He was so absorbed in play he didn't hear me. I leaped up from the bed and ran to the door to listen for a sign that things had returned to normal.

"Or Ma did," I went on. "Maybe she called the department and told them—"

But before I could finish, the deadly silence from downstairs stopped me. "What do you think they're doing down there in that bathroom all this time? Agnes hasn't made a peep since breakfast."

"Peep, peep," Jon said in his conductor voice.

I pictured Ma sucking on her Newport the way Jimmy had demonstrated, but when I tried to imagine Agnes, I couldn't. I returned to the window.

Just after eleven, Nancy's Studebaker rounded the corner of the street. "Maybe it's not her," I told Jon. "A lot of people have cars like that."

"This the coal car. It brings coal to that house right there. See?"

Sometimes one word can break your heart. I fought back tears as the Studebaker pulled into our driveway. Nancy climbed out wearing that green coat, her high heels clicking.

"You said you'd be here before nine," Ma said, flinging the door wide this time. "As if this isn't hard enough."

Nancy murmured something that sounded like an apology, but I didn't catch it.

Every cell in my body was listening for Agnes. When I heard the bathroom door open, I steeled myself. Would she cry or throw a tantrum like some kids did?

Silence.

In enthusiastic tones, Nancy rambled on about the Dohertys and the little girl who was right around Aggie's age and how lucky she was. She was no more convincing than Ma had been.

I waited for Agnes to tell her that Aggie wasn't her name, but she didn't even do that.

Finally, Ma told her to get her jacket from Zaidie's room. Just a day earlier, it would have been *your room*.

I stood at the top of the stairs, listening as the door opened and closed twice. "For goodness sake, not that jacket, Agnes. The one Dad—uh, Mr. Moscatelli bought you. And where are your new shoes?"

She was taking everything back, piece by piece. First the room, and now Dad.

Still, Agnes remained silent. Before I could stop myself, I was down the stairs.

Agnes stood impassively in the middle of the room, wearing the jacket with the dangling button. I hadn't seen it since the day she arrived. She had also dug out her old Keds.

"Agnes, you can't wear those. They're too small and besides, the snow will get in through the holes," I blurted out. "Where are the ones Dad bought?"

But Jimmy was right. It had all been a lie and Agnes knew it. She regarded me with the same stony expression she wore the last time I'd seen her in that jacket. I took a step backward, wishing I'd stayed upstairs with the door shut—or better yet, gone to school.

She didn't speak until Ma came out from the room holding the paper bag, which Agnes had apparently hidden under the bed.

"Agnes don't want." She touched the center of her chest where her heart was but didn't look to me the way she usually did when she corrected her own grammar. "I don't want it."

"Don't be silly, Aggie," Nancy told her. "You need your school clothes. And the winter coat Mr. Moscatelli was kind enough to buy for you."

"I don't want it," Agnes repeated. Though her tone was flat, I recognized her determination. And apparently, so did Ma.

"It's just some old stuff from the Goodwill anyway. I'm sure her new family will buy her something better."

Without a glance in my direction, Agnes turned and followed Nancy toward the door.

They were almost at the base of the walkway when she came running back—moving so quickly I was afraid she would trigger her asthma. I opened my arms in expectation.

But no. She stood calmly before me as she unclasped the shamrock barrette and pressed it into my hand.

"But that's yours," I told her.

She shook her head. "Zaidie keep it."

As she walked away, leaving as she had come, with nothing but the secrets she kept inside the jacket with the dangling button, I stood in the picture window, clutching the barrette so tightly it left marks on my hand just as her nails had done the first day we walked to school together.

Only after she'd gone did I realize she'd left her secret box in the closet.

CHAPTER FIVE

Already

AGNES

"YOU WEREN'T EXACTLY WHAT WE HAD IN MIND. NO OFFENSE."
Kathy stroked her bottom lip with her thumb just like Mommy
did. "You're too sickly for one thing. And no one told us you were
slow."

"Agnes have the asthma. Can't run."

"That's not the kind of slow I meant. But you know what they
say: 'Beggars can't be—'" When the words of the cliché failed her,
she shrugged. "Beggars are lucky to get anything so they should just
keep quiet."

We were alone in a bedroom that was at least twice the size as the
one I'd shared with Zaidie. The furniture was all white; there were
pictures of ponies on the wall, and we slept in beds with matching
bedspreads.

"Why our beds have roofs?" I asked. Would the rain come
through the ceiling the way it did in the corner of the attic before
Mr. Dean climbed up the ladder to fix it?

"Not roofs. Canopies, silly." Again, Kathy stroked her lip. "We
were hoping for someone who looked more like me so Mommy could
dress us up in the same clothes and take pictures. Like real sisters."

I didn't tell her I had a sister. Already. In the three days I'd been there, my new word seemed to describe my whole life. Don't need a bed with a roof. Already have a bed in Zaidie's room. A seat at the table, too, and a special blue plate with a crack in it that looks like the letter Y, too. Dog? Already have Princie, best thief in the world. If I said any of that, Kathy would cry. Then Mommy and Daddy would whisper about sending me back—and not to the Moscatellis, either.

Kathy leaped up from the bed. "Do you like Good and Plenty? I have some in my doll house."

I allowed her to pour the pink and white candies into my hand, and when she sprawled across the bed on her belly, legs kicked up behind her, I did the same.

"Mommy says you're a dwarf. Are you?"

"Agnes don't grow right or talk right or look right," I said, quoting Mr. Dean. Then I remembered what Ma taught me about lies. "Agnes just small," I said. "I . . . I small. I . . . am . . . small."

"I'm already taller than the sixth graders." A worried look crossed Kathy's face. "And, um, bigger."

"Big okay. Just like small. Zaidie told me that."

I expected Kathy to jump up and yell: *Mommy, she's talking about Zaidie again!* Or to stamp her feet hard on the floor and cry. *She was supposed to be my sister! You promised!*

This time, though, she was too worried about the word *big* to notice. She got up and went to the doll house and retrieved a white box. "A few Junior Mints won't ruin our supper. Long as we don't eat the whole box."

I held out my hand. "Jimmy gave me these one time."

Again, she ignored the mention of the people I wasn't supposed to talk about. She flopped back down on the bed. "Andrea James says I don't have any friends cause I'm fat."

"Andrea James lie."

"What makes you so sure? You never met her, and besides, Mommy says you don't know practically anything. No offense."

"People who talk mean lie. Ma told me that." It wasn't exactly what she'd said, but it was what I'd heard. And yes, I was sure of it.

Hope rose up in Kathy's eyes, but it fell just as fast. "Too bad she doesn't know anything, either. Mommy says that lady you call Ma is an old slob, and once, a long time ago—"

"Your mommy lie, too. Then." (If only Zaidie could hear me using the words she'd taught me!) "And Agnes is not slow."

Kathy leaped from the bed and barreled toward the kitchen. "Mommmyyyy! Agnes said you're a . . ."

I tuned out the rest as I allowed Zaidie's voice to fill my head. "I . . . not . . . slow. I . . . am . . . not . . . slow . . . either!" Every time I corrected myself, I touched the center of my chest and smiled. "See?"

"What's she saying up there now? Is she talking about those people again?" Mommy asked. And then more loudly, "Let's hope I don't have to call the department."

The Junior Mints were beginning to melt so I went into the bathroom to wash my hands, closing the door on Mommy's voice. If the Moscatellis didn't want me—like Mommy told me every day—would I have to go back to Mr. Dean?

When my hands were clean, I went to the front window. I hadn't seen the yellow station wagon since I'd landed at the Dohertys' but I knew he hadn't forgotten me. I stared into the coming night.

After a while, Kathy came and stood beside me. "Mommy made cube steak and mashed potatoes for supper. Gravy, too. And crescent rolls from a can like on TV. Don't you love those?"

It was Wednesday, the day Ma cooked the best supper: Franco-American, milk she made from powder and water, and that bread you can roll into little balls. I heard Jimmy and Zaidie arguing about whose turn it was to do the dishes, and Dad's voice: *Pipe down.* I saw the empty place where I should have been and the blue plate with the crack in it.

But the scents coming from Mommy's kitchen made my stomach

moan; Kathy needed a friend because she didn't have any; and I didn't want to be sent back to Mr. Dean's, so I said yes. Yes, I loved those rolls that were shaped like the moon outside my window at home. I followed Kathy to the dining room and sat in the seat that was not mine. Would never be mine. When Kathy smiled at me, I was almost sorry I couldn't be her sister.

EVERYTHING WAS BETTER at the Dohertys'. That's what the lady who brought me here told me. The yard was bigger, and the house was nicer, and every day after school Mommy took us somewhere in the car. Kathy had flute lessons on Monday and we put bathing suits under our clothes and swam at a place called the Y on Tuesdays—even though it was winter.

The first time, I sat on the edge and kicked my feet in the water. The teacher tried to take my hands and pull me in, but I pulled harder. *No.*

"Don't worry; I won't let you go," she said. I knew she wasn't lying because she called me *Honey* like the ladies at the hospital did.

So Mommy had to tell her how I wasn't like other kids on account of I had the asthma and some worser things wrong with me. Though she kept her voice low, I knew what she was saying. That's when I jumped.

The water was deeper than me, but Kathy gave me a red circle to hold me up and everyone clapped when I kicked my way across the pool. *Like she's been doing it all her life,* the teacher said.

By the second week, I didn't need the circle anymore. "She must have had lessons before," the teacher told Mommy. All I knew was that in the water, I jumped and danced and ran like the other kids did on the playground or in the yard. The next day, I could still feel it moving around me, holding me up.

"When we go back to that river again?" I asked at breakfast. That made everyone laugh like I had said a joke.

"Hush now," Mommy told Kathy, patting her hand when she saw how serious I was. Then she explained how it was a pool, saying it like that. Extra loud.

But I didn't give in. "For me, it a river." Then I patted my chest the way I did when Zaidie reminded me to say the word *I*. As if I was talking about myself and not just the water.

Mommy and Daddy looked at me and then at each other, like they wondered where I came from and what kind of secrets I had inside me, the way Zaidie did sometimes.

I wondered that, too.

"Did you learn to swim in a river somewhere?" Mommy finally said, like it was a bad word.

"Yes," I told her, though that was one of the secrets about myself I didn't know.

Then I counted how many days it took till we came back to Tuesday, numbering them by the things we did. Only I didn't call it Tuesday. I called it River Day.

Wednesdays were for shopping and on Sundays we all had a bath and went to church. On the other days, we visited people who gave me and Kathy cookies and stroked my hair the way I used to do with Princie.

"So shiny!"

"That's what I call blue-black!"

"She's a lucky little girl," the lady who said my hair was the color of a bruise told her.

"Much better off than running the streets like those poor Moscatelli kids," another one added.

Mommy cocked her head in my direction and put a finger to her lips. "Little Miss Big Ears," she said into her palm. Somehow everyone seemed to know about Ma. What she'd done.

"Can I go out to play?" I asked when they talked about that—even though it was so cold my face burned when it hit the air. Never argue with liars—not even in your own head. That's what Zaidie said when she knew I was thinking about Mr. Dean.

Alone in the yard, I wished I could tell her about the Y. How I remembered something about myself that I almost forgot. Zaidie would have liked my new clothes, too. Mommy bought dresses from stores where the clerks wrapped them up in tissue paper before putting them in a bag and called her by her name. On the way home, we stopped at another place where she searched for ribbons and barrettes clipped to little pieces of white cardboard to match. And when I told Kathy about my shamrock barrette, she said the ones from the store were better. *Because they're new, silly.* Sometimes people don't even know when they're lying.

She even thought their dog was better. "Cookie has papers, for crying out loud. And she went to dog school where she learned to sit and heel and never, ever to steal or to break out of the yard."

I closed my eyes and remembered sitting in the hole on the couch, with Princie's head resting on my lap, and all the kids squished in beside us, and I knew there was nothing in the world better than that. From then on, I stopped telling stories about the dog I already had and pretty soon, I stopped mentioning Zaidie, too.

I didn't forget them, though. Every night when we kneeled beside our beds to say the prayers Mommy taught me, I imagined I was back there on the couch, and I said their names instead of the Hail Mary: Zaidie, Jimmy, Jon, Princie.

I wondered if they knew they were the best prayer of all.

CHAPTER SIX

The File

DAHLIA

Looks like the Leaning Tower's got you stumped. You been working on that one for what—three weeks?" Louie pondered the puzzle pieces that were scattered across the card table.

I removed my glasses and stared at his fuzzy form as he rose out of his recliner.

When he wasn't asleep in his chair by nine, I knew something was on his mind.

"If you ask me, it should be called the Beautiful Tower of Pisa. Look at it, Louie. Did you know there are seven bells, one for each musical note?"

"The rest of the world sees a building about to topple over any minute, and you talk about the bells. That's you, Dahlia. To a tee." He shook his head as he headed down the hall. "Full day at the garage tomorrow."

He was still listing the jobs he had scheduled when the bathroom door closed.

I waited, and a minute later, he stepped halfway into the hall, toothbrush in hand. "Leave it alone; you hear me? For once in your life, leave it the hell alone."

"I have no idea what—"

This time the door slammed, cutting my lie in half.

The water ran longer than usual and I imagined Louie's thoughts running with it. All the things he never wanted to talk about circling the drain. He was forty-two that year, but when he came back into the hall, I saw a shadow of the old man he would become. In the morning, dressed in his uniform, face set for the day, he would be different.

"You think I didn't see that file sitting right there on top of your 'beautiful tower of Pisa'? I thought you were going to give that back to the case worker."

"It was a tough morning. None of us were thinking about the file."

"So burn it, then. It's not your business now. She's gone to another home and from what you said, they might even adopt—"

I fell quiet for a full minute before I spoke. "Of all the kids that passed through here, I never saw one like her."

By then, he'd reached the stairs, but he paused, one hand on the rail, and looked down at the worn tread of the rug while I took refuge in the Beautiful Tower of Pisa.

I fit a piece of the bell tower into the puzzle. "You know how scared she was of Mr. Dean? Well, the morning I tried to coax her out of the bathroom, I saw a different kind of fear. A worse kind. 'Please, Ma,' she said, talking like Zaidie taught her. 'I want to stay here.' And there it was in her eyes. The fear. As if for the first time in her whole miserable life, she had something to lose."

He scanned the room the way an outsider might. "This house. Us? A family that didn't even want her, for chrissake. Imagine if that was the best thing you ever knew?"

"Yes. Imagine."

"What did you say to her?"

"The only way you get through it is to be tough, Louie. Merciless. So I told her I wasn't her Ma, and she shouldn't call me that anymore." I paused, reliving it all. "After that, she went without a fight. Just walked into the room and took off all the clothes we gave her. When she came out, she was wearing what she had on that first day. That flimsy corduroy jacket meant for a boy. Her old holey sneakers. The fear was gone, too—but what replaced it—God—it was terrible."

"That dead look she had when she first come. I can see it now."

"It took everything I had not to go to her, but what could I do? Even if we could manage another one, it was too late."

Louie started up the stairs, his tread charged with anger. "Next time the department calls with one of their Emergencies, tell them the Moscatellis don't live here anymore. I mean it."

At the top of the landing, he paused again; and in that pause, I knew he was trying to shake the image of her as she'd been that morning in the bathroom. When she was afraid.

"And that file? Burn it," he hollered down to me. "You hear me, Dahlia? Put the damn thing in the fireplace and come to bed."

As if he didn't know it was too late for that.

I'd started reading the night before, just after he'd fallen asleep. For all the hell it contained, it was a thin folder—a couple of legal documents and a few pages of mimeographed notes from the social workers who'd been assigned to her case over the years. Most were handwritten, some with haste, others clearly labored over. They attempted to describe the first six years of the most grievously neglected and abused child who had ever stood at our door. And that was saying something.

It began with the removal of two children from the home of a Miss Carrie Rose Mellon. The author, identified as Evelyn Moore from the Department of Social Services, made an effort to keep her penmanship as neat as a schoolgirl's and her narrative dry.

The authorities were alerted to a situation at 405 Gardena Street, Apartment B after Mr. Cyril Reedy from Apartment A had become alarmed by the persistent cries from the children next door. He hadn't seen the woman he assumed to be their mother in several days.

I was accompanied on the call by Police Sargent Anthony Dutra. No one responded to our knock, so Sargent Dutra and I forcefully entered the apartment. Inside, we discovered two female children, one asleep on a mattress in the bedroom, the other in a crib. They were later identified as Maud-Marie Juniper, age 3 1/2, and Agnes Josephine Juniper, 14 months.

We suspected the children had been alone for a number of days. The older child, who let up a fierce howl when she awoke to find us standing over her sister, had been subsisting on crackers and dry cereal. There was a milk crate beside the crib and a sour-smelling bottle propped on a rolled shirt, indicating that she had attempted to feed the younger one until the milk ran out. The bottle was full of foul-smelling water. Both children were severely malnourished, unwashed, and infested with vermin. The baby was too weak to cry, naked and lying in the urine and feces of several days. There were conspicuous bed sores. The shape of her head was distorted, apparently from months of lying in the same position. She was distinctly small for the age recorded on her birth certificate, and her legs were bowed. We believe she had rarely been removed from the crib since birth.

The children were taken to Claxton Hospital for evaluation and treatment. The caregiver, Carrie Rose Mellon, who described herself as a former neighbor, was charged with gross neglect and abandonment.

On further investigation, the mother was identified as Melody J. Juniper, currently incarcerated in Graves State Prison. Apparently, Miss Juniper, a former ward of the state of Maine, had hidden her children with Miss Mellon prior to her arrest in the hope they wouldn't end up in care.

An appropriate placement, preferably in a home where the sisters can remain together, will be sought when they are well enough to be discharged. Family reunification is the ultimate goal.

In nearly two hours, I had only read the one page. The first thing that stopped me was that there had been two of them. What had happened to Maud-Marie? And why, five years later, hadn't the "ultimate goal" been achieved?

I also took in the mother's age: nineteen. I wondered how a ward of the state of Maine had ended up giving birth in Boston at sixteen. Alone, too, from the sounds of it, since the only one she had to turn to was a neighbor. Had she run away to avoid the maternity homes? Good Lord.

I couldn't help thinking of a couple of the girls that age who'd passed through our house in that situation—or remembering the angry words Jimmy blurted out the day they took Agnes away: *The kid hasn't got a chance of seeing happy till she's eighteen and busts out of the system for good, and by then, she'll be so messed up, it won't matter.*

I skimmed until I found that Melody had entered a rehabilitation program after her release in the hope of regaining custody. In the file's only personal note, someone had written of the mother: *Seems to care about her children very much.*

I read the line over several times, finding some hope in that emphatic *very*—though of course, I had to wonder where this Melody was now.

The next page answered my question. Apparently, she had maintained contact until two years ago, when she'd gotten married. From that point on, she was referred to as Mrs. Jackson. *Husband seems very domineering*, a social worker named Natalie Perkins had scrawled at the bottom of a report. And then only two months later: *Mrs. Jackson missed a scheduled visit and when we called, the phone had been disconnected.* I would go back to those two lines several times, but the only answer to my question was hidden somewhere in that tiny star.

I was forced to put down the papers several times as the odors of sour milk and shit rose off the page. There was no mention of garbage, but as I read the dry report, I inhaled that, too. I heard the cries of the toddler, the gasps of those who entered the apartment, the prim Evelyn Moore, who would not be at this job for long—I was sure of that—and the police officer, one Sargent Anthony Dutra. Was he a father or a grandfather? Did he still wake up in the middle of the night and find himself back in that apartment like I would after reading about what he'd seen that day?

But what I heard loudest was the silence of the child in the crib. The one who had turned her mouth toward a sour bottle of water, too weak to raise a cry for her own survival. Agnes. A kid who was none of my business, as Louie said.

Well, that was me. According to my mother, I spent my days, my life, worrying about things that didn't concern me. *Anything to avoid thinking about your own failures,* she told me once. One of many statements that could never be taken back.

I returned to the file, wondering who had lifted Agnes from the crib in that condition. Was it Miss Moore of the perfect penmanship or Sargent Anthony Dutra? Had they stood aside and waited for the ambulance? If I had been there, I would have done it myself, not even noticing the sores, the shit, and the bugs. I would have held her to my chest and told her what I told the rest, not just my own three, but the Emergencies, too.

There, there. Silly meaningless words, but sometimes all we've got.

Agnes had been different from the others, though. At six, there was still a shadow of that silent baby in her. If she turned to anyone for nurture, it was Zaidie. Now that I'd read the file, I wondered if she'd seen her lost sister in her. It was a natural role for Zaidie, too. I still remembered how she had tried to mother Jon when they first came.

Again, I paused, wondering if we migrate as naturally as birds in winter toward those who can give us back what we've lost. Was that how Louie had come to me? And Jimmy?

Nonsense, my mother would say. She'd been horrified, but clearly not surprised, when I first told her about Jimmy. Wouldn't it be easier to pick up a little job somewhere if Louie's not making enough money? Why take in other people's problems? Two digs for the price of one. Or maybe three.

"As if you know anything about me or my kids," I said out loud all these years later. When I finished reading the report the first time, I went up to Zaidie's bedroom, and let the hall light illuminate the empty bed where Agnes had slept. Across the room, Zaidie had pressed herself against the wall, the way she was forced to sleep when Agnes crawled in beside her.

I wasn't the kind of person to show my feelings, especially to my girl. Somehow it had always been easier with the boys. I could blame the way I'd been treated as a child. What happened to me later on. But maybe it was just how I was. Like Mother, for all my resentment toward her.

That night, though, I stroked Zaidie's pale hair and told her how grateful I was that she had come to us. And then I sat on the bed where Agnes had slept and stared into the black night like I sometimes caught her doing, wondering what she'd seen, until I heard Louie shuffling down the hall.

"Are you coming to bed or not?"

CHAPTER SEVEN

The Biggest Word in the Sky

JIMMY

I FIGURE YOU GET ABOUT THREE DAYS IN YOUR WHOLE STUPID LIFE when you feel so good nothing can touch you. Or more like three minutes. Anyway, there I was sitting on a rock at the edge of the woods in the freezing cold, wearing a jacket with a broke zipper, and yup—smack in the middle of one of my three. The reason? Debbie D'Olympio had just asked me a question that made me believe in those miracles Nonna was always going on about.

Debbie and I had been meeting at the Grainer School playground every Wednesday, three sharp, for almost six months—practically an eighth-grade record. At first, we sat on the swings like kids, teasing each other about dumb stuff, writing in the dirt with our feet. Then, a couple of months ago, we moved to the rock. It's not a place where I could kiss her or anything, especially since the little kids get out of school around the same time, but sometimes we horsed around like I do with my little brother and sister. Only different. Okay, way different.

On the way to the playground, I always stopped by Bruce Savery's house to ditch the hat Ma makes me wear and remind my buddies who I was going to meet. That day Brucie and Kev came up from the basement where they'd been playing darts to watch me Brylcreem my hair like it was some kinda spectacle.

Kevin stood behind me in the bathroom mirror, asking if I'd frenched her yet. As if he knew the first thing about kissing a girl, never mind frenching.

"I woulda had her at the Sugar Shack by now," Brucie bragged. He claimed to have gotten Janice Meachem to second base back in the fall when the high school kids first renamed an old cabin in the woods for that song on the radio.

I stuck Brucie's dad's Brylcreem back in the medicine chest and slammed the door a little too hard, hoping they didn't notice. I wasn't about to tell them I already had brought Debbie out to that dumb shack. Or how the old bum who used to live there ruined everything.

It all started in the summer when I was helping my dad out at the garage like I do every Thursday. I had just finished stacking oil cans into a neat triangle and I thought I'd sneak off for a soda when I spotted the bum, putting air in the tires of his bike. It was summer, hot as hell, but he was dressed in heavy clothes. And the smell? Whoa. I didn't want to make him feel bad, though, so insteada looking for a place to puke, I held out my pack of Camels.

"I'll spot you back someday," he said, hands shaking like old Mrs. Ryan's do since she got the dropsy.

"Thanks," I told the guy—as if he was the one who gave me something, right? Anyway, when I said it, I made the mistake of looking straight into his eyes. Maybe just for a minute I thought it might have been my old man or something. Hard to explain what happened next, but it was like his whole life was in those eyes. And now it was in mine.

Everyone in town musta seen that bum riding around on his crappy bike, but nobody knew who he was till they found his body in the woods around Thanksgiving. By then, Richard J. Cartier had been dead for a couple months.

"Awful fancy-sounding name for a hobo." Ma shook her head when she read it in the *Gazette*. "Imagine." But I could tell she felt sad, too.

So anyways, there I am at the Sugar Shack with Debbie D'Olympio and what am I looking at? A cup of coffee Richard J. Cartier left on his dang table. And I'm thinking how that day at the gas station when he passed his life into my eyes, he only had about a month left. Kinda made me shudder.

Oh, I snapped out of it fast enough, but by then, Debbie was spooked, too—which is how stuff like that works.

"Maybe we should go?" she said, chewing her Teaberry gum double time and staring at that coffee cup, almost like she could see it, too. "My mom's probably worried about me."

At that point, someone else woulda pushed her a little, gotten something to tell the boys about. But once you let yourself feel sorry for one person, next thing you know you're feeling sorry for the whole dang world. On the way out, I grabbed the bum's moldy cup a coffee and threw it hard as I could into the woods. It shattered on a rock.

Nope. I sure wasn't about to tell Brucie and Kev none of that. Instead, I said, "Oh, don't worry. Debbie'll be getting a good look at the inside of the Shack soon enough."

THOSE WERE GOOD times—Brucie and Kev watching the way I combed my hair with two fingers like there was magic in it. Walking down the street, pretending I was wearing a leather jacket and a white T-shirt that showed off my muscles like the guys in the movies did. I played it so good that other people saw the way I felt inside instead of the gawky kid in a jacket with a broke zipper and a striped jersey like my kid brother might wear.

But there was always that one minute before I turned the corner of the school when I remembered who I was. Sixty seconds when I was so sure Debbie wouldn't be there the breath froze up inside me.

That was when I remembered Dad. He wasn't one for talking much, but those Thursdays in the garage, I watched how he handled cars with tricky problems no one else could fix. Sometimes he'd stop and I'd see that same doubt pass over him. Then he'd let out a few swear words, set his face a certain way, and go back in. That was how he became the best mechanic in the whole world. Or at least in Claxton.

So I did the same. And there she was sitting on that rock in her pink parka like one a those mirages you read about. Every single time. Shoot. Soon as I saw her I was the guy in the leather jacket again. If someone was calling my name, man, I didn't even hear it. I lit up a Camel and passed it to Debbie even before I said hi—cool as heck.

Sounds dumb, but the biggest thrill of my life was watching her stick that cigarette between her lips and pretend to draw. Brucie and Kev woulda said it was a waste of a good smoke, but when she passed it back and I tasted her Teaberry gum? Man.

That day, she was acting funny, though. "It's awfully cold out; don't you think, Jimmy?" she said, doing this cute little shiver. "Maybe we should, um, go somewhere."

At first, I didn't get it. Was she asking me to go to her house and meet her mom? I came to my senses real quick, though. There was no way Debbie'd bring a kid like me over to that fancy split-level where she lived. I can hear it now: *Mom, this is my, um, friend, Jimmy Kovacs.*

Now it woulda been a fine enough name if the guy I was named after wasn't always landing himself in the court report. Ma hid the *Gazette* every time James Kovacs Sr. messed up, but someone— usually good ole Brucie—made sure to bring it to school and read it out loud in the cafeteria.

If only the guy coulda done a respectable crime every now and then, it mighta made kids think twice about crossing me. But not James Kovacs Sr. No, he went for weasely crap like "Shoplifting," "Drunk and disorderly," and "Domestic disturbance"—whatever the heck that means.

"So?" I always said, cool as I could be in a situation like that. "Guy ain't no one to me." I didn't even look up from my lunch tray. But after the bell rang, I went straight to the bathroom and puked.

"Do you think the little stove in that place you took me before works?" Debbie asked, interrupting my dumb thoughts. She peeled off one of her fur gloves and stuck her hand in the pocket of my jacket with mine.

"Don't worry; I'll get that old thing fired up, all right," I said, like I knew what she was talking about all along.

I had stomped out my cigarette, and we were halfway across the playground when I heard my name again. Next thing I knew Agnes was barreling toward me. *"Jim-meee!"*

My first instinct was to keep going and pretend I didn't know the kid. After all, she wasn't nothing to me. Just another one a Ma's Emergencies. I woulda got away, too—if only Debbie hadn't stopped to look back.

"Is that girl calling you?"

So okay, I didn't much like the way she said *you*—like she was seeing me different all of a sudden—but at that point, I coulda let it go.

"Never seen her before in my life," I said, squeezing Debbie's hand. I picked up the pace.

I woulda kept going straight for the shack and second base—if it wasn't for that creaky sound that came out of the kid's chest when she got too excited or tried to run to Tucker's store. Once when she caught a cold, it got so bad, I could practically hear it leaking through the walls of Zaidie's room.

So right after claiming I'd never laid eyes on her before, I spun around and made a liar outta myself. "What the heck, Agnes? You know you're not supposed to run."

Kid was so happy to see me she just stood there, wheezing and smiling, smiling and wheezing like some kind a fool.

"Didn't uhhh you uhhh hear uhhhh me, Jimmy? I was uhhh calling uhhhh you."

"And you're not supposed to talk, neither. Jeez, kid. You want to end up in a oxygen tent again?"

But when the kid had something to say, nothing stopped her. So I told Debbie to give me a minute. Then I led Agnes back to the rock that was supposed to be our special place.

"Shush now. Quiet," I said, patting her hand like I was Ma or something. "You gotta rest before this turns into one a your full-blowed attacks. Where's your teacher, anyways? Your new mom? And I thought you had a sister or somethin'."

She pointed down the street. "Kathy uhhh leaved."

Somehow in the middle of all the gasping and wheezing, she managed to explain how she snuck out of the dismissal line before anyone noticed.

So what could I do? I sat with the kid on the rock, holding her hand and shushing her every time she tried to tell me something—which was about every two minutes—until the wheezing slowed down. And the whole time the stupid kid was smiling at me like I was Wyatt Earp and the Easter Bunny all rolled into one. Jeez.

I musta been pretty worried cause I forgot all about Debbie. I didn't even hear her coming up behind us.

"What's wrong with her?" she asked, looking at the kid the way people did when they caught Richard J. Cartier going through the trash cans.

I mean, did she have to say the word *wrong* like that—as if it was the biggest word in the sentence? Or maybe in the whole stupid sky? Reminded me of Bruce Savery reading the Court Report at school. *Wrong*. Almost made me want to go out and commit a dang domestic disturbance.

"Didn't you ever see anyone with asthma before?" I blurted out before I could stop myself. "Maybe you're the one got something wrong with you."

Well, that was it. See, I'm pretty sure no one in her whole life said anything like that to Debbie D'Olympio. Least of all the likes of James Kovacs Jr.

I stared at the cute mouth where she'd held my Camel a few minutes earlier and wondered how I could take it back. I tried to chuckle like I was just kidding or something.

"Debbie, you know I didn't mean—"

But before I could get it out, I heard the rasp of the kid's breath, and it was just like that day in the dang shack. Instead of thinking about Debbie like I shoulda been, my mind went back to the days when the kid first came, and how she had stood in the picture window for hours, waiting for some guy in a yellow station wagon to come and beat the crap outta her for nothing. All while Debbie sat in that nice split-level house. And you know what? I wasn't sorry. Nah, I wasn't a bit sorry.

Not that it woulda mattered. Debbie D'Olympio didn't even say goodbye. She just walked away, picking up speed as she hit the pavement like she was running from a burning house. And heck, maybe she was.

Any kid in his right mind woulda told the wheezing Indian to scram and run after her. But me? I just sat there on that rock and let Debbie go. After a while, a shudder took hold a me as the cold came through my cheap jacket. I fired up another smoke, making sure not to breathe on the kid.

By then, my lungs were kinda burning, and every time I exhaled, the angry plume got bigger. "I hope you're happy. You just ruined the best day of my life."

"I made prettiest girl in the whole damn city go away," she said, nodding.

"Jeez, you don't have to smile about it. And Ma would wash your mouth out with soap she heard you curse like that."

"Ma," she repeated. As if the word tasted sweet in her mouth.

"Hah. You musta forgot what she's like—because she'd be giving you a whoopin' right about now." I reached in my pocket and gave her the Sky Bar I'd brought for Debbie. Not that she deserved it, but I didn't need no reminders. That's when I noticed the shiny red ribbons tied to the end of Agnes's pigtails, her fancy wool coat. She even had fur mittens like Debbie's.

"Looks like them Dohertys are treating you pretty good, huh?"

She bit into the caramel square first just like she always did. "Mommy takes us swimming on Tuesday. Even in the winter. And I have my own bathing suit. A green one." She scowled as she moved on to the fudge square. "Only she's not really my mommy."

"Yeah, well, real or not, she's probably going ape by now. From what Ma says, this cold air ain't good for the asthma, neither. You know the way home?"

She pointed toward Grainer Street. "That way. Mommy's house is on the corner. A white one with green windows."

"You mean shutters?"

"Shutters." She touched her chest like she did when Zaidie taught her something, like she was taking the word inside herself. "See?"

It was just an ordinary word, but when she said it, I could tell what she was thinking about. Or who.

"You still miss her, huh?"

"My sister," she whispered.

If Ma's name was sweet to her, Zaidie was like one a Nonna's holy saints. She couldn't even bring herself to say it out loud. I was sorry I brung it up. Or that I'd ever played that silly "See?" game with her.

So there I was feeling sorry for ninety-nine things that weren't my damn fault when outta the blue, the kid says, "Mommy was here looking for me."

"Here? You mean today? While you were sitting here with me?" I jumped to my feet.

The kid pointed to the playground, not the least bit flustered. "Over there. Kathy, too. They don't see us, though." Then she corrected her grammar, all proud a herself. "Didn't. Did not see us."

"What the heck, Agnes? You saw your mommy and you didn't say anything? How long ago?"

"Right before the prettiest girl left." She popped the marshmallow square into her mouth. "This is the Jimmy piece, on account of it's the sweetest one."

"For cryin' out loud, Agnes. Good old Mommy's probably home calling the cops right now and you're sitting here, naming the squares of your Sky Bar. Lady probably thinks you're kidnapped or something. And when they see me, they're gonna—"

I started for the street, pulling her by the hand. "Let's get going. One block down Grainer, you say? Hurry up—but don't run. No matter what, do not run." Okay, I wasn't making a lot of sense, but it had been a pretty messed-up day. And now I had to worry the cops and some crazed Mommy might be looking for us.

As we walked, I couldn't help noticing that all traces of the asthma attack that wrecked my life were gone. She even had the nerve to smile at me. It woulda been pretty aggravating, but I figured when someone hurts you bad as that Mr. Dean did to her, you go one of two ways. You either walk around scared shitless for the rest of your dang life, or you turn out like Agnes.

Her new home was so close that we could see it from the sidewalk of the school. Four houses down. No streets to cross.

"That the house with the green shutters you were talking about?"

Agnes let go of my hand and nodded. Then she pointed in the opposite direction. "You go that way and I go to the green shutters. Then Mommy won't call the cops on you."

"Heck, did you think I was really afraid of that? Let's go." I tried to reclaim her hand.

Agnes shook her head and touched the center of her chest the way she did when she learned a new word or had something important to say. "I go by myself, I said."

Like I told you, when that kid made up her mind, there was no changing it; and since there were no streets for her to cross, I didn't argue. I looked back a couple of times until she reached the house, though. And every time I did, she spun around and gave me that smile of hers. Almost like she could feel my eyes on her.

On the way home, the whole dumb afternoon tumbled around in my head—the taste of Debbie's Teaberry gum, the way she tilted her head when she asked me to go to the shack, and that thing that come over me when I walked around the Grainer School and saw her waiting for me in her pink parka. Best feeling I ever had in my life.

I walked a little faster. Maybe it wasn't too late. Maybe I could still go home and call her. But then the kid's dang smile came back to me—and the way Debbie looked at her when she said the word *wrong*. Shoot.

Worst part was I couldn't even blame Debbie for it. Just like you couldn't blame people in town for acting the way they did when they caught Richard J. Cartier picking through the trash. None of those people had ever got as close to the bum as I did the day I give him that cigarette. Just like Debbie had never seen the kid standing in the window, watching for the yellow station wagon. Sometimes even in the middle of the dang night. And Debbie hadn't been there the first time the kid laid down in the snow to make angels, neither. But I had. Suddenly, I was furious at Ma.

"Everything you do, no matter how small, has a consequence," she liked to say.

One of what we called her personal Ten Commandments.

"And everything you don't do," Dad chimed in, looking around the house. "That adds up, too."

But did either of them ever think of the consequences of bringing all those Emergencies into our house? How every one of them changed us? It made me mad till I remembered that once, someone had stood outside the house at 100 Sanderson holding a sorry-eyed kid name of James Kovacs Jr. And for some reason no one can ever explain, Ma had opened the door.

With my whole life and probably a little of Richard J. Cartier's rolling around in my head like that, it was no wonder I never noticed the kid was following me. My first hint shoulda been the happy howl Princie let up when she spotted me from the picture window. I mean, the dog's always glad to see me, but this was different.

Ma came and stood in the door, with Jon behind her. "Why is Princie barking like that?" But by the way his voice rose, you could tell he knew before he finished the sentence.

"Jimmy, what in the world—"

She was saying my name, but Ma's eyes were on the spot behind me. And when I turned around, there was the kid I thought I left on Grainer Street, smile blazing like a fire that nothing in the world could put out.

"I come home, Ma!" she said, as Princie and Jon pushed through the storm door and leaped on her. "Home!"

CHAPTER EIGHT

The Fifth Time

ZAIDIE

THE FIRST TIME AGNES RAN AWAY TO OUR HOUSE, MRS. DOHERTY came to pick her up.

She was the tallest woman I'd ever seen and she sat on the edge of the couch straight as a parrot on her perch.

"We thought you were happy with us, Agnes."

It sounded like an accusation, but I could tell her feelings were hurt, too. I studied her from across the room. Though I didn't like her much, I couldn't help thinking of Eleanor Roosevelt, who refused to make herself small for anyone. After I finished reading about her in my Biography for Young Readers, I'd torn her picture from the front of the book and tacked it on my wall. It wasn't right, but sometimes you need something so bad, no one can stop you from taking it. Not even yourself. That's what Jimmy says anyway and he would know.

Agnes was small and alone, but she had her way of not letting anyone make her feel little. She sat on the other end of the couch with her hands folded and said nothing until the girl who was supposed to be her new sister began to sniffle. Noisily.

"Sorry, Kathy, but I already—"

Ma stopped her there. "No, Agnes, you don't. Now please apologize to Mrs. Doherty—I mean, Mommy—for all the trouble you caused."

Agnes turned back to her hands, so Ma said the words for her—extra loudly like she did when she was speaking for two. "We're sorry we worried you, Mrs. Doherty, and we promise it won't happen again. Don't we, Agnes?" Her eyes remained on the mute Agnes. "Well, don't we?"

At that moment, I wished Eleanor Roosevelt could see my sister. The way she kept her peace.

"Don't worry," Jimmy said to fill the quiet. "I won't be going to the Grainer playground anymore anyway, so even if she wants to run away, she won't have no one to follow."

That might have convinced the grown-ups, but us kids? We all knew how quickly Agnes learned. When I tried to prepare her for school, she'd memorized the alphabet in a single day, and Jon only had to show her the twisty shortcut to Tucker's store once before she was cutting through yards and alleys like she'd been going there all her life.

WITHIN A WEEK, she'd run away to our house three more times. It didn't matter how angry Dad got when he had to drive her home again, or that after a call from Nancy, Ma lectured her about ruining her chance.

"If they can convince your mother to sign the papers, the Dohertys want to adopt. Do you know what that means?" she asked every time.

But Agnes just gave her the Eleanor Roosevelt look. Only when we were alone did she answer. "But I want you adopt me, Zaidie."

THEN, AS ABRUPTLY as they had begun, the visits stopped. When almost two weeks passed and she didn't come back, Ma said, "See. All she needed was a little time to get used to it over there. With any luck, this will be a permanent home for her."

Another week had slipped by when I picked up the extension in the foyer and heard Mrs. Doherty's voice on the other end of the line. "Don't even bother bringing her home this time," she told Ma. "I've already called the department. They can pick her up at your place in the morning. God knows where the child will end up now."

Ma hesitated. "Are you saying Agnes isn't there? How long—"

There was a minute of quiet in which both mothers forgot to blame or be angry with each other long enough to absorb what had happened. A minute in which I imagined the two of them, each in their separate houses, peering out their windows into the descending dark.

"Oh, dear God," Mrs. Doherty gasped. "Well over three hours ago. Where could she possibly be?"

CHAPTER NINE

The Trouble with Girls

DAHLIA

THE DAY I FILLED OUT THE APPLICATION TO BECOME A FOSTER mother I tried to tell them: boys only. I can still see the lady who came to do my home interview, looking up from her forms.

"Excuse me?"

"I'm just, um, better with them," I explained, feet crossed neatly at the ankle. If I had any idea how desperate they were for homes, I wouldn't have been so nervous. Even put on a scratchy pair of nylons.

The truth was I knew too much about how things go wrong for girls. Oh, they start off bright and hopeful enough. Take my poor Zaidie—inhaling all those biographies, a picture of her latest hero tacked on the bedroom door every week, even thinks she might become the president of the United States, for heaven's sake. No idea how the world would take back its promises one by one. You? A foster kid? A girl thin as a spindle, not even pretty? Did you really think we meant you when we said you could be anything you wanted to be? Sometimes she reminded me so much of myself I had to look away.

"There's no place on the application form for that, Mrs. Moscatelli, but I'll make a note," the lady said, pretending to jot it down. "Better . . . with . . . boys." She put her pen away and packed up to go. "All right, then."

I followed her onto the front porch. "And no hoodlums, either," I called after her. "In fact, no teenagers at all. Little ones are what I want. Well-behaved little boys." I didn't think it was necessary to add that these nice little boys should also be Caucasian.

She climbed into her car and opened the window. "No teens. No problem cases," she repeated, nodding. "Got it."

Little did I know that once they had me in the system, they'd do what they wanted. Just like they did with the kids. No problem cases? They must have had a good hoot over that one.

In the past eleven years, we'd had girls who blocked the toilet with their tampons because no one ever taught them better, and more delinquents than I can count, including the one who busted a hole in the garage window with his fist, leaving blood stains on the cement floor that will never go away. Colored kids, too. That always got the neighbors riled up, even though the twins who stayed with us for almost six months were probably the best behaved boys we ever had. Most didn't leave blood stains, but they might as well have for all we could forget them. And finally this—a sickly Indian with a growth problem no one ever took the time to figure out. Another girl, to boot. In the middle of all my worry, I was damn furious.

On the phone, Mrs. Doherty had insisted she call the department. "It's my responsibility—at least, for the next sixteen hours."

I imagined her consulting her watch, estimating to the minute how long it would be before Nancy arrived to take Agnes away.

"The cops, too. You need to get a hold of the Claxton Police Department. Make sure you tell them it's been three hours."

"My husband has friends on the force. How will it look if I . . . In any case, I'm sure the department will phone—"

"Good heavens. She's six years old and she's out there somewhere in the dark. Call every number you can think of. And if they don't find her, call again."

"Well." Within a minute, the shame and fear I heard in her voice had spun itself into resentment—a turn I knew all too well. "If your son had only stayed on his own side of town, none of this would have—"

"You can blame Jimmy or me or anyone else all you want later, but right now, you need to call the cops." I slammed down the phone harder than I intended.

Zaidie was the first to get her coat on when Lou and Jimmy went out to search. "Not you. You stay here with your mother," Lou told her, more gruff than necessary.

"But I know her best. I know where she'd—"

"Just Jimmy and me, I told you." Harsher still.

Finally, he turned to me like he always did. The universal translator. "We're going to be looking through the fields and alleyways she mighta passed. Last thing I need is . . . her slowing us down."

Both Zaidie and I heard the catch in his voice. In his mind, he was already surveying the vacant lots. We shuddered at the same time.

"But she's my sister," Zaidie whispered pitifully after they'd gone.

Defiantly, she opened the door and let Princie out—even though Louie had expressly forbidden it.

"Go ahead, girl. Find Agnes!" Zaidie told her. "Find. Agnes."

Princie stopped and barked once, almost as if she understood. Then she took off in the direction Lou and Jimmy had gone, almost knocking Lou's mother over as she climbed out of her car.

"*Dio mio!* Watcha my ricotta pie," she yelled after her, shaking a fist with one hand as she balanced her pie with the other. "Stupid *cane bastardo!*"

I sighed. My mother-in-law had the uncanny ability of showing up at exactly the wrong moment with one of her pies. As soon as she heard Agnes was missing, she pulled out her beads and started with the praying and pacing.

"Dear God, Anna, can you do that in the kitchen? My nerves are shot to hell as it is."

I'd never spoken to her like that before. She stopped, the way she had the first time Louie brought me home. Then as now, she gave me a good looking-over, deciding if all the rumors she'd heard about me were true. She took her beads into the kitchen.

I could still hear her, though. Spoken in emotional Italian, it sounded more like high opera than the rosary. Whenever she passed the stove her beads clicked against metal, marking the time since Agnes had gone missing. Made me jump every damn time.

Meanwhile, Jon had taken out two cars, his and Agnes's favorites, and crawled under the table where they had played the last time she was here, narrating the race for both of them. His form of prayer, I thought.

My way was to take up a bit of my long-neglected mending and to sit by the phone, pretending I wasn't watching it. That I wasn't willing Lou and Jimmy to walk through the door with Agnes, smiling with everything in her. When she was with us, that smile seemed like the most ordinary sight in the world. Even annoying at times. Only now did I see it for what it was: one of those *miracoli* Anna went on about.

Zaidie didn't allow herself any easy comfort. Never had since the day she first walked into the parlor, holding on to her poor brother's hand tight enough to cut the circulation, their mother only a week dead.

"No abuse or anything—not like the usual cases," the case worker said, filling me in. "These kids were well taken care of. The lady just got sick."

"And the father?"

"Apparently ran off with a young girl when his wife got pregnant with the baby. The mother just moved here a year ago, hoping to start fresh. A few months later, she got the diagnosis."

"If it's such a good family, there must be someone—"

"An aunt in New Jersey, who only just heard about the kids. Otherwise, well, it was a mixed marriage. Baptist father, Jewish mother—

both strict. From what I understand, neither side had much to do with them." She shook her head. "Sad—given how it all turned out."

"As long as no one expects us to take them to Synagogue." I shuddered. "Or church." Another silent shudder.

"The mother was non-practicing, and they haven't even been able to find the father." She handed me a card: LUCILLE MENDELSON, D.D.S. followed by a New Jersey address and phone number. "That's the aunt. You can expect her to visit from time to time."

"A lady dentist?"

"Says she'd take them herself, but with her work and all—"

"So it's likely to be long-term." I reached for the baby, already thinking how I would carry him into the sun, love him until he forgot the sorrows of his mother's house. As for the girl, they would have to find a placement elsewhere.

"We stay together, Jon and me," Zaida said. Only six years old but watching me with those narrow eyes of hers. "I promised Mama."

Like all Emergencies, she knew more than most adults about the bargains life drives—hard, unfair, implacable—to use a word I learned from a quiz in my *Reader's Digest*. She was a match for them, too. In spite of how I felt about girls, I couldn't say no.

AND THIS WAS the price of it. Sometimes I think she knows me better than I know myself. I hadn't even gotten the needle threaded before she was after me. "But what if she doesn't call the cops like you said? What if no one does, Ma?"

When Anna's rosaries hit the stove on cue, the needle punctured my index finger. I watched the blood pearl. "For goodness sake. Now see what you made me do?"

Zaidie continued to stare at me as if I hadn't spoken. Waiting.

I put my finger to my mouth and tasted the blood. "If she doesn't make the call, the department surely will. And besides, Dad and Jimmy probably already—"

"They been gone almost an hour. They woulda found her by now if she was on the route. And—"

"She's a ward of the state, Zaida. The department will take care of it. Haven't you got homework?"

"No one in Agnes's whole life ever did what they were supposed to do for her, Ma. Why would they now?" She pushed the phone in my direction. Like I said, if life was implacable, Zaida Finn was more so.

Apparently, Anna was listening all along, too, because the rhythm of the prayers she was reciting with feet and fingers and tongue abruptly ceased. She stood in the doorway, looking so small and hunched it was impossible to believe she had given birth to the towering man people nicknamed Frankenstein. But the authority in her voice and in the hand gesture that sliced through me like a sword belied her size.

"You hear the girl, Dahlia? I would call the *polizia* myself, but my English not so good. While you wait, that *piccola* out there alone in the dark." She hesitated for a minute, beads in hand, and spoke in a lower voice. "You gonna let those people keepa you afraid your whole life, Dahlia? *Madonne*. That Chief Wood—"

"For God's sake, Anna! Enough."

In thirty minutes, we'd both violated the unspoken pact that had kept the peace between us for twenty years. I'd let slip what I thought of the God who abandoned me when I needed him most, and she'd blurted out what she thought of the way I lived my life.

Even worse, she had spoken the name I had worked so hard to banish from my mind. Out loud. When my hands began to shake, I buried them in my mending.

It was Jon who convinced me. Crawling onto my lap, his eyes were as serious as they'd been when he stood at the door at fourteen months old. He held Agnes's blue car on his palm like an offering. "I want to play with her, Ma. Please don't let Agnes get hurted."

Good Lord. As if I had that kind of power. I nudged him off my lap.

"Get them out of here then, Anna. Take them for a drive—to your house, for an ice cream cone—anywhere. If I'm gonna do this, I need to be alone."

Zaidie studied me, looking deep as she could into the one part of my life she would never know. Then she went to the closet and got her coat. Hers and Jon's, too. "Come on, Jonny. We're going to Nonna's house."

CHAPTER TEN

The Coward

DAHLIA

THE HOUSE EMPTY, I TOOK UP ANNA'S PACING. BUT IT WASN'T long before I butted straight into the reason I took kids in the first place. Not for their sake—like those who thought me and Lou were some kind of heroes believed. Hah. And sure as hell not for the money, though there were plenty who assumed that, too. *The only way a mental cripple like you could make a living.* My mother had so much as said it.

But no. The real reason was because there's something louder than dogs barking and kids scrapping, doors slamming, newborns wailing, and the things of this world being shattered one by one. A noise I would have done just about anything to drown out, even if it meant taking a pack of kids, delinquents or otherwise. Taking them not just into my house, but into the deepest part of myself.

Soon as Anna left with Zaidie and Jon, there it was. When I could no longer hide my foolish shakes, I walked rhythmically like my mother-in-law with her beads. But instead of praying, I cursed every- one and everything, starting with Louie. What on God's earth was keeping him? If he couldn't find her, why didn't he come home?

Jimmy, too. Mrs. Doherty was right: If he hadn't been off preen- ing for some girl at the Grainer School, Agnes would be settled into her new life by now.

Then there was Nancy—in fact, the whole damn department—

going back to the woman who promised not to send me any girls. Incompetent liars, the lot of them. Couldn't even be counted on to call the damn police in an emergency.

And why was I alone here with the noise anyway? Walking miles in my own house to avoid the stupid phone? That was Zaidie's fault. I felt her eyes on me even now, heard her voice in my head: *You have to do it, Ma. Not someone else. You.*

Why had I ever let that one stay?

Yes, I cursed them all—from Agnes's no-good mother to my neighbor Josie Pennypacker, who was out on the porch yelling for her cat like all was right with the world. "Flufferrr-belllll!" Good Lord, was there ever a sillier name?

Then there was Anna . . . barging into my house with her rosaries and her pies, hanging her picture of the Pope on the wall like she had a right. She knew Zaidie never missed a trick but she said that name in front of her anyway. Said it in front of *me*. Well, she could keep away from now on, her and her manicotti with homemade gravy, the comments she pretended to speak to herself in the kitchen. *What kinda wife serves her husband macaroni from a can? Madonne.* I could see her shaking her head at me from across town.

Now that his name was out there, I cursed Calvin Wood, too. Chief Calvin Wood—him and his family and the whole stupid city that worshipped them. Bunch of know-nothing fools.

I WAS CAREFUL to avoid the mirror, but I didn't have to see my face to know the one I truly despised: the foolish young girl with a head full of crazy dreams and no idea what the world was. Or even what she was.

The wreck of a woman she grew up to be.

The coward. Oh yes, her I hated most of all.

I can't do it, the coward yelled at the phone every time she passed it. *Do you hear me? I can't do it.*

The only answer was the noise in my head: memory. Well, damn that to hell, too, because this time there was something that spoke even louder. My eyes gravitated to the manila folder on top of the bookcase.

"How long you gonna hang on to that?" Louie asked a week or so after I first read Agnes's file. "I thought I told you to throw that damn thing out." But as the weeks passed it had become part of the décor, like the table where I did my puzzles or Anna's Pope, who stared me down every time I walked past him.

Despite the horrors of Agnes's first year, with its stench of shit and garbage and near starvation, it was the second half of the file, the one that told the mundane story of all the kids that ever passed through my door, that haunted me. The child set loose in a world where no one ever looked at her the way Louie and me did our three, the ragged, mismatched clothes packed and unpacked in a series of paper sacks as she moved from house to house, unseen and unloved until she—or sometimes he—finally arrived on Mr. Dean's stoop or someplace like it. If there was one thing in the world there was no shortage of, it was those doors. Those stoops.

But what I saw most clear of all when I glanced at that file was the way she looked the day I sent her away. How she had stood up straight and gone. How she had set her face.

My hands were oddly steady when I picked up the phone.

It was past eight anyway, I told myself. Surely, the chief of police had gone home to his family by now. Even if he was there, he would have more important business to worry about than an Indian kid who got lost walking across town. Most likely she'd met up with someone she used to play with in the neighborhood and gone home to supper with them. It wouldn't have been the first time I got myself all riled up over nothing.

"It's about the Juniper girl," the officer who answered the phone at the Claxton Police Department called out after I stated my business.

His was the next voice I heard: "Chief Wood here."

Between those words and my own, I encountered the bendy nature of time. Probably less than a minute passed, but it was long enough to contain a lifetime—no, more than that. All the lifetimes that might have been.

Last time I heard that voice, he was thirteen and it cracked every time he spoke. Not yet Chief anybody, he wasn't even Calvin except at school. He was just Cal, the little brother I met when Bobby brought me to the house for dinner one Sunday. "Might as well get it over with and meet 'em all at once," Bobby had said, explaining that all five brothers, even the oldest who was a junior at Boston College, came home every Sunday for roast beef and custard pie. "The only one who ducks out sometimes is Silas, but you don't want to meet him anyway."

"Why not?"

Bobby shrugged. "Dad says he's the mailman's kid."

I looked at him curiously, thinking of Silas, the surly boy I knew from school. He seemed so different from the others I almost wondered if it was true. However, Bobby had already dropped it. As we climbed the hill to the mayor's house, he teased me about being nervous.

"Well, your hand feels sweaty," he said—though they weren't. Was he disappointed? Angry even? I brushed off the thought, but maybe I saw more than I admitted. Otherwise, why would I remember such a trivial thing all these years later?

That day, though, I just laughed. Nervous? Things that scared other people turned my skin rosy with excitement. With life. I hadn't even been afraid when I'd spoken in front of the whole school in my campaign for vice president of the junior class. I looked over and saw Bobby, the handsome son of the mayor, who was running for president, grinning at me as I finished. By the time the votes were tallied, I had won both the election and the boy.

I didn't feel afraid that day, climbing those wide steps with the ostentatious stone lions on each side, either. The family symbol, according to Bobby. I wasn't as pretty as some or as smart as others, but I walked around like someone who was born lucky and the Woods, natural politicians all of them, even those who never ran for office, knew that was what mattered.

At the table, they praised Dahlia's Place, the little Italian restaurant my parents had named after me when I was three. It was a hole-in-the-wall with stereotypical red-checked tablecloths and candles in Chianti bottles straight out of *Lady and the Tramp*, but on weekends there was always a line out the door.

"Best meatballs in the city," the mayor said, kissing his knuckles like a *paisan*, though I was pretty sure he'd never been there.

"Margie, you should have made some lasagna for our special guest. A nice Italian girl like this doesn't want a boring roast, do you, Dahl?" He winked as the nickname they would always use was born.

I tried to say I loved roast beef and that Mrs. Wood's was the most tender cut I'd ever had, but Bobby stopped me.

"She's only part Italian, Dad; I told you that. Her name's Garrison." Bobby grasped my hand under the table. That's when I noticed his was the sweaty one. Why, I couldn't guess. I stored it up in memory, though.

"My mother's family is from Naples," I said, pulling away from Bobby as I reveled in the attention. "But Dad's an all-American mutt."

Predictable as the laugh track, everyone at the table flashed perfect teeth, smoothing over Bobby's moment of temper. I had never met anyone so responsive as the Woods. In their presence, my jokes were funnier, my stories fascinating; even the color of my eyes felt deeper.

"An all-American mutt. You hear that, Marge?" the mayor laughed. "Bobby says you're already talking about college. Got big plans for the future. That's what we like to see; don't we, boys?"

Marge scooped more mashed potatoes onto my plate. "Any idea what you want to study?"

"I've been thinking about law," I told her. Before that, I had only allowed myself to dream of that when I was alone in my room or when I was busing tables at the restaurant on weekends.

I flushed, as if I'd taken too large a portion of the beef, revealing an unladylike appetite. "Or maybe nursing. One of my aunts is a nurse."

Mayor Wood frowned so briefly that someone who wasn't used to disapproval would have missed it. In an instant, though, his sunny expression had returned.

"Nursing is a wonderful profession for a bright girl like yourself," he said, pointedly ignoring my other choice. "In fact, my Margie was studying to be a nurse when we first met. Tell her, Marge. She looked pretty cute in that uniform, too."

Mom—cute? How ridiculous was that? The boys rolled their eyes—all but Calvin, who was fixed on me. He reddened when I caught him staring.

"Two important professions—though very different," Mrs. Wood said. She paused to take a bite of that tender meat, chewing it slowly. "Choose the one that sets your heart on fire, and don't let anyone talk you out of it."

I couldn't remember anyone talking to me like that. Even my guidance counselor had argued for practicality. I could almost feel something stretching, opening up, *becoming* inside me. Could I really do it?

"I think you should pick lawyer," Cal blurted out from across the table, as if he'd heard my silent question. He looked more like his mother than the rest, I decided. Reminded me of her, too.

"And I think little brother has a crush. Look at him; he's the color of that radish right there." Bobby laughed, pointing at his salad. I got the sense that laughing at Cal—albeit good-naturedly—was a family sport. For a minute, I wondered if Silas, too, was teased—perhaps less kindly—and that was the reason he avoided family dinners.

"Nothing wrong with that. We Woods know a pretty girl when we see one; don't we, Cal?" the mayor put in, interrupting my thoughts.

Did all politicians follow every statement with a question, subtly demanding consensus, or was it just the mayor?

Mrs. Wood moved the green beans around her plate with a fork. "Leave him alone, Russ. All of you." No one was listening, though. When our eyes met across the table, we both looked away quickly.

Looking back, the seeds of everything that would happen later were all there at that first meal, if I'd only had eyes to see. But of course, we don't.

For weeks, I bragged about my dinner at the house where the lions stood guard, marveling at the table setting, the conversation, the tenderness of the roast.

"Which of my brothers did you like best?" Bobby asked on the way home.

"They're all nice. Your mom and dad, too." Still holding his hand, I pulled a half-step ahead of him. He wasn't as smart as me, but he had a shrewdness I didn't possess. One look at my face and he would have seen I was lying. If I said I particularly liked Cal, that I'd seen something sweet, something different from the rest in the boy who'd sat across the table, I sensed he would pay for it. And probably I would, too.

"THAT YOU, DAHL?" Chief Wood said into the phone after the forever minute had passed.

How did he know? Had he memorized the sound of my breath all those years ago?

And that nickname. Dahl.

My silence was apparently confirmation enough. "You have one hell of a nerve calling this number," he went on, more confident than before. "Brazen as ever, I see."

Well, you would have thought I'd die. After all, words like that, spoken in the same tone, had imprisoned me in my house for twenty years.

But there was that folder on the shelf looking at me. And there was Agnes, before me in my mind, setting her face to go. When I looked down at my hands, they were oddly steady, my palms dry as the first day I walked up those wide stone steps to the mayor's house.

"Sorry, but I was under the impression this was the Claxton Police Department—not the Wood family's clubhouse."

If he had recognized my breath earlier, I knew his in the furious silence that followed. Only it was the others I heard, not Calvin. Had they ever been as different as I thought?

"I'm calling about the girl," I blurted out before my courage could fail me. "Agnes Juniper. Have you found her?"

"We got a couple of cars out looking for her now and from what I hear, you better hope she's found safe. Not that I'm under any obligation to share any information with you."

"I better hope? What's that supposed to mean?"

"Case worker says you been luring the kid over to your house all winter—in spite of being warned. Repeatedly." He sounded like a prosecuting attorney. "Foster mother corroborates it."

Had Nancy really used the word *luring*? Had Mrs. Doherty?

"If you're trying to scare me, Cal, it's not going to work. Not this time." It was as if I was ascending the stage in the auditorium junior year, the whole school applauding.

"It's Chief Wood to you."

A door closed. The sound of him shutting himself in the office. From across town, I felt myself closed in there with him. Just us and the rage of twenty-two years.

"Ever think about what my brother went through, Dahl?" He had lowered his voice, but there was no turning down the volume of his hatred. "That kid doesn't turn up, you just may get a chance to find out."

"Believe it or not, Chief Wood, this isn't about me and you. And it's certainly not about—him. This is about a little girl who—" Oh yes, I was shaking now, but not with fear.

"Can't even bring yourself to say his name, can you? Lying bitch. Well, how about this? I got a Mrs. Mary Jeanne Doherty who says the kid was headed to your place when she disappeared this afternoon. If Princess Winterspringsummerfall isn't located within the next twenty-four hours, I'll be sending dogs over there to Sanderson Street."

"Send whatever you want, Cal. Just find that kid."

I wasn't sure who slammed the phone down first. Nor did I notice that Lou and Jimmy had come through the door. I looked behind them, hoping to see Agnes, though I knew by their faces that they hadn't found her.

"It's been almost two hours, Lou. What—"

"We couldn't find her so we took the car and drove over to the Dohertys'," Jimmy said. "Any news, Dad figured they'd hear first."

"And?" I stared at Lou.

"The police found her three hours ago—even before the foster parents knew she was missing. Just took a while to figure out who she was."

Three hours ago? So Chief Calvin Wood had been toying with me all along. That, however, was the least of my concerns. "What do you . . . Surely she could just tell them." I had begun to shake so bad that Princie leaped on me and began to lick my face, knocking me into my chair the way she did with the kids sometimes. "Sweet Jesus, Louie, what are you saying?"

Louie didn't often touch me for no reason, but that night he put one hand on my knee, the other on the dog who was licking my face as if there was something in her saliva that could cure me. "She's safe, Dahlia. I shoulda told you that first thing. Safe and being taken care of."

"Safe where?" I said, pushing Princie away. "And what do you mean being taken care of? Is she hurt?"

Louie got up and headed for the kitchen, where he would stand at the sink and pour a glass of water from the faucet like he always did. "Goddamnit, Dahlia. Even if I wanted to know—which I don't—do you think they were going to tell me anything?"

I followed him to the doorway and watched him down his water like some men do a shot. He was still looking out the window when he spoke. "All's I know, the next placement is going to be so far away this will never happen again. Not to her. And not to us, either."

CHAPTER ELEVEN

Three Faces and a Clatter of Pennies

AGNES

THERE WAS A CALENDAR IN THE HALL AND EVERY NIGHT, MOMMY made a red *X* through it like she did with our chore list. Done. Eleven *X*s had passed since the last time Dad brought me back and I promised Jon I would see him soon.

Before she made the next *X*, though, I got the cough. Mommy gave me medicine and soup and told me to stay in bed. JimmyZaidie-JonPrincie . . . I started to pray. By the time I got to Dad, the asthma was growling.

At first the sound was real low like the kind Princie makes when she sees a dog three blocks away: *Don't come any closer, you hear?* But the asthma didn't listen and after two more *X*s, Mommy brought me to the doctor's. He talked to her about breathing treatments and when to call the ambulance, but he didn't say anything to me.

Mommy wasn't talking to me much anymore, either. *This isn't what I bargained for*, she said to Kathy when she set up a treatment. *Probably caught it from those Moscatellis.* (Here she gave me a bad look.)

I wanted to tell her she was wrong, but talking only made the asthma madder so I stayed quiet.

When Kathy went to school, I lay on my bed and whispered to it like a mean dog, asking if it would please go away so I could get back to my sister's house. It worked, too, because when Mommy took me back to the doctor, he said I was good enough to go to school.

Don't let her out of your sight, she said to Kathy, pointing her finger the way she did when she was really, really serious.

She told the teacher and the crossing guard, too. *If she runs away again, I'm going to have to call the state.* She was looking at them, but she was secretly talking to me like people do sometimes.

Two more red *X*s passed before I saw my chance. That made thirteen *X*s and Zaidie said thirteen was unlucky. But if I didn't go, Mommy might cross out the whole calendar before I got another chance.

I walked extra slow, talking to the asthma like Zaidie did with me after a nightmare. When we got there, I told it, I would put on my lucky shamrock barrette and ask Ma to make her tea with honey and lemon, and everything would be good. See?

Two streets from home I saw the first face.

Mr. Dean slowed his yellow car down and opened the window. "Well, if it isn't little Agnes Juniper. I thought you were living in some fancy house on the west side. You must've missed me."

He looked up and down the sidewalk. Then he smiled the way he did when he knew we were alone.

Inside me, I could feel the asthma growling like the dog was on the porch. *Don't run,* it was saying. *Don't you dare run.*

But Mr. Dean's face was meaner than any asthma I ever met. I ran.

"Jesus Christ," he spit out at me, and he wasn't praying like Nonna. "Are you trying to bring on an attack? Get in the car and I'll take you home." It was pitiful how slow the yellow car had to move to keep up with me.

Only two streets away. One. With any luck, Jimmy was out on his bike and he would get Mr. Dean with his baseball bat like he promised. But like Zaidie said, there's no luck on the thirteenth day.

At the corner of the street with the name that started with S for Sanderson, the rumble in my chest turned into a howl that knocked me onto the sidewalk. I tried to breathe, but the asthma was stronger. Inside, I was calling for Ma, but she didn't hear me.

Mr. Dean slowed the car again. He asked me questions and answered them himself like he did when he came up the stairs to the attic. "Never listen, do you, Agnes? Well, now see what you done. I wouldn't be surprised you die right there—and you know what? That's what you get. Yup, that's exactly what you get."

Then just when the breath was almost all pressed out, the best thing happened: A lady opened her door and came running down the sidewalk. "Good Lord!" she was shouting like Ma says sometimes. And then she hollered to someone inside her house. "Call the ambulance! There's a little girl out here who—" She never finished her sentence, but it was okay because only a few people were allowed to see how mean Mr. Dean really was and she wasn't on the list. He took off in his yellow car.

THERE WAS NO calendar to count the days at the hospital, but I knew I'd been there longer than ever. *Ma*, I called when no one heard me, saying the prayer I started at the Dohertys' house. *ZaidieJimmyJonPrincieDadMa. Maaaa.*

After a while, I must have said it out loud, too, because the nurse named Ellen patted my hand. "Who are you calling for, honey?"

I could tell she felt sad for me because whoever it was, they didn't come. Not them and not anyone else, either. That night she brought me an extra bowl of green Jell-O.

After some more days passed, another hospital lady came to my bed, smiling, and said she had spoken to my case worker (*Do you know what that is, Agnes?*) and they had a surprise for me. When I was ready to go home, someone very special would be coming for me. Isn't that good news?

I prayed harder. *ZaidieJimmyJonPrincieDadMa.* Still no one came.

Then one morning, I woke up and the second face was there at the foot of my bed. It was a lady I didn't know. Except I did. I blinked at her, but I didn't say anything, and she didn't, either. I didn't know her and I didn't want her there standing at the bottom of my bed like that. Except I did. Some part of me always wanted her and always would.

She had brown skin like me. And her hair wasn't the regular kind of black; it was very black black like mine and my doll's. I could see her earrings peeking out from under it: two little crosses. Or maybe they were *X*s like the ones Mommy made on the calendar, counting all the days that were done. She wasn't crying, but there was water in her eyes.

Finally, when the quiet got too big for both of us, the lady with the *X*s on her ears said my name—only wrong like I used to inside my head. Agnés. When she said it, a little of the water spilled onto her face.

"It's Agnes," I corrected her. "Agg-ness."

I don't know if she said anything else, cause saying my name right made me so tired I closed my eyes.

When I woke up, the second face was gone. I wasn't sure if I dreamed the lady at the foot of the bed, but when I touched my face, I found the water that spilled on her cheeks had also spilled on mine.

THE NEXT DAY the nurse named Ellen came and threw open the curtain around my bed. "Have you heard the good news yet?"

I looked at her but didn't answer.

She set a wrapped-up present on my tray table. It had a green ribbon on it, too. "Zaidie says my birthday doesn't come till summer."

"Well, Zaidie's right—whoever she is. But some days are so special they're almost like a second birthday." She put the present in my lap. "Go ahead. Open it."

The nurse whose name was Peggy and the lady who brought my supper came and watched me pull at the ribbon. They were all smiling and I could tell they wanted me to smile, too, and so did I. Except I couldn't.

Inside the box was a plaid dress like the one Mommy gave me to wear for my first day at the Grainer School. It was blue and green and there were green socks, too.

"Your favorite color." The nurse called Ellen traced a line of green through the plaid. "Do you like it?"

"Yes," I said, and "Thank you" like Zaidie taught me. I didn't tell her I already had a dress like that at Mommy's house or that I liked the secondhand one with a grape juice stain in the front that Ma gave me better. On account of it used to be Zaidie's.

"Don't you want to know why we bought it for you?" the lady who brought my food trays asked.

They stood there in a circle of three, still waiting for me to be happy.

"You're being discharged tomorrow. You're going to a home close to Boston," the nurse named Ellen said. "A wonderful family." Then she told me about the zoo and the swan boats, and the Christmas display at somewhere called Jordan Marsh.

"Zaidie has a book about swans." I closed my eyes and imagined riding on the back of a tall white bird in the place where I first learned to swim.

THE NEXT DAY, just like they said, the doctor came in, listened to my chest, and wrote on the paper that said I could go home. He looked at his watch and frowned a little. "I thought they said she'd be here by nine."

The nurse named Peggy checked the clock on the wall like it might say something different. "Probably got stuck in traffic on 128."

She turned away so I couldn't see her face.

After the doctor and the nurse called Peggy left, another lady came and washed my hair, buttoned up the new dress, and tied it in a nice bow in the back. Then she helped me pull on the matching socks like I couldn't do it myself.

Whoever was supposed to come and take me to the place with the swans still wasn't here yet, though. The nurse named Peggy gave me a picture book to look at while I sat in the lounge because someone needed my bed.

A little while later, I heard her talking to someone else when she thought I wasn't listening. "They should have told the couple she was an Indian right off the bat—especially since they were hoping for a kid who might eventually be free to adopt."

"Would have saved everyone a lot of grief," the other one said. "Especially the poor kid."

I didn't tell them that I was way too old for *The Three Bears*. Or that I wasn't a poor kid. I already knew about people who didn't come when they were supposed to, especially the fathers and mothers. Everyone in the homes knew that. They just couldn't; that's what Zaidie thought. Or they were no-good louses, like Ma and Dad said. But I didn't tell anyone that, either. I sat there looking at my book. I bet that girl Goldilocks had someone who didn't come for her, too.

At lunchtime, one of the ladies gave me a tray with the kind of ice cream you eat with a stick for dessert. But by afternoon, everyone in the hospital was so busy they forgot about me. I put two chairs together and pretended it was a bed so I could go to sleep and forget about me, too.

Later I woke up and I was hungry again and the nurse named Ellen was holding my hand and calling me those sugary names she used when she felt sad.

"I'm sorry, sweetie." She brushed my hair out of my eyes. "But the family from Boston isn't going to be able to take you after all."

"Can I go back to my room and have supper?"

"Oh, honey, I wish you could, but you can't stay in the hospital if you're not sick. Don't worry, though. Your case worker is sending someone to pick you up. Meanwhile, I'll have someone bring you a sandwich. Ham and cheese—how's that sound? And maybe a candy bar from the vending machine? Would you like that?"

I closed my eyes and thought of the lady with the cross earrings, she stood at the end of my bed and never said anything but my name. And I thought of the water that spilled on her face and mine. Somewhere that water spilled and spilled and never stopped until it became a great river.

"Yes, please," I told her. "I'll take a Sky Bar."

When she came back with my candy, I wanted to make her promise it wasn't Mr. Dean coming, but someone called her away before I had the chance. So instead of eating my Sky Bar, I just held it the way Nonna holds her beads or Zaidie clutches on to one of her books. Like just having it in my hand might make the world come out different.

After a while the nurse named Ellen and the nurse named Peggy went home and I fell asleep the way I used to do when I was in the attic and there was nothing to watch or do but listen for Mr. Dean.

When I woke up, a nurse whose name I didn't know was standing over me. She picked up my white hospital bag. "Is this all you have?"

Yes, I said with my chin.

"Someone is here for you. He's out there signing your discharge papers now."

He? I thought of Mr. Dean, stopping his car beside me while the asthma tried to steal my last breath. How he told me maybe I was going to die right there. And that would be good.

No, I said with my head. *No!*

The nurse who didn't tell me her name wasn't looking at me, though, and when I tried to say it out loud, all that came out was a squeak from the asthma.

But then I saw the third face coming toward me in the hall. It was a face that had a rule against smiling and wasn't about to break it for anyone. It was Dad wearing his long-day face and it was the best face I ever saw.

That's when I found out I could still talk, and better than that, I could yell. "Daaad!"

"You want to end up back upstairs in a damn bed?" He scowled. And then to the nurse, "I hope you told her this was just for a day or two till they can find out if the mother's back in Boston."

He said *mother* that way him and Ma always did when they talked about them. But when I ran to him, he wrapped his grease smell around me and hugged me same as he did the other kids and that was the only thing that mattered.

THERE WAS ANOTHER face, too. The trouble was I couldn't see it. I never can, not even when I have the penny dream like I did the night I went home to the Moscatellis to stay. It was after Ma gave me two Chips Ahoy on my Y plate and the kids let me sit in the best spot in the couch and Princie licked my face so hard I could still feel her scratchy tongue on my cheeks even when I went to my room.

In the dream, all I see is her legs next to mine. We are in the back seat of a car and it's hot, and the sun makes white stripes on our brown legs. Then the car stops and the door opens and the girl starts to scream, and when they try to make her stop, she bites someone. Hard. Hard enough to make blood. After that, people are yelling and saying bad words. Only I'm just listening to her.

I don't want to get out of the car, but someone pulls me by the arm and I drop the little change purse I'm holding.

"Agnés's pennies!" I yell as they clatter onto the street.

Then the car drives away—away without me—and the girl's scream is in my mouth. "Forget the stupid pennies," someone says, and when I look up, that someone is Mr. Dean. Only I didn't know his name because it was the first time I ever saw him. I try to tell him how the girl with the brown legs gave me a penny whenever she found one. I try to tell him they are lucky and I need them. Only he doesn't listen.

Even though the car is gone and I have to go inside, I don't forget the pennies shining in a puddle on the street. And I don't forget the girl with the brown legs, either. I can't see her face, but I don't forget.

Most of the time I only have that dream when my eyes are open. That night, though, after Ma tucked me in and Zaidie read me a book, I fell asleep and dreamed the girl with the brown legs and me were wrapped up together in the same bed. So close I could taste her very black black hair in my mouth.

But when I woke up, the legs wrapped up with mine were pale, and the hair was yellow and the scream I made on the street followed me from the dream right into Zaidie's room, where she was shaking me.

"Agnes! It's a nightmare, Agnes! Look, I'm right here with you! Right here. See?"

PART II

1962

CHAPTER ONE

A Stone in My Pocket

JIMMY

PEOPLE AROUND TOWN NAMED THE RIVER AFTER MY BUDDY Jools's family—partly because it was near their house, and partly because it's really not a river anymore. It's more like a half-dried-out creek where people throw shit the trash man won't take—old tires, smashed-up bikes, garden tools, stuff like that. There's even a refrigerator with the door off, lyin' on its back, in the middle, weeds swayin' through the rusty holes. Spend enough time here, though, and you almost get to like the stink of the place.

Anyway, me and Jools were down by Buskit's River like we were most every day when school got out. Okay, sometimes before. It's not like we intended to skip class. Nah, most of the time we'd just sneak out for a smoke between wood shop and math; then I'd look at him, he'd look at me, and next thing you knew, we'd be headed for Buskit's.

It was pretty much an ordinary day on the riverbank—me thinkin' about a girl so far out of my league we ain't even playin' the same sport while Jools sits there sketchin' his creek. Some of his drawin's are pretty good, too, especially the ones at the end of his book. Ma and the girls think so, too, but when Zaidie tried to talk him into showin' them to the art teacher, he looked at her almost resentful. Like she could never understand how the stuff kids said, the way they laughed, rung in his ears even when he was sleepin'.

"This ain't art, Zaidie," he said. "Art's pictures of . . . of beautiful stuff. Not crap people throw away. Besides, the pages are all dirty from the riverbank. Mr. Ferrante would laugh me outta town if I brought them into school."

He pointed at the bits of mud and weed stuck to some of the pages, a smudge of green water on others. More than a few also had a ring from the bottles of Wild Irish Jools clipped from his mother. Then he shot me one of those resentin' kinda looks, like it was my fault for askin' him to bring over his sketchbook.

"But look," Zaidie insisted, flipping through the pages. "You made ugly beautiful here. And here and here." She pushed the sketchbook at Jools, tryin' to make him see more than what was on the page. As if she was attemptin' to show the kid who he was. "I bet that if you brought these to Mr. Ferrante, he'd put them in the spring art show."

But by then the echoes Jools heard in his head had drowned out everything else. "In a art show? Me?" He stormed out of the house like she'd insulted him or somethin'.

He musta been hearin' echoes that day by the river, too. Outta the blue, he set down his sketchbook and started apologizin' for being a crappy friend. Even had tears in his eyes the way he gets sometimes, especially when he drinks his Wild Irish.

I aimed a rock at a rusted-out bucket—and hit. "Another three-pointer for Kovacs!" My hands were in the air like I just banked the winning shot in the game. "Man, that kid's on a roll!" In eighth grade, I played center for the school team, but these days, this was the only place I shot. Whatever was getting him all emotional, I didn't want to hear it.

Jools didn't let it drop, though. "You know, the other day when Larry Wood threw you against the locker?"

"Larry Wood—who's that?" As if I didn't know the name of the kid who'd been tormenting me since the opening bell of ninth grade. Without thinkin', I rubbed the shoulder that still hurt.

"Tuesday, when we was walkin' to English, remember? Him and Ace Feroli was comin' out of Mrs. Ruffino's class—" Nice kid and good with a drawing pencil, my buddy Jools, but the school didn't put him in the lowest track for nothin'.

I focused on the bucket that had landed cockeyed in the river—and missed. Proves what thinkin' about stuff like that will do to you.

But like I said, there was no stoppin' Jools—especially not on the day after his Ma got her check. He took a long pull from the Richards Wild Irish he stole from her stash.

"Listen," I started off. "Number one, that kid don't bother me half as much as he thinks he does. And two—there ain't nothin' you coulda done about it anyhow—except get your own ass whupped. Ace Feroli ain't no one to mess with, you know."

"If you were takin' a poundin', I shoulda took one, too. That's what friends do."

I gave him a sideways look, wonderin' what I'd done to deserve that kind of loyalty. Back in middle school, when I played basketball and baseball for the school teams, and had girls like Debbie D'Olympio hangin' around, you wouldn't have caught me dead with Jools Bousquet. Oh, I didn't throw pebbles at him at the bus stop or make B.O. jokes when he passed like a lot of kids did. But I wasn't about to sit at the lunch table where he hunched over his sloppy joe all by himself neither.

The worst part was knowin' my sisters would have—Agnes cause she never gave a damn what anyone thought, and Zaidie, well, she was just kinda born wanting to do the right thing. Her and all the heroes she had taped on the walls of her room. I thought about that a few times when I passed him sittin' alone, or tryin' to pretend the pebbles didn't hurt, but I never stopped. Somethin'—maybe it was the stench of Buskit's River—scared me away every time.

Everything changed the day I walked through the high school doors, though. It was like Jesus was standing there telling you which way to go. Sheep this way, goats over there—and just like in the Bible, there's no arguin' with the verdict. Instead of sheeps and goats, we called the groups rats and colleige.

Mosta my old teammates, and all the girls like Debbie D'Olympio, went colleige. Within a week, even my friends Brucie and Kev were splashin' themselves with Canoe, and putttin' on the colleige uniform, too—pastel button-downs with chino pants, these shoes they called desert boots. They even had a certain kinda belt.

As for me, what can I say? The hand pointed the other way.

The day she realized my old buddies weren't comin' round no more, Ma slammed around the kitchen, cursin' Kev. *How many times did I have that kid for dinner when I barely had enough to feed my own?* Then she went on about how she never trusted Bruce anyway.

But me, I saw it different. I mean, how can you blame someone for something so set it's practically in the Bible?

Still, Ma kept a button-down in the closet, just hoping that one day I'd wake up and be someone else. Poor woman. You shoulda seen the look on her face the first time I opened the door to Jools Bousquet's B.O. But soon as she tried to lecture me about runnin' with the wrong crowd, she walked straight into a mirror. If there was a bigger outcast in town than Jools, it was Ma herself and she knew it.

The next time he showed up, she was ready with his favorite Spam sandwiches with pickles and catsup and a lecture about how thin he was; he needed to eat.

Mangia, Nonna corrected her, like the word was more powerful when you said it in Italian.

Then Ma told him how he was saying his name wrong. "I knew some Boose-kays when I was in school. French, right?"

But Jools just shrugged and said people musta figured Buskit was a better name for his family. Them and the junk river by their house.

"Why's Wood always botherin' you anyway?" he said that day on the bank. "Ya'd think he had his hands full with student council and football, all that colleige stuff—"

"His family hates mine for somethin' that goes way back. Larry probably don't know no more about it than I do." When he didn't say anything, I tried to make a joke. "Frankenstein musta screwed up one of their cars or somethin'," I said, though everyone knew it was Ma the Woods hated.

Jools was lookin' out on Buskit's River of junk, but then he turned his face, and there was somethin' in his eyes I never seen before. That dumb love he had for me, yeah, that was there. But somethin' else, too. Pity. He tried to pass me the bottle.

I stared at the green glass with the stupid rose on it. The truth was I'd never tried it. Not when Kev stole a half-drunk bottle of his old man's whiskey the summer after ninth grade, and not at any of the rat parties, either. "Nah, thanks. Not my brand," I always said. "So what is your brand, Kovacs?" a kid had taunted the last time kids got together out by the sugar shack. "Fanta? Yeah, I bet you wouldn't say no to a nice orange soda." I could still hear them laughing, but the next time someone passed me the bottle, I tightened my jaw. Not my brand.

That was Ma's fault, too. She started in on me when I was about nine. I called it her "Promise me one thing" lecture—and for some reason, I was the only one that got it. Every time she saw anyone drinkin' on the TV, it was her cue to take off her glasses and stare at me all serious.

"They make it look glamorous, Jimmy, don't they? Everyone joking and happy. Well, that's not the truth of it for a lot of people."

And then, she'd say her line: *Promise me one thing* . . . like it was a sacred vow.

Only once—the week before I started high school—did she mention James Kovacs Sr., though I knew he was smack in the middle of the room every time it come up.

"You think he'd be getting himself in the paper all the time if it weren't for the booze? And what about your mother? Why do you think she gave you up—because she wanted to? Promise me one thing . . ." This time, though, she took one of her stupid rocks out of the basket she kept next to her headquarters and handed it to me.

I stared at the stone like it was a snake, but Ma didn't take it back. "Take this and any time you're tempted to give it a try, remember what you promised."

I'd said *yeah, yeah* to her before—mostly because I wanted to be left in peace. But that day, looking into the eyes that, even without her glasses, seen me clearer than anyone, I took the stone and I meant it. If fate thought it could destroy me with booze like it done to James Sr. and my first Ma, I wasn't gonna make it easy.

That day by Buskit's River, though, knuckles achin' from how much I wanted to smash Larry Wood, I felt the blame for everything that was wrong with my life shifting to Ma. Why did I have to put up with him and his friends? And she had the nerve to tell us how to live? Someone who hid in the house and let us take the crap that was meant for her? My fist tightened around the rock in my pocket.

It was like a match sparked inside me. The fire leaped higher as I remembered all the times when she needed to be someplace, but couldn't come. Every time I nailed a home run in Little League, I used to look up in the bleachers to the place where the parents sat, searchin' for the face I knew wouldn't be there.

So yeah, I was blamin' her for all of that—and a few things I couldn't even name.

Heck, at that moment, it seemed like everything wrong in the world had Ma's fingerprints on it. Who was she to make me promise?

I wiped Jools's spit off the bottle and brought it to my mouth, but it was as if she was watchin' me all the way from home, seein' me through the blur like she did when she took her glasses off.

Jools looked down at my hands, noticin' my balled-up fist for the first time. He hunched his shoulders in on himself the way he did, and turned his face back to the river of junk, lettin' that curtain of hair hide him.

I reached into my pocket and pulled out the stupid rock I'd been carryin' around for a year and raised my arm. This time I wouldn't miss. But somehow my hand wouldn't let go. Instead of heavin' the rock like I wanted to, I threw the bottle in my right hand, nailin' the bucket. It shattered so hard it sent out sparks.

Poor Jools looked like he was about to cry. "Shit, man. What do you think you're doing? That was half full!"

CHAPTER TWO

The Girl in the Waves

AGNES

WHEN HE WAS HOME, JIMMY SPENT MOST OF HIS TIME IN HIS room or in the foyer trapped between the mirror and the phone. Asked why, Ma narrowed her eyes like she did when she warned me to stay away from Buskit's River at night. "Just don't turn into a teenager." Sounded like a spell cast by the wicked witch in one of the fairy tales Zaidie used to read me.

"Not me, Ma," I promised every time. "I'm never gonna be no teenager!"

"Any . . ." Zaidie corrected from wherever she was. Sometimes just inside my head. "And yes, you are. Soon, too!"

The next time I caught Jimmy moping by the phone, I turned to her. "What's he doing out there?"

"Probably working up the courage to call that girl again," she said behind her hand. "Even though he's already tried at least seven times."

"More like eleven and she's not just a girl, Z. She's *the* girl," Jimmy said. "Most beautiful, most spectacular, most . . . most everything."

Zaidie made her voice lower. "Most snobby is what she is."

"Debbie?" I squinched up my nose, remembering how the girl who used to meet Jimmy behind the Grainer School had looked at me the day I followed him home.

"I forgot that chick a long time ago. Besides, she ain't nothin' to this girl. Right, Z?"

Zaidie rolled her eyes. "Um . . . I guess you have to be a boy to see it."

"Jane Miller," she said to me behind her hand. "He can call a hundred and eleven times; she still won't come to the phone—and she's not even pretty."

Good thing Jimmy had stopped listening. He picked up the phone and put it down twice, tuned to nothing but his own heartbeat. Finally he dialed.

"Hello, Mrs. Miller? It's Jimmy Kovacs? I was wonderin' if . . ."

It didn't get much further than him saying his name like that—as if he wasn't exactly sure he'd got it right. He was replacing the receiver when Jon burst in with a packet of snapshots he'd taken when he went on vacation with Jeffrey's family.

Oblivious to Jimmy's mood, Jon pulled his favorite picture on him. "Look, Jimmy, it's waves! At the beach."

"That's where you usually find 'em, Shad." Jimmy stared at the phone like he could still hear Mrs. Miller's voice in his head.

But then he must have noticed Jon's sagging shoulders. He flipped through the pictures quickly. "Nice. Glad you had fun, buddy." Abruptly, he started up the stairs.

"But you didn't even look at my horseshoe crab." Jon's disappointed voice trailed after him, but Jimmy had stopped hearing.

"Agnes and me want to see, Jonny," Zaidie said, patting the couch. "Bring them over here."

Wedged between us, Jon named the things in his pictures as he passed them to us—even though Zaidie had been to the beach many times with Cynthia or her aunt Cille and I knew what they were from TV and books: sandcastle, seaweed, the jetty, what he called a horseshoe crab even though the crab didn't live there anymore.

I looked at that one extra long. "So it's really a horseshoe crab house."

Jon snatched the picture away. "No, it's not. Tell her, Zaidie." He glowered at me. "Your body's a house."

"Maybe it is," Zaidie laughed, passing me the next picture. "Yours, too, Jonny."

I held on to that one so long Jon tried to snatch it away. "What are you starin' at? Haven't you ever seen a starfish?"

I clutched it tighter. "But why'd the star get turned into a fish? Did it do something wrong?"

"*Maaa!* Agnes is making fun of my pictures!" Jon wailed. Then to me, "You better stop or I won't let you see the one of my Dairy Queen."

"Stop teasing your brother, Agnes," Ma said, without looking up from her book.

I didn't bother to tell her that I wasn't teasing or making fun. I really wanted to know.

A FEW WEEKS later, when everyone was watching TV, I sneaked into Jon's room to look through his pictures again. It wasn't the star that got turned into a fish or the horseshoe crab's house I wanted to see, though. It was something even more mysterious: waves. I looked at them so long it felt like they were tumbling toward me.

Finally, Zaidie came to the foot of the stairs. "Agnes! What are you doing up there? Jon and me are gonna play Clue."

Before I could stop myself, I shoved the picture of waves under my shirt and took it to my room, where I hid it in my secret box.

"I'm Miss Scarlet!" I yelled, claiming the red piece as I slipped my treasures back into the closet, guilty as the culprit in our game.

By then it was late August and Jon had forgotten all about clams and sandcastles. He never even noticed that I'd swiped the ocean straight out of his room. But every day when I was alone, I took out my box like I did at Mr. Dean's and stared at the photo. As if there was something I needed to see. Something just outside the black-and-white square. I turned the picture over to see if it might have slipped onto the other side.

When I still couldn't find it, I begged Dad to take me there. "Just one time, Dad. Before summer's over."

"To the beach?" He snorted as if it was another planet. "You think I have time to sit around baking on the sand like a damn rock?" He walked away muttering about savage amusement.

Nonna, who was visiting that day, scooted closer to me on the couch. "I take-a you myself, *piccola*, but the sun no good for me."

Then she told me about a bad mole the doctor had to cut off her forehead. "Righta there." She pushed back her hair to show me her scar. Was it my imagination or did it look like a tiny starfish? I traced it with my finger.

"But when I was little like you? Every Sunday in summer, *mi mama* make eggplant sandwiches, pack up some *succo di pesca*, and we take the train to the beach."

When she talked, the waves were in her eyes, clear as the starfish in her scar. "Luigi used to like it, too," she said, looking toward the kitchen, where Dad had disappeared. "He just forget. It happen when you grow up."

"But you're grown up, Nonna."

She put a finger to her lip like she did when she was about to tell me something that was just between her and me. "Me, I get so old, *piccola*, I remember all over again."

I snuggled closer. "I'm not your *piccola* anymore, Nonna. Remember what Dr. Genova said? I'm practically average now."

IT WAS TRUE. At my last checkup, the doctor had slapped his knee and beamed, pointing at the size chart. "What did I tell you, Anna?"

Two years earlier, Nonna had taken me to see the man she called the smartest doctor in America, despite Ma and Dad's objection. "He's not even a pediatrician, Anna." (Ma) "Man's a quack is what he is! She just likes him cause he talks Italian and flirts with her—a seventy-five-year-old woman for chrissake!" (Dad)

Their protests only made Nonna more determined.

That first time, Dr. Genova spent so long reading my records, looking from me to them and back again, I started to think Dad was right.

"A dwarf?" he said out loud when he was done. Then he ripped up the paper and slapped the file shut. "What idiot wrote that?"

"Hah. A professional never calls another doctor an idiot," Ma said back at home.

"I told you he was a quack!" Dad added.

But Ma must have been thinking about it because the next time Nonna came over to drop off sausage and peppers, she brought it up. "So your Eye-talian doctor friend thinks Agnes might not be a dwarf after all?"

"Everything they write about my *piccola* is wrong; that's what Dr. Genova say. Except the asthma. She really have that."

But Ma wasn't convinced until he came for a house call the first time. Before he left, he stopped to put a puzzle piece in the field of tulips Ma was working on and to check out the books stacked beside her chair. Then he looked her straight in the eyes like people almost never do. A little too long, too—according to Jimmy, who had still been awake. "It's Dahlia, right?"

She nodded.

"Call the office in the morning and make an appointment, Dahlia," he said, starting for the door.

When Dad heard he didn't even say *Mrs. Moscatelli* like he was supposed to, he stopped calling him a quack and started calling him *your mother's boyfriend*.

Two days later when we were going back to the doctor's, Ma followed us to the door. "If she's not a dwarf, why's she so small? How about you ask your doctor friend that?" she told Nonna.

Dr. Genova didn't give the answer right away, though. Instead, he looked me over good like he did before. Then he told her to feed me lots of fresh milk and hug me eight times a day; he bet I'd grow like a weed. He winked at me. "No, not a weed—a sunflower."

"Eight, you say?" Nonna took out her pencil.

"That's right, Anna: Not *sette*. Not *nove*. *Otto*." But his eyes weren't on her; he was still looking at me the way Jimmy said he'd stared at Ma. Like a man who found sunflowers everywhere.

Nonna was almost finished writing down what he said when he took the paper and added something in his own clear handwriting: *FAILURE TO THRIVE*. "Give this to Elizabeth at the library and see if she can find something for Dahlia to read."

Ma kept the library book for so long she had to pay for it, and whenever she was reading, she always stopped and looked at me like she had the night we had the Franco-American. Or the way Dr. Genova eyeballed me in the office.

"What, Ma?" I'd say, but she just put her glasses on and went back to her book.

The next time Dad accused Ma and Nonna of having a crush on Dr. Genova, I piped in, "Me, too! I have a crush, too!"

"See what I mean? That quack put a spell on the three of yas!" But then he gave me an extra hug—just in case I hadn't gotten my eight.

It was fall when Ma walked into my room and caught me looking at my picture of waves. I tried to stuff it under my shirt again, but it was too late.

"Jon let me keep this one."

I could tell Ma knew I was breaking the one rule, but she didn't correct me. "You're still missing that beach, aren't you?"

I closed my eyes. "Missing." Though I wasn't sure I'd ever been there, it didn't feel like the wrong word.

Ma stroked my cheek the way she did with her baby Jon sometimes, but never with us girls. "If you're still here next summer, I'll find someone to take you. I promise."

I pushed her hand away and the words with it. *If you're still here.* Whenever the case worker talked about getting me back to my mother, I ran into the backyard to throw the stick to Princie. The idea of leaving the Moscatellis felt more impossible all the time. And yet, something leaped inside me when I thought of the one who looked like me and had my laugh, the one who gave me the treasures in my box. Would she really come for me someday?

THE TREES WERE flaming red and orange the Sunday morning when Nonna showed up wearing a pair of cat-eye sunglasses like the ladies in the movie magazines have. She announced we were going to the beach.

"Cripes sake, Ma; it's sixty-two degrees. Have you lost your mind?" Dad said. Then looking even more alarmed, "And where in hell did you get those *putana* glasses? Sure you're not meeting up with the quack?"

"Maybe I am." Nonna strutted around the living room. "And watch-a youself. I'm-a still your mama."

Ma flung open the curtain. "Doesn't mean they have to swim, Lou. It's a beautiful day for a picnic on the beach if you ask me."

Dad laced up his eyebrows. "Why do I sense a plot?"

"I make up a nice basket," Nonna said. "Eggplant sandwiches and pickle eggs. Some a those anise cookies the kids like, too." She lowered her cat-eyes and showed the ones that were brown and faded. "Who wanna come? Jonny? Zaida?"

When Jimmy and Jools came slouching down the stairs, she pounced on them. "You boys come to the beach, too. You and your friend need-a some sunshine, Jimmy."

"Thanks, Nonna, but we got plans." These days Jimmy said the same thing when anyone in the family asked him to go somewhere.

But Jools stopped. "Heck, it's been a long time since I been to the beach, Jimmy. And this time of year? Ain't like any girls'll be there to see us hangin' out with your grandma or nothin'."

"I don't think so . . ." Jimmy tried to say, but Jools had already started up the stairs to get the sketchbook he'd left in Jimmy's room. "Sometimes I wanna draw somethin' besides that ole river. Ya know?"

THE ONLY OTHER people on the beach that day were two old men combing the sand with their magnet sticks, but it took me a while to see them cause first of all—the sky. It was bigger here. So big that all you could do was open your arms wide as you could to take it in. And the water that had been black and white to me for so long was the color of the beach's name: Green Harbor. It sparkled like the lost jewelry the old men hoped to find in the sand. Even the waves were different. When they rushed at me like they did in the picture, they made noise.

Jimmy nudged Jools. "Look at Sky Bar. I think she seen the promised land." But Jools already had his sketchbook out and was staring like he saw it, too.

Jimmy spread out the blanket Ma gave us. Then Nonna told Zaidie and me to "set the table." She'd even brought real silver and cloth napkins like we used for holidays.

"Because it is," she told Zaidie when she mentioned it. "A very special holiday, right, my *piccola*?" She winked at me like Dr. Genova did when he said I was a sunflower. "Now set-a the most beautiful table you can. After lunch, I take off my stockings and you kids roll up you pants and we put our feet in the water."

Zaidie found an old pickle jar, which her and me filled with seaweed for a centerpiece while Jon hunted for six special rocks to mark our places. "I'm taking mine home to Ma," he said when he found a particularly smooth white one. From his voice, I could tell he was sad that she could never come to the beach.

The peach juice and sandwiches tasted better than they did at

Nonna's house. I didn't even mind the sand crunching in my teeth or the taste of ocean that got into everything. But before I finished my first half, the same thing that had made me steal Jon's picture came over me. In a second I was on my feet and running for the waves, kicking off my shoes and pulling off my sweater as I went.

"No, *piccola!*" Nonna shouted. "That water ice cold! You papa will— You ma—"

Zaidie was yelling, too, something about my asthma. "Agnes, what are you doing? You're not supposed to run!"

But like Jimmy when he was thinking about Jane Miller, I heard nothing but that thing inside me and the waves that were talking to it. Without stopping once, I jumped into the best feeling of home I'd ever had anywhere. Even in my own room with Zaidie.

"Look!" I heard Jonny yelling from the edge of the water. "She's swimming! Agnes is swimming!"

Whatever took hold of me, it must have been catching, because the next thing I knew he was peeling off his jacket, ditching shoes and socks, and running into the waves, too. Zaidie followed. Nonna was yelling and cursing in English and Italian, but no one heard her.

"Come on, Jools," Jimmy cried. "Like you said, it's not like there's any girls to see us makin' fools of ourselves."

"Shit, Jimmy! This water's freezin'-ass cold!" Jools yelled, forgetting he wasn't supposed to swear in front of us kids. But instead of reminding him that his kid sisters and brother were there, Jimmy just laughed. "First one to dunk gets a dime for Tucker's."

The next time I looked up at the shore again, Nonna was shaking her head, but she had stopped yelling, and from the look on her face, I could tell she was remembering again. A minute later, she peeled off her stockings.

It would have been the best day of my life if all of a sudden I didn't catch sight of what I'd been looking for in Jon's pictures. Right there in the waves and real as anything was another best day. I was playing in the water with the girl who had brown legs like mine, only we were both smaller. She was throwing water and laughter at me just like Zaidie and the boys were now. The girl was saying something, too, but I couldn't hear it because of the waves and because of my new brothers and sister and because of all the other stuff that had come between us before.

Mau Mau, I screamed. Except silent, like I always did when I called for her.

A minute later I noticed all the kids were watching me as I stood still in the water, seeing what no one else in the whole world could see, like I did on Franco-American night.

"You okay there, Sky Bar?" Jimmy asked. So I did the only thing I could do. I turned back to them and to the shiny green that surrounded me and to Nonna, who was smiling at us from the edge of the water, and when I looked again, the girl in the waves was gone.

THAT NIGHT, THOUGH, I got out the secret box I'd never shown to anyone. Then I flipped on the light and brought my very best present into Zaidie's bed. Lying in the palm of my hand, it looked like an ordinary penny, but it wasn't. It was the one I'd picked up from the puddle the night they took her away.

I wanted to tell her about the girl I'd seen in the waves and how it made me remember the thing I had made myself forget. Mr. Dean was standing in the attic door the way he did the night he took the hammer to me, only this time it wasn't cause I peed. I was calling for Mau Mau. I wouldn't stop no matter how many times he told me to.

He took a step closer, his hand raised up in the air, and I swear—I wanted to shut the hell up—I did. But it was like that feeling I had when I jumped in the water. Nothing on earth could stop me. *Mau Mau*, I yelled louder. *Mau Mau!*

But instead of whooping me like I thought he was gonna do, he dragged me to the window, opened it up, and pushed my head into the cold night air. *You know what your precious sister is, Agnes? She's a retard; that's what she is. Locked up in an institution and everything. So go ahead, howl all you want. She ain't never gonna come.*

Though I didn't know what a retard was or that other thing he called the place where she went, I knew by his voice it was something like a dope fiend or an Indian or nobody. Words he said when he wanted to tell me why no one wanted me. I tried to shake my head, but he was holding my neck so tight I couldn't.

No, she's not, I tried to say, but when I opened my mouth to call her name, the cold air rushed in and the asthma started to wake up and I couldn't make a sound.

After that, I tried to forget, but those words, like the other ones, they followed me. *Retard!* kids yelled at each other on the playground or sometimes in our yard. And whenever I heard it, I felt that cold air from Mr. Dean's window choking me again. Then once after Dad wrecked a tire on a nail Joe Junior left in the road, Ma said the O'Connor boy belonged in the place where Mr. Dean said Mau Mau had gone: an institution.

"No, he doesn't!" I didn't even know I was yelling till everyone stopped eating and stared at me. "And . . . and you shouldn't say that, either." But no one, not even me, knew why I was so upset. Or why I jumped up and ran outside without clearing my plate. Not till today when I saw the girl in the waves. Not just her legs or her hair, but all of her.

Zaidie took the penny from my hand and closed her own fist around it for a minute so she could feel what it meant.

I knew she had looked at my file cause I'd heard Ma yelling at her about it, so I asked the question I didn't dare to ask anyone else. Even myself. I said it so low that no one would have heard me but Zaidie: "Where did they take her? Where did my sister go?"

But she just looked sad and handed me back my penny. "Sorry, Agnes, but I don't know; Ma took the file away before I read that part."

For once I wished she was a better liar. And I wished I hadn't turned the light on because then I wouldn't have seen the tear that slid down her face.

I went back to bed and switched off the lamp and I didn't ask that question again for a long time. I didn't take out my penny, either, but some nights, I still woke up with my fist closed around the emptiness.

CHAPTER THREE

Killed by a Cat

DAHLIA

FOR WEEKS, JIMMY HAD BEEN WORKING ON THE BLOCK OF WOOD Jon brought home from Cub Scouts, carving and sanding it into a sleek race car. By the time he was finished, it flew across the kitchen floor so fast Jon and Agnes whooped like it had won the Pinewood Derby. After the little kids painted it, Zaidie added a perfectly even white stripe, and their lucky number: 100—same as our house.

Then wouldn't you know? Old Josie Pennypacker had to go and ruin everything by dropping dead on the night of the event. Right in front of our house, no less. I blamed Flufferbell. Damn cat disappeared regularly, but this time was different.

A WEEK PASSED and then two. Still, old Josie wouldn't give up. All hours of the night, you'd hear her calling that fool name—more desperate every time. Only the day before, Agnes had heard her whimpering on the porch and gone over to share her Hawaiian Punch.

"Sometimes they just don't come back," Agnes tried to tell her, as she passed her the glass of punch. "Nothing you can do."

Josie shook her head, rejecting both the drink and Agnes's words, and that night she was out calling louder and longer than ever—right outside the girls' window.

She was at my door first thing in the morning, too—bleary-eyed and still in her bathrobe. "Agnes was cruel," she blurted out, sounding like a kid tattling on a friend. "I didn't think she had it in her."

"She doesn't," I answered quick—like I always did whenever anyone said something about one of my kids. There was a lot more I wanted to add. *It's not Agnes that's mean, Josie; it's life.* My kids knew that practically from birth. I shook my head at her. *Look at you, half-toothless with a head of snowy hair, and you still haven't got the news? Sad—that's what it is.*

But before I spoke, I took in the rings below her eyes, the tear-stained ruts in her cheeks, and for once in my life, I held back. Good thing, too, because within twenty-four hours, the woman was dead. A massive coronary, the know-it-all neighbors were repeating even before they carted the body away.

"Killed by a damn cat is more like it," I told Louie, when I called him at the garage. "Imagine if your last word on this earth was Fluff-erbell? Dear Lord."

Louie took a breath so sharp, it cut through the phone. Then he fell quiet. "Poor woman," he finally said, sounding like his mother. "God rest her soul." A minute later, he reverted to form. "This couldn't wait till I got home? I'm in the middle of a damn engine job here."

Outside my door, Edna O'Connor from the next street and Jeffrey's mother, the one I called Gina Lollobrigida for the way she flaunted herself around, were carrying on. Like they ever gave a damn about the woman. Old Gina had even got herself all fixed up to go look at a dead woman.

I stepped out onto my porch.

"That little cat was all she had in the world," Edna sobbed when she saw me. If I felt like arguing, I would have told her Josie had a lot more than a fool cat.

She had my kids—though you wouldn't read about that in her obituary.

Oh, she'd started off like everyone else in the neighborhood—moaning about the trouble we'd brought onto their perfectly respectable street. When the cops had been called for one thing or another, Louie and me knew who it was right away. *That damn Josie Pennypacker*, he'd say before I added my bit. *The hag.*

But everything changed a couple of years ago when Jimmy went and told Agnes he loved her. Maybe the first time the kid ever heard the words. Did he have any idea how dangerous that could be?

Don't get me wrong; I'd thought about saying it a few times myself—especially when I caught her looking at me with those hungry eyes of hers. But you have to be careful about giving Emergencies—or yourself—the wrong idea.

Sure, Agnes was settled in like a member of the family and all, but as long as there was talk about getting her to a home closer to her mother, I held back.

THAT NIGHT WAS the high school dance, though, and well, you would have thought Jimmy was going to meet the queen. Boy spent twenty full minutes in the bathroom looking at himself. When he came out, it wasn't just his hair that was gleaming; it was like the whole world had a sheen to it.

"I love you, Z," he yelled to Zaidie, before telling Jon the same thing. Shad, he called him like always—short for Shadow. Then he'd picked up Agnes and whirled her around. "You, too, Sky Bar. I love you."

"Damnit. Can't you ever call anyone by their right name?" Louie snapped. But I knew what he really meant: *Be careful there, son.*

It was too late, though. Soon as Jimmy set her down, Agnes touched the center of her chest like she did when she first came and was claiming a new word as her own.

"Jimmy loves me. Me," she told Jon, talking like she'd just won one of their endless competitions.

"So?" Jon countered, sounding confused. "He loves me better. Right, Jimmy?"

The dance mustn't have turned out like Jimmy hoped because for the next few days, he was under one of those dark spells that gets cast on kids that age. It didn't break till one night in the middle of supper when Agnes decided to give the words back to him: *I. Love. You. Jimmy.*

Like each word was a sentence, or more than that—a whole book. And the way she smiled when she said it? It was as if something trapped inside her all her life had been set loose. Heaven help us.

Jimmy looked up from his plate of teenage miseries and laughed out loud. "Wha'd you say, Sky Bar?"

This time she stood up and repeated it like it was the Pledge of Allegiance, hand across her chest and all. Even Louie had to laugh. Well, almost.

Anyway, once it was loose, there was no stopping it. Within the week, Agnes wasn't just saying those words to the family, she was telling the whole foolish world—from the mailman to that bitch of a fourth-grade teacher (who rewarded her with a trip to the principal's office for inappropriate behavior) to Flufferbell—and always with that blazing smile.

First time she said it to Josie Pennypacker, the old woman hunched up her shoulders, wrapped her cardigan sweater around herself tight, and scowled. "Are you talking to me, little girl?" Like she'd cursed her or something.

Then, just as she had with Jimmy at the table, Agnes stood up straight and said it louder.

"Probably gone inside to call the cops," Louie muttered when the old woman walked away, mumbling.

But a couple of days later, Josie showed up at the door with a lumpy-looking cupcake on a plate. "Made it from scratch."

"Hmm. So I see." I left the inside door shut as I regarded her sorry-looking creation.

"It's for the little girl. Agnes," she emphasized—as if I might eat the damn thing myself.

"I didn't think you knew her name." Up until then she'd referred to our kids generically. The teenager. The blondie. The noisy little boy. The Indian.

I opened the screen and took it. A nice treat for Princie, I figured. But before Jon and Agnes had brought the dog back from the park, Josie was at the door again—this time with a whole tray of crooked cupcakes.

"I don't suppose I could give to one and not the others. There's a couple on there for you and Louie, too."

Dear God. What had Agnes gone and done now? Reluctantly, I accepted the plate.

Was I surprised when they turned out to be the best I ever had, or when Josie started remembering the kids' birthdays with two bucks and a card. She even came flying out of her house to defend Jonny when that bully, Tommy Collier, tried to steal his volleyball.

In return, Jimmy kept her walkway shoveled in the winter, the three younger kids went out to search for Flufferbell whenever she took off, and Agnes told her she loved her every day for the rest of her life—even though Josie ran away every time.

Like I say, sometimes the truest thing about a person never makes the obituary.

BY THE TIME school was out, the body and the terrible white of the sheet they used to cover it were gone. The pack of neighborhood gawkers had mercifully disappeared, too. I couldn't have the kids getting the news from strangers so I lined them up on the couch—the girls, the surly teenager (*Jeez, can't you just tell us whatever it is?*), the restless boy (*But Ma, I have to get ready for the Derby!*). Sensing it was some kind of family event, Princie took her spot between Jon and Agnes and watched me attentively.

Course they all got quiet when they heard. Even Princie, who must have caught the feeling from the rest. But soon you could see Jimmy hardening himself against it like kids do at his age, while Jon and Zaidie puckered their mouths up the exact same way and began to cry.

Jon only stopped blubbering as he realized the impact it might have on him. "But why did she have to die on the day of the Pinewood Derby?"

That earned him a nudge from Zaidie. "Stop being so selfish! Think of poor Miss Pennypacker."

Meanwhile, Agnes, who was closest to Josie of us all, just folded her hands together like they taught her to do in school when she really needed to pay attention and looked down, eyes dry as bone. I could tell she was drawing on what she knew, the mean truth she'd tried to tell Josie that day on the porch: Sometimes they just don't come back.

If death is a surprise to most people (*Such a shock!* my mother always said whenever it had the gall to come near), it was something my kids knew all too well. In fact, no one even had to die for them to understand. They were used to people walking through doors and vanishing without a trace. Poof. No explanation. Not even a pretty write-up in the paper or a guy standing on an altar who claimed to know where they'd gone. Or why. Or to promise you'd see them again someday because maybe you would, but most likely not.

Gone is gone, see? as Zaidie explained to Jon when his hamster got eaten—probably by Flufferbell. I wondered if she was thinking of the mother, who she'd seen lying beneath another terrible sheet, just like Josie.

All you could do was fold your hands and look out on the world the way it was and somehow, somehow try to keep them in the only place where they could be reliably found: inside you. And oh yes, you could—and if you were Agnes, you had to—go out on the street and give your *I love you* to someone else. Didn't matter whether they deserved it or not.

Glowering at me like I was the one who killed the woman, Jimmy grabbed that hoodlum leather jacket of his. "I'm going to Jools's. No need to wait up."

I was about to remind him he hadn't had supper and wasn't likely to get any at the Bousquets' place. Besides that, he was sixteen—he still needed to ask.

But before I could speak, Jon let loose with a stuttery yell, "B-but, tonight's the—the Pinewood Derby! You—you—you promised, Jimmy, you—"

Jimmy turned around, hand still on the doorknob. "For Pete's sake, Shad, did they have to do it on a Friday night? I got my own life to live here. Supposed to be a parent who takes you, anyways. Why don't you ask your mother?"

I'm telling you the way he said the word *mother*, the way he looked at me, I wondered if those Woods had gotten to him somehow. Told him God knows what.

There was no time to think about all that, though—not with Zaidie sobbing into her hands and Jon downright wailing over Josie Pennypacker or the Pinewood Derby or the both of them rolled into one.

"Maybe Jeffrey's dad can take you—"

"They're already taking their c-c-cousins, Ma. There's no room in the car."

"Well, Dad, then."

"But Dad hates Cub Scouts. And he thinks the Pinewood Derby's stupid. Says so every night. And 'sides that, he's had a long day."

"Don't worry, Jonny. Dad won't let you miss it. Not after all the hard work you kids have put in."

When Zaidie and Agnes looked up from their separate forms of grief, I could tell they were both thinking the same thing: Louie's not gonna like this.

SURE ENOUGH, LOUIE grumbled his way through dinner. "Nope, not doin' it." He set into his meat loaf, arguing with himself. "Is it my fault Jimmy backed out on him? Whose idea was it for Jon to sign up for the stupid Cub Scouts anyway?" (He shot me a look.) "Whole thing's nothing but trouble."

He paused to gulp his water. "Useless busy work. He wants a badge? Send him down the garage to help out and I'll be happy to give him one."

But when Jon's lower lip began to judder, Louie pushed his plate away and got up—just as we knew he would.

Jon rushed to hug him—probably about to blurt out the words that sent old Josie scurrying every time, but Louie stopped him.

"Hurry up and get that car of yours before I change my mind. And soon's that race is over, we're leaving, understand? Got a truck waiting for me in the bay tomorrow with a problem six mechanics ain't been able to figure out."

Agnes had been angling to tag along ever since she'd seen Jon's racer flashing across the floor, but had been told repeatedly it wasn't for the likes of her. "You're supposed to go to Girl Scouts like Zaidie," Jon explained with an exaggerated patience that almost made me laugh. "You're supposed to sew and sell cookies. Right, Zaidie?"

Ignoring him, Agnes went to the closet for her shoes. She was at the door, her shamrock barrette clipped to the side of her head all lop-sided and hopeful, before anyone else.

"Absolutely not," Louie said. "Tell her, Dahlia."

"If she really wants to go so bad, what's the harm, Lou?"

Louie shook his head. "Come on, then. With any luck, they'll throw us out."

CHAPTER FOUR

The Girl Beneath the Yellow Leaves

DAHLIA

NONE OF THE OTHERS HAD DONE THEIR CHORES SO I LET ZAIDIE off, too. She seemed happy to escape to the room where she had begun to live a life apart from us, just like Jimmy did at Buskit's River. Don't think I hadn't noticed.

It was fine with me—at least for that night. I hoped the clatter of the dishes might drown out the sound of Jimmy's voice in my head, the way he'd looked at me. Like he knew everything I'd spent my life trying to hide.

And maybe the water from the faucet would rinse away what I'd seen that afternoon, too. Poor old Josie under that terrible sheet, her whole life nothing more than a sorry heap. I suppose that was what really made Edna and Gina Lollobrigida carry on the way they did. The truth of it. When I thought of the old woman standing at the door with her lopsided cupcakes, face shining with the flame Agnes had lit inside her, I almost started bawling myself.

Soon's I turned off the water, I heard the strains from the record player Zaidie's aunt had sent her for "Hanukkah." Same song over and over, too.

Johnny Angel, cause I love him and I pray that someday he'll love me. She was only twelve, for heaven's sake. What exactly was she thinking about up there? Could there be some boy at her school . . . ? Before

I allowed the thought to take hold, the needle scratched across the vinyl and started again.

That did it. I stormed up the stairs and burst through the door without knocking as the simpering idiot on the record whined: *Together we will see how lovely heaven will be.*

Why, oh why had I ever let them talk me into taking a girl?

"I thought you were doing homework. You should have stayed down and helped with the dishes if this is all you have to do with your time." I pulled the plug on the record player as Shelley Fabares's voice skidded into oblivion.

Zaidie glanced in the direction of her desk, books lined up just so. "Already done."

I couldn't help noticing the way her color deepened, like she'd been caught at something. Growing up, I suppose. It wouldn't be long before she responded to my outbursts with anger like Jimmy's. Or mine toward my own mother.

I gave a perfunctory check of her geography assignment. Above the desk, right next to a picture of Marie Curie, she'd hung the chart where she tracked her life: homework done, pages read, even how many strokes she'd brushed her hair.

Her outfit for the next day—a plaid pleated skirt and a white blouse—were already over the back of her chair, slip, socks, underpants, and all. On my best day, I'd never been so organized.

I rubbed my hand over the smooth grain of the desk. "Your brother did a nice job, didn't he?" My way of apologizing.

Zaidie's smile still had some of her sadness over Josie, which made me regret breaking whatever comfort she found in her music.

"Best present I ever got," she said, repeating what she'd said on Christmas morning.

The compliment was for Jimmy—always the adored one—not me or even poor Louie, who dragged the damn thing home from a rummage sale on Parkington Street.

"Guess how much I paid for it?" he said that day when he lured me out in the garage for a look.

I traced the nicks and scratches with my hand, my eyes settling on the broken drawer. There wasn't even a handle. "Too much, whatever it was."

Louie's face caved in a little. "There's not a lot of extra for Christmas this year, so when I saw this—well, I thought Zaidie might like it."

I hadn't had much hope for that desk, but after Jimmy refinished it and Jools polished up an old handle he found in Buskit's River, it looked almost new.

I stared at the record player, hoping I hadn't scratched up *Johnny Angel* too bad. "Well, since your work is done, I suppose you can play your music awhile. Only not so loud. And not that same song over and over. Let me hold on to what little sanity I have left. Please."

"Sorry, Ma."

I was the one who should have been apologizing, but instead, I turned back to the chart and pointed at the last thing to be checked off. "You haven't brushed your hair yet."

"That's next."

ON THE WAY downstairs, I touched the gray mess I pulled into a bun every day like the old ladies did. Probably didn't hit a hundred strokes in a week. I liked to tell myself Louie didn't care about things like that, but a couple of times when old Gina Lollobrigida slunk past our window, I'd caught him watching. Even blushed a little like Zaidie when he realized I saw. "Christ almighty, Dahlia," he said. Like that was my fault, too.

I'd barely reached the bottom of the stairs when strains of a new song stopped me.

When people ask of me what do you want to be now that you're not a kid anymore . . .

There's just one thing that I'm wishing forrr . . .

I wanna be Bobby's girl; I wanna be Bobby's girl.

I almost turned and marched right back up the stairs, but then I remembered Zaidie's face after I scratched *Johnny Angel.*

Instead I went to the picture window and looked out at the spot where Josie had been, but was not now. Then I wrapped my cardigan around myself extra tight like she used to do—not sure if I was protecting myself from what was outside or the saccharine voice that was drifting down the stairs.

Like my kids, I'd seen too many people I loved come and go to be surprised by death's tricks. It wasn't just the babies who clung to me one day then disappeared into a social worker's car and were never seen again, or my own dead father lying in his coffin, either.

NO. TRUTH IS I'd been dead myself once. I'd lain down in the unfamiliar woods where it happened and stared at the sky until I couldn't stand to look at it anymore and then I'd closed my eyes and let the smell of the earth take me. It had been a cold summer and the yellow leaves were already starting to fall. If I lay there long enough, I knew they would cover me like the terrible white sheet covered Josie.

For a while—they said it was three days, but because I was dead, it happened outside of time—I wanted that. Yes, even as I drank the rainwater that kept me alive, I wanted it.

But then something inside me—later Louie would claim it was him, his voice, though I hardly knew him at the time—called me. *Get up and walk and don't stop till you find the road out*, the voice said.

And somehow, with seven broken bones and a bad concussion, I did. Barely made it to the highway before the sky collapsed on me again, but it was far enough.

First face I saw was my mother's. "You're going to make it," she said, squeezing my hand. There were even tears in her eyes. If I had squeezed back, maybe we could have fixed everything that was wrong between us.

I pulled away and turned my face to the wall. How could I tell her she was wrong? That Dahlia Garrison, the girl who stood up in front of the whole school without a trace of fear, who thought she might become a nurse—even a lawyer—had died out there in those woods when she closed her eyes to the sky. Died and been covered in yellow leaves. Now someone I didn't yet know, the one Louie called out of the dark, lived in her place.

Staring out the picture window, I almost let myself go back to all of that—to the hospital room where my mother gave up weeping for me, and to the woods where a foolish young girl was buried forever.

But wouldn't you know—just then, a thin, bedraggled Flufferbell came marching down the sidewalk like a soldier back from the wars, howling for food so loud she drowned out the past and the future—even the sound of that infernal song. And where did she stop, but right outside my door.

Dear God.

CHAPTER FIVE

The Maledizione

ZAIDIE

THE DAY AFTER MISS PENNYPACKER PUT HER HAND ON HER chest like she was about to make a sacred promise and dropped dead, Nonna came over with her holy water to bless the spot. She also made a pie in honor of the occasion: *crostata al limone.* Even the name was more delicious than the American kind.

Everyone was distracted so I took a double slice onto the porch, where I watched Nonna sprinkle the sidewalk and pray in Italian.

Eventually, Ma came and stood in the doorway. "For goodness sake, Anna. Josie wasn't even Catholic."

"This not for Giuseppina—it for you. You and *mi Luigi*," Nonna said, without looking up.

I glanced at Ma. Whenever Nonna called Dad *her Luigi*, we knew she was serious.

Nonna paused briefly to shake her hand in the direction of the doorway. "Someone die outside-a you door like that? It a *maledizione*, Dahlia. A *maledizione*." She returned to her sprinkling. "*Ave o Maria . . .*"

"A what?" Ma said. Then she raised her hand. "Never mind. I don't want to know."

However, the way she was staring at the sidewalk—as if she saw

Miss Pennypacker lying there beneath Nonna's holy rain—said otherwise. A shudder I will never forget passed over both of us at the same time. That's when I knew the *maledizione* was real.

I didn't even have to look the word up in the Italian-English Dictionary to understand that it was some kind of Italian curse. No longer hungry, I fed the rest of my pie to Princie and went inside.

AFTER THAT, I cut through Mrs. Guarino's yard out back and entered by the kitchen door, careful to avoid the contaminated patch of sidewalk. I snapped the drapes in the front room shut as soon as I was safe inside.

"What do you think you're doing? I can't even see my puzzle." Ma squinted at the Taj Mahal, still unbuilt on her card table, but I noticed she didn't get up to open the drapes.

It took a few days of working in the dark before she even mentioned it again. "You don't believe that foolishness Nonna was talking about, do you? That stuff about the *mala* whatever it is."

I wondered if I should tell her that three nights earlier I'd sat straight up in bed, certain I'd heard Miss Pennypacker's voice. Just a nightmare, I tried to reassure myself, but then Flufferbell, who had taken to sleeping at the foot of Agnes's bed, stirred and meowed in the direction of the window.

"You think those drapes could keep death out if it had a mind to pay a visit?" Ma said before I had a chance to speak.

"Better than nothing," I answered feebly, still hearing the voice that had cut through my dream: *Fluufferbell . . .*

"People from the old country believe some strange things, you know—especially the women. You can't listen to—"

"Jeffrey's mother believes it, too. She says the whole street better be careful."

Even though I knew better than to use her name, Ma bristled at the mention. "Gina Lollobrigida? So now you're listening to that paragon of wisdom?"

"She says death comes in threes."

Faster than I'd seen her move in years, Ma jumped up from her seat and flung open the drapes, drowning us in light. "With any luck, she'll be number two. Or I will—if I have to listen to any more of this claptrap."

"Ma!"

"I'm sorry, but I've had about all I can take of these superstitious fools. Your Marie Curie would be ashamed of you."

But before she was back in her chair, Ma's body contradicted her with another shudder.

SHE WAS RIGHT about Marie Curie, though. Maybe I wasn't cut out to be a scientist after all. That night I replaced the chemist's picture with one of Joan of Arc holding her sword. Now, there was a heroine who understood what I was up against.

"I thought you were supposed to be Jewish," Ma muttered when I caught her standing in front of it.

"Half, remember?" I said. "And why do you care? You didn't even want me to go to Hebrew school."

"Hmph." She folded her arms across her chest. "Who do you think gives you the bus fare every week?"

Ma and I had stopped talking about the *maledizione*, but whenever I caught her scowling at the street, I knew she was on the lookout, too.

WE DIDN'T HAVE to wait long, either. It was only a few weeks later when the car we all dreaded pulled up in front of the house and Nancy got out. I almost screamed when she marched right across the patch of sidewalk where Josie had fallen. Like most people, she had no idea where she was walking in this world.

It seemed Agnes's mother and her husband had moved again. Some place closer to home. "From what I hear, they're still having their troubles, so it's not likely she'll take her back anytime soon, but . . ." She lowered her voice, but I already knew the rest.

Afraid my sister might be number two, I shuddered like Ma had when the light hit her too hard that day in the parlor. Not that Agnes was about to clutch her heart and drop like Miss Pennypacker. No, if the *maledizione* came for her, it would be the other kind of death.

Ma described it as the kind that leaves behind a question mark instead of a corpse. "Sometimes those are worse," she said. "When they're in the ground, at least you know no one can hurt them anymore."

I took to watching Agnes when she slept just in case the department or the *maledizione* or Miss Pennypacker's ghost tried to spirit her away in the middle of the night. Sure, I was used to seeing kids come and go, but Agnes was my sister now. There was no way I was going to let them take her away.

But then a few days later, I heard Ma saying Mrs. O'Connor from the next street had a stroke. A bad one, Dad added, making it obvious that she was number two. For a minute I was almost relieved that it hadn't struck our house, just like I'd been a little glad that Agnes's mother was caught up in the same thing that killed Jimmy's mom and kept his father away. But that night I saw young Joe O'Connor walking through the neighborhood, clutching his head like Agnes held on to that penny in her sleep, and I realized the *maledizione* was never something to celebrate.

FORTUNATELY, AT TWELVE and three quarters, I had so many other things on my mind I soon forgot the curse. Every day after school, I went straight to Cynthia's, where I stayed till it was time to set the table for supper. "Just homework," I told Ma, when she asked what the heck I was doing over there all those hours.

"Your sister and brother miss you."

"They're little kids, Ma. They need to play with their own friends." Then, catching the stricken look on Agnes's face, I recited all the assignments they gave us in honors class. "I thought you wanted me to go to college." College. It was the word to end all arguments as far as Ma was concerned. Her holy grail.

There was another reason I went to Cynthia's, though, and it—or should I say *he*—was even more compelling than a death at our doorstep.

I'd known Henry Lee most of my life, but somehow never noticed the smooth roll of his shoulders when he walked, the contrast between his skin and the pastel shirts he untucked as soon as school got out (polished, but cool all at once), or the hair that was as black and shiny as my sister's.

I knew I shouldn't tell Agnes. She was already jealous enough of the blue diary I wrote in every night, never mind a boy. And besides, she was still a kid. But I couldn't help myself. I told her everything. Even when I'd first gotten my period, I'd blurted it out.

She studied me skeptically from across the room. "Nuh-uh. You're lying." So I'd showed her the box of Kotex and the elastic belt to prove it.

At first, she took it with her usual stoic quiet. But just when we were about to fall asleep, she flicked her light on. "You mean you're going to do that right here in our room? Every month?" Her eyes went round as coins as she stared at the twin bed where she still climbed in with me some nights. "Disss-gusting."

"Jeez, Agnes. You sound like those guys in the Old Testament who made the girls go sleep in a hut."

Her reaction to Henry Lee was even stronger.

"Only boys I like are Jimmy and Jon," she said, scrunching up her nose like she did when she smelled liver cooking in the kitchen. Then, when she'd had a moment to think about it: "You're not going to kiss him, are you?"

"How do you know I didn't already?" I teased. She raced out of the room with her fingers in her ears.

Once when I lingered too long on the phone in the foyer with

Cynthia, rhapsodizing about the wonders of Henry Lee, I caught Agnes standing beside me, jump rope in hand. I'd given up stuff like jump rope when I started junior high, but she never stopped asking me to play.

Her eyes narrowed. "Jimmy'll get him with his baseball bat. That's what he'll do to Henry Lee!"

I covered the receiver with my hand. "You're supposed to be outside playing. Go!"

But when she upped the ante by threatening to tell Ma, I hung up and followed her into the backyard. "What do you want to play—Chinese or plain?"

"No Chinese!" she said a little too quickly. And then, unconsciously mimicking Dad—stern face and all: "In this house, we play regular jump rope."

IT ALL STARTED a few months earlier when my aunt Cille got the same aggressive cancer that took my mother. She left Jon and me a generous educational trust, a weathered book of Hebrew that had once been Sylvie's, and a sorrow I couldn't explain to anyone.

Though I only saw her twice a year, Aunt Cille was my link with the lost part of myself. Who else knew that I had my grandfather's chin or my mother's endless (sometimes dangerous) curiosity? Who would tell me stories about how my grandparents had first come to this country, or remember the many times my inquisitive mother had wandered off and gotten lost—at the beach, in a museum, once on a crowded city street?

For two weeks, the mysterious alphabet contained in the book sat on my bureau beside Sylvie's picture like Agnes's cigar box. Then one day—perhaps propelled by that same spirit that made my mother wander—I picked it up. It was another week before I got up the gumption to tell Ma I wanted to go to Hebrew school.

"But you're not— I mean, we're not—" she stammered. "Heavens, I wouldn't even know where to begin, Zaida."

But when I told her that my friend Julie's mother had offered to introduce me to her rabbi, and that Jimmy would ride the bus to class with me, she stopped what she was doing. "You've got this all planned out, haven't you? Just like you always do."

It seemed significant that I went to Hebrew school to find myself and ended up finding Henry Lee. Though he lived down the street from Cynthia and was in several of my classes at school, he seemed different when I ran into him outside the synagogue.

"Are you . . . Jewish, too?" Then I took in the gym clothes and immediately felt my face go hot.

Pretending not to notice the dumb question or my even dumber red face, Henry smiled, indicating a dank-looking building next door. "I have a wrestling class in—" He paused to consult his watch. "Fourteen minutes. I've got this thing about being early, though."

"You study wrestling?" I asked, looking at him like a stranger. "I thought you liked, um, debate club. Stuff like that."

"A person can be more than one thing, right?" He laughed. "Besides, wrestling and debating really aren't that different."

By then it was time for me to go inside, but that day during class, I found myself thinking less about Hebrew and more about the smooth muscles that were usually hidden beneath Henry's button-down shirts, the whiteness of his teeth when he smiled, and the similarity between wrestling and debating. What kind of boy said things like that?

I glanced out the window at the place where we'd talked and shuddered like I had when I felt the *maledizione*. This was a different kind of spell, though.

From then on, I asked Jimmy to take me on the early bus so I'd arrive fifteen minutes before class started like Henry Lee did.

"What other boy at school is such a master of time?" I asked Cynthia when I watched him start his paper route every day at precisely 3:48.

"What's the big deal about that?" She giggled. "You must be the

first girl I ever knew who got a crush just because a kid is punctual."
Then we put Bobby Vinton on the record player and practiced danc-
ing slow together like we did every afternoon. It was easy to lean
against her smooth chest and imagine Henry Lee's cool, untucked
yellow shirt, but when she tried to think of Kevin Spinelli, my breasts
got in the way.

"You're not supposed to get them till you're thirteen, you
know," she said, like it was some kind of law. Then she glanced
down her shirt to see if something might have sprouted since she'd
last checked.

Ma agreed. "You want to know why I never wanted to take in
girls?" She stared at my chest accusingly. "There's your answer."

Nonna saw it differently. When we went bra shopping at Hanley's,
she barged into the fitting room and stared at the breasts that were
spilling from my first bra.

"*Bellissima*," she pronounced them right out loud. Fortunately,
we were the only ones in the store. Then to my horror, she flung open
the curtain to show me off to Mrs. Hanley.

"By the time she's fourteen, she'll need a C cup," the clerk clucked.

"Girl take after her Nonna." She put her hands on her hips, stuck
out her own drooping watermelons proudly, and strutted across the
store.

Laughing, the clerk did the same. "I was the first girl in my class
to get my friend," she boasted. "First to need a bra, too."

At that moment, it seemed as if for all the blood and mess and
ache, there might also be something fun about this whole business of
becoming a woman. Inside the dressing room, I stuck out my own
chest and laughed at the mirror. *Bellisima!*

On the way home, though, Nonna warned me to watch-a for the
boys, watch-a for the men. It sounded like one of Agnes's jump rope
singsongs, but Nonna was dead serious.

"Some-a the men, they don't know you still a little girl. And
some-a them"—(Here she widened her eyes like she did when she

talked about the *maledizione*.)—"they don't-a care. Tell you papa those kind bother you."

Dad? Was she kidding? I didn't know who would have keeled over from embarrassment first—him or me.

I glanced at Nonna, wondering if she knew it had already started. Drivers as old as my father leaned on their horns and whistled to me on the street; men who, only a year earlier, had petted my head like they did with Agnes and Jon winked at me in a new way; and some of the boys in class turned as red as I did when I caught them staring at the curves my baggy sweaters couldn't hide.

But when Jimmy's old friend Bruce Savery got me alone one afternoon at the playground and asked if I'd ever been to the Sugar Shack, Nonna's threats came pouring out of me, accent and all: "You want-a me to tell my father?" And then, reverting to myself: "Or should I just call the cops?"

"Hah. You think the cops care about you?" he spit back at me. "You're a foster kid. A Moscatelli, for crying out loud. Chief Wood hates—"

That did it. Forgetting I was Jewish, I said a quick prayer to Joan of Arc. Then, making use of Nonna's when-all-else-fails advice, I kicked him right in the you-know-where. Who knows what might have happened if a couple of Jimmy's rat buddies hadn't come along?

"You okay over there, Z?" one yelled to me, using Jimmy's nickname. I immediately recognized Crazy Duane, the kid who'd been thrown out of school for carrying a switchblade.

"Nice friends," Brucie muttered before he stumbled away, clutching his crotch.

Crazy Duane's laughter echoed from across the playground. "Good job, Z."

HENRY LEE, MASTER of time, was different. Though I was pretty sure he liked my chest, too, his eyes were mostly on my face. It wasn't long before he started walking me to Cynthia's house after school.

The second time it happened Cynthia shot me a look and discreetly fell back to walk with three eighth graders from pep squad.

I was so intoxicated with the smell of Henry's English Leather I hardly heard what he was saying, never mind what the girls were whispering behind us, but I could feel the envy. He might be in the advanced class with the kids they called finks, but Henry Lee of the untucked shirts and the wrestling muscles? He was cool. Even the eighth graders knew it.

Cynthia, too. She began to consult the clock when he started his paper route. "Three forty-eight again! How does he do it? Do you think he might go to the dance at St. Edward's?"

"No *might* about it. He is." I told her I planned to wear my new skirt. "All I have to do is convince Ma to let me go. And Jimmy to walk me there."

My face must have revealed how likely that would be since the dance was on a Friday—the night Jimmy reserved for "his own life."

At first, I'd been as offended as Ma and the kids by the very idea. But as I played records in my room or watched for Henry Lee to appear with his newspaper bag from Cynthia's window, I began to understand.

"If he can get Kevin to go, my mom will drive," Cynthia volunteered.

Henry Lee hadn't given me his tie tack like the older kids did, and (no, Agnes) he hadn't kissed me, but all of that was coming soon. How did I know? Because when I asked Cynthia's Ouija board if I was going to marry him, the needle swung toward YES with only the tiniest nudge.

As for children, the Ouija board predicted none. Not that I didn't like babies, but there was no way I was getting stuck in a parlor, fitting puzzles together and reading about other people's lives like Ma did.

IF I HAD any lingering fears of the *maledizione*, they were wiped out at the dance when, to the tune of "Roses Are Red," I leaned against Henry Lee's mint-green shirt for real; or later when we followed the kids who snuck outside for a Pall Mall or a Newport. Though neither of us smoked, the sweet smell of tobacco would always bring it all back: the cool Henry Lee standing in the dim light, hands in the pockets of his chinos, teasing me about nothing. And everything. The way the night air entered our bloodstreams, stealthy as hormones, and mysteriously remade the world.

He waited until everyone had gone inside to kiss me, but whenever I remembered the pressure of his mouth, I would taste smoke.

BY THE END of the school year, I was pinning Henry Lee's tie tack to my collar every day: "You're only twelve, Zaida. Much too young for this nonsense," Ma said in her exasperated voice every time she found the little pearl in the wash.

"Thirteen in a month," I reminded her. Then two weeks . . . tomorrow. "Thirteen!" I shouted on the morning I became an official teenager. "Now I'm like you, Jimmy," I told my brother at breakfast.

"'Fraid not, little sister. Cool like this only comes along once in a lifetime."

"Who is this boy, anyway? One of the Lees who own the tailor shop over on Oak Street?" Ma scowled and headed for the kitchen, her voice a trail. "As if your blood wasn't mixed-up enough already."

"His dad's an engineer, from the west side," I said, knowing how she got intimidated by fancy people.

"I knew I shouldn't have let you go to Hebrew school. If that boy gets you in trouble . . ."

"Ma!"

Exactly what did she think Henry Lee and I were doing? I might be a teenager with my own life to live, but the woman could still make me blush.

I WASN'T THINKING of any of that on the last day of school, though. I was too excited about the plans Henry and I had made for the summer. Once a week (at least, he begged), we'd meet at his friend Barry

Schuman's house. Barry had a built-in pool, a working mother, and a house generously stocked with things like salted cashews, Devil Dogs, and Pepsi—rare treats at home.

But that day, I was also full of the thing that bound Ma and I together in a way that no one, not even Henry Lee, could touch. The intersecting point of my charts and biographies and her dreams.

Inside my book bag was the best report card I'd ever received. It wasn't just the perfect string of *A*s (I'd received those before) but a note from Mrs. Galen describing me as a very bright student certain to excel in eighth grade and beyond. The word *very* was underlined twice. I'd already memorized what she'd written next: *I hope I live long enough to see what Zaida Finn becomes!*

I walked faster, imagining Ma's reaction. She wouldn't say much; nor would she give me a quarter for Tucker's like Cynthia was likely to get for her B-plus report, but I would feel the pride running through her like a current. And later, when she took out her book *Plan for College Now*, Mrs. Galen's promise would be on her face. I was so preoccupied I didn't pay much attention when Bruce Savery slowed his dad's car and called to me from the window.

Before I could decide whether to yell back or run, the car behind him honked and he sped away. I'd forgotten him by the time I reached the corner of Sanderson. Him and everything else but the future that was safe inside my book bag. *I hope I live long enough to see what Zaida Finn becomes.*

I saw Ma opening the report card, imagined how she would touch every A with her finger like it was more than a mark on paper. Picking up speed, I turned recklessly onto my own street. By then, the image of Nonna and her holy water had been eclipsed by Henry, slouching in the dim light outside the St. Edward's dance, and I'd forgotten all about the *maledizione*.

As I reached the house, I was yelling, "Ma! I got all As, Ma!"

I expected her to be waiting for me like she always was on the day we got report cards. The empty porch and the curtains fluttering in the open windows were the first signs that something was wrong. Then I noticed a familiar car parked out front.

I dropped my book bag in the driveway. What was Nancy doing here? My first thought was that they had finally come for Agnes. But the *maledizione* is nothing if not unpredictable. Hadn't Nonna warned me? Hadn't I seen it enough in my own life?

I thought of Miss Pennypacker, stepping onto the sidewalk that morning like she did every day, no clue that someone or something had counted out the steps she would take before her hand flew to her chest. The words. The breaths. Wasn't it supposed to be Flufferbell who was at risk of death?

I pushed open the door, calling louder, "Maaa!"

In the parlor, Nancy was drinking tea and eating Lorna Doones like she didn't notice they were months old, her legs crossed in a flirty way that reminded me of Gina Lollobrigida. I froze in the foyer.

"Come in, Zaidie," she said, like this was her house and I was the visitor. "Mrs. Moscatelli went upstairs to lie down."

Lie down—in the afternoon? On report card day?

"But it's almost time for *The Edge of Night*," I said weakly, my eyes settling on Jon. However, it was the way Nancy referred to Ma that really made me panic. Mrs. Moscatelli? My heart was hammering so hard I was sure everyone in the room could hear it.

Sinking into the hole in the couch, Jon looked like he was about to face the rifleman himself. I took it all in—the glass of ginger ale on the table before him like he was a guest, the unnatural quiet in the house. The only thing I didn't see—I refused to see—was the man who had taken over Ma's armchair.

"We have some good news for you, Zaidie," Nancy continued, beaming in the direction of the man. "Wonderful news, actually. Why don't you join your brother there on the couch?"

"They made Jimmy bring Agnes to the movies," Jon said from

the hole. "Even though it's a Wednesday and Jimmy didn't want to see no dumb kid's movie. They made him." He took a hiccuppy breath, looking at me like his last hope. "Tell them we ain't going, Zaidie. Tell them."

No longer willing to be ignored, the stranger stood up the way Ma taught the boys to do for a lady, but not for a kid, even one who had dropped a report card that pronounced her likely to excel in the driveway.

They say people you knew when you were little are smaller than you remember, but the man—I refused to call him my father—was taller than I recalled. More handsome, too. A pale blue cardigan, obviously chosen to match his eyes, was looped over his shoulders like he thought he was Tab Hunter. And though it was only June, his skin was a deep, cultivated gold. There were streaks of brilliant silver in the hair that was otherwise the same color as Jon's and mine, and he'd styled it like President Kennedy's. But it was the capped perfection of his teeth that really struck me.

"I can't believe how grown up you are, Zaida," he said. "Or how lovely." And then, unaccountably, Michael Finn began to cry.

The word that came to mind was the one Agnes used when she first heard about my period. *Disss-gusting.*

CHAPTER SIX

Chickens on a Conveyer Belt

ZAIDIE

WHEN I WAS NINE, DAD TOOK ME TO A PLACE ON THE EDGE OF the city where we sometimes picked up fresh eggs. This time, though, he was steeled up to confront Junior Littlefield, who owed him for the transmission he put in his truck three months earlier. The subject had dominated my parents' supper conversation for weeks. Mostly, we kids ignored it, but the chorus stuck:

"A hundred and forty bucks, Louie! That's the mortgage and the electric." (Ma)

"Don't worry; he'll pay or I'll take it out of his hide." (Dad)

That day, instead of parking in the front, we followed a dirt road to a large windowless structure in the back. I expected to visit the chickens in their coops like usual, but when I reached for the door handle, Dad's face darkened. "You stay in the car this time."

"But I want to see—" I began before I realized he was focused on the metal building that glinted in the sun. He strode toward the door, shoulders set like they were when Jimmy stayed out too late and Ma forced him to go out looking for him. Was he really going to take it out of Junior Littlefield's hide? What if someone got hurt? What if the police came like they did when Joe O'Connor Jr. beat up the mailman because he didn't bring his birthday card?

In an instant, I was out of the car, calling his name. "Dad, wait! Don't—" But as soon as I reached the building and pushed open the metal door, my voice was drowned out by the din. In the center of the room, a row of chickens attached by the necks to a conveyer belt squawked wildly. Junior Littlefield stood at the end of the line wearing a blood-covered raincoat and a pair of hip boots. An ax—also bloody—dangled from his right hand as Dad, intent on his hundred and forty bucks, jabbed a finger into his chest.

My eyes were on the chickens, though. The conveyer was paused, but they weren't fooled for a minute. Both the ones on the belt and the ones stacked in crates beside it screeched and flailed wildly, feathers drifting through the dusty air. The metal door flapped open in the wind, desperate as the wings of those chickens. I ran blindly for the road.

When Dad caught up with me, I was still crying. "For chrissake, Zaidie, do you have any idea how far from home you are?" He ordered me into the car. "And stop the damn bawling. Where the hell do you think we get that fried chicken Ma makes? From trees?"

"B-b-but they were scared, Dad. They knew—" I sobbed.

In between my sniveling, I caught bits of his lecture. "Your own fault." Hiccup. "If you woulda waited outside like I told ya . . ." Sob. "No more of this now, I mean it." Three loud hiccupy cries. "Knock it off before your mother sees you." But each time he spoke, his voice softened.

Finally, he pulled the car over and wiped my face with a greasy hanky. "There, there, now." Ma's words were all wrong in his mouth, but he had none of us own. "You're gonna go home and forget what you saw, okay?" He rested his large thumbs on my eyelids as if it was possible to erase it.

I only wished I could.

"IT WAS THE worst noise in the whole world," I told Agnes that night when she climbed into my bed for a story. As always, I needed her to hear what I heard, to see those feathers flying, feel the terror of the chickens. And when she turned on the light the way she did when she had a nightmare, I could tell she had. We fell asleep clinging to each other and for once, I didn't complain that she was crowding me.

The next morning, she marched into the kitchen like she did when she had a big announcement to make, stood at the head of the table, and told the whole family we were never eating chicken again. "Not Zaidie and not me, either."

Only Jimmy bothered to look up from his Frosted Flakes. "Hah. Good one."

So I might have to eat it, but no one could make me like it. When Ma served Chicken à la King the night after Michael Finn turned up, Agnes shot me a glance across the table. Neither of us said a word, but I knew we were both seeing those birds on a conveyer belt.

"I'm not hungry," I said, gagging.

Meanwhile, Agnes slipped her plate under the table for Princie when no one was looking.

Just this once, I would have been happy to hear that this wasn't a damn diner or that kids were starving elsewhere. But a silence like the one those birds left behind consumed the table. Jon and Ma picked at their food and Dad ate mechanically. Most ominous of all, Jimmy's seat was empty.

When I finally asked where he was, Agnes was the only one who bothered to answer. "He took off after the movie and didn't come back." And then, as a new horror occurred to her, "He's not taking Jimmy, too, is he?"

"Agnes!" Ma and Dad yelled simultaneously, as if they might reassure us. But then they fell quiet again.

I pushed my chair back and walked away without even clearing my plate, testing how far I could go without being noticed.

Apparently there was no limit. Agnes and Jon promptly joined me on the stairs.

Why wasn't anyone calling Michael Finn a louse or talking about how they'd stop him? And why hadn't Ma gotten on the phone to the Bousquets, demanding Jimmy be sent home this minute?

That night in my room, the case worker's voice echoed. "The earliest hearing we could get is in two weeks," Nancy said when Ma finally came down to the parlor. "That should give you some time to . . ." Her voice trailed off as if even she knew how unspeakable the idea was.

I'd waited for Ma to say something—that Michael Finn couldn't just show up and take us after seven years . . . we would fight . . . Louie wouldn't allow it . . . something. But the only sound was that of Michael Finn, clearing his throat as he looked pointedly at Nancy.

"In any case, it's just a formality," she added quickly. "There's never been any doubt that Mr. Finn is a fit parent."

Without making eye contact, she told Jon and me that our father would be visiting next Wednesday afternoon so we could get "reacquainted."

"We don't want to get re-ackainted, right, Zaidie?" Jon said. "Tell him he can't make us."

It was one of the only times he'd turned to me instead of Jimmy. Though I had once longed for him to recognize me as the big sister who had watched over him when our mother was sick, I had no more answers than Ma and Dad.

That night I waited up, hoping to hear what they said when they thought we were asleep. Around nine, Dad shuffled off to bed early. "It's been a hell of a day, Dahlia. I'm turning in." The defeat in his voice terrified me more than anything I'd heard up to that point.

Ma didn't try to stop him, either—even though Jimmy was still out somewhere doing God-knows-what with God-knows who.

Sometime after eleven, my brother slammed into the house, not even trying to be quiet.

"Dad's already gone to bed? What the hell?"

"Language, Jimmy," Ma said. "And for God's sake, keep your voice down. The kids are—"

"The kids are about to be taken away; that's what they are. And you're worried about me saying *hell*?"

"This is hard enough without you—"

"Hard enough," Jimmy repeated incredulously. "Hard enough."

I could hear him pacing up and down like a lawyer in the courtroom, allowing those words to vibrate through the house. His voice rose as he reached his summation. "So you really ain't gonna do shit, are you? Just let some asshole walk in and take half our family?"

"Jimmy . . ." Ma began before her voice broke.

At that moment, Dad's feet thudded onto the floor and his bedroom door flung open like a shot. "If I ever hear you talking to your mother like that again, I'll—"

But that night all the familiar threats, like all their promises and advice, felt hollow and he seemed to know it. When I went to the top of the stairs and looked down into the parlor, the prosecuting attorney had been replaced by my skinny brother. He was folded into Ma's arms, sobbing.

"There has to be something we can do, Dad," he said, swiping at his face as he pulled away. "What about all the money you been saving for our college? You could call that lawyer Brennan who got Duane off and—"

Ma shook her head. "He's their father, Jim, and like Nancy said, he hasn't done anything wrong."

"Just left them for most of their lives is all. Didn't even show up when their mother got sick and died. If that ain't wrong—"

"Not to the state, it isn't. Or not wrong enough. He's claiming their mother took them away and never told him where. That he's been looking for them—"

There was no point yelling that it wasn't true. Or that Aunt Cille

had told me the shit (yes, she'd even used that word right in our parlor) had abandoned us when our mother was pregnant and moved
out of state to avoid paying child support. Though he could well afford it, she always added. No point when we all knew Michael Finn
would show up in court, speaking his fancy words and wearing his
fancy clothes while Dad would be tongue-tied and reeking of the
garage in a rented suit. No point when Judge Reilly was married to
a cousin of the Woods and would have taken Michael's side even if he
showed up in court dressed like Junior Littlefield at the Egg Auction,
ax and all.

I ran to my room and shut the door on the whole pointless world.

I MUST HAVE slept late, because when I woke up, Agnes had dug out
every last picture of my heroes and hung them up so that wherever I
looked, one of them stared me down. What good had they ever done
me? I was about to tear Florence Nightingale from the wall, but the
sight of my sister in the doorway stopped me.

"You'll think of something, Zaidie; I know you will." Then she
handed me the lucky shamrock barrette I thought was long gone.

THE FOLLOWING WEDNESDAY, Michael Finn loped up the walkway,
carrying two pints of ice cream from Lannon's Dairy.

Inside, he tried to give me the carton in his right hand. "If I remember correctly, strawberry's your favorite."

"Black raspberry and vanilla are the only flavors I eat. I hate
strawberry," I said, violating Ma's one rule about telling the truth.

He hardly blinked. "What about you, Jonathan? I'm guessing
you're a chocolate chip kind of guy."

"Jon," I mumbled.

"I'm sorry. Did you say something, Zaida?"

"No one calls him Jonathan."

"Your mother and I always wanted our children to be called by their proper names." He set the ice cream on the coffee table, and took over Ma's armchair like he had a right. "Did you know I chose your name? After an old college friend—very lovely girl from Lebanon—though she pronounced it ZuhEEda. Your mother didn't like it much at first, but she came around." He smiled nostalgically.

So even my name had come from one of Michael's *friends?* The screen door slammed in the kitchen as Ma escaped into the yard.

"Get the bowls, Zaida, before that strawberry turns into a pink puddle for Mrs. Moscarelli to clean up."

Jon corrected him before I had a chance. "It's Moscatelli and she's our Ma."

I'd been proud of how little I remembered him, but when he drew his mouth into a thin, impatient line, it was as if I was back in New Jersey.

"Of course, your *Ma,*" he said, making it sound like the kind of word that could get your mouth washed out with soap. "Now would you get those bowls, Zaida."

I remembered that, too. The requests that should have come with a question mark but didn't. Jon drew closer to me as if he felt my tension. "I don't want none, either."

"You must be the first kids I ever met who don't like ice cream." Michael Finn was smiling again, but his index finger tapped out a menacing rhythm on the arm of Ma's chair. After all the years we'd been apart, I still knew the beat.

"I guess that means there's more for Daddy." He went into the kitchen, heading straight for the silverware drawer as if he lived here.

He struck me as the kind of guy who watched his figure like Gina Lollobrigida, but he plunged into the strawberry and ate it straight out of the carton to prove a point. "It's my favorite, too, Zaida. Did you know that? Another thing you got from me."

The tapping had stopped, but it continued to resonate in my ears.

How did he know what I always ordered? Not only would I avoid strawberry ice cream in the future, I vowed I would never again eat anything pink.

Finally, he set down the spoon and leaned forward, resting his elbows on his knees. "I'm really not such a bad guy, you know. No matter what she told you."

She. Was he talking about Sylvie? I scoured the memories from my life in New Jersey, and later with her on Elm Street. The only time I recalled her mentioning him was at the end, when she had called his name over and over, relentless as Miss Pennypacker crying for Flufferbell.

I sat still with my hands folded on my lap like Nonna Moscatelli had taught Agnes and I to do when company was visiting. *Had he ever had power over me?* I wondered. If so, I was free of it. Free. No matter what the court had to say, I would never go with him. If he tried to force me, I would run away as many times as it took just like Agnes had. As for the logistics of getting from Colorado to Claxton, well, I'd worry about that later.

I touched the shamrock barrette for courage. "Where's the girl you ran off with?"

"What?" And then before I had a chance to repeat it, "Is that what she told you—that I ran off?"

"Didn't you?"

"It was more complicated than that, Zaida—far too complex for a little girl to understand. You were what—all of five—when we split up."

"When you left."

His perfect tan took on a maroon tinge. "What kind of mother tries to turn a five-year-old against her father with a pack of half-truths? Did you ever ask yourself that question?"

"Things are either true or not. There's no such thing as half."

"Who taught you that little trope? No, wait. Let me guess— your Ma."

He stared me down waiting for me to say more, but I remained quiet till he was about to leave. Then I dug into memory and pulled out my one-word grenade: "Peggy."

He sighed as he sank back onto the couch. "I'm sure your mother had plenty to say about that subject."

"She never said anything," I said. "It was Aunt Cille who told me."

"A woman who knew absolutely nothing about our lives. Did she mention that after Sylvie and I got married, her family virtually disowned us?"

"They didn't do that. You were the one who poisoned her mind. Kept her away."

"Lucille knew nothing—" he said before I interrupted.

"Then you left us and ran off with a kid from your school."

"If you think you can goad me into discussing—"

"Peggy."

He was silent for a minute, but the hook was in deep. "Of course Lucille would make it sound as sordid as possible. If we stayed away from your mother's family, that was the reason."

My eyes burned. "Don't you dare say anything about my aunt."

By then, he was tapping again, tapping and staring at me as if he saw someone else. "All right, since you refuse to let it drop, Peg was hardly a kid. She was a graduate student who later became my wife. And she wasn't the cause of our problems. She was a symptom."

I'd heard the same line on Ma's soap opera. But he was eyeing me with the same wariness I felt toward him in his powder-blue sweater so I held my tongue and waited.

"And since you're so concerned, Peggy and I aren't together anymore."

"So that's why you came for us. Because you don't have anyone else."

"Enough, Zaida. When you're older, we can discuss—"

"I'm not going with you." I thought of how Rabbi Krieger had emphasized the importance of proper conduct for a Bat Mitzvah. *Say little, do much, and receive all men with a cheerful countenance*, I'd written in my notebook. A quote from the Torah. Obviously, the writer hadn't known Michael Finn.

Ma had come to the doorway. When I looked at her, I felt the presence and the strength of all those who had made me who I was: Sylvie and Aunt Cille, Jimmy, Agnes, Nonna, and all of those heroes on my wall. But above all, *them*. Ma and Dad.

Michael Finn reached for my hand and pulled me in the direction of the cloudy mirror where he stood beside me. "What do you see, Zaida?"

I jerked away, but not before my obvious resemblance to him was imprinted on my mind. His voice rose. "I see a thirteen-year-old child. And I also see my daughter—no matter how you—or to be perfectly candid, I—may feel about it at this moment."

From his expression, I could tell he heard the echoes of old arguments he'd had with Sylvie swirling around us. He shook his head as if to dispel them, then sat down again—this time on the couch beside Jon.

"I almost forgot I have something for you," he said, reaching into the pocket of his trousers. He pulled out five smooth marbles—the large ones they called boulders. They were the same ones that Old Man Tucker sold for a nickel, but when they caught the light, they looked like something rare and exotic.

"He doesn't want them," I said, rescuing a cat's eye that had rolled to the edge of the table.

"Yes, I do!" Jon blurted out before turning to me with contrite eyes. "I been looking for one like that, Zaidie."

"Of course you do, son." Michael slung a protective arm over Jon's shoulder as if shielding him from me.

"She used to call for you," I said.

Momentarily stunned, he released Jon. "What? Who are you talking about—"

"I thought she forgot, but at the end when no one was there but me and Jon and the nurse, I would hear her calling—*Michael, Miii-chaellll.*"

Ma took another step into the room as if to stop me. But it was too late. I was there, back in that apartment where no one wanted me to go. Not Ma. Not Michael Finn. Not even me.

"I didn't know how to pray, but I closed my eyes and imagined you coming home late at night like you used to. The first couple of times I really believed that when I opened them you would be there and everything would be okay."

"Jesus, Zaida." Michael Finn put his face in his hands, and for a minute I thought he was praying, too. Or weeping. When he looked up, I expected him to be sorry or to offer some reason. But instead, his face was pale with rage.

"So that's how you choose to remember your father? By her bitterness?"

Was that what he really thought—that she'd been bitter? I had been only five, but even then I knew how much she loved him. I would have told him, but he'd already taken so much of her; I wasn't about to give him any more.

"Memory doesn't choose," I said. "It just remembers."

"Memory doesn't choose," Michael repeated with a twisted pride. "Nice turn of a phrase. No matter how you try to deny it, no matter what lies they've fed you, you're still my daughter, aren't you?"

So he was taking credit for my words, too? He, who had bragged about the "journals" where he had published poems and stories. As if any of us cared.

From the kitchen where Ma had retreated, I heard the click of her wooden spoon and smelled onions frying. She had promised to make Jon's favorite: American chop suey.

"Our flights are booked for the day after the hearing, Mrs. Moscatelli. Please make sure the children are packed and ready," Michael Finn called from the parlor.

Then he kissed my cheek and winked at Jon before checking his appearance in the mirror one more time.

After the door closed, I heard the wooden spoon hit the wall, leaving behind a slash of red that would never be washed away.

CHAPTER SEVEN

My Father's Victory

ZAIDIE

FOR THE NEXT SEVEN DAYS, EACH NIGHT'S SUPPER WAS MORE OR-
dinary and wondrous than the last: tuna casserole with crushed
potato chips on Thursday, hot dogs and beans on Saturday, a Sunday
roast with mashed potatoes.

On liver and bacon night, Jon spilled his cherry Kool-Aid and
Dad dropped his fork, about to bark out the usual: *For chrissake, Jonny.
How many times have I told you—*

But before he got a word out, something stopped him. The same
force had Ma in its grip, too. She didn't jump up to get the mop or defend her baby by fuming at Dad: "Leave him alone, Lou; it was an accident." Nor did she yell at Agnes for overfilling the Flintstones jelly
jars. No one was denied dessert for goofing around at supper.

Without the blame, defensiveness, and tension we'd always fallen
into, we glanced around the table at each other and wondered how a
spilled glass of Kool-Aid had ever mattered.

Agnes laughed when Princie sidled into the room, hoping one of
us might sneak her a piece of liver from the table. "Watch out, Princie.
Your paws'll get stuck to the floor."

For a moment none of us knew what to do, but then we all joined
her. Even Ma.

"I got it, Shad," Jimmy said when Jon finally pushed back his chair to clean up the spill.

But the heartbreak was always close to the surface. The sight of my brother kneeling over that pool of Kool-Aid reminded me how he'd bent over Ma, sobbing; and the clock that had momentarily stilled ticked on, even more noisily. One day, twenty-one hours, and thirteen minutes before the hearing that would decide our fate. Just a formality, Nancy had said.

MICHAEL FINN DIDN'T call once that week; nor did we hear from anyone from the department. There were moments, whole hours, once an entire day when I allowed myself to believe he was gone for good. Maybe another girl like Peggy or the one with my name had caught his eye and he'd forget us for eight more years. Maybe, if I stayed up wracking my brain long enough, I could think my way out of this. But then his final words coursed through my sleep and jolted me awake in terror: *Our flights are booked . . . Have the children packed and ready.*

Sensing my restlessness, Agnes whispered to me in the dark. "Mr. Dean said he would come back to get me, too, but he didn't. He never did."

In my head, however, the words that tormented me answered her. *No doubt Mr. Finn is a fit parent . . . Just a formality . . . Have the children packed . . .* No, this was nothing like the threat from Mr. Dean.

When loudmouth Jeffrey let the news out, Cynthia pressed me every day. "You're not really going, are you?"

"No, of course not."

"Promise?"

"I promised yesterday, Cynthia. Please. Don't ask me again."

Sometimes saying the words scared me more. Other times, when I spoke up strong, I almost believed it. But it was never long before the clock resumed its infernal beat.

I still attached Henry Lee's tie tack to my shirt every day, but when he called, I told the family to say I wasn't home. Finally, sick of the endless ringing, Ma grabbed the phone from Jon: "Don't you understand? She doesn't want to talk to you."

It took a whole day to summon the courage to ask what he'd said. Ma scowled at a TV ad for Dial soap. "He said to tell you not to forget the plan. What's that supposed to mean?"

"Nothing," I said, my throat thickening, as I thought of how we'd promised to meet at Barry Schuman's house. Tuesday at one. Even as the clock ticked inside me, I hadn't forgotten for a second.

On Tuesday, as one o'clock passed and then two, I imagined him sitting by the pool, watching the gate. Henry Lee, master of time, would have been there by twelve forty-five. How long would he wait before he gave up?

At three, I went out in the backyard and threw the stick for Princie so long and so hard that for the first time ever, she wore herself out. When she lay down in the middle of the yard, I spooned her like I did when she snuck into my bed. Did Michael Finn really expect me to leave my dog, or the nicked picnic table where all the kids who'd ever passed through the house had told us their secrets, or the desk Jimmy had refinished for me?

Did he know Cynthia and I planned to try out for cheerleading next year and that Henry and I were in the same homeroom? Every object I'd ever used or tripped over felt sacred—from the jelly jars to the shoes Jon always dropped in the middle of the parlor to the window in my room where Agnes and I stared into the night and talked. Even the moon, our moon, would be different if Michael Finn took me away. I was sure of it. Burying my face in Princie's heat and softness, I cried for the life that was seeping away minute by minute.

I don't know how long I'd lain there before I realized someone was with me, stroking the dog from the other side. Henry's eyes had never been so dark, his olive skin never so smooth.

"So this is the famous Princie?" With his free hand, he swept a wing of black hair from his face. "I was expecting the most notorious thief in Claxton to be scarier."

I wiped tears from my face. Looking around the scrappy yard, I took in everything I had been embarrassed for him to see—the peeling paint of the house, the stack of old tires beside the garage, Ma's face in the kitchen window, lined with troubles. But now my fear felt as silly as Jon's spilled Kool-Aid. For once, it didn't even matter that my hair was uncombed or that I didn't have a tissue to wipe my eyes.

"So you were just going to leave without even saying goodbye?"

I looked toward that kitchen window, where Ma had disappeared. "I told Cynthia not to tell you. And besides, I'm not going." As the tears streaked down my face, I realized how unconvincing I was.

"But if you have to, we can write every week, and he might let you come back to visit your family in the summers. Then we'll—"

I shook my head. "Why would he do that? He doesn't even understand they are my family."

"You know my brother's girlfriend, Gail? They're still together even though she's in school out in California. He says the letters they had to write brought them even closer. He also says high school flies by, and maybe we could apply—"

"So even your brother's heard?"

"You know how you tell your sister everything—even if she's too young to understand? Well, that's me and Craig."

"Jimmy, too. Or at least before he became a rat." In the past, I might have been ashamed of that, too, but now it was just more spilled Kool-Aid.

And the amazing part? Henry didn't care. In his pale blue T-shirt, he lay in the dirt, one arm open to the sky, the other stretched across Princie to hold my hand. Nothing was said and he didn't sit up and try to kiss me or pull me out behind the garage to press himself, breath and bone and fire, against my chest. But I would always remember it as one of the most perfect moments of my life.

I was the one who finally bolted upright and checked the Timex watch that Ma had given me for my Bat Mitzvah. "Henry, look!" I held out my wrist, displaying the time: 3:57. "You're nine minutes late for your paper route!"

But Henry just lay there in my scrappy yard, stroking Princie and staring at the sky. "Yeah, I know," he said. And when he smiled at me, it was almost as if he'd seen that cherry Kool-Aid, too.

MICHAEL FINN SHOWED up on Wednesday afternoon just like he said he would.

Instead of a suit, he wore a pair of jeans and a blazer. A shirt that matched his eyes and the sweater he'd worn before was open at the collar. Unlike Dad, the obviously fit parent didn't have to prove his worth in the court room or anywhere else.

He and Nancy walked across the *maledizione* and climbed the porch, leaning close to each other to share a joke like a couple on a date instead of a pair who'd come to ruin our lives.

"Afternoon, Zaida. How's my girl?" He was so engrossed in Nancy, he seemed almost surprised to see me. Or was that calculated to throw me off, too?

His smile was a dare.

"What do you think of this guy?" he asked, capping Jon's head with his hand. "Is he a little heartbreaker or what? Just like the old man."

Nancy giggled. "No one's conceited in your family, right? You got it all."

I rolled my eyes at the familiar middle school taunt. How had I ever thought she was pretty?

"Where's your mother?" she asked.

When I refused to answer, Nancy approached the stairs. "Mrs. Moscatelli? You up there?"

If I had any hope, it disappeared as soon as I saw Ma's face. She'd obviously heard the judge's ruling by phone, but Nancy read it again before producing the paperwork for her to sign.

Meanwhile, Michael called me to sit beside him on the couch. He took my hands in his before I could stop him. "I don't know what I expected to find when I came here two weeks ago, Zaida. But since my first visit, you've made it clear that you're not the little girl I remember. Chronologically, you're thirteen, a child, but you're hardly typical, are you?"

Once again, I felt him puffing himself up, as if any positive quality I might possess was a credit to him, but I didn't pull my hands away.

"If you were," he continued, "I'd demand you do what the court thinks best—not just because I can give you a better life, but because—well, you're mine. I saw that when you were small, and it's even more apparent now. No matter how many years you live with this family, I will always know you better. Bone of my bone and all that."

Even as the words confused and incensed me, I felt he was speaking truthfully for the first time.

"I hope you decide to come with me today, but if you don't, well, Zaida, you've earned my respect. I'm going to allow you to make a choice."

At that, my brother was on his feet, his hands knotted into fists the way they were when he ran. He looked from Ma to me and back. "What? You mean Zaidie can stay, but not me? That's not fair! Ma! Tell him I'm not going!"

He flung himself at Ma, sobbing, and the two of them clung to each other as if nothing on earth could separate them. But I already knew it could. And so did Jon.

Momentarily unnerved—and undoubtedly embarrassed in front of Nancy—Michael Finn's mouth stretched into the thin line I remembered. The same line it had formed when I told him how Sylvie had called for him when she was dying.

Where had Princie come from? And Agnes? I didn't even hear them enter and would only later remember how Princie had run through the rooms of the house, barking, the way she did when we argued or she sensed danger.

Agnes, on the other hand, stood frozen in the center of the room, as if the sound of Jon's screaming and the sight of him clutching Ma's gray dress had taken her somewhere no one could follow.

I think Nancy was the one who stepped forward and wrenched Jon away, but I can't be sure. All I remember clearly was how Michael Finn dragged him from the house, a howl trailing him like smoke that would never be dispersed. But what would haunt me most was the way his eyes had scanned each of our faces and the house he would not see again.

"His things?" Nancy repeated.

"Forget them," Michael said.

Standing as still as Agnes, Ma covered her mouth and lowered her head, her eyes closed.

As they reached the sidewalk where Josie Pennypacker had keeled over, Jon broke free from Michael's grasp. But he must have known that there was no place to run.

Still sobbing, he turned to me. "You gotta c-c-come, too, Zaidie. Y-you—you promised our mama. You told her you'd always take care of me. You can't make me go by m-myself."

I thought he'd forgotten the times when, jealous of his bond with Jimmy, I'd reminded him I was his real sister. I told him how I'd gotten up with him in the night when our mother was sick. What she'd made me promise.

"Ma's my mother," he always replied. "And Jimmy is too my real brother. Realer than you."

I opened my mouth to explain all the reasons I couldn't go: because

Jimmy and Agnes needed me, because no one knew how Ma would carry on after this, because Dad couldn't do everything. But were any of those the real reason?

Or did I just want what Jimmy called my own life—Cynthia and my friends, cheerleading and the bench at Beth Shalom where I sat with Holly Simon's family? And most of all Henry. The way he'd made me feel at the dance that night when he stood there with his hands in his pockets, or the day before when we lay on our backs and opened our arms to the sky in the yard. I thought of how Michael Finn had dragged me to the mirror to make me see how much we were alike. How deep did it go?

"There's still time to change your mind, Zaidie. I didn't cancel your plane ticket," he said, coolly victorious. Again, I saw the smile, the dare he'd brought with him. This time, though, I understood it.

I turned to my brother. "We'll—we'll figure something out, Jonny, I promise we will. You have to go with him today, but Dad will . . . he'll do something to get you back. Ma will get a lawyer like Jimmy said and . . . and . . ."

Again, Michael Finn took his arm. This time, when Jon wailed, his cry had words: "I hate you, Zaidie! You know that? I hate you forever! You and Ma—all of you."

My only solace was that Ma had retreated to her room and closed the window so she didn't hear him.

After they left, I followed the car till I got tired. Then I went to my room and cried for my lost brother, but also for the part of myself Michael had forced me to see. The part that had chosen myself, what I wanted. Just like him.

IN THE WEEKS that followed, the phone rang every night at precisely six, just like usual.

"Zaaaa-deee!" Agnes called like usual when she picked up the phone. "It's that boy. Do you want me to tell him you're not here?"

She didn't even try to cover the receiver like I'd taught her, but it no longer mattered.

"Tell him not to call here anymore. It's over," I finally told her—loud enough that he could hear me.

"You're breaking up?"

I hated the water that filled my eyes. "For crying out loud, Agnes, just tell him." Then I tore the tie tack from the shirt I was wearing and ran out of the house. When I reached Buskit's River, I hurled it as hard as I could.

CHAPTER EIGHT

Get Up

DAHLIA

ONCE YOU'VE TRIED IT, THERE'S NOTHING SIMPLER THAN DYING. You just lie down where you are—in the woods or on the sidewalk or right there on your own messy sheets. Then you close your eyes and wait for the world to grow dim. Everything that seemed to matter—whether to make the meat loaf or the chop suey for supper, how to get your oldest to stop running with the rats, or what to do with the youngest girl, who was as bright as anyone—maybe brighter—but didn't care much about school—all of that rises like a cloud and drifts away.

The mole you've been watching on your husband's hand after reading the "Seven Signs of Cancer" in *McCall's* may bleed or grow—or it may sit there, harmless as a garden frog. Like the troubles of the Bauer clan on *Guiding Light*, the hour passes, the screen grows dark, and things reveal themselves for what they really are: vapors.

Once they took my baby away, I went to my room and closed the shades like I was switching off the set. Poor Agnes came and stood at the door.

"Are you coming down, Ma?"

I didn't open my eyes. I couldn't.

"Zaidie ran off chasing that car, and she didn't come back," she persisted. "Do you think she—"

"Give me half an hour," I finally said to make her stop.

But she must've seen me laying out straight, hands folded like I was in my coffin. The back door slammed, and I heard her running down the sidewalk, calling her sister's name. Princie, taking advantage of the open gate, followed, announcing her freedom with a series of joyful barks. And all the while I lay like the dead, unable to get to the window and yell about the asthma like I usually did: *Do you want to end up in an oxygen tent?*

Nor did I worry what mayhem Princie might wreak. The more, the better, far as I was concerned. Was I supposed to care that Gina Lollobrigida had her white dress ripped from the clothesline when the boy I'd carried around the house till he was two, holding on to his baby scent as if I'd never set it down, had been torn up like someone's morning glories?

Later, Zaidie came in, taking the stairs two at a time as if it was possible to outrun what's inside you. The door to her room was barely closed when the sobbing started up.

But the dead have no comfort left to give. I switched on the little transistor Louie got me for my birthday. The static it produced would have been perfect if it didn't make me think of the disappointment on Louie's face when he gave it to me.

"You bought this—for me? For heaven's sake, Lou," I'd said. "These things are for kids." No sooner were the words out than I saw that look and regretted it. Well, I was done with all of that, too. The guilt over who I was and who I could never be, what I could or couldn't hear. I slept to the static like it was a lullaby.

At six, the sound of Louie's work boots came tromping up the stairs. On another day, the heaviness in his step would've killed me. He stopped halfway up—like he couldn't bear to look at me, either.

"You coming down to make supper or what? The kids are hungry, Dahlia."

And then, after a minute of my deathly quiet: "Christ almighty."

When he walked back down, the heaviness was still there, but there was anger in his step, too. The closest that a man like Lou comes to it, anyway. I was glad of that. Rage, at least, kept you moving.

STILL, HIS WORDS echoed. The kids, he'd said, but what he really meant was the girls. Jonny was on a plane to a place I knew only through my jigsaw of the Rockies, and Jimmy had left before breakfast and hadn't come back all day, not even to say goodbye to his Shadow.

"I was supposed to be their big brother," he'd said the night before. "How many times did I tell them they didn't have to be scared of no one? 'Anyone messes with you kids, come to me.' Bad part was they believed it. Thought me and my stinkin' bat were a match for anything. Even worse, I believed it myself."

When they pulled Jonny off me, his howl was a cold wind that cut through all of us—even the ones who weren't there. I felt it in Lou and the girls, but mostly in Jimmy.

I didn't know where he'd gone—to Buskit's River or to Duane's or out to that old shack in the woods where the town drunk used to live; I didn't know whether he was running or walking or riding his bike. Nor was I sure if he was telling his friends what happened or laughing extra hard about some teenage joke like nothing was wrong in the world. The only thing I knew was the burning inside his chest, the heat behind his eyes. *Even worse, I believed it myself.*

"I'm not hungry," Zaidie called down when Lou asked for help with the supper. How long before she realized that man, her father, was right? He could give her a better life. How long before she reached for it with two hands?

I lay on my sheets and heard a pan clattering onto the stove. "Any Franco-American in the pantry, Dad?" Agnes asked, extra loud for my benefit.

"How the hell should I know?" Louder still.

Eventually, Zaidie was made to come down, and I heard their

chairs clatter into place at the table. Only after she went out and the TV came on did Agnes start pestering Louie. Full volume, of course. "She didn't even tell you where she was going, Dad. In the night. You're just gonna let her walk out?"

A silence like mine filled the house—as if death was contagious.

But Agnes was having none of it. "And where's Jimmy?" she pressed. "Ma woulda called the Bousquets by now." She lowered her voice, but it rose up anyway: "Do you think she'll come down tomorrow? If you talk to her, Dad, I know—"

"Damnit, Agnes, watch your show."

I switched on the static and fell asleep.

Later, when Louie was snoring in the couch, Agnes brought me a plate of cold noodles and some of the fresh milk that had made her grow. As if that might cure me, too. She flipped on the light and sat awhile, too, talking about the things that used to matter. "Did you hear Zaidie come home? Said she went down to Buskit's River." Here she paused, waiting for a reaction. "At night, Ma—when it was dark. Princie was lost, too, but me and Dad found her. She stole the O'Connors' dog bowl again, though."

Jon's gone and you're talking to me about dog bowls? I hollered inside. *And what about Jimmy? You, above all of them, know how he is. Sensitive, much as he tries to hide it. The sweetest of the sweet, like you say when he brings you those Sky Bars. Kid's been blaming himself for things that weren't his fault since he was two. How do you think—*

Why was she coming up here, trying to make me eat? Drink? Feel?

"Turn out the light when you go," I told her.

That night, mad and heartbroke as he was, Louie still put his hand on my thigh when the lights went out. After twenty-two years, it was the only way he could fall asleep. It didn't take long before he lost his patience, though. "Your boy was out all night, you know. You're not the only one hurting here."

He waited, but all I had was the silence of the woods.

"Can you give me a rough estimate of how long you plan to lay up here like this?" he asked a few days later. "Cause the house down there? It's fallin' apart."

If I had the strength, I would have told him that when it's your time to lie down, it doesn't come with a plan. It just comes. I would have told him something else, too. How the pain I experienced the first time I died came back every time I fell asleep—the real, physical pain—like I was feeling those fists all over again. Then the yellow leaves fell around me, thicker than ever.

"Not long, Louie," I murmured, too low for anyone to hear. "Not long at all."

The next day Anna came and filled up the space I'd left the way the living do. Filled it with motion and smells. Lemon Pledge, and Pine-Sol, homemade gravy simmering on the stove and manicotti in the oven after the pie came out.

As she swept and did the wash, she had plenty to say to me, though she pretended to be addressing God. "*Buon Dio*, what-a wrong with her? She need-a come down and take care her *bambini* like a good mama. *Mi Luigi*, too. I'm too old for all-a this, *Gesu*. And look-a the mess she make around the place! These puzzle and books? Who need that *giunca*?"

She tossed them in the trash, probably hoping to rouse me. But instead of being moved to fight, I agreed with her. Junk it was—all of it. My whole life. Nothing but *giunca*.

Every day Agnes came into the room and tried to get me to eat or to talk or to worry like I was supposed to.

"It was Dad and the kids who wanted you, you know," I finally said, hoping to drive her away. "If I'd had my choice—"

"I know," she said, without blinking. "So are you comin' down or what?"

I heard other things, too: Louie's heavy step, the sound of him snoring in his chair or beside me, Jimmy coming and going. Anna yelling for him to "keep away from those *bullos* who lead you the wrong way, to help you Papa now; he need-a you—and *Dio mio*, talk to you mama! She listen to you, Jeemy; you know she do. She love you more than anyone—even her *marito*."

"Don't you know this is America, Nonna? Talk English, for cryin' out loud," Jimmy said. The door slammed as he went out, listening to no one in any language—not even Princie, who barked like she sensed danger.

I DON'T KNOW how long I stayed in my bed like that—unable to eat or listen or care. A week? Two? It might have been a month. All I know was that when I finally put my gray dress on, it hung on me like it belonged to another woman. And it did.

It happened like it did before. Though I hadn't been physically beat, my body ached itself dry and every night I dreamed of the yellow leaves covering me like a blanket. The voice, when I finally heard it, seemed to come from nowhere, too. Just like the first time.

That's when I knew Louie was right all along. It had been him calling me out of the woods that day. Him pushing me forward as I dragged myself through the thick brush, my ribs throbbing, my head dazed by the concussion. He was the one who wouldn't let me fall until I reached the highway where I was found. I just didn't recognize it then. How could I have?

The voice came from back then, too. Back when Louie was young—at the beginning when we still believed we could make a good life in spite of everything. That I could forget. Before we'd seen all those broken kids come through here. Way back to the time when we thought we could take in our three—and then it was four—and raise them up as if they had no past. Back when we believed two people—even a pair like Louie and me, for heaven's sake—might be able to save someone. When I thought how foolish we were, I didn't know whether to laugh or cry.

But the voice wouldn't let me do either. *Get up!* it ordered me. *Get up and walk and don't stop.*

Don't you know I can't, Louie? I'm weak and dizzy and dear God, I've lost every shred of faith. Not faith like the kind that drives your mother through the house, beads clicking behind her. Just the faith to lift my arm, or to take another step. I can't.

Get up!

WHEN I OPENED my eyes, I was in my own bedroom. I wasn't alone like I thought I was that first time, either. Louie was right there standing beside the bed. And behind him were the girls—Agnes in the doorway, my poor heartbroke Zaida, just outside.

Louie's voice wasn't the same as the one I'd heard in my dream. It was made deep by the years and everything they contained, but it came through clearer than ever. He pulled back the covers and spoke again. "Enough is enough, Dahlia. Get up."

"You have to, Ma," Agnes said behind him. She came into the room, opened the closet, and pulled out the gray dress that would never fit me right again.

But it was Zaida who got to me. Even in the shadows of the hallway, I could see the sheen in her eyes, the narrow bones that had gotten narrower since I first lay down.

"Please?" Her voice was a whisper that no one heard but me.

PART III

1966—1968

CHAPTER ONE

Lilacs in November

ZAIDIE

Dear Jon,
Today you would have been twelve.

I TORE THE SHEET FROM MY NOTEBOOK AND CRUSHED IT INTO A ball. The next page was blindingly empty. Somehow my brother was twelve. A seventh grader in a school I'd never seen, waking up every morning to a house, a life that was locked to me. Did he still order the pizza with baby fish, then pick them off and taunt the nearest girl? Could he catch the lonely sound of a train when it was still miles away? Was he happy?

Maybe I had it right, after all. Today the brother I knew would have been twelve. Ma would have baked his favorite chocolate chip cake and invited Jeffrey to dinner. Then a ragged chorus of Moscatellis would have sung to him and cheered his most secret wish as he blew out the candles.

All I knew about him now was contained in the evolving signatures on Michael Finn's annual Christmas greeting.

Agnes pointed at the reindeer on the first card when I opened it in our room.

"Doesn't he know you're Jewish?"

"Oh, he knows, all right."

Inside, he'd written *Love, Dad* (two words that felt like more of a taunt than the reindeer). Beneath it, Jon's name was scrawled in familiar eight-year-old penmanship. I traced it with my finger. Had he forgiven me for letting him go alone? Or did "Dad" force him to sign?

The next year it was *Love, Dad and Evelina* with my brother's name tacked on like an afterthought. Jonathan, he was calling himself now. Who was that?

This December, there had been another addition: *Love, Dad, Evelina, and Marisa*, it read, with Jonathan's name set even farther apart. Still, I was filled with jealousy over this new sister, the stepmother with the exotic name.

A generous check fell from the cards as soon as I opened them, but I never cashed it. "A hundred dollars!" Agnes cried when I tore another one up. Then she listed all the things we might have bought— *roller skates with a real key!* when she was eleven. Birthstone earrings from Menard's Jewelers and fancy school clothes from Jordan Marsh as she entered middle school. This year she'd been dreaming of tickets to see Herman's Hermits. "For a hundred dollars, we could hire a limo and sit in the front row, Zaidie!"

"It wouldn't hurt to deposit it in your college fund," Ma put in. "If you were a little friendlier, he might call next time and maybe you could—we could—"

"He won't, Ma. And even if he did, he wouldn't let Jon come to the phone." I'd never told anyone how Jon had vowed to hate us forever.

It was months after he screamed those words at me before I understood why Michael had let me make my choice. Not because I'd earned his respect, as he'd said. No, it was what he'd seen—what we'd both seen—that day he dragged me to the mirror. My coloring and some of my features were indeed like his, but it was Sylvie who looked back at him from my face. Sylvie and all the ways he'd wronged her. Separating Jon and me—and forcing me to choose it—had been a final and devastating strike at my mother.

I began every letter to my brother the same way, attempting to bring him to the place where I was, make him see what I saw:

> *Dear Jon,*
>
> *I'm writing from your old bed, looking out on the lilac bush where you used to hide whenever we played hide-and-seek. Do you remember the day Jimmy asked why you always chose the most obvious spot? "Because I like the smell of the flowers," you said stubbornly.*
>
> *Since it was November, we all laughed at you. But sometimes when I pass that bush in winter, I swear I catch a whiff of those lilacs myself. It's all still here, Jonny—the worn spot by the garage where you parked your bike, even our picnic table, though no one has sat there much since you left. But you— sometimes you seem as distant and unreachable as our mother, Sylvie.*
>
> *I can't see her face anymore. No matter how hard I try, I can't, but I still feel how she squeezed me when her friend brought me to visit the hospital the day you were born.* We're going to be so happy, *she promised.* Just the three of us.
>
> *They're still the saddest words I ever heard.*

The first lesson I'd learned as a Moscatelli kid was how to forget. It was how Jimmy and the others survived, and it was what I needed to do, too. So I let go of my mother and erased the smell of sickness and death that permeated the rooms she'd painted sunny colors, filled with music and plants back when she still believed in her own promise. And when Aunt Cille brought me pictures of her when she was young,

I stashed them in my drawer. They didn't look like her anyway. The face I remembered, transfigured by heartbreak and illness—but even more by love for me and Jon—had been much more beautiful. So beautiful, in fact, that it hurt to look at her. For seven years I hadn't.

BUT AFTER JON left, everything changed. "You're too quiet," Ma complained, worry grooves forming between her eyes.

Agnes didn't like it, either. "Why are you always writing in that stupid notebook? Talk to me. Look at me. I'm right here, Zaidie."

Only Jimmy, who had been tugged away by a mysterious force himself, seemed to understand. One night when Agnes was complaining about all the time I spent alone, he slammed his fist on the table in the way that rattled everyone. "For chrissake, leave Z alone about her damn writing. Maybe she's gotta do it. Did ya ever think of that?"

It didn't help that I kept my notebook secret from everyone. Why had I started writing—to explain why I stayed behind? To apologize? To prove something to Michael Finn? Maybe even to win a skirmish in the long war between him and Sylvie? I didn't know.

Jimmy's explanation was the only one that felt true. I did it because I had to. I did it because no matter where I looked for Jon in the neighborhood or in the city, the only place I ever got a glimpse of him was on the pages of my notebook. Day after day, I filled them with swirly writing, doodles, and memory. But there was something else there, too: hope.

When Ma looked at me suspiciously and Agnes tried to hide my notebook, I went to the playground and sat in the empty bleachers at the field where Jon had played Little League. After many attempts, I even found my way to our old apartment building, where I sat on the steps and chewed on my pen.

Dear Jon,
    I'm sitting on the steps of a place you'd never remember.

That was as far as I got before the woman who lived in our old apartment came out and asked what I was doing there. When I had no answer, she reminded me this was private property. "Go on now. Move along."

I closed my notebook but stayed put. Then I pointed up at the window: "That was where my mother slept. My brother and me—our rooms were across the hall."

Maybe she'd heard about us, the fated young woman and her two orphan kids who'd lived there before her, because she closed the screen door gently when she went inside. A minute later she returned with a glass of lemonade. "Just don't make a habit out of it, okay?"

I nodded and then I began my letter again.

Dear Jon,

> *There are some places on this earth where no one has a right to chase you away. Places where all you can do is stand your ground. Even if you're scared.*

I'd never visited my mother's grave—even on the anniversaries when Aunt Cille begged me to go. But a few months after Jon left, I took the bus to the other side of town and walked to the cemetery. Soon I was visiting the stone marked SYLVIE MENDELSON FINN every week—another secret that separated me from my family.

Sitting with her name, all my letters ended the same way. *Has her promise come true, Jon? Are you happy?* But those questions would probably sound silly to a boy his age, so I always crossed them out.

By then I was living two lives—my own and the one I re-created for my brother in the stories I wanted him to feel as much as I did. I took care to listen well to Ma and Dad's conversations—both what they said outright—and everything that lay beneath—so he would catch every inflection. I wanted him to hear Flufferbell's caterwaul the night she was left out, smell Ma's pork chops frying on the stove, experience the loneliness and the immense peace of the field of stones where I sat with Sylvie Mendelson Finn. To feel the smoothness of her marker when I pressed my face against it. If he knew every detail of life in Claxton—from the wonder of Gina Lollobrigida's beehive hairdo to the modern elementary school they were building on High Street—a part of him would still be here.

I told him about Jeffrey's broken arm, and Jimmy's various jobs (though I omitted the hope that filled the house whenever he started a new one and the gloom that descended when it didn't work out). I filled pages with details about my new boyfriend, Charlie Putnam, describing every goal he scored in his soccer game, the plots of every movie we saw at the Claxton Drive-in. Though Jon probably wouldn't be interested, Charlie had infiltrated my mind so completely, I couldn't help myself.

Jimmy hates him, I admitted for the first time in a letter. *But do you want to know the real reason I fell for Charlie? Because he was the first boy I ever met who was as nice—okay, almost as nice—as the one who called you Shadow. Sure, it doesn't hurt that he's cute and smart, "popular" even. I suppose that's what drew me in. But it wasn't till I went to his house and saw him playing with his little sister, Abby, who has Down's syndrome, that I was hooked.*

Mostly, though, my letters to Jon were filled with what I didn't say. I didn't tell him about the day Jimmy left for Vietnam, or how Dad, haunted by the daily death count on the front page of the *Gazette*, had stopped reading his newspaper altogether. Nor did I tell him when Princie lost interest in running away—even if the gate was wide open. It wasn't long before she turned away from her food bowl, too. Nor did I say that on certain days—like this birthday or the day we first came—Ma still took to her bed like she had those weeks after Michael Finn took him away and how we all held our breath until she came back down. How fragile everything had become since he left.

After a while, I wasn't just writing to Jon anymore. I wrote to see.

I wrote to know. But most of all, I wrote because that was who I was. It was my brother's gift to me. Did it come at the most bitter cost? Yes. Just like the cigar box Agnes had kept in the closet since she was small. And for that reason, I held on to it like she did. Fiercely.

I looked around the room Agnes had made her own when she moved in two years ago. She'd searched every paint store in the city for the perfect summer green color and enlisted Jimmy and me to help her paint. Then she'd asked Jools to imagine Buskit's River without the junk and to draw what he saw. The five sketches she'd framed and hung on the wall were the result. Though it smelled of her—a mixture of chlorine and the rain-scented cologne she wore—though it was filled with her things, Jon was there in every corner.

Dear Jon,

Today you are twelve. Do you still order your pizza with baby fish? Can you hear a train from miles away? Do you still smell lilacs in November?

CHAPTER TWO

Come On, Agnes

AGNES

CLIMBING OUT OF THE POOL, I HEARD THE COACH CALLING MY name: "Agnes Juniper. Meet me by the bleachers after you change out of your suit. I need to talk to you." I knew things were serious when she used both my names.

"I'm sorry, Coach, but my brother's waiting, and he's gotta leave by—" I yanked off my bathing cap and shook out my hair as I turned to face the clock, confirming my suspicion that practice had run extra long that day: 3:31. "He's due at the factory by four and if he's late for his shift one more time—"

"Hmm. Sounds like late runs in the family." She fingered her whistle, as if she might blow it at any time. *Attention!* "Don't worry. I already told Jimmy I'd drive you home if he has to leave."

When I came out of the locker room, I was surprised to see him sitting on the bench with Coach Lois. Right away my heart clenched. Ma and Dad were so excited when he got on second shift at Larkin Leather. Had he already—?

As always, his grin was an arrow shot through my anxiety. "Coach here's been telling me about your pos-si-bi-li-ty." He opened his arms as if the word was a huge hug. "Not like I didn't already know."

He smiled at Coach Lois in a way that would have made me go

all red if I was like Zaidie. When he was younger, Jimmy fell in love once a day and three times on Sundays, but since he'd come home from Vietnam, he was different. Normally, I loved seeing signs of his old self, but when the lady he was gawking at was my coach, it was downright embarrassing.

"Great talking to you, Jim," Coach Lois said, smooth as could be. "Agnes and I will just be a few minutes."

"Oh. Um, yeah, sure." Even Coach couldn't help smiling back at him as he slouched off, patting the pocket where he kept his smokes. "I'll be right outside, okay, Sky Bar?"

Then he winked at Coach. And me. And at the whole world—the way he used to. Yeah, embarrassing.

"When it comes to brothers, I'd say you got pretty lucky," Coach Lois said. "Jimmy's a sweetie."

The sweetest of the sweet, I thought, imagining the mountain of candy I'd eaten since the day Jimmy renamed me. A year earlier, I'd gotten so sick of Sky Bars I thought I'd gag if I ate one more, but there was no way I could tell him. Especially then.

"Thanks." I slid onto the bench.

She gave me the kind of appraising stare I was used to getting from Ma. "Just one question, Agnes, and then I'll let you go. Why are you here?"

"You asked me to meet—"

"That's not what I mean."

"Um. My mother read somewhere that swimming might be good for my asthma, and—"

"That was four years ago when you started swimming at the Y. Now you've outgrown your asthma and you're on swim team."

"I know I'm late for practice sometimes, but Jimmy—" I began, anticipating what she was about to say.

"This is your sport, Agnes. Your team. That means you owe us. You. Not Jimmy."

I looked down at the blue and white tiles. "I know you were disappointed when I lost my last two races, but honestly, Coach, I—"

"No, Agnes. I wasn't disappointed that you lost. I was disappointed because you could have won. Easily. And you're right, I don't like it when you show up late day after day. I've been very patient because—"

I took a ragged inhale, certain she was about to kick me off the team. How could I make her understand how much I loved all of it—from joking in the locker room with my teammates to the smell of chlorine in my nostrils—everything connected to that moment when I dove into the pool and felt my body moving through the water. No matter what was on my mind, it disappeared as I gave myself up to its rhythm. It was like the time I made snow angels with Zaidie when I was six, or the first time I stood on my chair and told Jimmy I loved him. But how could I explain that to my coach?

"So okay, you signed up for swimming because of your mother. Or your asthma. Or because you like seeing your brother sit in the bleachers, cheering for you every day—even if it means he's late for work and risks his job."

I closed my eyes. "I—I just love to swim. Far back as I can remember, I loved it," I blurted out. "Isn't that a good enough reason?"

"Not for you it isn't, no. And not for this team. You're the most gifted athlete I've ever coached, Agnes. The natural people like me dream about. If you gave it the effort, I wouldn't be surprised if you made it all the way to the—well, the sky's the limit."

"But those girls at the meets have been taking lessons since they were three, and they swim like their lives depend on it. Like it's the reason they were born."

"And you?"

"I don't know; I just swim." This time I knew better than to ask if that was good enough.

She sat there, whistle in hand, waiting for me to say more. When

I didn't, she nodded. Then she started to gather her things, dismissing me.

"I watch you," she said before I left. "Socializing and laughing right up till the race starts while the other girls are totally focused. That's the difference, Agnes. In any case, if you ever decide you want to start swimming like your life depended on it, there's no end to your—"

We both set down our swim bags and opened our arms as we spoke the word together, letting it fill the room like Jimmy had: *pos-si-bi-li-ty.*

I had reached the door when I turned around. "Thanks, Coach." More than all the stuff about my gift, I was grateful for what she said about Jimmy and me. As if she saw we were alike. That just because we didn't look the same or have the same last name, we weren't a second-rate brother and sister. We were as real as anything.

"I'll see you tomorrow," she yelled back. "Two thirty sharp. Better yet—get here by two twenty. And remember, if you change your mind, I'd love to start working with you individually."

I smiled. That was Coach for you. Even when she claimed to give up on me, she was still trying to find a sneaky way to make me better. Just like Ma.

Jimmy was on the sidewalk when I came out, staring off the way he did—like he forgot where he was, same as he forgot time. One reason we had always been so close was we both knew how to let things be. I didn't ask why he wasn't at work.

"Ran out of gas over on Warren Ave," he said when he saw me scanning the street for a sign of his beat-up Falcon. "No need to mention it to Dad, okay? Brucie's takin' me to the gas station when he gets out of work."

Brucie? I didn't like him, but I let that be, too—unlike the rest of the family. Even Ma, who never complained about much of anything when it came to Jimmy, especially after he came home from the war.

Not the lost jobs or the rage he went into when he found out we had to put Princie down while he was away, or the even scarier way he sat out on the picnic table smoking half the night for days afterward.

"You killed my fucking dog and you didn't tell me?" he yelled when Dad tried to coax him inside one night around three in the morning. "Then you got rid of everything. Her bowl and her collar, her stupid bones, everything. It's like she never fucking existed. That's how it is around here, isn't it?"

It was the first time anyone had ever used that word in the house—never mind twice in one spiel—but no one said a thing. The fault line was already there, visible, and everyone was afraid that the wrong move—even the wrong look—might crack him in two.

"No, Jimmy—honey, that's not how it is," Ma said, stepping into the yard, her voice low. The lights in the neighbors' houses were already flickering on. "Listen to your dad and come inside, will you?"

For that night, at least, he had. He was right about how it was, though, and we all knew it. We'd hung on to Jon's trains and cars, his favorite cowboy bedspread for a while. Then one day I came home from school and they were gone. Gone like the treasures Princie had been collecting from the neighborhood all her life. No one asked where. Pretty soon no one spoke my brother's name, either, except when Zaidie got her annual Christmas card from Colorado. And even then, we didn't say it out loud. We just touched the place where he signed beneath his dad.

THE DAY MA spotted Bruce's gold Mustang outside the picture window, though, her old self returned with a vengeance.

"Is that who I think it is, Jimmy?" Instantly, her arms locked across her chest.

"If I'm old enough to fight in a war, I think I can pick my own friends, Ma."

"Not if it's that one, you can't. Bruce Savery might have a better address than Jools or Duane, but if I had to trust someone with my life, he'd be the last of the three."

"In case you didn't know, Duane's in jail, and Jools sits up at his house drinkin' all day. So if my life's in danger, they ain't available." Jimmy slammed the door behind him.

"I'd still call them first," Ma yelled back. By then, though, the only people left to hear were Zaidie and me.

"She's right," Zaidie said to the empty picture window, not even caring if she sounded loony as Ma. "Anyone but Bruce Savery." Then she turned to me. "If Jimmy ever tries to bring him around, make sure you stay away. I mean it."

THOUGH I WAS tired from school and practice and Jimmy was worn out from all the stuff that went on in his head, we took the long way past the Grainer School that day.

We never talked about the afternoon he led me home back when I was the most lost kid in the whole town. No, we preferred to make believe we always belonged to each other—blood—like Ma and Dad used to pretend before Jon got taken away. But we didn't have to say it. I knew what was on his mind when we walked that way, and he knew the same about me.

"So you ready to start winning like your coach wants?"

"You think it's easy? Coach Lois doesn't understand how good the other girls are." I'd taken a few more steps when another thought occurred to me. "What were you saying to her in there anyway?"

He stopped to pick up a stick, as if Princie was with us, and held it awkwardly. "I told her how Nonna always gave us a couple bucks for Christmas when we were kids. You spent yours the first day—usually on someone else. Didn't matter what you bought; you just couldn't wait to toss it to the wind."

"I did not . . . and even if I did, what's that got to do with winning a swim meet?"

When he didn't answer right away, I turned around and walked a few feet backward so I could see his face. "Jeez, Jimmy, did you really tell her that?"

"Yup. Told her you never gave a damn about winnin' nothin'—not even Monopoly or backyard kickball. You just wanted to play." He threw the stick as far as he could and paused, almost like he was waiting for Princie to fetch it. "Truth is, though, winning feels pretty damn good, Sky Bar. Remember the time I hit that walk-off homer in the tenth inning back in ninth grade? Best moment of my life."

"A stupid ball flying through the air was your best minute? Nuh-uh."

"Okay, maybe I had a couple better minutes with girls, but top three. Definitely top three. You know why?"

"Can't imagine."

"Cause sometimes it's more than a ball flying through the air. It's the minute—no, the second—when you hit back against everything that ever kept you down. The one second in your whole damn life when anything is possible." He shook his head. "Imagine if Z could swim like you? She'd have six gold medals by now."

As we passed the Grainer School, Jimmy stopped to light another cigarette like he always did at that spot. Reminded me of Nonna, who crossed herself whenever she passed a Catholic church.

"Zaidie's gonna be the first girl president," I told him. "She doesn't have time for stuff like swimming."

"Where have you been? President was last month. This week she's plannin' to be the next Louisa May Alcott."

I squinched up my nose the way I always did when anyone mentoned Zaidie's writing. That blasted notebook.

"So how come you're not goin' to work?" I said. If he could break our unspoken rule, so could I. "Did you lose—"

"Nah. Just called out sick."

"But you're not, and if you keep—"

"You know who you sound like now? Ma. Or better yet, Coach Lois." Just thinking of her made him beam. "Lady's got the bluest eyes I ever seen. Man."

"Don't be disgusting. She's old, for crying out loud—almost thirty-seven."

"I don't care. Cause when you see a scrap of pretty in this world, you gotta stop and give it a little respect." He straightened up and demonstrated his best military salute, cigarette still in hand. "You know why?"

"I'm sure you're gonna tell me."

"Cause there's a whole lot of ugly out there, Sky Bar. A whole lot of ugly. I guess you seen that already, though. Even before me, you seen it."

And then he gave another salute—this time for me.

"Did anyone ever tell you you're a goofball?" I said, pushing him off balance.

IT WAS COLD twilight by the time we got home, and despite the extra-thick bathing cap Nonna found for me at Hanley's, my hair always got wet. Still, I didn't argue when Jimmy told me to wait outside.

By the time he pushed through the bulkhead doors, the sun had set, but a particularly bright moon and stars illuminated the yard. He held his bat up triumphantly.

"What the heck, Jimmy? I haven't seen that thing since—jeez, I don't know how long."

"Ninth grade, when I made the all-star team. All that talk about winnin' musta brought back my glory days." He tossed me the ball in his left hand. "Come on, Agnes. Pitch me a few."

"Are you crazy? My hair's turning to icicles here and I'm starved. Ma's gonna wonder . . . Besides, I was never any good at pitching. That was Zaidie, remember?"

But I was already heading for the well-worn pitcher's mound.

"That was the first year I came, remember? You used to say you'd take that bat to anyone who tried to hurt me." Even after all these years, my breath caught when I thought about Mr. Dean.

"Still would, little sister." He took his best batter's stance. "Come on. Three pitches before it gets so dark I can't see the ball. If I strike out, we go inside."

I hurled it in his direction as hard as I could. "Stri-ike one," I yelled in the announcer's voice I once used when I called the games in the backyard.

The sound of the past must have drawn Zaidie onto the back steps. She wrapped her arms around herself for warmth. "What in the world are you two doing out here? It's almost suppertime, and it's getting—"

"Hey, there's no whining in baseball. Didn't I teach you that? You play the game in whatever conditions you find yourself." He turned back to me, dead serious, even in the shadows. "Come on, Agnes."

My next pitch landed in the dirt, but he swung at it anyway. "That's two. You got one more."

Zaidie jumped down from the steps. "Let me try."

"Not this time, Z," Jimmy said. "This is between Sky Bar and me."

By then Ma had come outside, Flufferbell at her heels. She was wearing the blue jeans Zaidie and I, embarrassed by her old-fashioned housedresses, had saved up to buy. But that night, looking at her in her jeans, dressed like everyone else's mom, I missed the old gray dress.

"Baseball? At this time of night? For pity sake," she said, but there was a lightness in her voice, like she was seeing the old Jimmy, too. Before the war. Even before he walked through the door at high school and found out he was a rat.

"Pitch him something decent, Agnes. Your father will be home soon and I still haven't got the pot pies in."

"It's Juniper on the mound tonight, folks, with batting champ

Jimmy Kovacs at the plate," I broadcasted. "But does she lose her cool? Not a chance. She looks, she sets . . ." I wound up like the pitchers on TV, extra dramatic for their entertainment.

Jimmy wasn't laughing, though. His eyes were on the ball that sailed through the dark, straight over the plate. He went for it with everything in him.

"Holy cow! That ball is . . . *gonnne!*" I yelled.

Zaidie and Ma were hollering, too, cheering like Jimmy had just won the World Series. Or we all had.

But Jimmy had hit that ball so hard the crack drowned out the sound of our voices. In fact, for that single second, as it soared over the Guarinos' fence and beyond, I swore it drowned out the whole world.

"Yes!" he yelled, throwing down the bat as the sound came back. "*Yesss!*" And then to me, "See what I mean, Sky Bar? See?"

CHAPTER THREE

James Kovacs Sr. Makes the Paper
One More Time

JIMMY

G OOD OLD JAMESY. GUY COULDN'T GET A SINGLE THING RIGHT IN
his whole life, not even dyin'. After Brucie brought me the paper,
I sat out by the picnic table, starin' at the words—the name, or maybe
just those two letters at the end he had no damn right to use—Sr.—
till it was past dark. Didn't even make it in time to pick up Agnes at
her practice.

If the man had a ounce of decency, he woulda died in a hospital
like you're suppose to. But not Jamesy. Guy didn't have one friend to
check on him till his body stank up the flop house so bad it became a
story. The bum was so damn invisible it took a week before anyone
realized what was causin' the whole roomin' house to reek worse and
worse by the day. Finally, one of the bright bulbs who lived there
thought to ask if anyone seen that guy in Room 2. That was who he
was to them—the guy in Room 2.

Think of it. Jamesy had lived in the rooming house for six years
and no one even knew his name.

"Never smelled anything like it," someone named George Stark
was happy to tell the paper—and from what Brucie said, the TV, too.
"They're gonna have to get the place fumigated if they want to see a
penny of rent after this one."

Course there was nothin' about services like most people have. No picture neither. Not that I cared, though I mighta liked to get a look at him for once. But nope. Just some talk about the stink he left behind. I guess that's what people like James Kovacs Sr. get.

I put that newspaper under my bed. Maybe I'd hold my own little service later, I thought, though I didn't say a word to no one. But the way Ma watches me, I could tell she knew. That night she made my favorite meal for supper, pork chops with mashed potatoes and beans, and no one hounded me about whether I'd followed up with the job Dad heard about at the garage, or asked why I left Agnes to walk home in the dark with her wet hair.

"You want extra potatoes? I made them with real butter the way you like," Ma said instead.

But all I could think of was that damn stink when they took the guy out of the building. *Never smelled anything like it,* said the famous George Stark, king of the flop house. *Didn't even smell like a body anymore. More like some kinda chemical poison.*

"Thanks, Ma, but I ain't hungry," I said, pushin' back my chair. No one tried to stop me when I left my plate on the table and went upstairs, either.

Alone in my room, I was sorry—but also mad as hell. It was how I felt a lot in those days. With nothin' else to do, I took out that stupid newspaper and read the story a few more times till the fumes practically rose off the print.

After Dad and the girls had gone to bed, tiptoein' past my door like they were afraid of waking a panther, I went down to see Ma. She was working on a puzzle of Van Gogh's sunflowers.

"I'm looking for a yellow piece that fits rights there," she said, pointing at a flower near the top. Like I could just forget everything and go back to the days when I helped her with her idiotic jigsaws.

I pulled up the chair like I used to, but instead of looking for her yellow piece, I dropped the newspaper on top of the puzzle like it was another jagged part.

"Guess you thought if you buried this deep enough in the trash you could keep it from me forever."

Ma looked at me as if she was considering whether to lie or not. She coulda easily claimed she had no cause to hide anything since I never read the paper anyway. Or that she hadn't seen it herself. There was no hiding the truth on her face, though. "He might've been your blood, Jimmy, but he was a stranger. I didn't think you needed to know."

I reached down and found the yellow piece she had been looking for the last couple of days and snapped it into the puzzle. But inside, I could feel the thing that happened to me sometimes, the turning— like I didn't know who to be angry at anymore. James Kovacs Sr. or Ma or the whole damn world. "You ever think maybe I'm just like him? Just another pile of stink like the old man?"

"Not if you don't want to be, Jimmy."

"And he did wanna be that way? Is that what you think? The guy wanted to die in a flop house with no one to speak for him but some asshole who never even knew his name?" I shook the paper at her. "Here it is—his eulogy and his obituary all rolled into one. *Worst thing I ever smelled.*"

"Stop it now. You're getting yourself all in a lather when there's nothing to be done."

"Are you listenin', Ma? What I'm trying to tell you is maybe I can't stop it—and you can't keep me from it neither—hard as you tried."

By then I felt the heat behind my eyes, as if I was going to cry again like a damn girl. A pussy. Wasn't that like what they called me in the Army? Scared to pick up a gun. Had to be a medic cause he don't want to hurt no one. That's right. A pussy. The mama's boy from Boston, they named me, even though I'd only been to that damn city once when Dad and Nonna took us to the Franklin Park Zoo.

I never told them about the promise I made her, or the stone I carried in my pocket that whole year. But they could tell. Wouldn't drink the hooch. Never shot horse like a lot of them done when things got bad. On account of I promised my Ma. No, I never told anyone, but in a place like that, people figure out who you are real fast.

"Leave him alone. He must be a Adventist or somethin'," my buddy used to say when he thought I couldn't hear. But I didn't even have church or God or anything to explain it. Nothing but a damn rock. I can't tell you how many times I wanted to chuck that thing in the jungle, but every time I tried, I thought of the night she give it to me. *Promise me, Jimmy*, she said. Serious as shit.

Without thinking, I swept the puzzle she'd been working on all week onto the floor. "Wouldn't it be somethin' I turned out just like him—a bum, Ma, like you and Dad always said he was?"

"He had his troubles—things I knew nothing about, Jimmy. I never should have said—"

"Are you saying you were wrong? That he wasn't a pile of stink—"

"I didn't know him, and neither did that other fellow at the rooming house. So yes, I was wrong. Him, too. We both should have kept our mouths closed."

"You said it about all of them."

She stood up so fast she almost knocked the card table over. "I didn't know any better at the time, Jimmy. Till this moment right here, I swear to God, I didn't know anything better. And to tell the truth, I was scared of losing what I had—you. Cause if he wasn't a bum, then maybe he would come back and take you someday like . . ." She let her voice trail off like she always did when she thought of Jon.

"If I was any kind of human being, I woulda been hoping for that," she continued. "But I wanted you to be mine. Don't you understand? I wanted the four of you for myself and if that meant your real folks had to stay drunk or lost for good, I suppose I wanted that, too. Dear God, Jimmy, I'm so sorry."

By the time we noticed Dad on the stairs, we was both cryin'.

He was six foot four, my dad, a powerful man in every kind of way—especially when he give you that John Wayne face of his. But that night, standin' there in his underwear? Man, he looked nothin' but old. Old and half-broke like me.

He came downstairs and kneeled on the floor to pick up the mess I'd scattered. With every piece he dropped on the card table, I could feel the strength comin' back into him. By the time he stood up again, he was almost back to his old self.

"Enough of this now, the both of yas. I got seven cars in the yard right now, includin' two that gotta be done by noon. So whatever you two are goin' on about, it's gonna have to wait till morning."

He tramped toward the stairs, where he abruptly turned around, more powerful than ever. "In fact, it can wait till never, cause you know what you're gonna do tomorrow? Get up and take care of what's in front of you. Just do that and you'll be too busy to worry about any of this other shit."

If only he knew how much I wished I could be as tall and sure as he was. I woulda even taken the ugly along with it. If only I could tell him how much I'd always wished that. Him and Ma, too.

THE NEXT MORNING, I woke up full of all kind of feelings—the way I did in country after I picked up a boy and lifted him on a stretcher, after I told him he would be all right even though I knew I was lyin', after I stayed with him, tryin' not to look at the wound where his life was seepin' away. It was barely light when I headed for the cabin in the woods where a bum named Richard J. Cartier had died just like James Kovacs Sr.

The Sugar Shack, we called it when we used to bring girls there. The path we used to take was so overgrowed I never woulda found the place if somethin' wasn't pullin' me there. If it hadn't been pullin' me there since I was a kid.

No one had been to the shack since a nor'easter knocked a tree on the roof back in junior year. It was mostly dead now, but weeds, vines, lichen—the whole wild world was scalin' the walls, burrowin' its way through brick and wood. When I managed to get the door open, I found it had even snaked its way inside. Made you wonder how long it would take for nature to take back everything we ever built.

The table where Richard J. Cartier set his coffee cup was still there, though, and the seat he pulled from a old truck, where we used to make out with our girls. Weird as it sounds, he was still there, too, looking at me like he had that day I gave him a smoke outside Frankenstein's Texaco. Some things you don't ever shake. I sat myself down on the cracked red vinyl and fired up a Pall Mall in his honor.

I inhaled good and hard, tasting all the things I was sorry for. The boys who gave one last cry for their girlfriend or their mama, the life they thought was theirs before their eyes went blank with the lie of it, for the dad I never knew and the one I loved as much as anyone ever did their own blood, but could never follow.

At that moment, though, I was mostly sorry for the shit I said to Ma, sorry for the broke puzzle she'd worked on all week. Sorry I blamed her for things that weren't her fault. Even though I knew I'd probably do it again, I was sorry. What the hell was wrong with me?

At first, I thought I'd just go out to the woods and see if the shack was still standin', but once I sat down, I didn't get up. I smoked half my pack, and when I got hungry I ate the Slim Jims and washed them down with a Pepsi from Tucker's, even ate the candy bars I'd bought for my sister to make up for not showin' the day before. Looked like I wasn't going to make it to the Y that day, either. As it got later, I went out and gathered wood for a fire in the old stove. No one had used it since Richard J. Cartier sat here drinkin' his last cup of coffee.

I don't know how long the fire had been burnin' when I heard footsteps coming through the woods and felt myself goin' into one of those cold sweats I used to get in Nam when I heard someone creepin' up. Who I thought it was—the ghost of Richard J. Cartier, or the cops, or just some gook with a gun—I don't know. But was I ever relieved when I got a familiar whiff of B.O.

"Shit, Buskit, you shoulda let me know it was you. Scared the piss outta me for a minute."

Jools looked as spooked as I was. "Tell you the truth, I wasn't sure what I was walkin' into here, either, man." He sat on an old tree stump someone musta dragged inside a long time ago and helped himself to my last cancer stick. "Just cause of a crazy hunch."

"A hunch?" I'd never even told him I used to come here, never mind the story of how Richard J. Cartier passed his spirit into my eyes that day.

"Not mine. Your sister's. Girl came up the house a little while ago, lookin' for you. Said she had a feelin' you were out here."

"What? She's supposed to be at swim practice."

"Not Agnes. The other one." With his hand, he drew the shape of an hourglass.

"Damn. It was Z who come lookin' for me?" I said. And then, "Watch yourself with them remarks about her body. She's still in high school, you know."

"Sorry." Jools dropped his head a little lower than it was already. "Ain't every day a girl who looks like that comes knockin' at my door."

"So what did she want you to do about it?"

"Bring ya back, I suppose. At least let 'em know you're okay." He looked around the cabin that was slowly being reclaimed by the woods. Like we all are, though not everybody knew it yet.

"Well, here I am—okay as shit," I said. "Guess your job is done." I pointed at the door.

Nodding, he lowered his head another few inches. Then he looked at me like he did back at school, before we decided to skip another class or just walk out for the day. "Not really the best way to put it," he said, with the sly half smile he used to give me in those days.

"What?"

"I mean, shit really ain't all that okay."

I don't know who started laughing first, but before long the two of us filled that cabin with the sound. Then all of a sudden we stopped same as we started. Like we planned it. When he looked up, I could tell he knew all about James Kovacs Sr.

Probably read it in the stupid *Gazette* just like Brucie.

I reached for the newspaper I'd set beside the vinyl seat and tossed it on the fire, watching the newsprint turn blue before it crackled and disappeared. Call it his funeral service.

Jools looked away. "Sorry, man."

And then he did the only thing he knew to do. He pulled a bottle from the pocket of his coat. Not the Wild Irish he used to drink, but Old Crow this time. He unscrewed the cap and took a pull before he held it out to me.

I kept my eyes on Jools the whole time—as I reached for it, as I put it to my mouth, as I felt the burn run through me, lighting me up inside like the fire that made short work of James Kovacs Sr.'s story.

To Ma's way of thinkin', Jools might as well of signed my death warrant that day, but when I looked in his face, I swear all I seen was love. Same as what had been on hers and Dad's every time they told me James Kovacs Sr. wasn't nothin' but a bum.

CHAPTER FOUR

Zaidie Writes a Valedictorian Speech

AGNES

WHEN I FINALLY GOT KICKED OFF SWIM TEAM, IT WAS ALMOST A relief—both for me and for Coach Lois. There was no need to mention the missed practices, the chronic tardiness, my general lack of seriousness. She didn't even bring up the clincher: A week earlier, she'd caught me out in the alleyway puffing on a joint with a couple friends. Nor did I try to explain that I was just goofing around. If I actually inhaled the stuff, I might have had an asthma attack. No, instead she just talked about making space for another girl. "Someone who really wants to be here."

I closed my eyes, which made me feel as if I was still in the water, the way I always did for the first hour after I climbed out of the pool. How could I describe the sensation? Was it freedom? Power? Peace? If I knew the answer to that, maybe I'd be the swimmer Coach Lois thought I had it in me to be.

"It's okay, Coach. I've been thinking of getting a part-time job anyway," I said. "Thanks, though. You taught me so much about . . . well, just so much."

Tongue-tied and strangely flushed, I got out of there fast as I could.

Jimmy rarely made it in time to watch my practice like he used to, but that day he was waiting in his car when I came out. In the past, he would have known something was up right away. Those days, though, his mind was too cluttered to think much about me.

He leaned over and cracked the passenger door, obviously impatient to be somewhere else. "What took so long? I thought you were never comin' out."

"No one said you had to pick me up. In fact, I'd rather walk."

Still, I climbed in and fiddled with the car radio, switching it from the hard rock he liked to top forty. As "I'm a Believer" filled the car, I waited for Jimmy to complain or for the sunny strains of the chorus to drown out the clamor in my head. But Jimmy was too preoccupied to notice and no matter how loud I turned up the music, I still heard Ma's voice. Still saw her disappointed face. I might be all right with quitting—okay, being kicked off the team—but how was I going to break it to her?

I needn't have worried. Soon as we pulled into the driveway and saw the family on the porch, the rest of the day evaporated. Even Spider Johnson, who'd been our mailman for as long as I could remember, was all hopped up.

"Your sister got something from that college in New York," he called out. "We been waiting for you. Better hurry up; I still got mail to deliver."

"Good old Spider," Jimmy muttered. "You'd think he was the one going off to college."

I laughed. Ever since Zaidie started receiving catalogues from places like New Mexico and Hawaii, the mailman had been fired by her dreams. Later, I would flip through the catalogues, studying the exotic locations, the endless subjects that it was possible to learn about in this world, just like he did. And after we went to bed, Ma pored over every word, took in every photograph like it held the secret of life.

Spider had been waiting on the porch for us the day the catalogue from Berkeley arrived. "You really think you might go out there to Califo-ni-a?" he said, pronouncing the word without the R.

"My first choice," Zaidie told him.

"This week anyway," Jimmy added.

Spider didn't hear him, though. "I always wanted to see those red-woods. Promise you'll send pictures."

This letter was different, though, starting with the heavy white envelope and the official logo in the corner, beneath the words DIREC-TOR OF ADMISSIONS. Even her name, typed in black ink, had weight: ZAIDA G. FINN.

"Don't open it yet!" Jimmy yelled, pivoting toward Ma. "Not till Ma gets the Polaroid. This minute here's one for the history books."

"What if it's a rejection?" Zaidie flushed as Ma headed inside for the camera. "Did any of you think of that?"

"Not a chance," Jimmy said, and we all nodded in agreement, even Spider. "Open it!" we sang out as Ma raised the clunky camera.

And just like that, the day turned from the one I thought it was when Coach Lois took me aside and lowered the boom to the crazy wide smiles captured in Ma's pictures—mine and Jimmy's, Spider Johnson's, and in the center of it all—Zaidie holding that blazing-white letter.

But the face I would always remember best was the one that never made the pictures. The one behind the camera. Ma studied the letter long after Spider went back to his route and Zaidie went off to tell her friends.

"Columbia University—and early admission, too." She fingered the expensive-looking paper, the raised seal at the top of the letter like it was braille. "Imagine." Even though she'd been dreaming of days like this as long as I could remember, she seemed stunned.

"Everything you done finally paid off, Ma." Jimmy slung an arm over her shoulder. "You should be damn proud."

"I wish I could take an ounce of credit, Jimmy. But no." Ma set down the letter, shaking her head. "Zaida did this all on her own."

LATER, AFTER EVERYONE had gone to bed, I slipped into the room we used to share and told Zaidie about Ma's reaction. It was a while before she spoke.

"Did she really say that?"

Whenever things were particularly good or bad—or just more confusing than usual—I knocked on the door of the room we used to share, slipped into her single bed, and checked on the moon outside the window. Our moon.

"Agnes, you're too old for this. You're squishing me," she always said. And then she moved over. This time was no different. I could feel her brooding beside me, thinking of what I'd told her.

"Well, she's wrong," she finally said. "First of all, Ma never wanted to take credit for anything. She wanted the glory—and everything else—to go to us. And second—she's more a part of it than I like to admit. Yeah, I did the work, but every test I took, every paper I wrote, she was there with me. Her face when she opened the report card, or when I handed her a paper with the word *Excellent* across the top was my rocket fuel. Her life was so hard, and after Jon left—" Like all sentences that included my brother's name, this one was left unfinished.

I reached out and covered her hand with mine.

"You know what it says in the Talmud? *Every blade of grass has an angel that stands over it, whispering, Grow, Grow.* That was Ma. That was the work of her life."

I lay still in the silence, feeling her mind work as she went on.

"You don't do anything by yourself in this world, and if it's worth anything, it's not just for yourself, either. You're either lifting up the people around you, or you're pulling them down, whether you know it or not."

"Who said that—Helen Keller?"

"No, Ma—even if she didn't use those words."

Though she didn't know it, though she was still months from being chosen, that night, as we lay squished together in her skinny little bed under our own private moon, Zaidie had begun to write the speech she would deliver as valedictorian. "The Most Ordinary People in the World," she would call it.

I shifted uncomfortably, remembering the scene by the pool. The resignation in Coach Lois's voice had been the worst of it. "Too bad there's not much credit for Ma to claim in my case," I said. And then I told her.

Like she always did, Zaidie grew quiet for a few moments before she responded. "It's probably for the best. You didn't want to do anything with it anyway," she decided, pragmatic as ever. "And you'll need those extra hours to focus on school. Pretty soon you're going to be putting in your own applications."

"Not everyone wants to go to college, Zaidie. Joellen Guarino got a good job down at the Claxton Savings and Loan after she graduated. And in case you haven't noticed, I'm a C student."

"C-plus. And that's only because you get Ds in the subjects you don't like. English and Social Studies you bring home As without hardly trying."

I groaned. "I think I heard enough about trying for one day, okay?"

But once she got started, Zaidie was as relentless as Ma. "You just have to get a couple of grades up a little and be ready for your SATs. And since you're not swimming, you'll need something else to round out the application."

I had drifted off to sleep when, a half hour later, the light flicked on. I swiped at my eyes. Again, I'd been dreaming that I was in the water.

"I know what you should do!" she said, sitting up in bed.

"What I should do . . . about what, Zaidie? It's like two in the morning."

"You should run for student council next year. With your talent for making friends, you'd be a shoo-in, and colleges go crazy for that leadership stuff."

"Hah. According to Coach Lois, that's my downfall; I'm too social."

"Yeah, well, that's how we become—I don't know—who we're meant to be. By turning obstacles into assets. It's the Moscatelli way."

I laughed. "The Moscatelli way? Dad goes to work and fixes cars all day, while Ma sits around, watching TV and doing puzzles. As for me and Jimmy, I don't want to talk about it. Is that the 'way' you're talking about?"

"Maybe it is. Did you ever think that maybe Ma was re-creating the world she hoped we would see every time she did one of those puzzles? That her whole life, everything she ever read about or thought about has been to figure out who her kids were and what we needed? And Dad shows us the way every morning when he gets up and laces up his work boots. The man just keeps going. Day after day. No matter what."

When she spoke those words at her graduation a few months later, she would receive a standing ovation, but at two a.m. in our old room, they were greeted only with the majesty and the stillness of the night.

It was too late for all this talk, her endless grand thinking, but like always, I took in every word. All of it, starting with my talent for making friends. This time, though, I didn't know who was right—her or Coach Lois.

"You'd rather socialize with the competition than beat them," the coach complained more than once. "And you wouldn't be late all the time if you came by yourself instead of taking the long way with that pack of girls."

There were six of us who walked home together after school, down Main Street, stopping to look at the Capezios we coveted in the store window, to flirt with the boys who circled around us, or to buy a candy bar at Kresge's.

Knowing my problem with tardiness, Ma had given me a watch for my last birthday. But all too often, I still arrived at the Y breathless and late, the ghost of my asthma rumbling in my chest.

"Anyone want to guess what she forgot today?" Ellen Morgan taunted.

I laughed and stuck out my tongue, but she was right. There was always something. My friends Judy Katz and Kathy Doherty had taken to bringing extra bathing caps, goggles, and shampoo for me.

Much as I wanted to agree with Zaidie, Coach Lois was right this time. Goofing around with my pack—even pretending to smoke a joint that made me cough—had cost me my sacred hour in the water.

THE FIRST MONTH, though, I reveled in the freedom from Coach Lois's eyes, which veered from me to the clock and then away. Free to stop for a Coke and fries at Junie Sweet's, I lingered on the red stools until the boys filed in from basketball practice, their cheeks blazing with the coming winter and their own wild energy.

It felt good to leave together, eleven or twelve of us filling the streets like we owned them. Next to Junie's was a dive bar called Coop's Tavern, and sometimes one of the boys would dare another to open the door and hold it till someone staggered out and chased us away. Meanwhile, the rest of us stood on the sidewalk, peering into that shadowy world where a lone drunk might be heard carrying on a passionate rant. Then we'd all laugh as we scattered down the hill into the gathering dark.

In those moments I felt almost as free as I had in the water. *Who needs swimming?* I said to myself one day. Immediately, I felt a tightening in my chest. Better not to think about things like that, I decided, catching up with a boy named Joey Lynch. I'd been hoping he might ask me to the dance at St. Edward's Parish.

When everyone was out of sight, he noticed that I'd forgotten my mittens at Junie's so he took off his own and gave them to me, holding my hand for an extra-long minute. And then he did it. He asked me to the dance. I raced all the way home, just daring the asthma to stop me.

"My goodness, did something . . . happen?" Ma said when I came into the house. "You look—I don't know—different."

And different I was. Every single day. But there was no explaining that kind of thing to your mother.

Zaidie and I huddled in her room for days, discussing what I would wear to the dance and experimenting with new hairstyles—twists and beehives and flips, though my thick hair inevitably escaped the clips and bobby pins and cascaded down my back.

Finally, she pulled out her best baby-blue cashmere sweater. It had been kept in tissue paper since her birthday. "This would look really good with your dark blue skirt."

"Are you sure? I thought you were saving it for something special."

"What's more special than my sister's first date?"

The sweater, still in its delicate paper, sat inside my top drawer, and every day, soon as I got home from school, I looked at it. Still there, I told myself, unable to believe my luck. That soft blue sweater was Zaidie and the dance and Joey Lynch's hand inside his mitten. His bright face in the cold.

And then one day, it was something else.

I WAS THE last one to leave Junie Sweet's that afternoon. Me and Susan, my old friend from elementary school who had just tearfully confided that no one had asked her to the dance.

"You can come with me and Joey," I told her.

"It doesn't work that way, Agnes." She giggled for the first time that day.

"Who says? It's my date and if I want to bring someone, I will." I almost told her about that crazy stuff Zaidie called the Moscatelli Way, but then I thought the better of it.

By the time we left, Junie was closing up, and all of our friends were gathered on the sidewalk outside Coop's. They stood slightly back, listening as Joey Lynch held the door, allowing one of the old boozers to broadcast his madness onto the street. As usual, they were laughing, and for a minute, so was I. Then I recognized the voice.

LATER, SUSAN, WHO had peered inside, would tell me Jimmy was the only one in the bar that afternoon—just him and his phantoms. But I was already gone.

I ran farther and faster than I ever had in my life—past the voices that were calling me back and the old Falcon squatting there on the street like the most forlorn hulk in the world, past the street where the Deans lived and the Dohertys' house with the green shutters on the corner of Grainer and the school, past the place where Joey Lynch had held my hand before he gave me his mittens, then on to Derocher Field, where Jimmy had hit that tenth-inning home run in the all-star game. The best minute of his life, he'd called it. I ran and ran till the asthma I had mostly outgrown caught me.

IN THE FAMILIAR white tent, I dreamed relentlessly of water. When I struggled for breath, I imagined myself in the deep, pushing myself toward the air. And when the nurses increased my oxygen, I thought of how I told Coach Lois that the other girls swam like their lives depended on it. For the first time, it made sense.

No one but Susan knew what I had seen and heard that day. Nor would they ever know, but they all saw the change in me. After I was discharged, I stayed home for a couple of weeks until I couldn't stand

Ma watching, trying to figure me out. If she stayed at it long enough, I knew she would. Just like always.

"You're not just lung sick like when you were a kid; this is something else," she concluded one afternoon when she delivered chicken noodle soup to my room.

I made no response, so she turned to leave. I knew that wasn't the end of it, though. And just as I expected, she stopped at the door. "It's that boy, isn't it? The one you were planning to go to the dance with."

Again, I said nothing.

"He called a couple of times, you know."

"Tell him I don't live here anymore," I said, stealing the worn-out line Dad used when the department asked Ma to take another kid.

"Already did. To be honest, Agnes, I had a bad feeling about that kid from the first."

If I wasn't lung sick and heartsick and some other kind of sick I couldn't identify, I would have grinned. When it came to boys lurking around me and Zaidie, Ma always had a bad feeling. And to be honest, so did I. I should have trusted myself more.

Again, she started down the hall—and again she turned back. "Best cure for what's bothering you now is to get moving. Plan on going back to school tomorrow."

AT SCHOOL, I avoided my old pack and ate lunch alone with Susan; and as soon as the bell rang, I set out walking. Sometimes I heard my friends calling my name, but driven by the memory of Jimmy's voice, I picked up my pace. At home, Ma and Zaidie were thrilled—and just a little baffled—by the amount of time I spent studying.

"What happened to you? Get struck by lightning one day when we weren't looking?" Dad asked when I went straight upstairs to work on a project after supper.

"Yeah, I did," I whispered.

Still, there was something missing. Something I mourned even more than the loss of my friends.

THE AFTERNOON I showed up at the pool fifteen minutes before practice Coach Lois hardly looked my way. Nor did she glance in the direction of the bleachers, where I sat in Jimmy's old spot during practice. My old teammates clearly noticed my presence, though; and once I saw Kathy Doherty whisper something in the coach's ear before she pointed up at me.

I waited fifteen minutes after everyone left, hoping Coach Lois might come and talk to me. Finally, just as I was about to leave, she appeared and sat beside me on the bench. We both stared into the empty pool.

"They look pretty good, don't they?" she finally said. "Did you hear we took second at the Southeastern Mass Regionals?"

"No, but that's great."

I realized I didn't have much time so I blurted out what I'd come to say. "Coach, I know I don't deserve it, but I wanted to ask—"

She turned to face me. "If you were hoping to get back on the team, I'm sorry, Agnes. We have a full roster, and Rebecca, the girl who replaced you—she works hard every day. To be honest, you're right. You don't deserve it."

"But I'm different now. I swear, I—" I stammered. If I were Zaidie, I could have told her about Jimmy's home run and the cracked wishbone in my treasure box. I would have explained the Moscatelli Way—how you don't just win for yourself; you do it for all the people who never won a damn thing in their whole life and never would. People like Ma and the mother I hadn't seen since I was small and Mau Mau. For my beautiful brother hollering like hell in an empty bar.

But I wasn't Zaidie and I didn't have those words. Still, it was as if Coach Lois heard them anyway. Or saw them on my face. Felt them.

"Remember when I told you that if you were ever ready to commit a hundred percent, I'd like to work with you individually?" she said.

Like my life depended on it, I thought, remembering that feeling I had in the hospital or when I was walking to the Y that day.

But all I said was, "Yes, I remember." Then I gave her a hug that would have even embarrassed Jimmy.

CHAPTER FIVE

The Magnet

ZAIDIE

HISTORICALLY, 1968 WAS THE YEAR OF MANY THINGS, AND BY fall, everything would change. But for Agnes and me, it began as the year of winning. Swim meets and competitions, scholarships and acceptances. Until Penn interrupted my streak and Agnes lost a 100-meter breaststroke to a girl from Waltham, it seemed like no one and nothing could say no to us.

I tyrannized Ma with lists from my favorite magazines, starting with "Plan your College Wardrobe Now!" from *Mademoiselle*.

"Who wrote this? The Filene's company? No one in the world needs all these clothes." Ma read the list out loud:

"Four blouses. Three skirts with matching sweaters. A black dress and a pair of heels. For what exactly? Are you going to college or to fancy parties?"

"Both, Ma! What do you think?"

"Two blazers. And what's this? Three pairs of pajamas—new ones? Good Lord, Zaida, who's gonna see you?"

I imagined myself drinking hot chocolate in the lounge in my cute pajamas and matching slippers, hair pulled up on top of my head the way the model's was in *Mademoiselle*, but I couldn't tell her that.

I let her cool down for a week before I showed her "Must-Haves for Your Dorm Room," culled from *Seventeen*.

Then there was my major. When I told my parents what I'd chosen, they were even more befuddled.

"English?" Dad said. "What's the use of that?"

Desperately, I turned to Ma, the one who had been buying me notebooks for years. "But I want to be a writer. You know—"

"No one's prouder than us of that prize you won, but you don't want to go to college and spend all that money on something that will most likely . . ."

"It's like dreaming you'll be a baseball player," Dad chimed in. "Or a girl singer with the Beatles, for chrissake."

"She wanted to be those things at some point, too, remember?" Jimmy called from the foyer, where he had just come in. Late to supper as usual.

"I never wanted to play baseball! That was you." I burst into irrational tears. As always, that brought out Jimmy's protective streak.

"I guess they might as well pave over Fenway Park and close the record shops, then," he said, switching sides. "Same goes for book writing. Hell, Dad, someone's got to give it a shot—even if ninety-nine percent of 'em's gonna fall on their face."

I headed for my room, crying harder.

LATER, MA CAME up with a plate of Chips Ahoy like she did when we were little. As if a few store-bought cookies were the cure to everything.

"All Dad's trying to say is that not everyone gets a chance like you, Zaida. People like your Aunt Cille and that Michael Finn out there in Colorado"—she never called him my father—"maybe it's different for them. But families like ours? Moscatellis and Garrisons? A couple of generations back you would've had to drop out of school when you were fourteen and go to work in the factory. For a hundred generations—maybe forever—no one ever got the chance. You're coming up in a golden hour, Zaida. It wasn't always this way, and it won't last forever. Don't waste it on some impractical dream."

"But this is what I want. What I always wanted—even though I didn't know it. How else can I live all those lives I've been dreaming about?"

A light came into Ma's eyes the way it did when she saw one of our hopes, but then just as quickly something inside her, *someone*, jumped up and snuffed it out.

"Maybe you could get a job on the paper. Study what do they call it—journalism—"

"That's not the kind of stories I want to tell, Ma. I'm going to write my own."

"Made-up, you mean. Fiction novels." The disdain in her voice, much as she tried to keep it out, cut through me like a January wind.

"It's not something less like you think. I want to use everything I know—not just the so-called facts. I want to tell the stories that are truer than true."

Again, I saw that flicker. Like for just a minute she understood. But it was promptly extinguished with one of the long sighs that had squelched so many of her own dreams.

"It's your choice, Zaida. Your life. All I'm asking, all your father wants—is that you honor your chances."

Though I didn't change my major, I would remember her words enough to write them down later the way I'd once inscribed words from Eleanor Roosevelt and Joan of Arc in my notebooks. And then a few months later, when I rose to speak to my class, I would talk about the golden hour, and would end my speech the way she had that night in my room.

We, the class of 1968, are graduating at a unique point in history. With that comes untold opportunities, but also a great responsibility. Honor your chances. Many generations who came before you and many more who will come after may not have them.

After that, people would rise and clap; my teachers would congratulate me; and my classmates would swarm around.

But that day in my room, the last thing I wanted to hear was some talk about how things had been for her and Dad and a bunch of poor people who came from Italy and Ireland or wherever in steerage. I couldn't wait till she left so I could call Charlie and talk about something—anything—else.

Even though I kept my door closed, our nightly conversations—or maybe just the spirit of them, the goofy teenage elation—always managed to seep under the door.

Jimmy, in particular, could pick it up from a mile away.

"Never heard so much damn gigglin' in my life. What kind of idiot is this kid?" Since I'd begun to date Charlie, or maybe it was even before that, maybe when Spider Johnson dropped the first college catalogue in our box, a gulf had opened up between my brother and me. He was glad for me, but it was hard not to see my success as an indictment—especially after Charlie came on the scene.

To him, my boyfriend was everything he could never be. "Look at the two of yas. With your golden hair and your perfect teeth, you look so much alike it's practically—whaddya call it—incest."

And when Nonna asked what my new *amore* was like, Jimmy spoke up before I got a chance. "Colleige, that's what he's like. The ultimate colleige."

He sounded like he was back in high school when he and his rat friends used to hang out at the picnic table, laughing and blowing smoke rings at the world that excluded them.

"Be fair, Jimmy," I tried to say. "You're not just your car or who you hang out with—your job—are you? Well, Charlie isn't, either."

"Tell you the truth, Z, those things there? That's exactly who I am. A car on the verge of shittin' the bed? That's me, sister." He stood up and thumped his chest in a way that scared me. "Best friends with a kid who lives by a dried-up river of junk. Me again." (Another thump.) "And your Charlie? He's the same."

I hated the way he said *sister*—not as an endearment like he used to, but as if it was something hard—a hand pushing me further away. Was I the ultimate colleige in his mind, too?

"Only thing you got wrong is my goddamn job," he added. "Cause at the moment, I ain't exactly got one."

Ma, who was in the kitchen drinking coffee and pretending to pay attention to Nonna as she instructed her on how to make eggplant rollatini (*Luigi's favorite!*) got up and came into the doorway like she'd been listening all along. As if she'd been listening since the day we were born, even before she knew us.

"What did you say? I thought you liked that job at Simpson Spring—" And then, not needing to wait for an answer, "You should have told us, Jimmy."

I was almost grateful when the rage that was visibly rising up inside him was transferred to her.

"Why? So you and Dad could sit up talkin' about the trouble with Jimmy half the night? You think I don't fucking hear you?"

When Nonna, who had followed her into the room, hands covered with egg and breadcrumbs, gasped at his language, he turned back to me like it was all my fault. Everything from the lost job to the forbidden word that had worked its way from the backyard directly into the parlor.

"Thanks a lot, Z."

AFTER ANOTHER ACCEPTANCE came in—this one from Smith, who offered a full scholarship—the gulf widened. "You see those pictures in the catalogue? They have teas, Z. And they dress up in gloves—inside—like they're expecting the flippin' Queen. In a few years, you won't even wanna know me." He grabbed his jacket from the hook. "Hell, maybe you don't already."

"That's not fair, Jimmy! You're the one—" I cried out, but before I finished, the door slammed, and I was left to wonder if what he said was true. Did I resent him as much as he seemed to hate the colleiges of this world?

I complained to Agnes that Ma and Dad paid more attention to a hook in the foyer where Jimmy hung his jacket than to anything we did. It was an old leather bomber he wore year round—even in the summer, as if it wasn't just weather that made him cold. Or as if the seasons had stopped mattering to him; he was governed by something else now.

Soon as Dad came in after work, he checked the hook. Was Jimmy home?

If it was empty, he'd ask Ma where the boy had gone. As if she knew. If not, he'd look up the stairs in the direction of Jimmy's room, obviously wondering what kind of mood he was in that day.

As for Ma, she must've seen that hook, in the shape of a giant question mark, in her dreams. It didn't matter whether the leather jacket was there or not; the question it asked was never entirely answered: Where was Jimmy? What was happening to him? Even when we heard the stereo blasting from his room—usually Hendrix or Jimmy Page—no one knew.

Sure, Ma was still proud of Agnes's and my accomplishments, but there was something muted about it now. As if the hook, that twisted question mark just inside the door, was always before her, obscuring everything else.

IT WAS MARCH, the day of the state finals in swimming and Agnes's friend Susan came running up the driveway, her face flushed, yelling to me where I was waiting on the porch. "Zaidie! Did you hear?"

And then, when Ma stepped outside, "Mrs. Moscatelli! Zaidie! It's Agnes, she—"

"Dear God—what?" Ma called out, clutching her heart. "Were they in an accident?"

Ever since Josie Pennypacker had died in front of our house, it seemed that Ma was just waiting for the next bad thing to happen. And that day she'd been particularly apprehensive. Though Nonna had offered to drive to the meet in Springfield, Jimmy had insisted they go in his car. "Nonna's fine in town, but you ever go out on the highway with her? She drives like the little old lady from Pasadena."

"He's got a point there," Dad said, though I was pretty sure he'd never heard Jan and Dean.

"Not a great option either way," Ma said when Jimmy left the table. "You sure you can't take the day off?"

"I got two brake jobs and a total engine, Dahlia. Someone's gotta keep this joint afloat, you know."

However, before she could say it out loud, Jimmy's Falcon peeled into the driveway with Agnes in the passenger seat. All four doors gaped open at the same moment and they started up the walk, Jimmy leading.

"Did she win?" I yelled before I saw the answer in his eyes.

"Win? That's not the half of it. Tell 'em, Sky Bar," Jimmy said.

"Yes, *piccola*, tell them what you do before they hear it on the radio," Nonna added, brushing off her dress as she hopped out of the back seat a minute behind them.

"Broke the state record in the hundred-meter freestyle is what she did. Our Agnes is All-American. Fifteen years old, only started swimmin' serious last year, and she broke the freakin' state record."

"They're coming from the paper to interview her tomorrow," Susan added, obviously disappointed that she hadn't been in time to break the news. "I wouldn't be surprised if they put her picture on the front page."

My eyes were on Agnes, though. Though she was smiling, there was something subdued about her happiness—not a word anyone had ever used to describe my sister.

"Oh, honey; I couldn't be more proud," Ma said, opening her arms, but there was a question mark as big as that hook in the hallway in her voice. Clearly, she saw what I did.

When Jimmy passed me, I caught a whiff of booze on his breath. *Was that it?* I wondered. Had he and his Old Crow spoiled Agnes's victory? Couldn't he even hold back for one day? We looked at each other the way we did a lot those days. Rats and colleiges facing off like they did when he was in high school.

Agnes remained quiet at dinner, and later when her friends called to congratulate her. In my room, I watched the door, waiting for her to squeeze into my little bed and tell me what was on her mind as we both stared into the night sky.

Around three in the morning, she still hadn't come, so I went to her.

"Come in."

In the light from the moon and the tiny plug-in Dad had bought for her when she was small and afraid of the dark, I caught the glimmer of Agnes's trophies, including the large one Jimmy had proudly carried in that day. Mutely, she slid over to make room in the bed.

"You want to know what winning is like?" she finally said. I lay still beside her.

"A magnet. It attracts all kind of things. Trophies like those up there, and new friends—some who like me cause I'm me, and others who just got pulled in by the force of it. Even people like that reporter who all of a sudden think I belong in the newspaper."

"It also attracts opportunities; don't forget that."

"I haven't, but you know what, Zaidie? The magnet itself—it's a force that doesn't know the difference between good and bad. It draws them both."

"What are you saying?" I asked, but deep down, I knew. I thought of the gulf that had opened up between Jimmy and me since I first began to win my own race. Even my growing separation from Ma and Dad. My eyes filled with water.

Again she was quiet for a few minutes.

"You know who was at my meet today? Right up in the front row like he'd always been there. Dead center. Watching me like he told me he would."

I sat up straight and switched the light on. "You can't be talking about that guy from when you were little? What was his name—Mr. Dean? It couldn't have been him. I'm sure he forgot you a long time ago."

"The one and only. And he will never forget. You wanna know why?" Again I waited. "Cause I'm the one who knows who he is. Up there in that attic, I saw everything he hides from the world."

"But what would he be doing way out there in Springfield? Besides, it's been so long . . . How could you even recognize him?"

"Oh, I know him, all right. Just like he knows me. The minute I won the race, it was like my eyes went straight to him—just like that magnet I told you about. He was the only one who wasn't clapping. And then, when I looked in that direction again, he was gone."

CHAPTER SIX

All Saints

DAHLIA

I WAS STANDING BY THE PICTURE WINDOW, WAITING, WHEN THE car pulled up. "You're never gonna guess who bought Tucker's store," I blurted out soon as Louie closed the door.

"That dump? You might want to ask me if I give a shit first." He headed for the kitchen, where I could hear the faucet running, the sound of him slugging down his water.

"Okay, I won't tell you, then. And I won't say who he hired to run the deli, either."

"Thank heaven for small mercies," he replied, rinsing out his glass. One of his mother's sayings.

Hmph.

The subject didn't come up again till after the kids were in bed. "Since when did Tucker's have a deli?" Louie asked, casual as heck. Like he hadn't been stewing on it all night. "Packaged bologna, and hot dogs dangling out of his filthy meat case; is that the deli you're talking about?"

"Hmm," I murmured.

"Well, whoever it is must be a damn fool. They'll spend more money than the place is worth before the board of health lets 'em even open the door."

Another *hmm*.

"Be that way, then, Dahlia. Like I said before, it ain't like I give a shit."

Well, the next day who do you think came in busting with the news? "Drove by Tucker's old store today—just in time to see them hanging the new sign."

I lifted my eyebrows, not even dignifying it with a murmur.

"Joe O'Connor's really lost his mind this time," Louie said, referring to our longtime neighbor from the next street. "All those years living with that crazy son of his finally got to him."

Zaidie exhaled her disgust into the kitchen, where she was doing homework at the table.

I set down my mending. "Thought you didn't give a damn."

"I'm telling you, he hasn't been right since Edna died," he went on, shaking his head. "First he starts draggin' poor Crazy Joe to Mass every morning with the old ladies. Now he's gonna open a store?"

"Hmm."

"Man's a retired welder, for chrissake. Probably never set foot in a damn market till he lost the wife. Church, either."

"Who's going to look after his boy? That's what I want to know," I said, no longer able to hold my peace. "The kid'll be out wandering the neighborhood getting into God knows what."

"Hah. I guess you didn't hear the best part. Crazy Joe's gonna work there, too."

"You shouldn't call him that, Dad," Zaidie finally yelled from the kitchen. "How would you feel—"

"That's his name, ain't it? What do you want me to call him—Crazy Paul?"

Zaidie slammed her book shut and started upstairs to her room. "You two are hopeless!"

Normally, Louie wouldn't have let that pass. *Hopeless, am I? Me the one who works fifty hours a week to keep you in fingernail polish and encyclopedias?* And I would have taken issue with the fact that she included me in her hopeless category when I hadn't said a damn word.

But Louie was too caught up in his story to bother. "You haven't heard the clincher, Dahlia. You know what he's calling the place?"

Before he could tell me, Jimmy slammed through the front door, ushering in a rush of heady spring air. Jools was right behind him.

Usually it took a court order to get two words out of Jools, but not that day. "The Nothing's Perfect Market and Deli!" he spat out.

"Nothing's Perfect," Jimmy repeated. "No joke, Ma. Got a sign painted up and everything." He painted the shape of a rainbow with the flat of his hand.

I hadn't seen him in such a good mood since the day Agnes broke a record in the state finals. Even paused to kiss me on the cheek just like he used to. No booze on his breath, either—at least none I picked up.

The boys were so busy laughing at Joe O'Connor's foolishness that no one noticed Agnes when she came in the back door. In the past, she would've wanted to know what all the chuckling was about, but ever since the state finals, she'd been acting funny. Quiet. Maybe the swimming was too much pressure. Right away, she started laying the table for supper.

Without needing to ask, she set a plate for Jools in Jon's old spot. Somehow it always made us feel better when the chair was occupied—as if just for that one meal we were whole again. It didn't even matter that it was the likes of Jools Bousquet taking his seat.

The jokes continued through dinner, starting with Jimmy. "Might as well call the place Lousy Sandwiches and Moldy Cheese."

"You say your meat's rotten?" Jools piped in, more animated than I'd ever seen him. "Slipped on a spill in the aisle and broke your leg? Hey, nothing's perfect."

"At least they're honest," Jimmy said. "Imagine Crazy Joe workin' the deli? Probably be razor blades in the pickles."

"Joe Jr.'s a grown man. Older than you, Jimmy. And he's got a mental illness," Zaidie said, speaking up for the first time. "How would you feel—"

Jimmy used to say you could put those four words on her tombstone, drawing a crescent with his hand the way he had with Joe O'Connor's sign.

"Not a bad idea," Zaidie had said in return. "Might be a good question for the living to ask themselves when they walk through a graveyard."

This time, though, Jimmy was in a more conciliatory mood. "You're right, Z. Sorry." But then, he looked at Jools and they broke up all over again.

"Just don't eat the pickles, right?" Jools said, lowering his head before he, too, apologized to Zaidie.

Even Louie emitted a grunt that faintly resembled a laugh.

Finally, I cleared my throat. "Ahem. You might not think it's so funny when you hear who's running the deli for him. The manager, he calls her."

"A deli manager? In that tiny store? Ten steps and you hit the back door," Agnes said, her mind off her own worries at last. She covered her mouth to suppress a giggle as she glanced at her sister. "Zaidie, you gotta admit—"

"Okay, that is kind of funny," Zaidie conceded—though I wasn't sure if she really thought so, or she was just happy to hear Agnes laugh.

"Let me guess," Louie said. "I bet it's what's-her-name—Jeffrey's mother. Old Joe's had his eye on that dame for years."

Course, I bristled right away. "Gina Lollobrigida? That might be who you'd pick, but Joe O'Connor's got his mind on a higher plane these days."

"Higher plane, my ass. You saying he's got the Sisters of Mercy to run the joint?"

"Closest thing to it," I said, interrupting the laughter that had now consumed the bunch of them. "From what I hear, he's talked his church friend into making up the potato salad and whatever else he plans to sell in that imperfect deli of his."

The truth slowly seeped into Louie's brain as he wiped his mouth. "Church friend? But Joe's been going to rosary group with . . ." He threw down his napkin. "What the hell are you tellin' me here, Dahlia?"

I looked out on five sets of lifted eyebrows, mirroring my own, some in curiosity, a couple in disbelief—and one in plain horror.

"From what I hear, he's made up a sign for her, too." Though I usually left the theatrics to the kids, I stood up like Agnes did when she made a big announcement and painted one of Jimmy's imaginary banners: "Anna P. Moscatelli, Manager."

"My mother? That Anna Moscatelli?" Louie gasped. "Impossible. She's seventy-five, for chrissake—and she's never had a job in her life. Besides, I—I won't allow it."

"Seventy-seven last September," Jimmy corrected him. Louie stared at me as if it was all my fault.

"It's 1968, Dad," Zaidie said. "Women want their own jobs; we're tired of husbands or fathers telling us what we can and cannot do."

"Or sons," Agnes added gently, almost as if she felt sorry for the world that was crumbling around people like Louie. Me, too, I suppose.

"That might be fine for you girls, but good Lord, Nonna's almost eighty," I said—more defensive than I intended.

"You always said she's got the energy of a woman half her age, didn't you?" Zaidie put in.

"Two women," Agnes added.

A hush fell over the table as everyone focused on their meat loaf and creamed corn.

"Nah. Not buying it," Jimmy finally said, looking up. "Even if she wanted a dang job, Nonna would never work in a store with that name. Nothing's Perfect? I mean, have you ever seen a speck of dust in her house?"

"He's right; she wouldn't set foot in the place—on general principles." Louie shot me another look of blame. "Where on earth d'you get that crazy rumor anyway?"

"Hmm." That was all I had to say to him and his blame. Him and his boss routine. Maybe my girls were right. Us women were tired of being told what we could and couldn't do. Tall as a queen, I got up to clear the table.

THE FOLLOWING SUNDAY, Anna showed up with none other than Joe O'Connor himself. Even dragged poor Crazy Joe—excuse me, Joe Jr.—along, though he shook his head when Anna tried to coax him inside.

Realizing this wasn't the typical visit from Nonna, who hadn't even brought a pie, the girls drifted down from upstairs and took a seat in the parlor. By then, Joe Jr. was pacing up and down the porch, carrying on an argument with himself about his duties at the store. "Sweep the floor. Help Anna in the deli. Say good morning to the customers. No! I'm not saying it and you can't make me. Smile, Joe, make sure you smile. No smiling! I won't."

Thank goodness nothing's perfect, I thought to myself, plunking a plate of stale Lorna Doones in front of the guests. "Tell us, Anna. Are you really planning to work in a store called—"

"That just the front. In my deli, everything"—she put her fingers to her lips and kissed them, *paisan* style—*"perfetta!"*

Louie opened his mouth to speak—probably to say he wouldn't have it. But before he got a word out, Joe looked toward the stairs. "We were hoping to catch your Jimmy. Is he here?"

Nonna glanced in the direction of the hook that told the story of Jimmy's life. Or everything we could discern of it. Since the leather jacket was there, he was most likely upstairs sleeping it off.

"I just remember. Jeemy tell me he have to help a friend on Sunday," she said, covering for him like we all had learned to do. "You talk to his papa, Joe. He tell Jeemy."

"Or to his mother," I put in. Some independent woman Anna turned out to be.

Across the room, my girls smiled at me.

"We're gonna be hiring someone to help with the painting before we open," Joe said.

"That dump needs a lot more than a coat of paint—" Louie began.

I hurled a look at him before he got any further. With any luck, Jimmy might get a month's work of it.

"And after we open up, we'll need a delivery driver."

"A delivery driver, huh? Sounds like you got big plans for the place, Joe. The Nothing's Perfect Market and Deli, huh?"

If Joe caught the sarcasm, he didn't seem to care. It was like he was just waiting for someone to ask. His eyes ignited. That's when I realized it wasn't just the name of a market; it was some kind of religion.

He raked his cottony white hair till it stood on end as he leaned in with his story. "Ya know, ever since the trouble started with Joe Jr., I been nursing a grudge against God. Me, I mighta deserved a curse like that—especially in my wild days. But an innocent kid? What had he done? And my Edna was an angel on earth. How could God—"

An angel on earth—Edna O'Connor? The woman was the worst gossip in the neighborhood, her and her friend Gina Lollobrigida. Besides that, I'd never forgiven her for calling the dog officer and trying to get Princie put to sleep when the dog tore her dress from the line. Thought more of that white dress than my kids, I thought. Course I wasn't about to say any of that.

"Hmph," I blurted out in spite of myself.

Fortunately, Joe was too caught up in his story to hear me. "Twenty-plus years, I never set a foot in a church, and when I went back, it wasn't to pray or none of that. I went cause after all those years of Catholic school, listening to how the Church knew the answer to everything, I felt like I deserved an explanation. Or a refund.

"So day after day, I sat there with the foolish old ladies—sorry, Anna, not you of course—waiting for someone to answer one simple question. Why? I didn't kneel, I didn't stand, and I didn't get up when it was time for Communion. I just sat there waiting. And every day the priest stood up there delivering nothing but the same old rigamarole I been hearing since I was a kid."

Louie cleared his throat loudly. Then he got up and opened the window a little wider. "I'm sure all this is leadin' to some kinda point, Joe, but we got things to do, and your boy out there—" By then, Joe Jr.'s walking and ranting had reached a fever pitch.

But Joe had my attention and he knew it. "Let him talk, Louie— and Joe Jr.'s a man, not a boy."

Joe lowered his head and when he lifted it, he ran his fingers through his hair again. He'd forgotten everyone else and was talking directly to me.

"Then one day, just when I was about to give up, I got what I came for." He rose as if to leave.

"Well, don't keep us in suspense," Louie said, arms folded across his chest. "I just wasted ten minutes of my life listening to the buildup—"

"You already seen the name of my market, didn't you?"

"Nothing's Perfect? That's it, Joe? You sat in Mass months and months to come to that—excuse me—idiotic conclusion? Like I said before, we got too much to do around here to sit around listening to—"

"Where you hear that, Guiseppe?" Nonna said, as if this was the first she'd heard of his revelation. "Not in my church."

"That's exactly where I heard it, Anna. Right there in St. Anthony's. Third pew. Aisle seat. It was the Feast of All Saints or Souls— one of those—and the Father was saying how saints weren't what we thought. Sure, some of 'em were brilliant thinkers who wrote books and founded orders, but others couldn't even read and write.

"And some were drunks or sluts or so broke up by grief they didn't think they could take another step. But they did. They did. And then there were saints with bad tempers like mine. Even after they became saints, they were still popping off sometimes."

"Saints—popping off? *Dio mio*," Nonna said, crossing herself.

Joe didn't hear her, though. Standing by the window where his son was in a full-blown rant, water filled his eyes as he held me with his gaze. "But that's not the best part, Dahlia. The best part is it's all right."

"We all know you been through a rough time, Joe," Lou said. "Maybe you should see one of them doctors like your Joe goes to. No shame in it." He was starting to sound like Zaidie.

"The whole world and everyone in it is all fouled up, and it's all right, cause you know what? It wasn't never meant to be perfect. Not in your heart or mine and sure as hell not in this life. All we gotta do, all we can do is be what we were made to be. You hear Junior out there? He's not just fine, Dahlia. He's a living, breathing saint."

"The kid who used to put nails in the road to ruin people's tires—a saint?" Louie muttered. "The one out there cursin' up a storm on my front porch?"

But no one heard him. In a heartbeat, Agnes was on her feet like his first convert ready to step up and be immersed in the water. "Um, Mr. O'Connor?"

Joe, who had started for the door, turned around. He was so focused on his story, on me, he looked startled, as if he'd almost forgotten my girls were there, taking in every word.

"You know that job you were offering Jimmy? He'll take it."

CHAPTER SEVEN

The Inferno

ZAIDIE

JIMMY TOOK MOST OF THE WEIGHT WHILE I WALKED BACKWARD UP the attic stairs, angling the desk through the narrow passage.

"Man, I almost forgot what a beast this thing is," he groaned when we reached the top floor. "Last time I drug that thing up a flight of stairs, I had Jools on the other end."

"He offered this time, too. Did you see his face when you turned him down?"

"No need to worry about Bousquet's hurt feelin's, Z." With a cloth, Jimmy wiped a dusty window and peered into the empty street. "Cause right around now, he ain't got nothin' on his mind but that bottle of Old Crow he sent Stewie out for this afternoon. Just hope he saved me a coupla shots. My back's killin' me."

I winced at the mention of his familiar comfort, but since Jimmy had taken the job at the market, we'd started to get close again and I didn't want to say anything that might ruin it. Together we pushed the desk into the space I had cleared and stood back to admire it.

"Damn. I forgot how hot it was up here. What are you plannin' to write—a sequel to that book in your room? What's it called—Dante's *Inferno*?" He pronounced the name as if it rhymed with *ant*.

"It's Dan-tay," I laughed. "You know—Italiano? You should read it sometime."

"Yeah, I was thinkin' of it, but then I decided I'd save myself the trouble and take the trip myself. Some of the things I seen, Z? Bet I could teach old Mr. Dan-tayy a thing or two about infernos." He circled the shadowy space, kicking at the boxes that littered the floor. "Sure is a lot of crap up here. Whaddya think Ma's savin' in all of these?"

"Probably the story of every kid that ever came through the house. I hardly dare to look."

"Talk about infernos. Open one and the whole place'll go up in flames." He drew an explosion with his hands. In its wake, we fell quiet, thinking of the kids we'd called brother or sister for a month or a year, the ones whose report cards and school pictures had been meticulously saved just like ours. Now we watched for their names in the paper. One of Ma's twins played football for the high school team; he came by to say goodbye before he headed out to Ohio on a scholarship. We saw a couple of their names on the wedding page, too, and several of them were listed among those who had joined the military. When we spotted a familiar name in the court report, however, we hid the paper from Ma.

"You didn't really hurt your back, did you?" I finally asked.

Jimmy clutched his lower spine and deepened his voice in a perfect imitation of Dad's. "Get the heating pad, Dahlia. I really did it this time."

Then he settled himself on an empty crate and swatted at a network of spider webs as he surveyed the dim lighting, the nails protruding from the unfinished walls.

"You gonna tell me why you wanted to move up here? Like I said, this place is hotter than Dante's worst nightmare. Haunted, too." Looking at the crates in the corner, he made a cross of his hands as if to repel a vampire.

I reached for the broom, hoping to give him a hint. "Charlie and I have plans to meet at Junie Sweet's in an hour and I want to get the place cleaned up before I go."

He didn't budge. "You still haven't answered my question."

"What——?" I avoided his eyes. And then, when he continued to stare at me, "No big mystery. I just wanted some quiet; that's all."

"Quiet?" Jimmy pronounced the word like a curse. He peered into a corner of the attic where Jon's train lay in a heap of broken tracks. "Ask me, the place has been quiet since Shad left. Everyone thinks my nightmares started after the war. But the first time I woke up shakin' was the night that bastard took him away."

Then, remembering who Michael Finn was to me, he quickly added, "Sorry, Z. Sometimes I'm just an asshole."

"It's okay. You called him by the right name."

"Maybe so, but bastards or not, bums or not, they're still a part of us, ain't they? That's somethin' people don't understand. Even Ma and Dad didn't get it for a long time."

"And they do now?"

"Yeah, they do. Since I come home, they been forced to look at a lot of stuff they never seen before."

His eyes drifted back to the train we thought they'd thrown away. "I used to hear that damn thing runnin' in my sleep. When I woke up, the silence practically kilt me. You wanna know why I started blastin' that music Ma and Dad are always complaining about? I wanted somethin' to drown out the quiet he left behind. Part of the reason, anyway."

My eyes moved from the abandoned train to Jimmy's face. Sometimes I forgot that I wasn't the only one who'd been affected by Jon's abrupt disappearance.

"And now that you're busy with the Ultimate Colleige and Sky Bar spends half her life at the pool, the place is a damn tomb," he went on. "Whaddya think it'll be like with the both of yas gone?"

"You're not here much yourself these days, you know. By the time Agnes leaves for college, you and Jane will probably be married."

His eyes took on that dreamy look they always got whenever he heard his girlfriend's name. "She'd look pretty damn cute in one of them white dresses, wouldn't she? Diamond ring sparklin' on her finger like a little piece of the sun? Man. Do you really think she'd ever . . . to me, Z?" Then he shook his head. "Nah. Let's not talk crazy."

A COUPLE OF years earlier, I would have agreed. The thought of my brother and Judge Miller's stepdaughter going to a movie together, much less getting married, seemed about as likely as life on Mars. Even Jimmy had given up, though occasionally we still caught him dialing the number. "Just an old reflex," he'd say, looking embarrassed. "Not like I expect her to talk to me."

The Millers weren't even trying to be polite by then. "Jimmy Kovacs, is that you? How many times do you have to be told?"

"Seventy times seven. Ain't that what they say in the Book?" Jimmy said into the dead phone after they hung up on him.

"You already called that many times, son. At least," Dad said from his armchair. "And I don't think the prophets were talkin' about chasin' girls when they wrote that."

I still remember the day Jane left for college in New York. It was only weeks before Jimmy would be leaving himself—boarding the bus for boot camp.

"Just hope whatever colleige ends up with her knows what he got," he said, gazing out the picture window. "That girl deserves . . ." He drew increasingly large circles with his hand. "Everything."

"So do you, Jim," Ma quickly put in. "Don't ever forget that."

He kissed her on the head before heading off to who-knows-where. "Accordin' to my Ma, anyways." Though she'd been telling him all his life—we all had—somehow he never seemed to believe it.

Jimmy was on a base in California and was preparing to leave for Vietnam when the news hit town: Jane Miller had left school and disappeared. Some said she'd been trundled off to a home for unwed mothers; others claimed it was an abortion in someone's garage, followed by a nervous breakdown. Still others believed she'd run off and eloped, causing her family to disown her. I did my best to ignore the subject whenever it came up.

Then, just when everyone had almost forgotten her, she was back in town, waitressing at Rusty's Hideaway on the south side. Jane had always had an edgy side, but now her old friends described her as downright hard. If anyone asked where she'd been, she was quick to tell them off in language that confirmed their worst suspicions.

Again, the rumors started. Those who knew her father's harsh reputation in the courtroom speculated that he was punishing her by refusing to pay her tuition. If she wanted to go back to school, she'd have to earn it, the Millers' elderly neighbors said. But according to Jane's friends, it went deeper than that. "It's all her," Allison Hillman was heard saying at Junie Sweet's. "After what her parents made her do, she's rebelling against everything. Talk about cutting off your nose to spite—"

I walked out before she could finish the cliché, not wanting to hear the inevitable buzz about what exactly Jane Miller had been forced to do. To be honest, I couldn't imagine that girl being pressured into anything.

Then one morning I walked out the door and found her waiting for me. Despite everything I'd heard, I was shocked by the sight of her. The planes of her narrow face were sharper than ever and there was something steely in her eyes. I pretended not to see her, but she fell into step beside me.

We walked the three miles without saying a word. Only when the school came into view did she break the silence. "So I hear your brother's over in Nam."

I thought of all the times she'd refused his calls. The look on his face when he stood in the foyer holding that dead phone. Eyes straight ahead, I walked faster, joining the crowd that was headed for the door.

She scrabbled to keep up. "Listen, Zaida, I know you don't want to talk to me, and that's fine cause I don't have a lot to say to you, either. Just give me the address and I'll be out of your hair for good."

"Why—so you can play with his heart one more time? Not a chance." While heads turned, I slipped into the high school, leaving her on the stairs.

SHE WAS STILL outside when school ended six hours later. Only sheer aggravation made me stop. "Have you been out here waiting for me all day?"

"I took a lunch break." She looked at me obliquely as she lit a cigarette.

"Well, you should have stayed home because—"

"You wanna know one thing I learned from your brother?" She inhaled a long, slow drag and exhaled as if she was releasing much more than smoke. "Persistence." Was it me, or did I hear a catch in her voice when she mentioned him?

"You don't even know Jimmy. If you could have seen—" I stopped myself, unwilling to give her the satisfaction. "Listen, the *Gazette* prints the names of soldiers who want mail every Wednesday if you're looking for a pen pal . . ."

She stopped abruptly. "You wanna know how we met?"

"You were in the same graduating class, for crying out loud. You saw each other around all your lives—just like everyone else. Like I said—"

She flashed the tiny flame of her cigarette. "It was ninth grade and I had just started smoking. Maybe that was the first sign I'd turn out—well, like I did. Neither of my sisters would have thought of picking up one of these nasty Camels. But I was, you know, the black sheep.

From birth, you might say. I might've lived in the Millers' house, but hard as my mother tried, hell, hard as I tried myself, I could never be like them.

"Anyway, before homeroom, I'd sneak outside for a smoke by the dumpster—and there he was. That's when it started."

"You and Jimmy talked?" All this time, I'd thought it was some inexplicable out-of-the-blue crush.

"Every day. At first, that kid Jools was with him, but once we started hitting it off, Jimmy made sure to come alone. Some of the best conversations I ever had were over my morning smoke. After he dropped out, I missed him like crazy—though I never admitted it."

"So why didn't you take his calls if he meant so much to you?"

"Half the time my parents never told me he called. And the other half—well, the one thing I did right was get good grades. College was my ticket out. The last thing I needed was some local kid, a Moscatelli no less, holding me back. I mean, no offense . . ."

"Leave my brother alone," I repeated as I picked up the pace. She moved in front of me, blocking my path.

"It's not like I want to go out with him or anything, Zaida. That hasn't changed. But the past year, I had a lot of time to . . . think . . . and my mind kept going back to Jimmy. Sometimes it seemed like no one ever cared about me—me, the real Jane Miller—like that kid by the dumpster did—and I don't just mean as a girl. Is that weird or what?" She shrugged her bony shoulders. "Least I could do is write him a letter or two."

I lowered my book bag and stared at her. "Persistence, huh? So you're saying if I don't give you the address, you'll be outside my door tomorrow morning?"

She gave me her hard smile, revealing teeth perfected by braces. "And the day after that. Seventy times seven."

So he'd even shared his favorite aphorism from the Bible with her? I pulled out a notebook. "Just promise you're not gonna make him think—"

"We're friends, I told you. Even Jimmy knows that."

After I scribbled the military address, she looked it over—almost like she didn't trust me. Then she jammed it into her pocketbook and walked away without even a *See ya later.*

When Charlie caught up to me, I was still fuming. "What my brother ever saw in that girl, I'll never know. And she's rude to boot!"

Charlie looked back at her narrow bottom, the thin hair pulled into a ponytail streaking out behind her as she turned a corner. "Beats me."

JIMMY'S LETTERS HOME had grown shorter and more obtuse as his tour wound down, and if Jane wrote to him, he didn't mention it. He did his best to keep it upbeat and "normal" for Ma and Dad—Agnes even—but when he wrote to me, I heard a Jimmy I didn't know. The last letter consisted of three lines in the center of the tissuey paper. No heading or signature.

> *maybe we are all just figments of our own imagination.*
> *did you ever think of that, Z? stop believing in yourself for even*
> *a minute, and poof—you're gone.*

It was the kind of philosophical stuff I would later hear in college, usually late at night after a few joints had been passed around. But not from my brother. Never from my brother. Though I carried the letter around for days, the only one I showed it to was Charlie. He read the lines over a few times before he handed it back. The sympathy in his eyes was unmistakable.

"So? What do you think?" I finally asked.

"I hear there's a lot of drugs over there. And—I mean, you can hardly blame him. It's gotta be hell." He circled my wrist with his finger. "I'm sorry, Zaidie."

But by then, my mind was racing. Was that it? Had Jimmy become a dope fiend, like they said of Agnes's mother? I shuddered.

Besides death, it was the only affliction I knew that was powerful enough to keep a mother from her own children. I hid the letter in the back of my closet so Ma wouldn't see it. Just like Agnes stored her treasures.

What's that supposed to mean, Jimmy? Are you okay? I eventually wrote back.

Then, realizing what a ridiculous question it was, I scrapped it and began again. Turned out it didn't matter. He was home before he received another letter.

When there were no tracks on his arms like I'd feared, I began to wonder if I was wrong: Maybe there were scourges worse than dope. The only time he seemed anything like his old self was when he was leaving for Jools's. Though we knew they would be drinking, we were almost relieved. "At least he's interested in something," Agnes said. The next day, though, his mood was blacker than ever.

I expected he'd call Jane—no matter how friendly she kept her letters. Probably become a regular at Rusty's Hideway, too, but he never mentioned her.

Finally, one summer day when I found him wrapped in an afghan on the couch, I couldn't hold back any longer. "Aren't you supposed to be at—"

"Ain't nowhere I gotta be, Z. Nowhere in this entire world." He was staring at the TV screen, though he clearly wasn't focused on the game show. "Think you can get me a Coke out of the fridge? I'm feelin' a little . . . under the weather."

I cracked the green bottle and set it on the table beside him, feeling desperate. "Maybe you should call that girl—what's her name? The one who asked for your address?"

"Jane Miller?" He drank his Coke slowly, his mind clearly elsewhere. "You know, she wrote to me almost every day. Letters almost as long as yours, too. Still got every one of 'em up in my room."

"So why don't you—"

Jimmy wrapped the afghan around himself tighter and lay back down. "Last thing that girl needs in her life is someone like me—even if she was a little bit interested. Which she ain't."

THINGS HAD CHANGED since he'd started at the N. P., though. It wasn't as if the problems disappeared, but Mr. O'Connor—or Saint Joe, as people around town mockingly called him—had us believing again. If you could stumble a couple of feet toward what you were meant to be one day, who knows where you might end up in a month? Or a year.

"Reason most of us are miserable is cause we think we gotta figure everything out, get it all right," Joe would say, not caring a bit if he was mocked. "But truth is it's always gonna be screwed up and we're never gonna understand it. All we gotta do is get through the day the best we can. And trust. That's it!" By that point, his hands would be in the air, he'd be smiling like crazy, his cottony hair standing around his head, making it almost impossible not to listen.

Sure, Jimmy still woke up with the crashing nightmares a couple of times a week, which meant that soon he'd be out late with Jools. And after those nights by Buskit's River he still had a hard time getting up for work. But if he didn't show, Joe Jr. would come and bang on the door. "Like he was trying to wake the dead," according to Ethel Sylvia, the neighbor who'd moved into Josie Pennypacker's place. And in a way, he was. When that didn't work—as it inevitably didn't—Junior would march up and down the sidewalk, fearlessly crossing and recrossing the *maledizione* as he sang out the number of minutes they were late. "Thirty-eight minutes late for work, Jimmy Kovacs! Thirty-nine minutes. Got to get to work, Jimmy. Forty-one minutes late! Got to go to the Nothing's Perfect Market and Deli and sweep the floor. Say hello to the customers. Smile. Be polite." Here he began arguing with himself. "I won't. Don't have to. Forty-three minutes, Jimmy Kovacs! . . ."

That went on until Ma and Ethel were both screaming with him. "Damnit, Jimmy! Get the hell up for work!"

"Joe Jr. thinks he's Paul Revere," Ma said at supper as she and Dad developed a new routine. "The only thing he needs is the bell."

"Don't give him any ideas," Dad added.

When Jimmy asked, Joe hired Jools, too, and before long, Joe Jr. was stopping at the house by the river after he left our place. "Gotta be clean for the work. Wash your shirt. Underwear, too. No one ever got bit by a bar of soap, Jools Bousquet! Gotta be clean for . . ."

I'd been subtly trying to tell Jools the same thing for years, but there was nothing quite like Joe Jr. marching up and down in front of your house reminding you to take a bath to get your attention. Eventually, at the sight of him rounding the corner, Jools opened the window to yell, "Awwright, I hear ya!" The next sound coming through the window was the shower running. Without missing a beat, Junior continued on his way. "Gotta sweep the floor. Smile. Be polite to the customers. I won't. Don't have to . . ."

Then one day when I stopped into the N. P., as we kids called it, I noticed Jools's old sketches of Buskit's River hanging on the wall. They were matted and framed as if they were in a gallery. Behind the register, Jools's face couldn't decide whether to be proud or embarrassed.

"Saint Joe—I mean, Mr. O'Connor—caught me drawin' when it got slow so he asked to see my sketchbook . . ." he said, a patch of crimson spreading up his neck. "Next thing I know he's at the frame shop. I tole him no one would wanna look at any of this stuff, that the only halfway nice pictures I ever did were hangin' in Agnes's room, but you know Mr. O'Connor when he gets excited about somethin'."

"I sure do." I smiled, walking the length of the store, studying the sketches one by one. "They really look great, Jools. Some of them are almost like collage."

"Mixed media. That's what the lady said last week—right before she asked how much I wanted for one." He pointed at a blank spot on the wall. "Heck, I woulda give it to her for free. But before I could open my mouth, Mr. O'Connor come out from the back, yellin', 'Twenty-five dollars.' And she forked it over right there. Can you believe it, Zaidie? Twenty-five bucks for a junk drawin' by Jools— 'scuse me, Julian Bousquet. Even asked me to sign it."

It was the first time I'd ever heard him pronounce *Bousquet* correctly or use the name they called him in school. "Next time, Mr. O says, we're askin' for fifty."

Jools had been the first one to tell me about Jimmy and Jane, too. Every day just before closing, he said the deli got an order from the Hideaway Lounge. Joe, who knew nothing about the girl who waitressed there, complained it took Jimmy an hour to make a delivery that was five minutes away—and wondered aloud why someone working in a damn restaurant needed takeout anyway. But once he figured it out, he stopped griping and told Nonna to throw an extra sandwich in the bag so the two lovebirds could eat together. "On me."

"Lovebirds? Are you talking about my Jeemy?" The next day she brought in some of her homemade cookies and a chocolate heart in foil to pack with the sandwiches.

Since then, there had been days, sometimes whole weeks, when it was almost like the old Jimmy—the one before the drinking and the war had changed him—was back. It didn't last—maybe it couldn't— but we savored every minute.

That was the Jimmy who looked at me pointedly in the attic. "You think I don't know why you really moved your stuff up here?"

I picked up the broom and started to sweep again. "I already told you. I wanted a quiet place to write." With my eyes, I tried to pull his attention to the clock I'd hung on the wall the day before. "I'd really like to talk, Jimmy, but like I said, I'm meeting—"

"'Fraid you're not gettin' rid of me that easy," he said from his crate. "Not after I wrecked my back dragging the beast up here."

I swept faster, avoiding his face.

"It ain't no accident you picked a college in California, is it, Z? Couldn't put any more miles between yourself and us Moscatellis if you try."

"That's not fair, Jimmy, and you know it. I always wanted to go to Berkeley. And what do you mean us Moscatellis? Like I'm not one?"

"All's I know is ever since Shad left, you been movin' further and further away.

"Like you feel guilty for choosin' us. Heck, you'll be livin' out on the roof next. And after you leave, well, sometimes I wonder . . ."

"Stop right there," I began, but just then I bumped my shin against one of Ma's old boxes. "Shit," I howled. "Now see what you made me do?"

"That's what you used to say when you were six," he said, rubbing my shin the way he used to when I fell off my bike or roller-skated a little too fast. He looked up at me and the tenderness in his eyes almost broke me.

I jerked away. "So what are you—Sigmund Freud now? If I wanted someone to psychoanalyze me—"

"I don't have to pscyho-nothin' you, Z. I'm your damn brother, like it or not. You think you were the only one who felt it when Jonny left? He was my friggin' Shadow, capital S."

I sank onto my own crate and put my face in my hands, wondering how he knew so much. I'd never talked about my guilt over Jon to anyone.

"But I was supposed to take care of him. I promised, Jimmy," I said, tears streaming down my cheeks. "And I let him go with . . . with the bastard."

"The bastard's your father. Shad's, too."

"You wanna know the worst part? I remember living with his moods—and I can never forget what he did to my mother."

"You were what—three or four?"

"I might've been small, Jimmy; I might not recall a single detail, but I know what it felt like in that house. As soon as I heard the sound of him strumming his fingers on Ma's armchair, it all came back. There was always this tension—even when he was being nice—because we didn't know when it would turn. All we knew was that sooner or later it would. That's where I let Jon go."

"You were a kid, Z; you didn't let nobody do nothin'. The court did—probably that son of a bitch, Judge Miller."

"But if he had to go, I should have . . ."

"Woulda only made it worse. Jonny was a clean slate. He didn't remember nothin' about your mother and when the bastard looked at him, he didn't remind him of no one but himself."

"At first, I told myself I stayed cause of school and because I had my first boyfriend. Of course, I couldn't imagine leaving Ma and Dad—or you. Then I thought it was just because I hated him, that being with him would destroy one of us—most likely me. And all of those things are true . . . But the real reason—the biggest reason—"

Jimmy nodded slowly. "Sky Bar."

"Do you remember what she was like when she first came? How she used to follow me, cling to me, ask me a question every two and a half minutes? When Michael Finn showed up, she was still climbing into my bed almost every night. And sometimes I heard her crying out for the sister she hadn't seen since she was five. What would happen if I left her, too?"

"And you been punishin' yourself for it ever since. Takin' it out on Sky Bar, too—though you might not know it. You think she doesn't feel you pullin' away? You didn't even go to her big meet, Z. I know you gotta live your life, but have you seen her lately? She ain't been herself ever since."

"Whoa—wait a minute, Jimmy. You can blame me for a lot of things, but what's bothering her since the meet has nothing to do with me. In fact, I'm the one who's been trying to help. Did you ever wonder why she stopped walking home from practice alone?"

"That old buddy of yours—Henry Lee—picks her up. Seems like he don't mind much, either. Ever hear the two of them gigglin' in the driveway? Almost as goofy as you and the ultimate colleige."

"So maybe he's figured out how great Agnes is and he's got a crush, but he's only there cause I asked him to drive her. Mr. Dean had been hanging around at practice, sometimes on the street—"

At that, Jimmy was the one on his feet. "What the hell? That son of a bitch's been at the pool and you go to someone else instead of me? What's Henry gonna do about it? Kid like him wouldn't wanna get his chinos dirty."

What had I done? In my eagerness to change the subject, I had accidentally let slip the one thing I'd promised to keep from Jimmy. "He's been doing so good," Ma warned. "If there's one thing that could send him over the deep end . . ." She didn't have to finish the sentence.

I channeled Eleanor Roosevelt the way I did when I gave a speech in school so no one would know how flustered I felt. "I would have gone to you, of course. Heck, Agnes would have told you herself, but it turned out it wasn't him after all. It was just someone who looked like the guy. But by then, I'd already called Henry. And like you said, he doesn't seem to mind. Kathy Doherty says he even comes early to watch the practice."

Jimmy's eyes probed me, but I revealed nothing.

"Okay, well, if anything like that ever happens again, you come to me, you hear," he said with only a little doubt in his voice. "False alarm or not."

ONCE I HAD cleaned up the attic, I tried to write, but for the first time I couldn't sit at my desk for more than a few minutes. Everything—the cards, the boxes of broken lives—including my own, hard as I tried to prove I was different—pulled me up out of the seat. Was Jimmy right? After sacrificing my brother, had I abandoned Agnes anyway? I was drawn to the window. Whenever I looked through it, I saw the tiny one in Mr. Dean's attic where Agnes had sat for over a year, listening for the sound of his feet coming up the stairs. And he was still coming.

"I don't understand. Why does he care after all these years?" Charlie asked when I told him about it.

"Because he thought he destroyed her—and for some sick reason, that brought him satisfaction. Now every day, he gets older and weaker and Agnes grows stronger. The way he sees it, if she wins, he loses. He couldn't even beat a poor little Indian girl."

"She knows the truth about him, the part of himself he's hidden from everyone else, and he can't stand it." As he spoke, I thought about Ma's twisted connection to the Wood family, and my annual confrontation with Michael Finn and his check. I reached for Charlie's hand.

"Remember when Mr. Deveney talked about the nature of evil in ninth-grade English? Best class I ever had. Well, that's it." I shivered in the heat.

Sometimes, pacing up and down the attic, I felt the hold Mr. Dean still had on her, and the same chill I felt that day passed over me.

THEN ONE SATURDAY afternoon when I came in from the library, I heard the sound of Ma and Jimmy arguing about something in the kitchen—probably another late night by the river. But the only thing on my mind was my history project. I climbed the stairs to the attic, determined to hear nothing until I got my work done. But halfway up the stairs, I stopped.

"Agnes. What are you—"

She was perched on the box where Jimmy had sat. Instead of answering, she cocked her head in the direction of my Royal. "If you moved up here to write, you haven't done much."

"I've written a lot, actually, and I was just gonna—" I felt my face flame like Jools's had when I looked at his framed art on the wall.

"To be honest, I've changed my mind about becoming a writer," I admitted, pulling up a box opposite hers. "Ma and Dad are right. If I'm going to spend all that money on college, I should study something more practical like—" Before I could finish, Agnes was shaking her head.

"What? I thought you'd be happy. You hated my writing so much you used to hide my notebooks, remember?"

"I didn't understand until I started swimming. Or more like till I tried to quit. That's when I found out there's nothing more practical than being who you are. And if you have something you really, really love, it's the only practical thing you can do."

"Jeepers. Keep talking like that and Joe will have you working at the N. P. with the rest of them." I laughed.

"Speaking of the market, I got you a couple of presents." She moved aside, revealing the bags hidden behind her crate. I opened the small one from the N. P. and inhaled Nonna's homemade chocolate cookies.

"Far as I know it's not my birthday or anything. What's up?" I passed her a cookie before I bit into the gooey sweetness.

"Nine years ago today Dad brought me home from the hospital to stay."

"Really—you remember the date?"

"May first. I can still see that calendar you kept in your room. That night, before we went to sleep, the number was practically glowing."

"Heck, you're the one who should be getting a present, then."

"Already got a couple." Grinning, Agnes pulled the lucky shamrock barrette from her pocket and pinned it on the side of her head. "That and our moon."

"I can't believe you still have that thing."

"And I can't believe you lost yours." She held out the second bag. "Don't forget this one."

Inside were a set of curtains, obviously handmade from an Indian bedspread I'd admired.

"Wow, Agnes," I said, holding them up to the light. "These are beautiful. Did you make them yourself?"

"With the help of Mrs. Lee's sewing machine . . . and Mrs. Lee, who did the actual sewing. Okay, since we're being so honest here, all I did was buy the bedspread and picture it in your window. I figured you'd get more work done if you had a little color around you."

"Mrs. Lee, huh? I never thought she liked me when Henry and I went out—or whatever it is kids that age do."

Agnes seemed glad for a chance to turn away and hammer the curtain rod fixtures into the wall, even though that kind of thing was usually my job. "You wouldn't think it was weird if I—not that I'm even sure . . . or he's asked . . . or—"

"No," I interrupted before she could say more. "Of course not. In fact, I'd be happy that it's actually someone I like."

"Dating, that kind of thing, you know, it's never been for me." She set down the hammer and faced me. "But Henry is—I don't know—different . . . Is this how you felt when you met Charlie?"

"Probably something like it, and I'm pretty sure that kind of thing is for everyone," I said, laughing as I threaded the curtain onto the rod. "You know, since the wrestling coach got him lifting weights . . . wow. Half the girls in the senior class have their eye on him."

"That's another thing; Ma will say he's too old for me. And isn't he going out with Caroline Rubin?"

"So that's the reason you came up here today—not to give me cookies or hang curtains." I laughed. "You want to milk me for information about Henry."

"Part of the reason." She sat back down on her box, helped herself to another cookie. "But mostly, I just wanted to spend some time with my sister before she . . . Sheesh, I can't even say the words."

I took both of her hands in mine the way Charlie sometimes did when I worried about leaving. "It's going to be okay. Really."

And when she still looked doubtful, I broke into the chorus of "Ain't No Mountain High Enough." That, too, was borrowed from Charlie, and I knew he meant it when he cranked up the song on the radio or called it our song. But when I sang to Agnes, when she joined in, it had a different weight. After that, we pulled up the crates where I'd sat with Jimmy and talked until the cookies were gone, until the light outside the window turned a dusky lilac, and we forgot time.

It was an almost perfect afternoon, an hour when it felt like everything would be okay—no, better than that—fine. But whenever I look back on it or taste one of Nonna's cookies or remember the great light that was in Agnes's face that day, or hear our silly laughter mix with the sound of Ma and Jimmy, their quarrel obviously over, joking about something downstairs, it's always colored with sorrow. Little could any of us know that when Agnes jumped up, suddenly remembering that she promised to meet Coach Lois for an extra practice, life was about to change for all of us.

And yet maybe somewhere inside me I did know. How else would I remember the sounds that followed so vividly? Her feet clattering down the stairs as she sang out, "Hey, Jimmy, think you can give me a ride to the pool? I forgot I was meeting Coach and I need to be there now."

A few minutes later, the Falcon roared to life in the driveway.

CHAPTER EIGHT

Why I Stopped

JIMMY

THE WEEKS AFTER I WRECKED MY LIFE FOR GOOD, IT FELT LIKE the whole city of Claxton wanted to file in one by one, all askin' the same dumb question. Why I done it. Man, anyone coulda figured that out. The only question worth askin', the only halfway innerestin' one was why I stopped. No one cared much about that, though.

Guys in the jail musta thought I was somebody big cause when they took me down for questionin', it wasn't with no ordinary detective. Nope, it was straight to Chief Wood for me.

Handsome bastard he was when you got up close, too; hair Brylcreemed just so, like I used to try to do mine in junior high when I was meetin' Debbie D'Olympio. He sat tall in his chair, rosy color of someone who eats good, takes primo care of himself, while I slouched in my seat, head about to split like a pomegranate.

Still, if there was a imposter in the room, it was him, not me. Even sittin' there feelin' like I was about to puke all over the desk where he had everything lined up neat as his hair—I saw what he worked so hard to hide. It was somethin' no amount of hair cream or fancy cologne could cover.

Worst thing was he knew I seen it. He sat up straighter before he asked the question.

"So, Mr.—" He stopped to look down at the paper, as if he didn't know damn well who I was, as if he hadn't had a eye on me for years— the weak link in the family. The one he could use to break Ma. Yup. Freakin' imposter all the way. My head thumped like Bonham's back-beat.

"Mr. Kovacs, would you like to explain why you initiated an un-provoked attack on a stranger last night?"

An unprovoked attack. Was that what they called it? I picked up his shiny name plate, looked at it real good, and set it down. Then I stared across the desk at him, leanin' back in my seat. "You got any water around here?"

"Water?"

"You know that wet stuff comes out the faucet?" I clutched my throat so he'd get the idea. "I'm feelin' a little dry."

He narrowed his eyes, like he was decidin' whether to call some-one to rough me up or just do it himself. Then somethin' made him reconsider. He picked up the phone and asked a secretary named Shirley to bring a glass of water.

"For Mr. Kovacs." This time he said my name like I was the gov-ernor or somethin'. Shit, never seen anyone so polite in my life. If I weren't sittin where I was, it woulda been downright fascinatin' to watch the guy work.

After she brought it—nice-lookin' chick, too, this Shirley— Wood watched me chug it down like a animal at the zoo. Shirley stood there, too, maybe waitin' for him to tell her she could go. Or more like she was standin' outside a cage herself, eatin' popcorn, waiting for the ape to do something that would seal his fate.

"Don't know if that made me feel better or worse," I said, handin' Shirley the empty glass. "But thanks." Then I smiled like I always do at pretty women. Even one who's lookin' at me like somethin' that should be swingin' in a tree somewhere.

When we was alone again, the imposter kept up his new approach, like we was buddies chattin' in the parlor. He repeated the question. "Now that you've had your water, do you want to tell me why—"

"Nope," I said, stoppin' him right there. "Can't say's I do."

His skin flashed a shade darker. "I believe your family—I mean, the Moscatellis—have engaged an attorney on your behalf. Do you want to wait till he arrives? That's your right, of course. But to be honest? With all the evidence we have, it's not going to make much difference."

I rose to my feet with as much dignity as someone who had initiated a so-called unprovoked attack and was still half drunk could muster. "It ain't my rights I'm worried about, Chief. What I'm sayin' is I ain't tellin' you shit. Not here, just the two of us. Not with twelve lawyer types present. Never."

If it was possible to commit suicide twice in twelve hours, I'd just done it. But at that particular minute, I didn't care.

The imposter filled up with somethin' the color of purple. "Listen, you little w-w-wiseass," he said, sounding like his nephew, Larry, who took on a stutter when he got pushed too far. "Who the h-h-hell do you think you are?"

"Me? I'm exactly what you're lookin' at. A drunk wiseass just like you said. The real question here is who you are, Chief Wood. You wanna answer me that?"

His cheek muscles twitched like he was fighting the impulse to pull an unprovoked attack himself. "You're gonna pay for that, Kovacs," he said through his polished-up teeth. "And the price is gonna be higher than you ever imagined."

Just then, the guard knocked on the door. Wood called him inside. "I bet I will," I said, like it was just him and me in the room. "But you know what? It was worth it."

I mighta been the dumbest punk goin', but when I walked out of there, I swaggered like I did when I was a fourteen-year-old kid off to meet the prettiest girl in town. Back when I had no idea how hot the inferno could get.

NEXT PERSON I saw was the lawyer they hired with the state money Ma had saved up all these years, hoping I'd go to college. Well, here it was: my big education. Sitting in a cell with attorney Samuel L. Chisholm, listening to him explain how it all worked. Right away he started with the same question.

"It's not always what you did, James. It's how the jury perceives what you did. That's why your story is so important. Do you understand?"

I looked at the pocked floor of the cell, irritated by the name he called me: James. How many times had James Sr. sat here, sweating out one of his weaselly crimes? Only thing I could do was keep my eyes on the floor and hope I didn't puke all over the lawyer's fancy shoes.

"We'll definitely be asking for a jury trial," he went on. "No matter which judge we draw, he's likely to be a friend of the Wood family." He peered over his glasses, obviously wonderin' how much I knew about all that.

Then, when I didn't show him nothin', he went back to his papers. "Now I hear the victim—Martin J. Dean—had been harassing your foster sister. According to your guardian, there was some severe abuse in the past. Is that correct, James?"

Normally, I woulda just corrected the guy, but with my head hammerin' and the sound of that locomotive getting closer, I didn't have a lot of patience.

I snapped my head up so fast the room spun. "Nobody calls me that, okay? You wanna tell a good story, at least get the names right. I'm Jimmy, and my sister ain't no foster nothin'. My dad neither."

Like I say, it wasn't how I generally talked, but after you pound a guy to an inch of his life, people see you different. Least I could do was give them their money's worth. If I was really as tough as I pretended, though, I wouldn't've felt sorry right after I said it. Poor bastard was only tryin' to help me and here I was takin' his head off.

He cleared his throat. "I'll make a note of that, Jimmy," he said. "Now, if you could tell me a little bit about the events that led up to your encounter with Mr. Dean." I nodded my head like I did in school when somethin' like photosynthesis all of a sudden made sense. So beatin' someone to a pulp with a baseball bat was now a encounter? Made it sound like we run into each other at the beach or somethin'. Locked eyes across a bar maybe. Yeah, I was beginnin' to understand how this lawyer thing worked.

"See, I was up at my buddy Duane's house when my sister called me—" I told him.

"Duane Hillyer, correct? Your father mentioned the name when we spoke."

"Yeah, that's the one."

He cleared his throat again—a habit that seemed to go along with the lawyer trade. "Unfortunately, Mr. Hillyer is very familiar to the court . . . So you were with an old friend from school—doing what? Watching TV?"

"Yeah, I s'pose the set was on," I said, getting the idea. "His grandmother's always got one of them sitcoms runnin'. Even though she sleeps through most of 'em."

"All right, you were visiting . . . a friend and his grandmother . . . when your sister called for help," he said as he wrote out every word in his book. "Very good. And during the visit, you and your buddy shared a beer or two perhaps? Or maybe his grandmother offered you something?"

"Beg your pardon, Mr. Chisholm, but I ain't never let it go with a beer or two in my life."

He made no response so I dropped it. Yep, this was the education Ma saved up for her whole life. How smart people been runnin' the world since Adam and Eve messed everything up. When I went in the direction he wanted me to go, he took out his pen, repeating my words back to me like he was writing in stone. But if I veered off track a little, he sat back and waited.

I scratched my head. "Tell you the truth, after I talked to Sky Bar—I mean, my sister—things get a little fuzzy. Heck, even before that. I think she told me she was in a phone booth over on Penniman Street, and that son of a bitch—Dean—had just parked the car and got out."

Piece by piece, it came back. "Shit, the whole thing was my fault," I said more to myself than to him. "Agnes had a night practice cause of some big meet comin' up and I was s'pose to pick her up. So while I was waitin', I thought I'd kill a little time at Duane's place. Then I got hung up . . . um, watchin' TV with his grandmother, right?"

I paused to look him in the eye like Ma was always after us to do. "You really think anyone's gonna believe that crap? The cops seen me, Mr. Chisholm. They seen me and they knew I wasn't drinkin' no cherry cordials with Duane's grandma. Not that bein' drunk as shit was any kinda excuse. Nah. I wanted to kill that bastard with everything in me. Have for years. Only thing Duane's bourbon did was give me the courage."

At that, attorney Samuel L. Chisholm closed the leather notebook in which we was supposed to be makin' up—I mean writing— somethin' good enough to stop a train.

"I see," he said, checkin' his watch, like to see how much time he'd wasted on me and my crap story. He rose to his feet. "Your arraignment is at nine tomorrow morning. They're charging you with attempted murder, Jimmy, but I'm going to try to get it reduced to aggravated assault. I advise you to plead not guilty to all charges."

"Not guilty? All due respect, how's that gonna work? First of all, I done it. Didn't even try to deny it when the cops came. Least, I don't think I did. And second, I seem to remember a witness."

"You were defending your sister, were you not?"

AFTER THAT, WE talked a little more, him arguin' like he was on the other side. Devil's advocate, he called it. But the way he looked at me when we were done—it was like he knew I didn't have a chance.

"According to the witness, Mr. Dean was walking down the street, minding his own business. If you can't convince anyone of your motive—or that Agnes was under serious threat—then we lose. I'll be honest with you, Jimmy: It's a tall order."

AFTER HE LEFT, I walked up and down my cell, holdin' the head that was now explodin' with a lot more than a hangover. Now it was full up with the key words Chisholm had dropped on me.

Unprovoked attack; that was the first one and it musta been big cause Wood used it, too. When I tried to explain the guy had showed up at her meet on the other side of the state before he started comin' to her practices, that he was followin' her that night, Chisholm took the role of the prosecutor.

"Are you aware that Mr. and Mrs. Dean had no children of their own? It was only natural that they would be proud of their former ward, wasn't it? Mary Jeanne Doherty, another former foster parent, has also shown an interest in her success, from what I understand."

"Mrs. Doherty was the first one who brung Agnes to swimming lessons, and her daughter's on the team. So yeah, of course, she took a damn interest. You think Dean ever gave a damn about Agnes— aside from the pleasure he got outta torturin' her? The man used to follow her around in his stupid yellow station wagon when she was a kid."

"Did he ever accost her?"

"A-what her?"

"There are a lot of yellow cars in this city, Jimmy. How could you be sure it was him? Did the man ever get out of the car and harm Agnes in any way in all these years?"

"He harmed her by drivin' by. By livin', for chrissake. Every damn breath the son of a bitch took did her harm—"

There were words that were even more important, though. Dean had apparently claimed that on the night in question, he was just walkin' down the street. Like the citizen of the damn year. If I didn't wanna get sent to the slammer for tryin' to murder the bastard, I had to convince the jury he posed a serious threat to Agnes. A threat that justified gettin' beat nearly to death.

Even though this guy, Samuel L. Chisholm, seemed decent enough, there was no way I could make him see the stuff I seen.

"The guy kept her in the attic like a animal. Did you know that? Made her bang on the floor with a stick when she had to pee."

"Is there documented proof of that, Jimmy?" There was real pity in his voice by that point.

"Agnes told me. She told all of us. How's that for documented proof? You wanna know what he did a coupla days before they took her away? He picked up a hammer and broke every bone in her hand. She was fucking six years old, Mr. Chisholm, and that hand still ain't right. It's never gonna be. How's that for a unprovoked attack?"

"Mr. Dean claimed she had an accident, and his wife corroborated it. No charges were ever filed. And you better not use language like that in court."

"So the language I use, a fuckin' word, is a bigger deal than takin' a hammer to a six-year-old?"

"The records say it was an accident."

"The records? The fu—excuse me—freakin' records lie about more shit than you can imagine." I raked my hair. "How about you answer me a question for a change? What kinda accident could do somethin' like that?"

But Samuel Chisholm knew when to sit there in silence. Another lawyer thing I was s'pose to learn.

"They took her away, didn't they? And they never let the Deans take in another kid neither. What's that tell ya?'"

"No charges were filed, Jimmy," he repeated. "That's all the court cares about."

"And you wanna know why? Cause you think someone's gonna get a whole courtroom together, bring people in for questionin' like this over Agnes? Waste valuable jail space that could be used for someone like me or my old man? That bastard Dean said it was a accident and even though everyone knew it was a damn lie, it was good enough for them. Just move the kid to another home and forget about it. Who was gonna complain?"

The question sat between us in the jail cell. Just like it had sat in the house on 100 Sanderson Street ever since the first night I seen Agnes standin' in the window, watchin' for the yellow car.

"Well, how about we say he had a little accident himself over there on Penniman last night? That's a different story, ain't it, Mr. Chisholm? Hurt a hair on the head of a fine upstandin' guy like Marty Dean, and someone's gonna pay. They're gonna pay big. Ain't that how it works?"

As I was talkin', I seen Chief Wood sitting in front of me. Those sparklin' teeth of his when he told me what I already knew. And I seen the fear on my sister's face lit up like neon inside that telephone booth when I showed up. By then Dean was standing outside, poundin' on the glass. Just wanted to ask when she'd be done with the phone, he said when they took his statement in the hospital. Had some car trouble and he needed to call his wife; that was all. Bad as I hurt him, he could still lie good as ever.

But yeah, I seen all that. Seen his fists poundin' glass like he wanted to shatter it the way he did Sky Bar's knuckles, and then I seen his face when he turned around and spotted me comin' toward him. Me and my Louisville Slugger.

"You wanna know who was gonna complain about the stuff he

done to Agnes? It mighta been ten years too late, but in that minute, the bastard finally got his answer. I was. Jimmy Kovacs was."

I WISH I coulda been that cocky next day in the courtroom. It was easy in front of Wood or Chisholm, the guys in the cells, but with Dad, Nonna, Zaidie, and Agnes lined up—even Jools—behind 'em on a bench, it all become real. The O'Connors had closed up the N. P. to come, too, but Joe had to take Junior out when he started hollerin' to me about how many minutes I was late for work. The face I searched for, the one I saw when I closed my eyes in the cell, didn't show up till the thing was half over. Jane took a seat in the back row.

Seein' Zaidie cry and Nonna dabbin' her face with a lace hand-kerchief was bad enough, but when Dad started up, it about killed me. Only thing worse was Jane's hard look—and Sky Bar, whose cheeks were dry as the Sahara. Even when Princie died, they said she hadn't broke. And I knew why, too. Back in the years she spent in Mr. Dean's attic, she learned it wasn't no damn use. I hated the bastard for that, too.

Then there was the empty space where Ma shoulda been. The empty space that was always there, and me knowin' she was at home, beatin' on herself for everything she couldn't do. Everything she couldn't be. Probably even blamin' herself—the way I used to blame her. When Chief Calvin Wood come into the courtroom, I could almost feel the Slugger in my hands all over again.

IN THE WEEKS that followed, they all come to visit me, one by one, each carryin' that dumb question like they thought it all up them-selves. *Why'd you do it, Jimmy?* Then Nonna and Zaidie sat there cryin' like they did in court.

A day or two later, they brung Dad into my cell with Joe O'Connor. Right away, Dad comes at me with the same question: "You been doing so good. Why, son?"

"You know me, Dad. Whenever things are goin' too good, I gotta do somethin' to mess it up."

I turned to my ole boss, half jokin', half serious as hell. "Tell 'em, Joe. Nothin's perfect—least of all me, right? Tell 'em." Anything to stop my dad from crying like the girls.

But Joe just sat there, like he was thinking maybe he should change the name of the market. He draped a arm over Dad's shoulder. Much as Dad hated stuff like that, he didn't shove him away.

JANE WAITED TILL after I got my sentence to visit. I hoped she mighta softened up a little, but I felt like I was getting beat with the Slugger myself when she talked about all our ruined plans, when she accused me of lyin' when I said I loved her. I closed my eyes and tried to imagine her in that dumb white dress the way I used to, as if I ever deserved anything that fine in my life. When I opened 'em, she was gone. What I'd told Dad about ruinin' any good thing that came my way never felt more true.

They wouldn't let me see Sky Bar, not right away, on account of she was too young—and not even a real relative, accordin' to what people think. Not till the sheriff, who knew Dad from the garage, snuck her in one Tuesday afternoon when all the snitch types were off.

For a while we just sat there, the two of us, with Penniman Street between us. Then she asked me the only question that mattered: why I stopped. Actually, she didn't even ask it, she led me to it myself when she filled in the final piece, the part of the night that was still blacked out.

"I thought for sure you were gonna kill him, Jimmy. I was screaming for you to stop, but you heard nothing. You just kept hitting him. But at the last minute, when you had him on the ground—by then, he was begging—you raised the bat high in the air—and—"

"I stopped," I said, closin' my eyes as I finished it for her.

As she said the words, I saw Dean layin' there, seen his face beat to a bloody pulp, heard him pleadin' for his pathetic life. And in my mind, just like I done that night on the street, I dropped the bat.

Not cause I didn't want to kill him, cause I did. I still do. But when I looked down at him that night on the street, all's I could think of was the soldiers I carried off the field over in Nam; I heard their voices, too, some screamin', some cryin' like the kids they were. You might say I stared straight into the inferno itself. And when I looked one more time, the bastard I wanted to kill had disappeared and I seen my own Ma lyin' there.

CHAPTER NINE

Louie Takes a Walk

Dahlia

I WAITED TILL LOU AND THE GIRLS LEFT THE HOUSE THAT MORN-
ing. Then I went to the closet to look for my good blue dress, the
stockings my mother had given me for my birthday some years ago.
They were still in the wrapper. *If you ever have an occasion to wear them*,
she'd said in that way of hers, proving that even a present with a bow
on top could be an accusation.

Well, I won't, I told her, accusing back—as I pushed the gift in her
direction. She left it there on the table before she walked out.

Foolish words you play over and over in your mind, I thought as
I pulled those damn stockings on. As if those silly arguments matter when you come to a day like this—my mother too old and sick
with the rheumatism to come by anymore, and across town, the boy
she refused to call a grandson slouching in the new suit Louie had
bought him in the same courtroom where, decades earlier, I left a part
of myself forever. After I checked myself in Zaidie's full-length mirror to make sure the seams were half straight, I put on my shoes. I'd
only worn them twice in twenty-six years—first on the day I married
Louie with only his mother and his aunt Leona in attendance, and
then when the department come to interview me. I even dug out the
hat Anna had bought me, thinking that if only I put it on and went to
Mass with her, I'd be cured of what ailed me. Hah.

I might have got myself out the door, too—if I hadn't passed the other mirror, the one in the foyer that captured Zaidie as she moved from a skinny little wren to the girl she became, and made a joke of all the predictions the doctors and case workers made about Agnes. A dwarf, for heaven's sake.

Jimmy never stopped to study himself in front of that mirror like the girls did, but it drew him just the same. The night he left to drop off Agnes at practice was no different. He glanced quick at himself on the way out, raised his eyebrows a little and pushed back his hair, as if he was startled by his good looks. Since the Nothing's Perfect and Jane had come along, there was something else there that surprised him—the happiness he never thought he deserved. Remembering that look, seeing it, broke me even more than what was going on across town.

Still, I might've got myself out the door if I didn't catch a glimpse of someone I'd almost forgotten. The coward stared me down, strong as ever. *Dress yourself up all you want, Dahlia Garrison,* she taunted. *You'll never make it to that courtroom. You don't have the courage to walk across the street and you know it.*

I WAS ON the sofa, laid out like someone in a coffin, hat, shoes, and all, when Louie came up the front steps, his feet heavy as if they were carrying three men. He stood in the doorway like he hadn't decided whether to come in or not. "Six years," he spat out.

He finally came inside, but not like he wanted to—more like a man who's got nowhere else to go. Like a man who was doing a sentence of his own.

"There'll be nothin' left of him in six years, Dahlia. Nothin'."

Right about then he noticed me, sitting up in the clothes that were supposed to make me look like what I never was: respectable. "For chrissake," he scoffed. "Did you really think you could—"

If I hadn't seen the turn in him at the door, it was impossible to miss now. In all our years, he'd never talked to me like that. Never looked at me the way he did, either. He shook his head and headed for the kitchen.

"At least a half dozen of them Woods were there. I know them by those ghosty blue eyes of theirs. All waiting for their big comeuppance. Even if you coulda got there, you would never . . ."

He opened the cabinet to take out a jelly jar, then turned on the spigot, drowning the words he didn't say. His daily ritual. When we were first married, it had been whiskey like his father drank. A single shot, never more than that. Just a little something to draw a line between the work day and the life we claimed for ourselves. But once he saw what the smell of it did to me, he'd given it up for good. Men will do those sorts of things in the beginning.

"All's I can say is if you take to your bed this time, you can stay there," he said when he came back in. "I won't be calling you back again. I ain't got it in me, Dahlia."

"Right about now, Louie, I don't much care what you got in you and what you don't. The only thing on my mind is my son." Then an afterthought—as I suppose they'd been all along. "Where are the girls?"

"Agnes is where she always is. At the pool. Every day, the girl swims further and further away from us. Best thing we can do is let her go, too. And Zaidie—I s'pose she's with that fancy boyfriend. Her way of swimming off to something better. A year or two, they'll both be gone and there'll be no point—"

"The fancy boyfriend has a name," I interrupted. Anything to stop him from finishing that sentence.

Louie headed back to the kitchen. Apparently, this was a two-shot night.

LATER, WHEN BOTH girls had come home and went—no, fled—to their rooms, neither of them hungry for supper, Louie and me found ourselves in the parlor without a word to say. Not that we usually talked much, but when he put the TV on and I settled in with my puzzle, there was something between us you could feel. Something I didn't much notice till it was gone.

"Isn't there something you usually put on on Wednesdays?" I finally asked, more desperate for noise than I dared to admit.

In answer, he heaved himself off the chair and started up the stairs. "I ain't got it in me . . ." he repeated, though this time it was less clear what he was talking about. To sit with me in the parlor? Turn the TV switch? I didn't dare to ask. It was just past eight.

I got up and followed him to the bottom of the staircase. "Now who's taking to his bed?"

He slammed the door to the room.

That night, I stayed in the parlor extra long, waiting for him to call me up the way he usually did. Sometime past midnight I gave up. Though Louie was turned away from me in bed, I could feel his wakefulness. We probably lay there for an hour or more like that, unmoving and sleepless, before either of us spoke.

"What the hell have we been doing all these years, Dahlia?" he finally said, addressing the wall. "Can you answer me that?"

"The best we could, I suppose," I told the ceiling. "Just like Joe O'Connor says."

"Don't start with that crap, all right? Not tonight. Joe's a decent enough fella, don't get me wrong. Been in the courtroom every day, too. But none of that bullshit of his stopped Jimmy from going out that night and . . ." He paused, still unable to pronounce the crime. "Hell, he couldn't even help his own son."

"Joe Jr. does all right. Fine, if you ask me. And Joe never claimed he could save anyone. That's the point."

He grunted as he rolled onto his back. "You think so much of old Joe, maybe you should move in over there. Get some of those books from the library that were supposed to fix everything wrong with our kids, and see what you can do for Junior. The two of you together? Now that would be a pair."

Then he got up, switched on the harsh light, and put on the bathrobe I bought one of our first Christmases together. It was a sad-looking thing now, all its clear blue color faded to something dusty.

"Do you remember the day he first come?" he asked, still not looking at me.

As if I could have forgotten. "When I called to tell you, you closed up the garage and came straight home. Only time in history that ever happened."

"You had lunch ready on the table—peanut butter and fluff like we were all kids. Afterward, we took him out in the backyard."

"Best afternoon of my life," I said. "I can still see the boy running up and down the yard, showing off everything he could do."

We called them back and forth to each other the way we had so many times over the years. Always in the same order.

"Somersaults. Or his best effort at them." At that, we chuckled. "Even at two, he had an arm on him when he threw a ball to me."

"You made him believe he did, Lou. Sometimes I think that's why he loved baseball so much. Because of the fuss you made."

"He wanted us to see how high he could jump—though he only got a couple inches off the ground. Right in that spot out there." He pointed toward the window. "And after everything he did, he stopped and laughed at us. Like he couldn't believe we were still there, watching."

"You looked at him like everything he did was a wonder."

"The wonder of a lifetime, Dahlia. That was how I saw that boy from the first day."

"He showed us the thing no one could take away, didn't he? The happiness we never believed we had a right to," I said, deviating from our script as I thought of how Jimmy had looked in the mirror the last night he went out. Sometimes we were so alike it was hard to believe we weren't blood.

"We thought that if we just kept our eyes on him the way we had that day in the yard, we could make it all go right. Whatever he'd been through those first coupla years, whoever he come from, we could wipe it all clean. All we had to do was keep beamin' on him."

"Not just what he'd been through, Lou." I could almost feel those yellow leaves falling on me, the trials of our early marriage.

"Coupla damn fools is what we were."

Again, he shook his head before he got up and walked to the window where he lifted the shade, as if it was possible to recapture the sunlight of that long-ago afternoon, as if he half expected to see that two-year-old boy running across the yard, falling, giddy, when he turned back and found we were still there. Or maybe it was us he thought he might see. Us when we still dared to hope. But the yard was full of nothing but night. He snapped the shade shut. Then he tightened the belt of his bathrobe and headed for the stairs.

"I thought you had a busy day tomorrow," I called as I followed him into the hall. "Where are you going?"

By then he was in the foyer, lacing up his work boots. "Out for a walk," he yelled up to me. "Go to bed, Dahlia."

"In your pajamas? You can't—"

He snorted. "Oh, I *can't*? So Joe Jr. can walk around the neighborhood yellin' anything he damn pleases, and his father can open a market with a foolish name like that; hell, my own son can go out to pick up his sister at swim practice and turn the whole goddamn world upside down, but when it comes to me, you're tellin' me I can't? Well, those days are over, Dahlia. If I feel like walkin' down Main Street buck naked, I'll do it. And if a cop comes along, hey, I'll just tell him nothin's perfect. Ain't that the idea?"

The door slammed behind him.

IT WAS NEAR morning when he came home. Instead of explaining where he'd been all night or even coming up to talk to me, he changed directly into the uniform he'd hung on a hook in the bathroom the night before. Four forty-five a.m. and he headed for work. Didn't even ask for coffee like usual.

And that night when he come home with a brown paper bag, I didn't have to ask what was in it. It was the end of Louie trying to please me. He went into the kitchen and poured himself a shot. After a mostly silent supper, Zaida headed upstairs to the attic where she did whatever she did, and Agnes followed her. A little while later, Louie also went up.

"Taking to your bed again?" I taunted him, not wanting to say how desperate the quiet felt.

"It's Jimmy's bed I'm taking to, if you want to know," he said. And then he paused on the landing, sounding tired more than anything. "I'm sorry, Dahlia, but I just don't have it in me."

When I heard the door to Jimmy's room close, it felt like the whole world was shut tight against me.

IT WAS A week before he had it in him to talk to me about it. A week before he sat in his chair while I worked on a puzzle of Van Gogh's *Starry Night*. Instead of turning on the TV, he told me about the walk he took that night.

"First place I went was over to Buskit's. I figured it was one place where a man could sit around in his bathrobe and boots like he didn't know whether he was headed to work or to bed without attracting much notice. I stayed there for a good long time, too, staring into that so-called river. Never seen so many empty booze bottles, so much broken stuff. Place smells like rotten eggs, too—like someone's been dumpin' chemicals in it. Was this the place where it had all gone wrong? I asked myself. When I didn't get an answer, I got up and headed for the high school, where them college types looked down on him. Seemed like that was when the trouble started."

"They were just kids like Zaidie and her friends. He thought they looked down on him is all."

"Same thing, ain't it? Anyways, after that, I walked by the garage, where he first got spooked by that bum—Richard whatever his name was. By then, it was startin' to get light, and I heard a car slow down, someone callin' my name—'You okay, Louie?' I guess the poor bastard never saw anyone tromping through town in the middle of the night in a bathrobe and a pair of Sears and Roebuck's Wearmasters."

Louie chuckled a little himself, but there was bitterness in the dregs of it. "I shoulda pointed the son of a bitch in the direction of Joe's store, he was so damn curious. Told him to take a good look at the sign."

"Did you know who it was?"

"Didn't even look back. Just kept walking, searching like someone or something was lost and I couldn't go home till I found it. Like one of your damn puzzle pieces that always go missing under the couch. Was it in that shack in the woods? Or did it happen even before that sunny day we took him out in the yard and watched him run? Was it in some house we never even seen? Some place I never knew the address to and never will?"

"You could walk the city for twenty years, Lou. You'll never get an answer to that one."

"Not for him—and not for us either, Dahlia," he said softly. "Could be some things are just wrong from the start."

And then he got up and went back to Jimmy's room.

CHAPTER TEN

Freedom

DAHLIA

OF ALL THE JIGSAWS I EVER FACED, THAT PICTURE OF MR. VAN Gogh's whirling, demented stars was the one that gave me the most trouble. Four weeks after Jimmy went to jail, it was still staring up at me from the card table.

Keep busy, busy! those frantic stars said every morning, echoing the Dear Abby types who tell you to take up a hobby or clean out the basement when your life goes to hell. Sure. That'll fix it.

The girls were out so much now it felt like I'd lost all three kids in one swoop.

Them and Louie, too, for as late as he stayed at the garage these days. Sometimes I got a hint he stopped off at the bar on the way home. Anything to avoid the landmines that surrounded me: the table, the parlor with its infernal quiet, that door Jimmy was supposed to walk through but didn't. I could hardly blame him.

When they were home, the girls huddled together up in the attic with the door closed. A couple of times I got so lonesome I went to the foot of the stairs, where I heard them laughing.

Laughing? After everything this family'd been through? "What could possibly be funny?" I said to the fool cat, who kept a good eye on me as if I might be the next to disappear. I stalked away, nursing my outrage—and something else, too.

"You're not getting into my things up there, are you?" I asked one night at the table, keeping my voice as neutral as the girl who does the weather.

"What things? We're just doing homework and stuff, Ma," Agnes said, focusing on the lousy ham sandwich I'd put out for supper. In the past, Louie wouldn't have abided it, but no one seemed to care what was on the table anymore.

Zaida, who never could tell a lie to save her life, got up from the table so fast she almost dumped her milk.

"I stopped by the deli this afternoon and Nonna gave me some eggplant with peppers," she explained, carrying her half-eaten sandwich to the garbage.

In the past, Louie would have weighed in at this point, told her that in this house we eat what's in front of us. But now he just sat there, chewing like a cow, concerned with nothing but how quick he could finish his crappy sandwich and escape to Jimmy's room.

After that, the girls avoided the place more than ever, which increased my suspicions about the attic. I even thought I caught Zaida looking at me like the rest of the town did. Like she knew. "Now, wouldn't that be the Woods' ultimate victory?" I asked, talking to the only one who was around. "To chase me into my last refuge? Drag their hate right through my own door?"

Flufferbell meowed and sauntered off to the kitchen in an effort to lead me to the food bowl. Even she didn't want to hear it.

Sometimes I almost wished Anna would come by, rosary beads and all. I wouldn't have even minded the dust swirling through the house like Van Gogh's stars as she attacked the place with her manic broom. But when she finally showed up, all she brought was another worn-out Dear Abby lecture. Not even a pie to sweeten it up.

"Not good to just sit there, Dahlia. Me, I gotta church in the morning, work atta Nothing Perfect all day. Then atta night, I cook meatballs for the deli. Don't even have-a time for my rosary, never mind for think." When her eyes settled on the coffee cups from the last three days that were still on my card table, I could almost feel her twitching.

"Hah. Some people could do with a little more thinking, you ask me." I added a piece to my puzzle. "It's what separates us from rocks and such."

Finally, unable to resist, she scooped up two of my half-empty cups and carried them into the kitchen. "If you thinking of the cure to the polio, then go on. Sitta there all day, Dahlia," she called back. "But iff-a you just think about things that can't be change? All you do is make youself crazy." Emerging from the kitchen, she made a hand gesture that seemed to describe both Van Gogh's tumultuous night and the ceaseless worries that churned through me. "You need-a to get up, Dahlia. Move."

Get up. Inside, I flinched at the words Louie had said to me twice before but didn't have in him to say again. I tried my best not to show it.

"Well, since Mr. Salk found the cure for polio fifteen years ago, Anna, I guess that leaves me free to think about whatever I damn please, doesn't it?"

She reached for the last coffee cup, but I covered it with my hand—even though the film on top was greenish. "I'm still drinking that if you don't mind."

God, I hated the way she looked at me as she set that cup down. The pity in her eyes. She picked up her old black sweater and had almost made it out the door when she stopped. "This Saturday, two o'clock. Jeemy have a visiting time. Iff-a you can't go, I take the girls."

Iff-a I can't go? So she couldn't come in here without swirling up a little dust, after all. Reminding me of all the ways I failed my kids. Her precious Luigi. I took a sip of coffee, hardly noticing the bitterness, that green film.

"I'll tell them to be ready." I looked down at my puzzle like Jonas Salk peering into his microscope.

I SUPPOSE I might have sat in that chair, staring at those broken stars for the rest of my life, cups of half-drunk coffee growing mold around me, if it hadn't been for Agnes. First she started missing practice and then she skipped supper.

"Just a cold," she claimed, doing a poor imitation of a sniffle when I confronted her in her bed. That's when I noticed she'd tacked the print from my puzzle above her bed. Maybe that damn picture cast a spell on the two of us, I thought, tempted to rip it down.

A couple of mornings later, I looked up and found her sitting in the straight-back chair Jimmy used as a kid when he helped me with my puzzles.

She picked up the box I propped in front of me as a guide. "You know where he was when he painted this?"

I waited for her to tell me.

"Looking out the window of an asylum."

"That explains a lot. It looks like a five-year-old did it with crayons, for heaven's sake. Why your dad ever thought I'd want something like this, I can't imagine."

"Actually, I was the one who picked it out," she said. "Most kids at school don't care much about this stuff, but there's this one boy . . . he really loves that painting."

I watched her slyly—noticing the secret pleasure she took in talking about this one boy. As if I didn't know exactly who it was. I could almost hear them laughing in the driveway like they used to before the rides abruptly stopped. When I asked where Henry was these days, she said she didn't want to talk about it.

"The guy went so crazy over a girl he cut off his own ear," she continued. "May have been why he ended up in the asylum."

"Another reason to throw the stupid thing in the trash. I've got enough problems myself without keeping company with a lunatic."

She laughed for the first time since her cold had come on. "You make it sound like Vincent himself came in the puzzle box."

"I'm not so sure he didn't. That's what those artist types do, you know—try to get in your brain, make you see the whole world like they do. You have to be careful with people like that."

"Whatever was torturing him, he tamed it into a present to the world." She stared into that cardboard picture, seeing much more than those stars.

"Hmph," I said, blinking back at the puzzle. Was this her version of Nonna's happy advice?

"So you've seen him, I gather," I finally said, not looking at her.

"Who?" Now, my Agnes doesn't go red like Zaida, but her color deepened just the same.

"The *Starry Night* boy. Who else?"

She buried her face in Flufferbell's fur. "A couple of times he came to my practice. He didn't sit on the bench and watch like he used to or anything. Just stood in the doorway a few minutes and left. And once when I was walking home, he stopped his car and asked if I wanted a ride—"

"Did you get in?"

"I told him I'd rather walk."

"And—"

"He left me alone like I asked. Even avoids me at school," she said miserably. "Then a week ago, he sent me the print. Just that. No note or anything."

"So that was what brung on the cold."

She was so lost in her own thoughts she didn't hear me. Finally, she got up and began to meander up and down the parlor. "What happened to me, Ma?"

"No one ever said growing up was easy, my girl."

"But you know I never cared about boys. Not like other girls, anyway. Not like Zaidie." She almost sounded angry.

When the cat leaped from her arms and went to the door, I got up to let her out, grateful for a moment to think. Then I went back to my chair. The poor kid had never looked more confused.

She looked around the room as if searching for a place to escape.

I nodded slowly. "It's that Dean fellow. He put you off men. Well—"

"It happened before that." She eyed me warily, as if deciding whether it was safe to say more. Whatever she remembered of the years before she walked through the Deans' door, we'd never spoke of it.

Go on, I told her with my eyes.

She pulled a wishbone from her pocket. It was so old it had turned white. "Last time I saw her, she gave me this."

"Her?" I took a long look at that bone. "You mean, your mother?" I whispered, almost as if the woman was sleeping in the next room and I didn't want to wake her. "It's okay, Agnes. You can talk about her. I'm sorry if I ever made you think different."

"She used to visit pretty regularly, but I hadn't seen her for a while. And when she finally came, there was this man with her. Mr. Jackson, they told us to call him. Her new husband."

"Us?"

"My sister and me. I knew right away he didn't like us."

"I seem to remember the file saying that after she got married, no one heard much from her."

"She was so different that day. Even though she had her troubles, she always laughed when she was with us. Like I do, Ma. You know, really laughed. And when it was time to go, she always promised we'd be together and hugged us so hard she made us believe it. But that day, well, Mr. Jackson was so . . . in charge. She kept looking at him before she spoke to us, as if she had to get permission. When they were leaving, even her hug felt different—as if he was there in the middle of it. We waited to hear her laugh or to promise us she'd come again soon, but all she did was hand me this bone."

I reached out and rested my hand on hers, wishing I could tell her not to count Henry out before they even got started. To say that no one had been more done with love and all the rest than me. And then that homely boy showed up at my door. But how could I? When I thought of Louie sleeping in Jimmy's room, the door closing on me night after night, I felt my eyes tearing up. I took the wishbone that had been bleached by time and fingered it, thinking of everything her mother had wanted to give her, but didn't—couldn't—and I swiped at my eyes so she couldn't see what I felt.

"All I want to do is swim, Ma. A boyfriend isn't in the plan," she said, reclaiming her wishbone. Unconsciously, we both turned toward the foyer and stared at the silent phone. When Agnes first started missing practice, Coach Lois had called every day. But Agnes had refused to come to the phone and now it seemed even the coach had given up. Again, there were things I wanted to say, but sometimes you say more by not speaking at all. Especially if you're a mother.

"You want to know why I've been avoiding the pool? Every time I leave the Y, I think of that night. If I hadn't called him, Ma, none of this would have happened. Jimmy would be home."

"Oh, honey, how could you have known—"

She held up her hand, determined to go on. "It was what I'd always done when I was in trouble—turn to Jimmy. Ever since that night at supper when he told me he loved me. Even my own mother was afraid to say it. She said she didn't deserve to till she took us back—"

"You know Dad and me—we loved you from the start; the both of us did. But we were still expecting your mother to come for you. Guess we were afraid, too. Just like she was."

"It's okay, Ma. I loved that it was Jimmy."

And of course, I knew that was true. It didn't matter that he was just a skinny kid himself; she believed him when he said he could protect her from Mr. Dean. Every time she was scared she'd run to his room and make him promise again, make him get out the bat and show her his swing. Then we'd hear them both laughing. I swear Mr. Dean got a little smaller every time he swung that bat.

Eventually it wasn't just that bogeyman, Mr. Dean. It was anything that scared her. If she was worried about an algebra test or some kid didn't invite her to their party, all she had to do was go to Jimmy and he'd take out his bat, tell her he'd take care of it.

Between that and his grin, Jimmy could crush any fear.

"I never should have let it go on, though—especially after he came back from the war, after the nightmares started. And that night—"

"He wanted to be there, honey. That's one thing he's clear about. Jimmy said you were terrified when he saw your face lit up inside that booth. That's why he went for the bat."

"I was. Terrified. At first. But . . . but then I was something else. For the first time, I didn't need Jimmy to protect me anymore."

I watched her.

"Because he'd already shown me something better. He just didn't know it," she said, gulping breath the way she had when she was small and tried to run. "Do you remember the night he took me out in the backyard with a ball and a bat and taught me how to win? He was just trying to get me to go back to swim team, but when he sent that ball soaring, he taught me something else. Something most people never learn in their whole life."

"I was out there that night. I didn't hear him say—"

"I didn't say he told me, Ma," Agnes said. "I said he taught me. Winning's never about what anyone else does. It's something that happens between you and yourself. You don't look to the left or the right. You just jump in the water and swim with everything you have. You swim for your life, Ma, and when you reach the finish line and look up, whoever you thought you were competing against is gone. Poof."

"But what does that have to do with what happened on Penniman Street? With Mr. Dean?"

"Don't you see, Ma? Since the first day I went to that house, Mr. Dean was the guy in the next lane. Even after I was safe with you and Dad and there was nothing he could do to me, he was still there.

"But that night on the street when he came toward me, I saw him for what he was—nothing but a coward and a bully. The weakest man I ever met in my life. He wouldn't have dared to touch me—not now when I'm old enough to fight back, or worse—to tell. No, the only place he could hurt me was in my head. And when I looked at him and he looked at me that night on Penniman Street?" She paused dramatically, bringing me onto that dark road, the claustrophobia of that moment. "We both knew I was done with that."

I got up and sat on a hassock directly facing my daughter. Then I took her two hands in my own, like I had so often hesitated to do.

"Do you know what all that means? You have to go back to school, Agnes. You have to swim, for heaven's sake. It's the least you can do for Jimmy, for all of us. You have to go back to your life."

She stood up the way she did when she had a revelation to share, her face as bright as it must have been in that phone booth when she realized Mr. Dean could never hurt her again. "And so do you, Ma. I need you at my meets. And Jimmy . . . Do you really think you can stay away from him for six years?"

I attempted to jerk my hands away, but she refused to let me go.

"I'm—I'm sorry," I stammered. "But this . . . this is my life right here. This house. You kids. My God, Agnes, you know I can't—" In spite of myself, I started to cry. But still, still she held on to me.

"Yes, you can, Ma," she said. "Just like Jimmy showed me. You can. Me and Zaidie are going to help you."

CHAPTER ELEVEN

A Gun Appears in the Story

ZAIDIE

FOR THE THIRD TIME IN MY NEARLY EIGHTEEN YEARS, LIFE SPLIT into a jagged Before and After. Before Jimmy's arrest, I'd been focused on graduation and preparing to leave for college. If I worried, it was about being separated from Charlie, who was going to school in Maine.

By then, we'd been together for two years and three months—practically a senior class record. On weekends, we parked his Mustang in Barkley's Woods for hours, daring each other, daring ourselves to go a little further as the year wound down. For the rest of the week the spark of everything we weren't supposed to do followed me, taking my breath at odd times, pulling me back to that dark car, the smell of leather seats, sandalwood cologne, and night.

Once in calculus—calculus!—I looked over at Charlie and thought of the last time we'd been together. His finger grazing my nipple. I flushed so bad that even Mr. Weintraub took notice.

He stopped the class. "Are you all right, Zaida?"

"Um, I feel like, uh . . . I think I'm coming down with something," I stammered, the eyes of the class on me. "Can I see the nurse?"

The whole thing was turning me into a blathering idiot. Headed for Mrs. Bonner's office, I could feel the heat on my face. She poked a thermometer in my mouth and looked at me skeptically: No fever.

She should only know.

THAT NIGHT ON the phone, Charlie talked to me in the low voice he sometimes used in the Mustang and I told him about the abandoned shack where older kids like my brother used to take their girlfriends, my untraceable fever rising. A storm had toppled a dead tree in the path and littered it with brush, but I was sure we could get there.

He got quiet for a moment. "When?" His voice curled around me like smoke. There was nothing wrong with it, I told myself. Charlie and I loved each other.

And after two years and all those nights in Barkley's Woods, the moments when I was stopped by the memory of his mouth, his secret fierceness, there couldn't be anything wrong with it. Well, could there?

Jimmy would have known the answer, but it wasn't the kind of thing you discussed with your brother. Especially not a protective one like mine. And when I tried to tell Agnes, she just wrinkled up her nose and told me to talk to someone else; she wasn't interested. She made it sound worse than Nonna or my friend Cynthia, who talked about Sin. Confession. Penance.

Not knowing where else to turn, I went out one night and sat in the alley outside Rusty's Hideaway, where Jane waited tables. If anyone would understand, she would. *Fair enough* was the motto she'd adopted after her own bitter experience. Pronounced in her edgy way, eyes flashing left and right as if on the lookout for who-knew-what, it almost sounded like a threat.

Everything about her seemed different now—from her appearance to her speech patterns. These days she sounded more like a lifer at the factory than a judge's daughter, or stepdaughter, as she always emphasized. Agnes and I suspected it was her way of getting back at her parents. Maybe Jimmy had been that for her, too—at least in the beginning. *Fair enough.*

"What are you doing here?" she said when she came out for her break. "I got fifteen minutes to eat supper and pull body and soul together for the rest of my shift. If you got somethin' to say to me, this ain't the time."

"But it's . . . it's important, and I can't talk about it at the house."

She lit a cigarette and looked at me, annoyed, but maybe a little curious, too.

Undeterred, I blurted out everything—from how I felt that day in calculus to the plan to go to the shack. The whole ugly confusing knot of it.

Jane sat there on an old milk can, hunched over her cigarette. The only signs she was paying attention were the way her eyes shifted back and forth when I spoke and the restless tapping of her foot, which sped up when I got to something significant.

After her smoke, she wolfed down a cheese sandwich oozing French's mustard while I shifted uncomfortably on my seat, wondering why I'd come. I didn't even like Jane.

She consulted her watch. "I got three minutes before I'm due back on the floor." I was about to leave when she wiped her mouth with her apron and told me to wait; she had something for me. Her cigarette was still burning. She returned with a small square packet. Instead of taking it, I shot her a puzzled look.

"You don't even know a friggin' rubber when you see one, do you?" she said. "Obviously, you need it more than I thought."

"But I—" Feeling my color rising, I held it between two fingers, as if mere contact with the thing was dangerous. "I mean—we're not going to do *that* . . ."

"Humor me, will ya? Put it in your pocketbook." She took a couple more sweet puffs from her cigarette, mashed it out, and started inside.

I wanted to leave her disgusting Trojan right there. Sure, I might have gone a little too far with Charlie, I might even have liked it, but I wasn't the type to need one of those. But for some reason, I dropped it back into my pocketbook. If nothing else, it would be fun to shock Cynthia.

"SO WHY ARE you still holding on to it?" Cynthia asked when I told her the story about Jane. We were sitting in her bedroom, surrounded by the same lilac wallpaper that had been on the wall since we were six. She reached for the tissue box she kept on her bureau. "Wrap it up and throw it away," she ordered. "Now."

Though it was what I intended to do, I wasn't about to take orders from her. I closed my fist on the packet.

"Are you crazy? Someone might see it. Your ma, for instance, and—"

"And what?"

"Remember what Mr. Ryan said in English composition? If you introduce a gun in the beginning of the story, you'll use it by the end. It's a rule."

"Chekhov said that, not Mr. Ryan. Besides, this isn't a story, and that's not a gun." I dropped the packet back into my pocketbook. With the way things were progressing in Barkley's Woods, though, and with Charlie pressuring me about the shack, I wasn't so sure.

I had other things on my mind, though. That day, I was picking up my perfect prom dress. Unlike the flowing pastels everyone else was wearing, this one was a sleek deep purple. Agnes said it was almost the color of my eyes when I was excited about something. But the real reason I loved it was because it reminded me of the sky that entered our room when we had our best talks.

AS IT TURNED out, though, the dress would sit in the closet, draped in its plastic bag, unworn on prom night. I blamed Mr. Dean for my breakup with Charlie, my spoiled graduation—and for just about everything else that had gone wrong in our family. It wasn't only the horrible things he'd done to Agnes when she was little or the sly torment she endured for years; I didn't just hate him for trailing her home from practice (why, why?) or for walking toward that glowing phone booth on the night Jimmy's life was ruined. The damage, the threat had rippled through all of us from the first day Agnes stood in the picture window, watching for his car. As I'd learned in Saturday school, one small act of goodness spreads outward, leading to untold benefits, as did the opposite.

"What's any of this got to do with me—with us?" Charlie said the day I told him. "I'm sorry about your brother and everything, but do you have to wreck our senior year—wreck us? How's that supposed to help?"

I looked at him sorrowfully. How could I explain that senior year just didn't matter anymore? Or that after Jimmy was arrested, I was no longer sure I even wanted to go to college, much less the dumb senior parties. One day I'd decide to take a year off and stay home where I could visit Jimmy on Saturdays, maybe even see if Jane could get me a job at the Hideaway. The next I wanted to bolt as soon as I could. Leave for California and never come back.

"I wanted to tell you now so you'd have time to get another date," I said. "I'm sure there's lots of girls who would go—"

"Gee, thanks, Zaidie. That's big of you." He walked away shaking his head while I felt the tears rising up inside me.

THE ONLY ONE who understood was Agnes. Everywhere one of us went, someone seemed to be whispering behind their hands. *Her brother, her brother* . . . Or worse, something about the Moscatelli kids. As if we were all guilty.

Though Agnes had gone back to swimming—harder and faster than before, she claimed with bitter satisfaction—and I remained diligent in my studies, we spent our free time huddled in the house, sitting in the hole as if Princie were still alive and Jon and Jimmy crowded us on the couch. In some ways, though, I felt stronger than ever.

FINALLY, ONE NIGHT, just before six, I was driven out of the house where nothing was cooking on the stove, Ma moped over a puzzle she would never finish, and Dad refused to walk through the door when he was supposed to. That night even Agnes was out—probably with Henry. Though she hadn't talked about him since I broke up with Charlie, I'd heard Caroline was going to the prom with someone from another school.

I walked faster, propelled by the confusion that swirled inside me day and night.

Just two days earlier, I'd convinced Jane to come with me to visit Jimmy. He barely spoke until we were ready to leave. Then he told us not to bother coming again.

"The hell, Jimmy," Jane said, wavy lines appearing on her twenty-two-year-old forehead.

"You heard me. I don't want no visitors."

But it didn't take long before he read our crestfallen expressions and the sweetest of the sweet resurfaced. "Don't ya understand?" he said, his voice cracking. "It's not that I don't want to see yas. It's just . . . the two of you? You don't belong in a place like this."

I tried to tell him that he didn't, either, but he stopped me. "Everything they said I done, I done, Z. And in my head—more."

Jane, however, wiped her eyes. "Fair enough." The words seemed to mock all three of us.

So all of that was inside me the night I left the house—Jane's tears—"Not angry tears, pissed-the-hell-off tears," she called them, as if that was a whole different category of anger—and the defeat that rose off Jimmy's skin. I had totally forgotten it was the night of the prom.

I swear I didn't plan to end up outside Charlie's house, but all of a sudden, it felt as if there was nowhere else to go. I tossed a rock at his second-floor window the way I used to. He lifted the shade, and then a few minutes later, appeared in the front door.

As soon as he came out, heck, probably before I left the house, I was crying. What could he do but wrap me up in his arms, his pale hair grazing my cheek, the smell of his skin—musk and grass—pulling me back to *before* faster than the speed of light?

"I wish I knew what to say, Zaidie," he whispered. "I wish . . . I could make it go away."

And when that made me cry harder, what could he do but kiss me? It was a light, consoling kiss at first. But when I kissed him in return, it quickly became the locus of all my confusion and hunger, a kiss that had forgotten nothing. I don't know who suggested we take a walk, but I was the one who led us to the shack in the woods.

Sometimes I tell myself I didn't plan for it to happen or want it to happen; it just did. By then, we both knew that what we had was over. That whether I went away to college or not, he would soon be gone. But more than that—I wasn't the Zaidie he'd fallen for, the one who was still open-hearted enough to love him back.

But then I'm forced to remember the deliberateness with which we moved those trees out of the path, dragged away the brush, wrenched open the door. I'm forced to see him, taking off his jacket, then his shirt; how I touched the muscles of his chest before he laid his clothes across the plank bed where Richard J. Cartier had slept.

If anyone hesitated, it was Charlie. "Are you sure?" he said, taking my face in his hands. Though the light was dim, the mixture of fire and gentleness that had made me love him was in his eyes. "We don't have to, you know——"

But it seemed we did. I reached into my pocketbook for the foil packet I'd carried around for months. Somewhere, Chekhov was laughing.

CHAPTER TWELVE

A Basket of Stones

DAHLIA

THIS WAS HOW I DID IT: ONE HOUSE AT A TIME, WITH ZAIDIE ON one side of me, Agnes on the other, and a fool cat bringing up the rear. I carried a paper bag for the times I couldn't breathe. Slow? My God, the first day it took me over an hour to make it past Josie Pennypacker's old place. But wobbly as a baby learning to walk, heart thumping like Edmund Hillary scaling Everest, I reclaimed the street I lived on. The city—or you might as well say the world—because aside from my jigsaws, Claxton was it for me—had come into view.

There were days I started out so dizzy I was sure I'd collapse before I made it off the porch. "I got one of my migraines coming on," I'd say, holding my head. "You want me to drop dead out here like poor Josie? Is that what you girls want?"

But they were merciless, those two. "Just to the corner today. Then you can go to bed the rest of the day if you want." Zaidie tightened her grip on my arm till I felt a jolt of her determination.

Agnes nodded and held me fast on her side. "Remember what I told you, Ma. Don't look to the right or left. Just keep swimming. And when you're afraid?"

"Yeah, yeah, swim faster. Fine for you to say." But somehow my feet kept moving. The only one who seemed to have any idea how I felt was Flufferbell, who opened her mouth wide as a lion and let out a fierce howl every day when I stepped off the porch.

At home, the girls tried to show me a textbook Mrs. Kelly had found for them at the library: *Anxiety and Panic Disorders.*

"Anxiety? Panic? For heaven's sake, I don't have anything like that," I said, switching on the TV so they wouldn't notice the red of my face. "And even if I did, your father's right. When did those books Mrs. Kelly sent home ever help any of you?"

"In case you haven't noticed, Agnes and I turned out pretty good," Zaidie said. "Maybe we got more from you and your books than you know."

I suppose that was meant as some kind of compliment, but all I heard was the first phrase: *in case you haven't noticed.* Truth was I'd been so fixed on the boys, I'd noticed far less than I should have. Trying not to think about that, I made it to the next house, but by then I was shaking so bad a car slowed down to gawk at me.

"Since when is a woman walking down the damn street some kind of spectacle?" I yelled. When I turned to give them a good glare, who was it but Gina Lollobrigida. In full war paint, too.

"Good to see you out and about, Dahlia," she called.

The strumpet. Even though the girls said she was just trying to be nice, I straightened myself up the best I could and pretended I didn't hear.

"I told you to let me stay home," I hollered at the merciless ones. "Now see what you've done? Even the likes of Gina Lollobrigida are laughing at me."

"Keep going," Zaidie said. Did I say they were merciless?

A minute later, I heard Agnes laughing. "Look, Ma. You got so mad at Gina Lollobrigida you went a whole house further than you were supposed to."

BY THE TIME I made it around the block, everything, including my own house, looked different.

"How long has it been since your dad painted this porch? It's a sight," I told the girls. The next day when Joe Jr. came by to deliver some of Anna's meatballs, a new idea occurred to me.

"Run to Creeley's and pick me up some paint for the porch, will you, Joe?" I told him. "A nice forest green. Tell him Louie will pay later. And two brushes, one for me and one for you."

"Me—Joe O'Connor Jr.? Go to Creeley's Paint Store?"

"Yes, you. I've got a job for you, Junior."

He backed up—nervous as I was every day when I crossed the *maledizione*. "Can't, Mrs. Moscatelli. Gotta work. At my job. Gotta work at the Nothing's Perfect Market and Deli. Can't. Gotta . . . At my job. Sweep the floor. Say hello. At the . . . Can't, Mrs.—"

"I already asked your father," I lied. "A nice forest green, and two brushes. I suppose we'll need some of that turpentine, too. What do you think?"

Sensing he was about to repeat his spiel, I pulled out my ace. "Jimmy wants you to do it, Junior. He called from the jail just this morning and told me so."

He looked at me skeptically. "Jimmy called—from the jail? Jimmy Kovacs?"

At first, I wasn't sure he was buying it, but then he blinked. "Turpentine and a scraper and some sandpaper, Mrs. Moscatelli. We need sandpaper. And paint. A nice forest green."

If he hadn't paid the bill at the paint store, I might have thought Louie was unaware of my project. He didn't even say a word when he come home and caught Joe and me scraping the porch.

Finally, a couple of days after we finished painting, I was forced to ask what he thought of the job.

He chomped his BLT like he didn't hear me. I stared harder.

"You wanna know what I think, Dahlia? I think you better send Junior to the store for a ladder and a few gallons of white. Better learn how to climb it, too."

"Climb a ladder—me? You know I'm scared of heights . . ."

"You'll have to get over it, then. Cause all you done with that bright green porch is make the rest of the house look like hell."

He got up and chucked his sandwich into the trash from halfway across the kitchen.

"Moscatelli sinks a three-pointer," Agnes sang out.

I shot her a look. "Good Lord. Do you think this is some kind of sporting event?"

"Kind of," Zaidie answered for her.

Louie had already slammed the door to Jimmy's room by the time I'd recovered enough to follow him to the stairs.

"Maybe I will; just you watch!" I yelled. "And for the record, it's not bright green. It's a nice forest . . ." I heard Jimmy's stereo switch on to drown me out. That music Louie always hated, too.

"The hell with you, then," I hollered louder.

THE NEXT DAY, still peeved by his suggestion that I get on a ladder and paint the house, I walked past three extra houses before I noticed. Then, realizing what I'd done, I went a little further. "To hell with him," I repeated to myself with every step.

Back at home, though, my eyes were drawn to the stones Louie had given me when he first came courting.

"Some fellas come with flowers, some bring candy," I told the girls before they could escape. "That's what your father brought me."

"Dad gave you a basket of rocks? When you were dating?" Agnes asked gently, still thinking of the words that had powered my walk.

"Not all at once. One at a time, he brought them. Every day till the basket was filled." Holy God, was I about to cry?

Though I knew they had things to do, they sat beside me on the couch and took my hands.

"It's all right," Agnes said, like I used to tell the kids when they had a bad dream.

But we both knew there were some things that could never be made all right. Not what Mr. Dean did to her in the attic. And not the three days I spent in the woods or anything that followed. The trial. The afternoon I watched my mother typing a letter to inform the Massachusetts General School of Nursing that I would not be a student there in the fall. Remembering, I felt every key in the typewriter pummeling my body. My parents' faces at the supper table when people stopped coming into Dahlia's Place. Fearful, dismayed, but most of all angry. It wasn't long before that rage—mostly Mother's—settled on me.

You couldn't have kept quiet about it, could you? What did you accomplish, dragging it all out in the open, taking on the Woods of all people? Just ruined yourself and us, too.

The only peace I had was when they were forced to take jobs out of town. I didn't tell the girls any of that, though. What was the point? I began with the day the story changed.

"I was home alone that afternoon. It was just a little after three— God knows why I looked at the clock, or why I remember—when Louie Moscatelli came to my front stoop and rung the bell."

"Did you let him in?" Agnes asked.

"I wouldn't have gone to the door for anyone back then—least of all Louie. I hardly knew the boy for one thing, and he was considered . . . something of a homely-looking fella at the time."

"Considered? At the time?" The girls giggled. "People still call him Frankenstein, Ma."

"After I heard him walk away, I went to the door to make sure he was good and gone. That's when I found the first stone."

"How did you know he left it? Or that it was for you?" Zaidie asked. "It might have been an ordinary rock from the garden."

"I suppose I didn't. Not at first. But when I picked it up, it was so smooth."

I paused and passed a rock to each of them. "See? He'd polished them up in his shop. From then on, he showed up every day with another one. In the beginning, he rang the bell like the first day, but once he figured out I wasn't going to answer, he stopped ringing. I'd hear him coming up the steps, then I'd wait a little while and go out to collect my rock."

"So why'd you keep them?" Agnes said. "I mean, if you weren't interested . . ."

"That's the question, isn't it?" I figured this wasn't the time to explain my theory of how Louie had come to me as mysteriously and purposefully as they had. I hadn't asked for it, and I certainly didn't recognize it when it came. But for some reason, I went to the basement and found a basket for the rocks he left behind.

"And then one day when I heard him on the porch, I looked out the window and found myself staring directly into that homely face—and seeing . . . seeing, well, my whole life, I suppose—though I didn't know it at the time."

"And then?" both girls said at once.

"What else could I do?" I laughed a bit for the first time since all the business with Jimmy. "I flung open the door and asked him what he wanted."

"What on earth I wanted; that's what you said," Louie corrected from the foyer, where he had slipped in unheard.

I was about to ask him what he was doing home two hours early, but he went to the kitchen for a shot of water before I had a chance. And after supper, he headed straight to Jimmy's room like he'd been doing. Something was different, though.

Halfway up the stairs, he stopped and looked at me on my chair. Soon as he caught me looking back, though, he cleared his throat and kept going.

It was long past midnight when I woke up and found him in bed—motionless, but awake. We lay there quiet for a few minutes.

"People been sayin' they seen you, Dahlia," he finally said. "Out walkin' around the neighborhood. Far away as Grainer Street, someone seen you. Is it true?"

"Hmm . . ." I said, wondering if it was Gina Lollobrigida who'd stopped near the Grainer School. Somehow it didn't seem like so much of a big deal as it used to. "You know what it's like, Lou?"

He grunted.

"The walk you took that night after Jimmy . . . It wasn't streets you were walking. It was like you were traveling up and down Jimmy's whole life, looking for something. Except this is my life I'm walking."

I paused, but he stayed quiet.

"We made it as far as Papa's old restaurant this afternoon. Me and my girls."

Louie grunted again.

"One of these days, you know what I'm gonna do, Lou? I'm gonna walk into that jail and see Jimmy."

The sky was so black that night nothing in the room was visible, but I saw him just the same—hands folded behind his head. "You know the question you asked me at the door that first day?"

I chuckled to myself. "What you wanted."

"What on earth I wanted," he corrected again. "Well, in case I never answered you proper, this was it, Dahlia. The all and the everything of it. This was it."

And then he reached for me.

CHAPTER THIRTEEN

Einstein and Me

DAHLIA

Turns out that while I huddled inside the house, confining the world to the shape of my picture window, nothing stayed put. Businesses changed names, houses were fiddled with till you could barely recognize them, lives and buildings were swept away, replaced by fields of glittering glass or markers in the graveyard. What shocked me most was the damn smell of the place. Even that was different.

"What's that?" I asked, sniffing as I reached the corner of Hope Street. I didn't realize I'd stopped to clutch my heart until the girls laughed.

"It's honeysuckle, Ma. What did you think?" Zaidie picked me a sprig from the bush and attempted to press it to my face. I shoved the tender thing into my pocket and pulled away.

"Hah. Only time I ever smelled that was from a bottle." I thought of the Muguet des Bois I splashed on myself in high school, Bobby leaning in to inhale my neck: *Sweet*, he said in my ear. I shuddered.

"When did the Juneaus start growing that?" I said—as if it was all their fault. The whisper I heard, the breeze on my neck as if Bobby had come back to nuzzle me one more time. All the things I could never tell anyone.

"The Juneaus?" Agnes said.

I took in the name on the mailbox: ANDREWS. "Hmph." I kept walking, touching the stone wall as I passed. "Well, at least the rocks haven't changed."

Even Dahlia's Place—renamed Cafe Roma after my family sold it—had turned into Sheehan's Irish Pub. But walking past it, I still inhaled the pungent scent of my mother's marinara; I felt myself at fifteen or sixteen, pushing through the door in my work shoes, putting on the green apron in the back, joking with the customers as I bussed tables. I took a deep breath, filling my nostrils with the stench of stale beer and something else—a jolt of my old strength.

"Someday soon you'll go anywhere in the city without thinking twice," Zaidie said. "And you won't even need us."

"But we'll be there if you do," Agnes quickly added.

"Hmph."

The first few steps away from the house were always the hardest, but the further I got from the *maledizione*, the easier it got. For thirty-four days I kept going, even when I was sure I couldn't. One house and then another, one step, one heartbeat . . . The girls tugged me along with their voices, their faith, like I was a damn toddler.

"You're doing good, Ma! Great! Just a few more feet. One more house. Yay!"

"You did it!"

Dear Lord.

I had made it six blocks and two houses from home when on the thirty-fifth day I came upon a sign halfway up Maple Street. A nice green sign painted in gold lettering with a border to match:

SILAS P. WOOD, C.P.A.

If the girls weren't there to hold me up, I tell you I would have dropped on the spot. It must have been five minutes before I was able to speak. "Silas? W-when did he come back to town?"

"That's been there long as I can remember," Agnes stammered, shooting her sister a confused look. "We're so used to seeing it, I guess we don't even notice it anymore."

"Silas Wood," Zaida interrupted. "That's Larry's dad, isn't it?"

"I think so." Agnes then clamped her mouth shut, but not before I caught the glance that passed between them.

"Larry?" I repeated.

"A kid who was in school with Jimmy," Zaida said, knowing I wouldn't dare to ask further.

When I felt myself beginning to shake, Agnes took my hand. "We should go back," she said. "She's had enough, Zaidie."

"Yes, I need . . . to go home." Why, oh why had I ever let them talk me into this?

But Zaidie remained unmoving as she spoke to Agnes like I wasn't there. "If we go home now, you know what's gonna happen? She'll never cross the porch again." Finally, she faced me, hands on her hips and all: "Then you know what happens?" She cocked her head at the sign. "They win."

I jerked my hand away from Agnes, trembling even harder. "Dear God, Zaida, don't you understand anything? They already won. Twenty-nine years ago, they took everything I had. And then some. I was foolish to think I could—"

When Zaida shook her head, I remembered the vocabulary word from my old *Reader's Digest* quiz that always made me think of her: implacable. Yes, that was her, all right. Implacable. And merciless. Heaven help me.

"That's not how it works, Ma," she said. "People don't just beat you once. They come back to do it over and over. In your case, every single day for the last twenty-nine years. Till now, that is."

"You don't understand," I repeated. "I need to go—"

"No, Ma. You're the one who doesn't understand." Zaida's voice lowered to almost a whisper. "Do you know how many times Frankenstein's Texaco's been vandalized?"

"That's—that's . . . not true. Louie would have—"

"Oh, he would have? Do you think Dad tells you about half the crap he takes? Half the stuff we kids . . ." Here she stopped herself, as if knowing she'd gone too far. "He's been protecting you for as long as you've been married. We all have. But every year, at least once, the Woods make sure to remind us."

I gaped at her. "Remind you? What are you talking about?"

"That they're still winning."

"This isn't the time, Zaida," I managed to say between gasping breaths. "Can't you see I need—I need to go home." I thought of the half-drunk cup I'd left on my card table that morning with an almost desperate longing.

"She's right, Zaidie. We can—" Agnes said.

But again, the implacable one shook her head. "This is exactly the time. This is where we've been walking to every day without knowing it. This building. This moment." She gestured at the sign before returning to me. "Come on, you still have four houses left to go."

"Good Lord," I said, reaching for Agnes. "Can't she see—"

But something Agnes saw in Silas P. Wood, CPA's window had caused her to turn.

Her eyes fixed, she let her hands fall to her side. "It's only four more houses, Ma."

"Agnes—I thought you understood."

"I do, but you know what I see up there in that window? I see Silas Wood—him and Larry and his whole family, looking down at you. And not just you. Us," Agnes said. "Dahlia Moscatelli and her crummy foster kids."

"Stop, please, Agnes—"

"That's what he thinks of us, Ma. What all those Woods think of us. Them and their friends, too. No matter what we do, we'll always be nothing but low-life Moscatelli kids."

"They're sure you'll turn back," Zaidie added. "One glimpse of their mighty name and you'll scurry home to your cell and slam the door. That's what they think."

"I told you, Zaida . . . I made my peace with that . . . I—" I squeezed my eyes shut.

But when I opened them, I was mysteriously drawn to the window the girls were forcing me to look into. It was empty, which was their real victory: They didn't even have to be there to scare me away.

My anger steadied me. "You say Jimmy knew his boy—Larry?"

Agnes nodded. "Larry went away to college around the time Jimmy got sent to Vietnam, but Jools told us—" She paused, obviously worried how much I could handle.

"Go on. Jools told you what?" For a minute, I forgot everything, the six blocks I'd have to walk to get back home to my chair, the name etched in gold lettering.

Everything.

"Back when they were in school, Larry made Jimmy's life pretty miserable; that's all."

Was that when Jimmy had become a rat? I wondered. Dear God, why hadn't anyone told me?

"Like I said, winning isn't something people like that do once," Zaida added. "It's something they do every day. They need it."

"It's their oxygen, Ma. Their life's blood. Just like it was for Mr. Dean," Agnes said. But when she looked me in the eye, she was no longer the frightened girl watching for the yellow car. She was Agnes, who could swim like a dolphin, and she was truly free.

"Imagine that," I murmured to myself with something like awe. I glanced up the street toward the corner. "Four more houses, you say?"

Walking slightly ahead of the girls for the first time, I reached the third house and stopped abruptly. "Are the lions still there?"

"Lions?" The girls glanced at each other.

"You mean the statues in front of the old mayor's mansion?" Agnes swiveled toward Zaida. "It's a historical site now."

"Yes, they're there. Someday, we'll—" Zaida began.

"No, not someday, Zaida. Today. Now."

"It's a good mile from here, Ma, and you've already walked pretty far."

"You think I don't know where it is?" I said. By then I had resumed walking. "I could practically tell you the number of heartbeats it takes to get there."

"As long as you feel strong enough." Zaida was a step behind me, with Agnes beside her.

"You said it right. If I don't do it today, I'll never set foot off the porch again."

The girls thought I was driven by courage like they were. Like they had been their whole lives. They were wrong. They thought this determination was something that came over me when I looked at the Wood name in gold letters and didn't blink. That was wrong, too.

What gave me my strength was the other name she'd said: Jimmy. And behind him were all the rest: Louie, Zaida, Agnes, Jon—even the kids who'd only been with us a few months. While I'd hid myself up in the house, the Woods had done their best to punish everyone I loved. I walked to the end of the street and turned left toward the west side like the place was on fire and I was the only one who could put it out.

Einstein or one of those types said that time bends; that sometimes an hour's not an hour; it's more like a minute. Other times it stretches into a week, or infinity.

Something of that nature. Well, that day, I, Dahlia Moscatelli, discovered distance is the same. A mile can be so far it might take a woman traveling by foot twenty-nine years to cross it—or so close that all she had to do was close her eyes, take a breath and she's there.

I can't explain it, but between the moment I stopped at the third house on Maple Street and the one when I found myself standing in front of those stone lions, I saw nothing; I smelled nothing; I didn't even think anything.

I wished I could say I didn't tremble when I saw the place, that my breath didn't catch inside me when I looked up that long driveway to the house on the hill, but that would be a lie.

Sensing it, the girls came to my side. "Are you okay, Ma?" Agnes seized my hand.

"I'm going to call Dad and tell him to bring the car," Zaidie said, merciful for once. "It's a long walk back and you're . . . you're tired, Ma."

Trapped in Mr. Einstein's bendable universe, I hardly heard them. Hardly saw their anxious faces. What I saw was Bobby Wood, holding my hand, as we walked up that driveway for the first time. What I saw was the door to that magnificent house opening, and the family gathered around the dining room table.

You're late, Robert, his father said. *You almost missed grace.* Though I could tell he wasn't sure about me—not at all—his smile was an irresistible blaze.

When I finally looked away from that table, the handsome young boy was gone; I was a middle-aged woman with streaks of ash and snow in my hair, and good heavens, I was blubbering again.

"I knew we shouldn't have come here," Agnes said, her eyes full of the heartbreak she held close all these years but never released.

"It's not your fault; it was me. I'm sorry, Ma. I just—I didn't want Agnes and me to go away to college and leave you there, sitting in that chair." The resolve on Zaida's face was replaced with a watery mess of grief and makeup. "And Jimmy, he needs to see you."

Though I wasn't given to that sort of thing, I pulled her to me right there on the street and felt her heart, her sorrows, her mascaraed tears, but most of all, the great life force she always had, pulsating against mine.

"There, there, now," I said, patting her back like it had all been a nightmare. Only this time I'd been the one living in a dark dream. "No more sorries. All you've done"—I paused to pull Agnes into our circle—"all the two of you have ever done since you come into the house was lead me back to myself."

Then I stood apart from them, and wiped my eyes with the back of my hand, done with the coward.

THOSE TWO MILES home, we must have been a sight: A grown woman walking through the streets holding hands with her teenage daughters like she was lost or blind. Crazy Dahlia Moscatelli, people would say, talking about me like they did about Joe Jr. But I didn't care who gawked. The truth, if they had eyes to see, was I'd never, in all my life, been less lost. Never less blind.

At home, my cold coffee was right where I'd left it. While the girls took their places on the couch, with Flufferbell a silent witness, I sat down on my chair and told them everything I'd kept to myself for twenty-nine years.

CHAPTER FOURTEEN

The Golden Tree

DAHLIA

SILAS WAS NOTHING LIKE THE REST OF THEM. IF HE HADN'T BEEN A Wood, the boy would have slipped through four years of high school unnoticed. Average to look at, not much of a student—and he had this, um, closed way about him. No personality, kids said, but I suppose that's a personality, too, isn't it?

The only reason he got picked for teams or invited to parties was because his brothers made sure of it. They were that way, the Woods—loyal to a fault. Here, I had to stop myself a minute. Yes.

He was only a year ahead of me at school, but the first time I ever paid him any mind was that Sunday Bobby brought me to dinner.

"To the mansion with the lions?" Agnes asked. I nodded.

What kills me is that even knowing everything that came of it, I'm still impressed when I think of that table—the sparkling glasses, gleaming silver, a tablecloth—on an ordinary Sunday. A maid serving the courses, for heaven's sake! But mostly, I was dazzled by all the bright young faces glittering around it. Five sons, all destined to be SOMEONE; that's what people said. As if the rest of us aren't.

In my mind, I saw them all as clear as I had at sixteen. Michael, a college student in Boston who still came home every Sunday, my handsome Bobby, the one they called Ray Ray—he excelled at hockey—shy Calvin, who was soon to come into his own . . . and him. The closed-off one.

When the mayor asked about my plans for the future, they all jumped in—like I was the most fascinating girl they ever met, and nothing was more important than my plans. Later, I realized that had nothing to do with me. It was who they were, how they had seduced a city.

Meanwhile, Silas looked down, focused on the beef he was cutting into tiny squares. I was acutely aware of his presence, though. He cleared his throat a bit too loud a couple of times, but then said nothing. No one seemed to notice but me. And Mrs. Wood.

"Silas, dear, sit up straight," she said, nervous, the way she'd been when they teased Calvin. A feeling I know myself as a mother.

He pushed back his chair, leaving that precisely cut plate of beef. "Can I be excused?"

Though he was speaking low, I felt the—what's the word?—volatility—that was just below the surface in all of them. The mayor, too. He released him with the same look my mother sometimes gave me. Who knows? Maybe that's why I was drawn to Bobby, why he was drawn to me. It was what I knew.

Anyway, it's strange the things you remember. The way Silas cut his beef, the sound of him clearing his throat. Almost as if you know it's significant long before you understand why. Or how. As if something warns you: *Pay attention. This is going to matter.* Hmm.

I suppose I felt sorry for him. I even tried to talk to him a few times when I ran into him at school, but he was always quick to get away.

"Silas is the mailman's kid; that's what Dad says," Bobby told me once after his brother missed an easy shot in a game of pickup basketball. And when I asked if that hurt Silas's feelings, the unpredictable anger flared.

"If there's one thing a kid's gotta learn, it's how to take a joke."

Was that something his father taught him? I wondered. Another Wood secret of success?

But before I could ask, Bobby got up and walked away—as he often did—abruptly leaving me to wonder what I'd said. Now, of course, I know it wasn't anything I said. It was what I might say. The questions I might have asked, but never got the chance.

"But why did Silas matter? Bobby was your boyfriend," Zaida said when I paused. "He's the one in all those pictures up in the attic."

I tensed up as I thought of them up there in the attic, going through my things.

How much had they seen? Obviously not enough to know Silas's part in it—but of course there were no pictures of that.

"You looked so happy, Ma," Agnes added, as if to reassure me.

Happy? Hah. I took a belt of my coffee the way Louie does with his water. I suppose I was for a while; we both were—though things were never right. There was always this anger in him, this need to . . . squash me, it felt like, and it got worse the longer we were together. Still, what did I know? Bobby was the first and only boy I went with in high school.

He was jealous of my friends, of where I went, who I was, it seemed like. And after I got accepted to nursing school it escalated, until finally I got the courage to break up with him. It wasn't easy, but somehow I managed to avoid him all summer. I'm telling you I never felt so free—so happy as I did that summer. Of course, the family was furious. The way they saw it I'd never been near good enough for Bobby, and yet they'd taken me in, encouraged me, even hired a tutor when I struggled with my chemistry. Who did I think I was? How dare I?

I was leaving for school in six days when it happened. Can you imagine? Six days and my entire life would have gone different. Both our lives.

I paused awhile before I went on.

Silas was the one who brought me out there, I began, knowing I didn't have to explain. After the kids blamed me for letting Jon go and for allowing everything to go to ruin while I lay up in bed, Louie had tried to make them understand it wasn't my fault. That I'd been left in the woods. That I hadn't been right since they found me on the highway three days later. He even showed them the clippings from the newspaper.

I wasn't there when they read it, of course, but I could see their faces just the same: Zaida's eyes filling, Agnes turning in on herself. And Jimmy? Probably got up and walked out. It's hard for boys to know what to do with those things. Later, when I saw the pity in them, I grilled Louie about how much he had said.

"I told them some boys . . . they took you out in the woods—and they hurt you, that's all. They hurt you bad."

I suppose he thought he was defending me, but I was outraged. And even madder that he'd reminded me of it. Crazy, isn't it? Though it's been with me every day since, I never let myself think of it.

I had gone back to those days I lay beneath the yellow leaves. I'd let myself remember the morning when someone or something called me out, told me to get up, and led me to the highway. But never, never, had I returned to the night it happened. Never.

Unconsciously, the girls reached their hands across the hole in the couch to each other. Their hair, their eyes, the light and the dark of them, were shining. Never had they been so beautiful to me—or so vulnerable. Was I really going to foist my nightmare on these poor girls? My children, for heaven's sake?

But now that it had risen up, demanding to be told, who else was there? Louie would have dropped like Josie Pennypacker if he was forced to listen to the details. Should I go down to Joe O'Connor's silly market, sit Saint Joe and Anna down, and let them know just how damn imperfect this world could get?

Like she often did, Zaida read my mind. "It's okay, Ma. You can tell us. I'm almost eighteen, you know—the same age you were. And Agnes—well, she probably went through worse before she was five."

Yes, worse. So many of my kids.

"Mr. Dean always told me that everything that happened to me was my fault. Mrs. Dean, too. They said I deserved it and more," Agnes added. "It was only after I told my story to all of you that I knew how wrong they were."

"Now is the time," Zaida said, like she did when we were standing under that green sign. "Go on, Ma."

LIKE I SAID, Bobby and me had broke up in the spring. Right after that pretty prom picture you might've seen in the attic, it happened. I know he took it hard. People said he hardly left the house all summer. There were rumors he changed his mind about going to Boston College like his brother. He was talking about a school out in Texas. Maybe even joining the military—like he couldn't get far enough away. His father didn't just object. He forbid it.

I still shuddered every time I thought of the man at the table.

Anyway, I had just got off work and was heading to my friend Murph's that night when Silas pulled up. He said Bobby wanted to see me one more time before we both left. He had something for me.

I paused, seeing that blue Chevy with the open door, Silas at the wheel. There weren't a lot of nineteen-year-olds with cars in those days and I was still young enough to be impressed by what the Woods had. Who they were in town. But that wasn't the reason I got in.

There was so much unsaid between Bobby and me, I wanted a chance to try. I wanted it so bad I didn't see what I should have seen.

Agnes narrowed her eyes. "What was that?"

Silas's face. The hardness of it. Later, those leaves falling on me, I would peer back in that car and see it clear as day, but that night . . .

Well, like I said, all I was thinking of was Bobby. I jumped in the car. I didn't even question where he was taking me till we left the city and headed for the wooded area outside town.

"Has to be some place where no one who could report back to my father might see you, okay?" Silas explained.

I nodded my head in the dark car. "Okay."

We drove deep in the woods till we came to a clearing. There, he handed me a flashlight and pointed to a narrow path. "He'll meet you down there. Not far, maybe a half mile."

"He's not here yet?"

"You know Bobby—always running late. Don't worry; it'll only be a few minutes." As soon as I got out of the car, he put it in reverse.

"You're leaving me—alone?" I called after him.

But he just backed out, taking out a few bushes in the process.

If I had any sense, I would have been afraid, but in those days there was this dumb strength running through me all the time— whether I was putting on my apron at the restaurant after being up all night studying for a test or getting up to give a speech at school. The only thing on my mind was what I would say, how Bobby and I would act. Still, I was grateful for the chance.

I looked at my watch: 7:05. Silas had told me the plan was to meet at seven. No doubt Bobby would be there soon. The light was still streaming through the trees as I started down the path. Ever since I was small, I'd loved to play in the woods. I'd find a fallen tree, sweep out a corner with a branch, and imagine I was in my own private kingdom. Nowhere had I ever felt more safe.

As I got closer to the second clearing, the place where I was supposed to meet Bobby, the tree came into view. My God, I wish you could have seen it! It was so beautiful it stopped me where I was, stopped me and then pulled me forward. It was early for the leaves to turn, but that one was already shimmering with color.

In the dazzling light, the leaves were pure gold. I could hardly wait for Bobby to get there so I could show him. That was what was good between us—especially in the beginning. Every song we played for each other was the best tune ever; a new pizza place wasn't just good, it was fantastic. If we only remembered that, I thought . . . I don't know . . . Maybe we could separate as friends. He could move on to his own life in peace.

I looked back down the path where I'd come—still not scared, though I was alone in the unfamiliar woods, just worried that he might not get there in time to see the spectacular gold tree before the light turned. That's when I heard the approaching car.

"Bobby!" I called out when the door opened. "I'm down here." And then, unable to resist, "You have to see—"

But before I finished, I heard a second door open. And then a third. "Bobby?"

Sitting in the parlor, I swear I heard those footsteps on the path. The unfamiliar voices. Felt the fear taking hold. Trembling right there in my own chair, I wasn't sure I could go on.

"Was he with them?" Zaida asked.

It was a while before I could answer, but the girls waited, pulling me deeper with their eyes. I shook my head.

IT WAS HIS cousin and a couple of other kids from out of town. Boston, we thought, though no one ever found out for sure. Thugs, they were—all of them—the Woods, too, for all their polished silver and fancy ways. At first, they stopped there in the clearing and stared at me, like they'd forgotten what they were supposed to do. One kid— the youngest of the group—he looked like he wanted to bolt himself. He turned from one to the other of them. "Chick hasn't done nothin' to us. Maybe we should—"

"Bobby," I repeated. "My—my boyfriend will be here any minute and—"

"You hear that?" a heavyset boy said, turning to the other two.

"She thinks Bobby's comin' to rescue her." He laughed, and then without warning, his fist was in my jaw.

I didn't know it was possible to be hit that hard. I went down, hitting my head against the trunk of the golden tree on the way.

It wasn't just the pain, but the . . . the intent of it. The power it had. The knowledge that this—hate, this violence—was there, around us all the time. I just hadn't known it. Up until then, I'd walked through the world like a damn fool, scared of nothing.

I looked over at the girls, expecting them to be horrified, but all I saw was courage. What had been such a shock to me was something they'd been forced to reckon with all their lives. Agnes in the attic. And Zaida, struck in a different way when she was abandoned with her dying mother and baby Jon in that apartment.

"Did the other boy—the younger one—did he help you?" Agnes asked. No matter how harsh life treated that one, she always searched for the way out.

I shook my head slightly, looking down at myself lying at the foot of that golden tree, the way they say you do when you die.

THE ANIMAL INSTINCT must have kicked in. Him and the big one took turns kicking and hitting me until finally, the third boy, who had stood back from it all—Walter, I heard them call him—came over and tore my blouse.

Without thinking, I covered my bosoms there in the parlor, as I was unable to do the night of the attack.

"We're not supposed to do that, Walter. You heard him. He was strong about that," one of them said. "Just rough her up; that's it."

"Hey, she ain't looking too good," the beefy one who started it all said. "There's blood coming out the friggin' mouth. Son of a bitch. I told you not to kick her so hard."

"Me? You were the one who—"

Yes, that was another funny thing I remembered—that he called it *the* mouth, instead of *her* mouth, as if he, too, was looking down at me from a great distance. Like I was no longer human. And I suppose I wasn't to them.

"Shit," someone else said. Were there more than three of them? Or was I just hearing echoes. "I told you to scare her, not . . . not this. The girl's dead, or you did anything else to her, you don't get a red cent. That was the deal. Go on, get the hell out of here, the three of you."

Who was the girl they were talking about? Was it me? That's how far away I was. And that voice. Where had I heard it before? My head throbbed, reminding me I was still there in my body.

"You heard me—go before you end up getting charged with something."

I struggled to open my eyes, but it felt like they were weighted with heavy coins. I heard the footsteps again, moving away. The one that was left, the voice, bent over me and tried to cover me with that torn blouse, almost as if he wanted to help. But then he stopped.

It was his eyes I felt before anything else. Next thing I knew his hands were on me, everywhere. "Bitch," the voice was saying, as he tore at my pants, pushed himself into me. "Messed up Bobby so bad he wants to scrap college and go off to fight the war. Probably get himself killed and doesn't even care. All over a little nobody like you?" I think he was crying by that point. Crying for himself—not for me. See, I was a corpse to him. Less than that.

The sun was going down, taking with it the gold of the tree. I tried to pry my eyes open enough to see, but they were swollen almost completely shut. Still, there was enough light to make out Silas's face looking down on me, and he caught the slit between my puffy lids.

"Even think about telling and next time it will be worse," he said, though at that moment, neither of us could have thought I'd live to see a next time. Then he ran away like the others and left me there alone.

I'D GOTTEN SO lost in the dark dream, the story I hadn't told anyone, not even myself, I almost forgot who I was speaking to.

When I looked up, Agnes was on the side of my chair, her arm sloped over me, hand holding mine with a different kind of force. The opposite of what I felt in the woods. Zaida sat on the floor, her face wet with my own unshed tears.

"I'm sorry. I shouldn't have told you all that . . . but once I got started, it just came."

"It's all right," Zaida said, wiping her cheeks and chin with the flat of her hand. Then she laughed at herself, which felt like a relief to us all. "I'm such a dope."

"We knew anyway, Ma," Agnes told me. "Not the details, of course, but we knew . . ."

Zaida nodded.

"That wasn't the end of it, though," I said, not wanting to leave them there with Silas, not wanting to let him win another minute.

By then, memory was pouring through me like light through that tree.

After the pain and the cold of those nights when the animals howled and the temperatures dropped, the tree was still there. It wasn't gold like I thought when I first saw it, either. It was plain yellow, but when the leaves began to fall on me, to cover me—how can I describe it? It was as if they were blessing me. That's when it came on me, that great peace I told you about. The peace they say you have at the end. In all my life, I never felt anything like it.

Agnes nodded as if she felt it, too, as if she could see that tree I wanted to show to Bobby clear as day.

CHAPTER FIFTEEN

Before

AGNES

MA WAS AFRAID WE WERE TOO YOUNG TO HEAR, THAT WE'D crack if we looked too deep into those woods, saw her walking that path, heard the sound of those car doors closing, first one, then another and another. She thought the fist that knocked her to the ground would reach through the years and shatter our tender bones. But the truth was we'd lived with that story all our lives. We just didn't know its name.

I had them, too. *Befores*, Zaidie called them, like they were places on the map. A whole country of them with a capitol and its own flag. Even after I told the Moscatellis about my life in Mr. Dean's attic, there were things I could never say. And in their own way, they kept me a prisoner just like Ma. I couldn't talk about Mau Mau, couldn't even say those two syllables out loud. But I still called for her in my sleep, still whispered her name whenever I stopped to pick up a penny on the road. People like Nonna call it prayer.

And it wasn't just my lost sister I kept secret. I remembered—no, I felt myself sitting in Mr. Dean's attic window, waiting for someone who used to come, but didn't anymore. *Yourmother*, they called her. As soon as she got out of her taxi, she'd be yelling the name no one else used: *Ahn-yess!* And when she saw my face, she always laughed. Not the way you laugh at a joke. No, it was more like the happiness that bubbled up inside her was so powerful she had to release it. Glory, Saint Joe called it when he heard me laugh the same way. *Yup, the glory is what it is. You just got a little more of it than most people.* I wasn't much for religion like Nonna or Zaidie—and neither was Joe when it came down to it—but somehow that sounded about right.

Whenever I thought of my mother and her glory laugh, I'd go to my room and take out my treasure box. Then I'd touch the gifts she had given me, one by one, looking for answers. Where had she gone? Why didn't she come back? And finally, the question that made me snap the box shut every time: Was she okay?

But once I hit high school, I was so preoccupied with swimming and friends and everything that was changing inside me, I hardly thought about the mother who was living in the house with me, never mind the one I'd lost.

And then from nowhere, there was something else. The thing I feared more than anything. The one that had taken away all the glory the dope hadn't managed to steal from my mother. A boy. Much as I fought it, he was there when the teacher called on me in geography. *Miss Juniper, are you with us today?* There when I swam laps, faster and faster—to escape him or to reach him—I wasn't sure which. At the end of the pool, I was startled to find Coach Lois with her stopwatch, beaming: *Your best time yet.*

AT FIRST, HE treated me like Zaidie's annoying little sister—the way he had when I was ten. He complained I was too slow getting changed. (Didn't I know Caroline was waiting for him? That she wasn't particularly happy about him driving Zaidie's kid sister around . . . that he had better things to do?) As we got to know each other on the daily twenty-minute ride, Caroline's name filled the car—as if to remind me what this was and what it could never be. As if to remind himself.

"I have to stop at the flower shop," he said one afternoon. "It's a whole year for Caroline and me. Aside from Zaidie and Charlie, it's the senior class record."

"Can I help? I love flowers."

Inside Meninger's, I held up a pale yellow rose. "This is the one."

"It's supposed to be red for a girlfriend. Don't you know anything?" he teased.

"About love and stuff? Not much." I wrinkled up my nose at the thought. "But if it was me, I'd rather have the yellow one. It's the color of—I don't know—a promise."

He laughed—but bought the yellow one.

Whenever I turned up the radio to hear Smokey Robinson or the Temptations, he grimaced. "Really, you like that goopy song?"

I cranked it louder. "What does *goopy* even mean?"

"Look it up in the dictionary. Probably says, 'Agnes's taste in music.' For someone who's not interested in love, you sure like songs about it."

The flash of his white teeth when he laughed made me laugh, too. Just like I had when the one who didn't come around anymore stood at the door and let loose her glory.

And then one day, he took the long way home and stopped at the N. P. "Just got thirsty all of a sudden," he said, handing me a Pepsi. Though soda was forbidden on my training diet, I didn't say no. When we reached the house, we sat in the car and drank it slowly in my driveway. Was that when it started? Or was it the day I caught him singing along to "My Girl"?

"Now see what you've done? You've got me singing goopy songs myself."

"You like it, too. Admit it."

He grinned. "I wouldn't go that far."

BUT A FEW days later, when we reached the house, he stopped me as I reached for the door handle. "Wait," he said. "I need to ask you something."

I looked at him, my hand still on the handle.

"Okay, this is gonna sound dumb, but . . . how'd you get that way?"

I checked myself up and down, wondering if my colors were mismatched or something. "What way?"

"It's just—I never met anyone like you before. Not in my whole life."

"You mean—an Indian?" I was used to people telling me that, asking about my tribe and how I ever landed in Claxton. Sometimes it made me feel the way I did in Mr. Dean's attic. Like the last one left. But part of my secret was not to show it.

"No, not that. Just the way you are. It's like you give it all away, everything—every minute. Nothing holds you back. I never met anyone like that before."

I laughed. "You're crazy, you know that?"

But then I jumped out of the car and bolted for the house, almost tripping on a boulder that had been in the yard since I was six.

Inside, the mirror where Zaidie and I stopped every day to see if we were pretty enough stopped me. This time, though, I saw what Henry saw. The girl who wasn't afraid of anything. The one who was unlike anyone he'd ever met. Had he really said that?

Once again, I felt the glory bubbling up.

A FEW DAYS later, I reminded him that we needed to deliver the anise cookies Nonna had tucked inside my school bag. For Giuliano. "Tell you boyfriend to drop them off on the way home from swim. Last time I see Giuliano, he look too thin."

"Jools has always been skinny, Nonna, and, sheesh, Henry's not my—"

"*Fa*. You think I don't hear you out in the driveway when I come here? Go—and tell Giuliano next time I send him manicotti." Nonna waved me away before I could tell her that whatever she thought she'd heard was wrong.

No one answered the door at the Bousquets so I left Nonna's package on the stoop.

When I turned around, I was surprised to find Henry behind me. "Feel like taking a walk by the river?"

Not waiting for an answer, he started toward the path. I hated Buskit's River—suspecting it was where Jimmy first started drinking—but it was one of those days when you first feel spring coming on. There were even a few crocuses in bloom. I picked one, imagining the delicate flower in one of Jools's drawings. Then I followed Henry. We walked until we came to a part of the stream that was still uncluttered by junk and sat down, him on one rock, me a few feet away on another. He tossed a pebble into the stream. "Okay, you want to tell me what's wrong?"

"Wrong?"

I didn't even know my mood had changed, much less that it was visible until he pressed me. "You've been different ever since we ran into Mike Sampson, outside school."

At that, the force of the secret I never let myself feel surged up inside me.

"Did you hear him? He was making fun of Jay Rodale, calling his brother a junkie because he got arrested last year." I crushed the crocus between my fingers. "My own mother . . ."

"You have a mom? I mean, I didn't know . . ."

"What did you think—I was dropped here from outer space? Yeah, I have a mother who actually gave birth to me. A sister, too. I mean, another sister."

He watched me like he was waiting for an explanation. As if I had one.

"She just—she couldn't take care of me is all. Cause of the dope and things. That's what the file says, anyway."

He was quiet awhile. "What about your dad?"

I peered into the water that was higher than usual. "Don't know much about him except that he's lighter than me. A white man, probably. And a fool. That's all she told me."

In the silence that followed, I felt myself growing hot. And small. Miniscule. Who did I think I was talking to—Jimmy? Did I really expect someone like Henry to understand files, and dope fiends, and fool fathers with no names? The kid lived in a brick house with a fancy iron fence to protect him from all of that.

On the way home, I turned up the radio to drown out the silence. "Ain't No Mountain High Enough" . . . my song and Zaidie's. Somehow hearing it always gave me courage.

Henry switched off the engine and stared through the windshield when we reached the house.

"Well, the guy can't be that foolish," he finally said—stopping me before I could escape. "I mean, you're his daughter, right?"

I looked at him, dumbstruck.

"And next time Mike talks like that, I'll deck him."

I laughed. "You?"

With his wrestling muscles and skill on the mat, Henry was strong enough to tackle Mike or most anyone else in the senior class, but I doubted he'd ever been in a fight in his life.

"OK, I'll tell him to stop, then. Stop, please." He grinned at me and it was like peering at myself in the Beautiful Mirror all over again.

Without thinking, I scooted across the seat and hugged him. Okay, it was impulsive. But it still might have been okay if I hadn't topped it off by telling him I loved him. Yup, just like I did as a kid when I used to go around blurting that out to everyone, from friends at school to the neighbors. Because I did. Or because they needed to hear it. But this was Henry Y. Lee I was talking to! Henry Y. Lee I had wrapped my arms around, like he was my brother or sister or the girls from my team after a victory.

Face flaming, I jumped out of the car as fast as I could. "I didn't mean . . . I . . ." I stammered.

"I know," Henry said. But by the confused way he was looking at me, the mixed-up way we were looking at each other, I wasn't sure either of us knew anything anymore.

"See you tomorrow," we both mumbled at the same time. I was in such a hurry to get away I dropped my geometry book on the driveway. I didn't go back to it till I heard his MG pull away.

So okay, I wasn't about to say that again—maybe not to anyone ever. But it didn't matter. The words were out. After that we stopped by Buskit's River every day on the way home, and every time we told each other more. Dumb stuff that didn't matter, but other things, too.

Even though I was tired from practice and homework, and every story I released into the air made me feel scared and ashamed, I didn't stop. No matter what I said, Henry kept walking, nodding, taking more of my life—more of me—into himself with every step.

After a while, he began to talk, too. "Sometimes all we can do is forget," I murmured, when he told me about what his family had gone through in China. Isn't that what Ma told me? But when I felt the river in my eyes, I knew that we might bury, but we never forget. Not really.

When I wondered aloud whether he'd told any of this to Caroline, he just shook his head and repeated what he'd said before. "You're different."

"YOU'RE COMING HOME awful late these days," Ma said one afternoon when I walked into the kitchen for a glass of juice.

"I'm training for a competition, Ma." I peered into the refrigerator so she wouldn't see my face. "Coach Lois is working me extra hard."

"Hmph."

She turned from the sink where she'd been washing dishes and dried her hands with a dish towel. Then, before I could get away, she removed her glasses.

"You're only fifteen, you know—and that boy—he seems to bounce from one girl to another. Isn't he going with Zaidie's friend? That's right. The Jewish girl."

As if she didn't know. "Jeepers, Ma. He's given me a few rides; it's not like—" I tried to say.

"And he's going away to college in Pennsylvania or somewhere soon anyway. He's toying with you is all."

"It's a few hours away, not the moon, Ma. Not everyone stays in the same town their whole life, you know."

"I just don't want to see you get hurt."

"I . . . I have no idea what you're talking about," I stammered, escaping for my room. But when I passed the mirror in the foyer, the truth was on my face.

THE NEXT DAY, more confused than ever, I was relieved to see the rain. This time there would be no chance for a walk. However, Henry quickly produced two umbrellas.

"Always plan ahead, that's my motto," he said, pulling up a street on the south side. Usually we went to Barkley's Woods or Buskit's, or one of the other wild places that still dotted the city. This was something new.

"You have a motto?"

"My dad says everyone does, whether they know it or not."

"I guess mine would be something like, 'See what happens and take it from there.' We couldn't be more opposite if we tried. Listen, I've been thinking—"

But before I finished, he got out of the car and stood on the sidewalk, holding out an umbrella.

"It's pouring, Henry. Where the heck are you taking me?"

He smiled mysteriously but didn't answer.

We were halfway up the street before he spoke again. "If that was really your motto, you never would have made honor roll this year. And you wouldn't be at the pool every day, week in, week out."

"True, I guess," I said. And then, a little while later, "I like the way you think about things before you say them. I never do that."

He grinned. "That's for sure."

He led me past the tailor shop his grandparents had once run. It was still called Lee's, though his grandmother was dead, and his grandfather spent his time tending a small garden behind Henry's house and reading Chinese newspapers.

"It used to embarrass my dad how hard they worked, even when they were old and they didn't have to. Especially my grandmother."

"Why'd they do it?"

He shrugged. "It was what they knew—and they were proud of it. Grammy used to brag she was the best seamstress in town."

By then we were standing in front of the building. "You want to know the worst thing I ever did?"

"No," I laughed. "Who do you think I am—Nonna's priest?"

"Don't joke. It's pretty bad."

He began to walk again, as if looking up at the shop was too painful. "It was my grandparents' anniversary, okay? A big one. Fortieth or fiftieth, I'm not sure, but anyway, we were having a party at my house. Grammy always took her shoes off at the door before she came into the house. Then she'd put on these little slippers she carried with her—even though my dad thought it was old-country. Anyway, that day, he sent my cousin and me out to clean up the neighbor's dog poop from the yard, and . . . I don't know how it happened, but someone dared me to scoop it into Grammy's shoe. By then there were a bunch of kids around and they were all laughing. Even my brother."

"So you did?"

"I thought I could clean it out before it was time for her to go, but us kids got involved in a game of hide-and-seek and . . ."

"I bet she gave you a good whaling," I said, imagining what Nonna would have done.

"I wish she had. Grammy was like you in a way. Up until that day,

I'd never once seen her shed a tear . . . I had just come in when she put her foot in the shoe."

I stopped short on the sidewalk. "And?"

"She froze. Then when all the kids looked in my direction and she realized it was me—her favorite sunzi—she started to cry . . . silently, though, the water pouring down her cheeks. If she yelled at me, even wept out loud, it would have been better, but she didn't make a single sound.

"All I wanted to do was make the kids laugh. I never thought how she would feel . . . or that I'd ruin her anniversary. A few months later she was dead."

"You're not blaming yourself for that, are you? Henry—"

"You don't understand. Grammy's life was nothing like mine. All she did was work. She hardly ever had a day to dress up in a silk dress, to stand there in candlelight, hear people toasting her."

By then the rain was coming down harder, lashing us in spite of the umbrellas. "So now that you know, do you still want to be—whatever we are?" he asked. Was I imagining it or did his color deepen?

It was how I had felt when I told him about the mother I hadn't seen since I was five, my fool father. Dropping my umbrella, I let the rain pelt me. "You have to ask?"

Then, despite all the times I'd promised to check myself, especially around Henry, I stepped under his umbrella and kissed him. At first, the boy who planned ahead clung as tightly to his umbrella as he'd clung to the future that had once seemed clear. Then he let go of everything, and kissed me back, both of us with our eyes wide open.

After we chased the tumbling umbrellas down the rainy street, we drove home with the Four Tops filling the MG and parked discreetly a block from the house to kiss one more time. *Bernadette, you're the soul of me . . .*

"Wait." He seized my arm when I was getting out of the car. "I . . . I just wanted to look at you one more time."

I laughed. "It's not like you won't see me tomorrow."

"Too far away."

As if it was a place, not a time.

I thought of how he'd told me I was different; and for just one minute, everything that had ever shamed me or made me feel set apart became beautiful. How had he done it? But all of that happened in another country with another flag. Before the night Mr. Dean followed me home and I ran into that telephone booth to call Jimmy.

Before the moment when my brother climbed out of the Falcon, holding his bat.

Before Zaidie began packing up her life, piece by piece, for California.

Before Ma opened the door, left the house, and told us the truth about the golden tree.

Before—it seemed like a hundred years before—I had the dream that would change my life. It was another dream about Mau Mau, but this time it was different. I was different. I couldn't hide from my sister's fate anymore.

I WAS GLAD that it was also before Henry had a chance to break up with Caroline. More than ever, I was aware of the towering mountain of hurt that stands in the center of this world. How could I, knowing what I knew, add another pebble to it? How could I risk being its next victim? Even a solid couple like Zaidie and Charlie had been broken apart by the tornado that hit our house that spring. Heck, Ma and Dad had nearly crumbled.

Henry must have seen the change in my face, because he didn't try to touch me when I got into the car. I was too distracted to turn the radio on so we drove in silence until I was nearly home. Finally, he switched on Stevie Wonder.

I reached for the dial. Silence. The last thing I needed was another seductive voice crooning to me about love.

Though Henry was a cautious driver, he veered to a stop so sharply that we ended up half on the sidewalk outside my house. In the past, I would have told him about Josie and the *maledizione*, but I had shared too much already. Besides, I figured, it was better if he didn't know.

"Okay, you wanna tell me what's going on? I thought we—"

"You shouldn't be giving me rides every day like this. It's not fair to Caroline."

"That's over. It's just . . . I've been making excuses when we were supposed to go out and I haven't even kissed her since . . . I have to talk to her, but it's tricky with all the senior stuff coming up and—"

Again, I stopped him. "No."

"What do you mean—no? Agnes—"

"It was a mistake, Henry. All of it—starting when my sister called and asked if you'd pick me up. From now on, if I need anyone to protect me—which I won't—I'll ask my family."

I reached for the door handle, but he stretched out his arm and held me in place, a kind of fury in his eyes. "A mistake? All the things we said to each other? The way we felt? And don't try to say it was just me—"

"Let me out of the car, Henry."

He released my arm, but held me even more forcefully with his eyes. "So you think I'm just gonna go away and forget it all? Is that what you want me to do?"

"Yes, that's what I want."

"See you tomorrow," he called after me before he gunned the engine and took off.

Somehow I managed to hold back the river until he was gone.

FOR THE NEXT two weeks, he was at the pool every day, even though I pretended not to see him. Then one day I looked up from the water, and the bench where he usually sat was vacant. The space outside where he parked the MG, too. I stood there a minute, looking at that empty spot, taking it into my bones the way Henry and I had taken in each other's stories.

So I did what I always did when I gazed into the contents of my treasure box too long and thought of all the vacancies in my life: I kept moving.

Walk faster; swim harder; don't turn around. It was what I'd been doing ever since the day I spilled the pennies on the road. The day the car drove away with my sister wailing inside it. For a long time it had worked, too, but not anymore.

Maybe I needed a new motto.

CHAPTER SIXTEEN

The Most Beautiful River I Never Saw

AGNES

AFTER I SAW WHAT HAPPENED TO MA WHEN SHE TOLD THE truth, I knew I could no longer hide from Mau Mau. I had to know what happened to her. What had caused Zaidie to hide her face from me when I asked? Was she really taken to an institution like Mr. Dean said?

Dad was dozing on the couch like always; Zaidie was upstairs studying and Ma was alone in the parlor, reading one of her *Reader's Digest* condensed novels. I pulled up the chair Jimmy used to use when he helped her with her puzzles and sat in front of her card table.

She kept reading.

I cleared my throat. "I think I'm coming down with something."

"Hmm." And a moment later: "Again, Agnes?"

After a quick appraising look, she returned to her book. To convince her—and myself—I made plenty of noise rattling around in the medicine chest and took to my bed early.

"The grippe's been going around school," I called from under my blankets the next morning when I heard her padding down the hall. "Zaidie already took my temperature."

On cue, Zaidie stepped out of the bathroom. "A hundred and one," she sang out.

One of the only lies I ever heard my sister tell.

Ma stood in my doorway. "Hmph. I just hope it's not like that cold you had earlier this year. The longer you stay home, the harder it gets, you know."

"For crying out loud, Ma, I have the grippe . . . I'm not like you." As soon as I said it, I felt like Henry after his grandmother put her foot into that shoe.

"I'm sorry," I murmured, but she was already gone.

AFTER EVERYONE ELSE left the house, I wrapped a blanket around myself and went down to sit in the living room. Ma brought me a glass of the dark ginger ale she always gave us when we were sick and switched on the TV. Even though I didn't exactly have a fever—or any other sickness I could name—the predictable rituals made me feel better.

In the morning, she usually made some motion to clean up or do the wash, but when we were home sick, she stopped the day to keep us company. She sat before her puzzle—that week it was a map of the world—while I sipped the peppery-tasting drink through a straw and watched her reassemble the continents, piece by piece.

"Remember that golden tree you told us about?" I said out of the blue. She set down her puzzle piece.

"Well, I saw something like that once. Only for me it was a river."

"A river?" The lines appeared between her eyes. "I hope you don't mean that dirty stream that runs by the Bousquet place."

"No, a great, powerful river. The kind they call mighty. Except I don't know where it is. Maybe I didn't even see it; I just heard about it."

She waited.

"Mrs. Jackson told me about it," I said, using the name they called my mother in the files. It was one of the only times I'd spoken about her to Ma and I was afraid she'd get up and walk away. She didn't. Nor did she set her face the way she used to when the subject of our "so-called parents" came up.

"It always bothered me that I don't even know what kind of Indian I am. How we ended up in Claxton. Nothing. She told me once when I was five, but I was so little I forgot." Mau Mau was older. She would have remembered, I thought, and once again the old grief washed over me.

"Apache or Cherokee," Ma said, listing the ones we knew from TV. "That's what I always say when busybodies like Gina Lollobrigida ask."

"It's neither of those, though. The only thing that stuck with me is the river part. That's what they call us up in Canada: People of the Beautiful River."

"People of the Beautiful River," Ma repeated slowly, tasting the words in her mouth. "Well, I'll be. From Canada, you say? And you never told anyone?"

It took a minute for me to answer. "Only Henry."

"Hmph. What did he have to say about it?"

"He said someday he'd like to go there and see that river. Those people. And then he took me by the tenement his Chinese grandparents used to live in when they first came here and told me how kids who worked in the factories used to shoot peas at them on their lunch break."

"Little bastards. Probably a couple of my ancestors among them, too."

"He said they never forgot how it stung . . . but that only made them more determined. Just like it did for me." I paused, almost seeing his face before me. "He understood, Ma. Like almost no one ever did, he understood."

"He's a smart boy, your Henry," she said, studying me the way she did. "You . . . care for him quite a lot, don't you?"

"Smartest I ever met," I replied, though his understanding was something bone-deep. It had nothing to do with intelligence.

I picked at the nubs on the couch, leaning into her question. "No one ever told me this could happen to me. You should have—"

"Hah. You think it's something anyone can warn you about?" Ma chuckled. "Good grief. You can't even describe it yourself—and you're in the thick of it."

I wondered if she was thinking of the boy in the pictures Zaidie and me had seen when we opened one of her boxes in the attic.

"Yes, even your old Ma remembers what it was like," she said, as if she heard the question I didn't ask. "And in case you're wondering, it was never Bobby Wood—though I thought so for a while."

I felt my face grow hot as she looked down at her puzzle.

"No, the only one in my whole life who ever made me feel that way was Louie Moscatelli. My all and my everything. It took me a while to realize it, though. And even then, it wasn't like it was for other people."

She hesitated like she had on the street when she told us about the golden tree, as if wondering whether I could handle it. Then she continued. "For the first few years, I couldn't stand for anyone to touch me. And course you know I didn't much leave the house. But your father married me anyway, married me and, eventually, I got used to . . . his touch and all.

"After the beating I took, though, I'd been damaged inside. I couldn't have kids like we wanted. But he stood by me. Even though his mother's church, his church back then, said he could have walked out once he knew what he'd gotten into. And I have to give your Nonna credit. Much as she wanted grandchildren, much as she believed all the stuff about a wife's duty, her love was bigger than that."

She picked up a piece of blue and fitted it into the ocean. "In the end, it turned out for the best."

"But you wanted—"

"If we'd been able to have our own, we would never have had all of you. Did I ever tell you about my theory about the migration of souls? Incredible thing, it is. Once you begin to see . . ."

She shrugged, seeming to change her mind. "Maybe another time."

Then she got up, went to the kitchen, and put on the kettle. After she'd fixed her instant coffee and brought me more ginger ale, she returned to her chair. "Where were we? Oh yes, we were talking about your Henry, weren't we?"

"Not my Henry, Ma. I haven't even talked to him since . . ."

"Well, you should. Before it's too late, Agnes." She looked me straight in the eye. "Go to your Henry now before he packs up and goes. And while you're at it, you should see if the department has a number for . . . for that Mrs. Jackson. I expect she'd be right proud to know her girl's swimming in the nationals."

"She hasn't bothered with me in years. Why should I—?"

"I expect she bothered about as much as she was able. Like we all do. And besides that, you're almost grown now. You don't have to sit here waiting anymore. You can go to her. But first—Henry."

I must have looked alarmed.

"Not today, of course. You wouldn't want to give anyone the grippe." She glanced at me slyly, a smile trapped just beneath the surface.

"I'm sure Henry's heard about the nationals. What am I supposed to say to him, Ma? I can't—"

"Good Lord, Agnes, just walk up the steps and knock on the door like Louie did. When he opens it, well . . . you'll know."

I planned to skip practice so I could visit Henry in the afternoon when his parents were out. *Feel like taking a walk?* I'd ask when he came to the door. Then the two of us would get in the car and head for Buskit's River. After that, well, everything would fall in place.

I even pictured how Henry would look when he saw me; how he'd fling the door wide and pull me inside before he went for his keys.

But as soon as I saw him, I knew it was all wrong. This was nothing like Dad, showing up with his stones. Though I'd tried not to add to the Great Mountain, I had obviously made things worse—not just for Caroline, but for all of us.

He cracked the door partway open. "Yeah?" Was this the boy who had promised he would never give up?

"I . . . I just thought you might want to know I'm going to the nationals. After all the rides you gave me, I wanted to tell you." As if everyone in the city hadn't seen it in the paper. I shifted from one foot to the other.

"Yeah, so I hear. Congratulations." He moved to close the door, but I put my hand on it—the way he had done that day I tried to get out of the car.

"I was going somewhere and I thought maybe . . . you could come with me?"

When I left the house, I didn't know I was going to the department, but something about being around Henry always made the muddy waters clear.

"Sorry, but I'm kinda busy . . . and I'm not the one you should be asking." Again, he attempted to close the door.

Then when I still refused to go away, he released his hand and sighed. "There's someone coming over." And when I still didn't budge: "A girl."

He closed the door.

I waited a full five minutes before I knocked again. It was another five before he opened up.

This time he was angry. "Listen, Agnes, I'm not sure why you're here, but you need to leave before—"

"You promised, though."

He gaped at me. "What?"

"You said you'd go to the river with me. You promised."

"That river you told me about . . . where your people came from? You're asking me to go to frigging Canada, Agnes? Now?" For the first time, he laughed.

"No, I'm asking you to walk across town to the Department of Social Services. I want to see if they have a number for my . . . mother. I have to find out what happened to her—and to . . ." Somehow I still couldn't say my sister's name out loud. I felt the water rising in my eyes.

He reached out to touch me, but then seemed to think the better of it. Instead he took a step back into the shadows of the house. "I hope you find them, and that . . . everything's okay."

Still, there was no mistaking the gentleness in his voice. Again, I fought tears. "Henry, I—"

He shook his head almost imperceptibly, but it was enough to stop me.

"Like I told you, someone's coming over and—and even if they weren't . . ." He paused, and for just a moment he looked at me the way he had the day he told me I was different, the day he made me feel the power of that.

"You don't need me to go with you, Agnes," he said. "You never did. This is between you and them."

I think I nodded at him before I turned to go, but the only thing I know for sure is that I didn't turn back. Not once. Not ever. Still, I felt him watching me as I left and for a long time after that, his face as clear and beautiful—if you can say that about a boy—as anything I'd ever seen.

WHEN I REACHED the white building where the Department of Social Services was housed, I almost went home. Was I really ready to hear a stranger tell me my mother was dead? Or that she hadn't called once in six years? I wasn't sure which was worse. As for my sister, I'd given up the idea of asking about her—at least, that day.

One piece of potentially devastating news at a time. With any luck, my new worker—Julie—wouldn't be in.

I was so distracted I almost collided with a woman in the hall outside the office. When I saw the familiar files poking from the top of her briefcase, I realized she was a social worker—though she didn't look like any of the ones I'd ever met. She was wrapped up in a bright colored caftan thing like someone's birthday gift. But it was the tiny silver elephants dangling from her earlobes that got my attention.

"My favorite animal," I said when I realized I'd been staring a minute too long.

"Most girls your age would choose horses. Or kittens." She touched one of the tiny animals pinned to her ear, almost as if she'd forgotten they were there. Then something flashed in her eyes. "Oh, my goodness. You're Agnes, aren't you?"

I stretched out my hand like Zaidie taught me to do. *Practice now so it will seem natural when it's time for your interviews*, she'd said, demonstrating the firm hand clasp. *And say both your first and your last like you're proud of it.*

"Agnes Juniper."

The woman with the elephants in her ears set down her briefcase, took my hand in her two, and said it with me in unison.

"You must be looking for me. I'm Julie Rocher." She consulted her watch before setting down her case and unwrapping herself from the caftan thing. Then she led me back inside.

"Priscilla, could you please call Mrs. Benedetto and tell her I'm running a little late? No, on second thought, I'm going to cancel. Tell her I'll give her a call in the morning."

"You don't have to do that. I can come back."

But Julie Rocher was having none of it. She led me into the office, where she immediately began to clear away several cups from her desk. "Forgive the mess. I'm one of those people who can't think without a cup of tea in her hand." She switched on an electric kettle. "Will you join me?"

"No, thanks." I looked around the room, taking in the posters of France, the small collection of elephants on her desk.

"Are you from France?" I asked, cocking my chin at a print depicting a French country scene.

"Not me, but my grandmother was and she painted such beautiful word pictures it became an obsession. Unfortunately, every time I plan a visit, something comes up."

She laughed, poured her tea, and settled herself behind her desk, indicating the seat opposite her. "Now I sit here and imagine. Sometimes that's even better; don't you think?"

Her eyes were pale with age, but they sparkled when she talked.

"Yes, sometimes," I said, remembering the river. Almost unconsciously, I picked up one of her elephants.

"Better than a puppy, huh?"

I glanced up at her. "After one dies, the other elephants return to the grave to mourn. They even cry."

It seemed like a perfect segue into my question about my mother. But before I could ask, she produced an article about my win at the state meet from the *Gazette*—laminated and everything.

"I hope you know we're awfully proud of you around here."

"It's not like the department had anything to do with it," I blurted out, angry that the ones who had sent me to Mr. Dean's, the ones who sent Mau Mau away in that car, were now taking credit for my victories.

She watched me calmly. "This is a hard job, Agnes. We see so much that goes wrong—and sometimes, yes, we even play a part in it. We need to be reminded that sometimes, even in the most challenging situations, things turn out right. Better than right."

She pointed to a framed picture of a yellow feather on the wall. Beneath it was a quote from Emily Dickinson written in a fancy script:

HOPE IS THE THING WITH FEATHERS

"Some days it's pretty hard to hold on to that little feather around here, but if we don't, we might as well close the office."

What about my brother? I thought, still nursing my grudge. *Do you have any laminated copies of the stories that were printed in the* Gazette *about him? And Mau Mau? Any poetic lines on the wall to describe her life?* But I held back—partly because deep down, I knew it was unfair. None of that was Julie Rocher's fault. Maybe it wasn't anyone's. It just was. And partly because her feather reminded me of something Zaidie would have hung on her wall.

I picked up the article she had preserved and for the third time in one stinking day, I felt my eyes filling up.

"Do you think my mother knows?"

Julie set down her teacup and without answering went to her cabinet. I felt my jaw tightening when she produced the manila file that contained every ugly thing that had ever happened to me. Did she have to drag that out?

She leafed through the pages to the end. "Last we heard, Mrs. Jackson and her husband were living in New Orleans. I believe the man's a musician, isn't he?"

"When was that?" I asked, refusing to look down at the typed forms or to admit how little I knew about my mother's life.

"She called . . . looks like it was about three years ago. Yes, three years ago in December. That's when we often hear from them," she mused, almost to herself. "Unfortunately that was before I transferred here so I didn't have a chance . . ." She flipped the page. "Oh, wait. It says she had a gift for you and wanted to make sure you were still at the same address. Did you receive anything?"

I shook my head—again feeling ashamed for all kinds of vague things. For those pages of misery and craziness that were supposed to be the story of my life. For the mother who only called once in three years and never made it to the post office with her gift. And most of all for myself, tricked into caring one more time. What a fool.

Apparently, I was more like my "father" than I thought.

"Nope, never came—which was probably a good thing. Everything she ever gave me was worthless. Once she even brought me a chicken bone and called it a present." I stood up so fast I knocked two of Julie's elephants onto their sides.

"She gave you that strong beautiful body, didn't she? The spirit I see in your eyes right now. Be careful what you call worthless, my dear." And then with the force of a revelation, she added, "You know something? I bet that wasn't the reason she asked for your address at all."

I looked at her blankly.

"I bet she just wanted to find out if you were still with the Moscatellis. So she'd know she didn't have to worry about you."

She hated the homes, I wanted to say. *And Ma hated her.* But before I could speak, I saw Ma sitting in her chair, urging me to find her. Now. Before it's too late.

"So she's—okay?" My voice was a whisper.

Julie closed the file and touched my hand. "I wish I could answer that question for you, Agnes."

I shook my head. "My mother—Ma—she figured the lady might want to know I'm swimming in the nationals. But since she hasn't called in three years—"

"I'm sure she'd be very proud," Julie interrupted. She picked up the shiny copy of the article that was still on her desk and looked at it as if seeing that mysterious feathery thing she talked about before. "I'm not sure if she's at the same address, but I'll put this in the mail for her on the way home. If there's any . . . follow-up, I'll let you know."

"I won't hold my breath." When I looked down, I noticed I was still clutching the little jade elephant I'd picked up when I first came in. I returned it to the desk.

"You can have that if you like."

"No, I . . . It looks expensive."

"I'm not even sure where I got it, but I doubt it's real jade. Please. It's my gift to you and I don't give away my elephants often."

"Thank you, but I'm not much of a collector." I hitched my pocketbook up onto my shoulder.

My hand was on the doorknob when I caught sight of my reflection in the glass and remembered the Agnes Henry saw. The one who was different. The one who was never afraid. When I spun around, the files were still open on the desk. "Do those records say anything about my sister?"

Julie gave me a long look before she returned to her seat and to the first page of the file. "Maud-Marie Juniper. Born April 18, 1951," she read.

"Yes. Where she is now? What happened to her? When I was little, Mr. Dean told me they put her in a . . . a place for retarded kids. Mrs. Dean said it, too. All these years . . . I was just . . . I was trying to survive myself. I didn't ask. But now—"

Julie looked down at the sheaf of papers. "Unfortunately, these are your files, Agnes. They make mention of her during the years you were together, but after that . . . it appears she was moved to another district."

"I know it says something."

She flipped through the pages, pausing to read some passages more carefully, skipping over others. Finally, she looked up.

"The foster mothers in your early homes made note of your good nature from the start. Your sister, on the other hand, was called . . . troubled. Difficult. It was one reason they had such a hard time finding a placement for the two of you. The caregivers made mention of fits, tantrums that grew more violent as time went on. According to their notes, she couldn't follow simple commands."

"They didn't know about that thing Ma read in her book—failure to thrive? It's what happens when no one ever talks to you or holds you. I didn't even learn to talk right till I came to the Moscatellis. How could they say—"

"Yes, there's mention of your growth problem and you were also labeled slow—obviously wrong. But the case of Maud-Marie—that was different. There were tests, visits to various doctors."

She closed the file. "I'm sorry, Agnes. I know it's not what you want to hear, and the Deans were certainly insensitive. After you were placed in their care, Maud-Marie was taken to St. Bridget's Home for the Mentally Disabled in the western part of the state." I wanted to shout that they were wrong—all of them, but as I sunk into my seat, a memory—fuzzy and long buried—surfaced. Mau Mau flailing wildly and screaming, whipping her head back and forth while I tried to comfort her. Maybe it was when we were leaving one home to go to another. Or when they took her somewhere without me. To one of those doctor visits perhaps.

There was another memory, too. Someone telling me that there was nothing we could do but forget. Though I could remember the sorrow in her voice, I still couldn't see who it was. Ma? One of those foster mothers who called me good-natured but slow? Or was it her—the one who had given birth to us?

Unconsciously, my hand closed around the little jade elephant. "If you don't mind, I think I'll take this after all."

If I had it in me to cry, I would have woke the whole city with my wailing, but I was the stoic one. Mau Mau had howled for both of us. I put my hand in my pocket, held on to my elephant as tight as I could, and walked straight home. No looking to the left or right, no looking back.

When I got to the house, I would put the elephant in the cigar box with my mother's presents and the stone I had retrieved from Jimmy's bureau the day he was sentenced, the one Ma gave him when he first went to high school. To me it was what Julie Rocher saw in her feather: the fragility of hope. And its strength.

As for the elephant, that was the promise I made to my sister. No matter if the whole world already forgot her, I wouldn't. Never.

CHAPTER SEVENTEEN

The Last Brave Thing I Ever Did

DAHLIA

BY THE TIME I VISITED JIMMY, THEY'D TRANSFERRED HIM UP TO Lovell—the same prison where Silas was sent. At the time, thinking of my tormenter in a cell must have brought some satisfaction. I don't remember much about those feelings, though, and walking through the doors, actually seeing those concrete walls . . . well, all that remained was the sorrow of it. And now, here was my Jimmy in the same place.

If I live to be a hundred and two, I'll never forget how I felt that moment the guard brought him in, my heart galloping off without me. Or how he stopped short at the sight of me.

"Ma? *Ma?*" His eyes veered sharply from me to Louie. "What the hell, Dad? You coulda at least . . . Shit. Ma?"

It wasn't what I expected. None of it. He sounded like he did when he first come home from the war, but it didn't take long before all that anger showed itself for what it was and he started bawling. He didn't even notice the fella to the right who had forgot his own visitors to laugh at him. The guard was saying something, too, but whatever it was, I couldn't hear anything but Jimmy. My son.

The girls had tried to warn me.

"HOLD ON TO her hand, Dad," Agnes told Lou the night before at supper. "Don't let go no matter what." *Just like they had done*, I thought.

Then Zaidie had wiped her mouth with her napkin. "He looks . . . different, too. It's hard to explain, but when you see . . ."

"I wish we could be with you, but they only allow two visitors at a time."

"You remember that picture of Joan of Arc I used to have on my wall?" Zaidie said. "Before I go through the door, I close my eyes and imagine I'm holding her shield in front of me."

"I never in a million years thought I could walk to the end of the street," I told them. "If I could do that—if I could sit you both down on that couch in there and tell you what I told you, well, then I suppose I could do just about anything."

"Joan of Arc's got nothing on Ma," Agnes said, but I saw the flicker of concern in her eyes. She reached under the table and squeezed my hand.

Still, the sight of him in that jumpsuit, his face . . . well, nothing could've prepared me for it. For a minute, I thought I just might drop right there like Josie had. Or worse, let loose with every last tear I'd ever held back in my life.

But for Jimmy's sake, I had to keep standing. I held on to Louie's hand just like the girls told me, and imagined—not St. Joan and her shield—but them at my side the way they were when we walked deep into those places I thought I could never go. So close their shoulders were touching mine. By then, my face was wet, but I didn't feel it until Louie reached into his pocket and handed me one of his hankies. Somehow the familiar scent of grease anchored me.

"What? When did you—how? Shit, Ma, is this one of those mirages?" Jimmy said before looking back to Louie. "Is she really here, Dad?"

Louie grunted—as if to say more might make him as emotional as Jimmy and me. "Yes, Jimmy," I answered, my voice steadier than I believed possible. "I'm here."

After we took our seats, him on one side of the plexiglass, us on the other, I told him how the girls had led me house by house back to my life, listing all the places I'd been. Jimmy kind of closed his eyes like he was traveling with me: the bank over on Westerly. The five-and-dime. And on the way home, a stop at the N. P.

"Joe Junior writes to me every damn day. I can't believe he never said—"

"Your Ma made him promise," Louie put in. "She wanted to surprise you."

"Surprise? Jeez, you almost gave me a heart attack. And the way I started blubberin' like a girl? I'll be catching crap about that for weeks."

"Junior's got a new routine these days," I went on. "Soon as he sees me, he steps out onto the sidewalk and makes an announcement, even though there's usually no one there to hear it. 'Mrs. Moscatelli's here! Right here at the Nothing's Perfect Market and Deli! Jimmy's Ma!' Between him and Jools, you'd think the queen had just dropped into the store.

"Nonna even dragged me to Junie Sweet's one day and made me sit on a stool and order a cup of coffee. Course, with all the people gawking, and those tin-plated walls pressing in on me, my hands shook so bad I couldn't drink it. The place hasn't changed since I was in high school."

"But you stayed?"

"You think Nonna would let me leave?" I launched into the impression I'd perfected over the years. "'Leesen, Dah-li-a, no one looking at-a you, and iff-a they do? I speet on them. You hear me? I speet on every last-a one.' Then she looked around, just daring someone to try it."

Jimmy laughed. "Pray like crazy and don't take shit from no one. That's my Nonna."

"So I suppose you heard about Agnes swimming in the nationals?" Louie asked after we all had a good chuckle.

"Have I heard? Damn, Dad, everyone in this godforsaken place knows about that. And they're all rootin' for her, too." He turned to the guard in the corner. "Or else. Right, Roly?"

"That's for sure," the guard said, briefly dropping his stern demeanor. "And we all know about the sister accepted to all those fancy colleges, too—unless he's putting us on. Z, right?"

"Tell him, Ma." Jimmy crossed his arms in front of his chest. "Smartest girl in the damn state, our Z."

"About to be the smartest in California, too," Louie added. Almost in unison, we wagged our heads at the wonder of it.

"You never know, Ma. I might go to college myself someday just like you wanted," Jimmy said. "Did Z tell you I'm studying for my diploma? Got me a real nice teacher name of Joan. Lady believes in everyone so much we can't fail if we try."

But then, a moment later, his face darkened. "I don't suppose either of yous have seen Jane around?"

I gave a quick glance at Lou. We'd heard she quit her job at Rusty's Hideaway, and there were rumors she'd returned to college, but we weren't about to tell Jimmy any of that.

"She hasn't been up?" I lifted my eyebrows, innocent as I could.

"Since I got here, my letters been coming back 'address unknown' just like the friggin' song." He slumped in his seat. "Probably for the best. Girl deserves the whole world like I always told you."

I waited for Louie to speak up and say what he normally did when someone hurt one of his own: *Well, the hell with her, then.* But when he looked down at his hands, I rushed in to cover his silence.

"The right one will come along, Jim. Just wait."

"In six years? Heck, Ma, I'll be too old to care." Then, seeing our stricken faces, he said, "Heck, I'm just teasing you guys."

He turned to the guard. "With all my good behavior, I'll be makin' parole in no time. Right, Roly?"

Roly made a sound that reminded me of Louie's grunts. A few minutes later, he reminded us that our time was up.

"Do ya think you might come back?" he asked, looking straight at me. "This ain't like a one-shot deal?"

"We'll be here, Jim. Every visiting day."

Yes, he was different, like the girls warned me—bulked up, cocking his chin—as if he had a new awareness of what life was, as if at every moment one had to be prepared to fight. But I also saw the little boy I'd sent out with a lunch pail on the first day of school.

He had started out of the room, when all of a sudden he asked Roly to wait, there was one more thing he needed to ask. He stood there for a long minute, unable to get it out. Again he teared up.

Finally, the guard took his arm. "Okay, Kovacs."

He shook him off. "So you did all that so you could come here? Leavin' the house, walkin' all over the damn town. You did it—for me, Ma?"

The question stopped me where I was, and it must have stopped the guard, too. He let him go.

"I did it for myself, Jim," I finally said. "And because it was time."

It was true, of course. But Jimmy was also right. The only thing he'd gotten wrong was the preposition. It wasn't for, it was because. What we felt the day he came to us—the overwhelming love—it had opened us up to the whole world; to all the other kids who came after him. Though we didn't know it that afternoon in the yard, right there in the dazzling sun, Jimmy Kovacs had become our because.

WITH TRAFFIC, IT was a two-hour ride home. There was nothing to fill it but the blaring of Louie's horn. A couple of times he rolled down the window to yell, "Learn to drive, will ya?"

But no matter where we looked, whether it was the white line of the highway or the trees flying by like the brief minute that is our lives, we saw Jimmy's face. And we saw the place where we left him. For once, I wished Louie had a radio in the car.

About an hour into our silent trip, something must have built up in him, too, though.

He cleared his throat.

"You want to know when I first decided I was going to marry you?"

I looked at him sideways. "Funny time to bring that up, isn't it?" But after another stretch of mind-numbing quiet, I said, "You told me you noticed me in the high school auditorium when I was giving a speech."

"Long before that, Dahlia. We were probably in sixth grade and you were wearing a blue dress with a lace collar."

I touched my throat, remembering a dress my grandmother had made for my birthday. Too fancy for school, my mother said, but I loved that dress so much I wore it anyway.

"That was the day I noticed you. The day I set my mind on you— well, that happened much later."

I removed my glasses and looked at him as if I'd never seen him before. "Do tell." Louie paused to curse an old man dawdling in the passing lane before he went on.

"It was the morning you got up there and testified against Silas Wood. I remember the dress you had on that time, too. A dark green. Very plain, but nice just the same."

I'd never spoken about that day. Never even allowed myself to think of it. And now Lou had me feeling the scratchy tag inside the neck of that new green dress? My mother's tension when she flung the bag from Hanley's onto my bed—I felt that, too. *You'll need something decent to wear.*

After the afternoon we'd had, it was about the last thing I wanted to talk about. He probably would have dropped the subject, too—if I just stayed quiet. But somehow I couldn't keep my peace.

"You were there, Lou? Good Lord, in all these years, you never told me . . ."

His eyes remained fixed on the road. "The whole town was against you. I figured you needed at least one person on your side."

I closed my eyes, seeing that packed gallery, the sea of Woods and their allies. My mother and father were seated behind my lawyer, their faces contorted with shame when I desperately needed to see faith. But him—the man who would become the most important person in my life, the one who had always been on my side—he was still invisible to me.

"No, you didn't see me, but I saw you, all right. Flesh, bone, and spirit, I saw you," Louie said, as if he was privy to my thoughts. "Took a helluva lot of guts to get up there and tell that story. Straight through without breaking, you told it—even when his lawyer came at you the way he did. Well, that's when I knew."

"It was the last brave thing I ever did, Lou, and if I had any idea how it would turn out, most likely I wouldn't've done it at all. So if that's why you married me, you were duped."

"Yes, you would have," he said, like he knew me better than I knew myself.

"I was so young, Lou—a kid who thought courtrooms were where the guilty got punished and the innocent were set free. Hah."

"But Silas was punished."

"Not long. The conviction was overturned on appeal in less than a year. No, he never had to pay like I did. Or Bobby . . ." I gazed out the window, remembering everything I'd tried to bury. "Those days I was in the woods, when everyone was sure I was dead, they changed him."

It was then that he'd written the first letter, hand-delivering it to our mailbox.

When I got out of the hospital, it was lying there on my bed— the only one I ever read. Course he blamed himself—just like I did for a while. Questioned everything from my ambitions to the audacity it took to say no to a Wood to my foolishness getting into the car that day.

I was so deep in memory Louie's voice, when he spoke, startled me. "That was when Bobby enlisted, wasn't it?"

"All the boys were signing up, but Bobby wouldn't be eighteen till October, and he was supposed to go to college in the fall. Another thing the family cursed me for. The enlistment and . . . everything that followed."

I could still see the screaming headline in the newspaper my mother dropped on the table that day:

MAYOR WOOD'S SON KILLED IN ACTION

Even in death, his father's identity came before his own.

Again, my mind returned to that dining room the first time he brought me home. I no longer saw the elegant settings or the blindingly white smiles, but the dark weave of emotions beneath it all.

"AND HIS BEST friend there. What was his name? He paid a price, too. From what I remember, his old man lost his job—just because the boy told the truth."

"Phil Gregory." After all these years, I still said his name like it was something holy. "If anyone was brave in that courtroom, it was Phil. Can you remember the noise that broke out when the prosecutor called him to the stand?"

"What I remember was how straight he stood when he marched in, and how loud he spoke up. As if the whole courtroom was deaf."

I nodded. "Most of them still are. But on that day, like it or not, they were forced to open their ears and hear. All of us were."

"You know what else I remember? I remember his father, nodding after every word, even though he had to know it would cost them. Him and his mother both."

Again, something clenched up inside me. Oh yes, I remembered. It was what I'd wanted from my own family, but hadn't gotten.

"I suppose that was where he got it—character—or whatever you want to call it. All I know is if it hadn't been for Phil, there was no way in hell he would have been convicted. Not a Wood."

"After his testimony, what choice did they have?"

We both fell quiet as we thought of the story Phil had told so loudly it filled the car twenty-eight years later. He described how a desperate Bobby had come to him a couple of hours before Silas picked me up in the car. Come to him and told him he'd overheard his brother planning something with his cousin and some kids from Boston. Something that was to happen that very day. He even knew the money those boys had been paid.

Fifty bucks apiece. Something about that detail shook me as much as anything else he said.

"And how did you respond?" the prosecutor asked Phil.

"I asked him why he was wasting time telling me. He needed to find Dahlia right away. Warn her."

"What did Mr. Wood say to that?"

"He said he was afraid she'd go to the police. The chief was a friend of his father's opponent in the upcoming race. If he did it— well, he'd be disowned. Or worse."

"Worse?" the prosecutor prodded.

"'They might hire someone to come after me the same way,' Bobby said. Breaking family loyalty was considered the worst thing a Wood could do."

By then the defense attorney was yelling hearsay.

Sustained.

Though it couldn't be stricken from the jurors' minds, Silas Wood still might have walked if that was all Phil had to say.

"Can you please tell the court what you did after Mr. Wood left you?"

"I tried to warn Dahlia myself. But when I called, her mother just accused me of stirring things up. Said they had enough trouble with the Woods already. If I could have explained, I know she would've listened. I mean, she's a mother; she had to. But she slammed the phone down before I got a chance and refused to pick it up again.

"So I tried Murph—Margaret Murphy's house. Dahlia's best friend. The sister who answered must have thought I was calling on Bobby's behalf. Murph wasn't home, she told me, and she hadn't seen Dahlia in a week. Then she hung up on me, too. That's when I remembered the restaurant where Dahlia worked. If I'd had a car like Bobby, I would have made it in time, but by the time I got there, she had just left."

By then, the defense attorney was on his feet once again, asking to approach the bar. "Where is this going? The witness obviously saw nothing."

"We're getting to that, Your Honor," the prosecutor insisted. "Where did you search for Miss Garrison next?" he asked when he was allowed to continue.

"Well, I had a hunch she might be headed for the Murphys' house over on Cushing Street—her and Murph were pretty much inseparable, and there was something I heard in her sister's voice. I knew she was lying when she said Murph wasn't home."

"And was your hunch correct?"

Phil nodded. "She was a couple of blocks away when I spotted her. I called her name, but like the rest of them, she must have thought Bobby sent me. She walked faster. Even though I was pretty tired, I still would've caught her. But just about then, I saw the car stop . . ."

"And did you recognize the vehicle?"

"Yes. All the kids at school were jealous of that blue Chevy."

"And did you know who owned it?"

"It belonged to Silas Wood."

At that, the courtroom gasped. The judge again sounded the gavel.

"After Dahlia got in, I chased them as far as I could till they made the turn for the highway. Then I—I didn't know what to do so I called the police."

"Were they of any help?"

He gave a terse shake of the head. "'We're not in the habit of arresting people because of what they might do. They gotta actually do something, son.' And when I mentioned Silas's name, he actually laughed at me. 'The mayor's boy? Is this a prank?'"

At that point, Phil had forgotten the rules. He looked directly at me.

"I'm sorry, Dahlia. I would've kept going. I would've found someone with a car, even if I had to go to my dad. I would've kept looking, but I had no idea where they were taking you." His eyes glittered with tears. "I just didn't know what to do."

Thank you, I mouthed to him.

I think there was another objection then, but it didn't matter. That moment, more than anything, the sheen in Phil's eyes, the words I could only breathe, had convicted Silas and everyone knew it.

RUMBLING ALONG IN the car these many years later, I closed my eyes and let out a long sigh.

From the start, I'd known I couldn't go back to the girl I was, but I still believed some kind of justice could come out of it. And I had no idea how dearly my family would pay for bringing down the Woods. How much it would cost me.

It was too late to head off to nursing school that year like I'd planned, but I thought I could leave town and forget. Maybe we all could—like Phil and his family eventually did. But the hospital bills wiped my parents out, and after everyone boycotted the restaurant, there'd been nothing to start over with. It broke my father, turned my mother meaner than ever.

But it was the hate that got to me more than anything. The force of it. It felt like something physical, like those kicks I took in the woods, the blows that killed the babies we never had. It murdered something in me, too.

As if he read my mind, Louie reached over and covered my hand with his own. Just the way he'd been doing for twenty-eight years.

"To be honest," I said, "if you hadn't started leaving those rocks on the porch, I wouldn't be sitting here."

"Most likely you'd be riding in some Cadillac with a doctor or a lawyer; that's where you'd be. Smart and pretty as you were—"

"No, listen to me, Lou. I'm telling you about the day you called me out of the darkest woods."

In the mirror, I caught sight of his eyes.

"When I got out of the hospital, Doc Magee sent me home with sleeping pills, and something else for my nerves. They helped for a while, but after the trial, after all the threatening calls, the stones thrown through the windows of the house and the restaurant, the way people looked at me whenever I went outside— There's nothing ugly as hate, Louie, though you don't know till you experience it yourself. And once that arrow burrows deep enough, there's no getting it out. No running away from it, either.

"There seemed like only one way out. Every night when my mother gave those pills to me, I stashed them in my jewelry box instead of taking them . . . I'd just about saved enough when you walked up those steps and knocked on the door."

CHAPTER EIGHTEEN

The Flutter

ZAIDIE

As Ma ventured further into the world she had once disowned and Agnes spent more time at the pool, I became the one who stayed home. There was still school and my part-time job at Hanley's, but otherwise, I lived in the walls of the gray house on Sanderson Street. I lived in three suitcases that were lined up, small to large, in the corner of my room. I lived at the top of the treacherous flight of stairs that led to the attic. And most of all, I lived in the typewriter on the old desk Jimmy had given me.

Flufferbell had taken to following me around the way she had once trailed after Ma. She regarded me suspiciously whenever I added another item to my suitcases, meowed in protest if I went to the closet for my shoes, and howled every time I crossed the *maledizione*. Soon I would leave her for good and we both knew it. With no money for a plane ticket to come home on holidays, I might not be back for a year. Maybe longer.

Sometimes I felt as lost as I'd been the day I came.

Alone in the attic, I filled journals and typed out long letters to my brothers—some of which I mailed—others too filled with unanswerable questions to foist on anyone.

When those questions got too big to fit into a notebook or an envelope, I turned to fiction.

I called my first story *Betrayal*. Wasn't that my inheritance—the weight I couldn't set down or leave behind no matter how I tried? Just like Jimmy carried his parents' alcoholism and Agnes her abandonment, my father's repeated treacheries—and the secret fear I might be like him—trailed me wherever I went. Alone in the attic, I gave them to "Colleen," a character named after a dark-haired model in *Seventeen*. But without my permission, Colleen's life, my life, refused to be about any of that. Somehow, it kept turning into a Love Story.

The only question was when it began. Was it the day Ma opened the door to Jon and me, first hesitantly, and then wide? Or before that, when I, at five years old, had risen from bed at three in the morning to comfort my screaming baby brother, my mother instructing me on how to prepare formula from her sickbed? Writing about them, I was keenly aware of how much I missed them. But more than that, I was overwhelmed with gratitude that I'd had them while I did.

And then I was pulled back further, back to New Jersey when Sylvie and Michael Finn and I had lived together as a family. I must have typed a hundred pages before I realized that no one ever knows for sure where and when the spark ignited their Love Story. Or why. Or where it's heading. We can only pick up the thread where we are and continue. Best we can. Day after day. I kept typing.

Between the clanging of the rickety fan I had dragged up to the attic after Flufferbell clawed a hole in the window screen and the transistor radio that kept me company and the tap of my typewriter keys, I didn't hear the banging at the door, even though it was coming from a girl who knew how to use her fists.

Apparently, she was aware of where I spent my days because she pinged my window with a rock. Thrown one bit harder, she might have shattered it. When I switched off the radio, I heard her yelling, "What the hell, Z? You gonna come down and open the friggin' door or what? I been banging for a half hour."

Even if I hadn't recognized the voice, I would have known who it was. Not only had she appropriated Jimmy's nickname for me, Jane had even mastered his syntax.

She plowed in, dropping a large duffel bag in the foyer with a thump as soon as I opened the door.

"Holy hell, what's in that thing?" I asked. We seemed to have dispensed with stuff like hello.

"What does it look like? Everything I own."

Then, before I could ask what it—and more importantly she— was doing in our foyer with everything she owned, Jane Miller, tough- est girl I knew, sank down onto her bag and began to cry. I looked wistfully in the direction of Ma's headquarters, momentarily wishing I'd never encouraged her to go out. At least she would have known what to do.

"It's like ninety degrees out there, Jane. Can I get you some- thing to—"

She blew her nose angrily. "A beer would hit the spot. And what the hell are you looking at? You never seen a chick cry before?"

By the time I'd poured her a lemonade, she had moved into the parlor and was sitting in the hole on the couch. The duffel bag rested in the middle of the floor like a large, feral animal. I almost tripped on it.

After she downed her drink, she held out the glass for a refill. "I just hitchhiked from somewheres north of Boston. And I had to walk from Main Street, where the trucker let me out. A good mile and a half." She cocked her head at the duffel bag. "That thing's heavy as a mother."

"You hitchhiked? From where? And why didn't . . . your parents pick you up?"

"If I had to drag that thing across the Sahara I wouldn't call them. Are you gonna get me some more lemonade or what?"

I started for the kitchen.

"And while you're in there, think you can fix me something to eat?" she called after me. "I was so nerved up this morning I couldn't even think of breakfast."

"My mother should be back in a little while." I scanned the street hopefully as I set a ham sandwich on the coffee table.

"Not unless the movie's a bomb, she won't."

"The movie?"

"When I passed the Colonial, I saw your ma and that crazy kid that used to work with Jimmy buying tickets to the matinee."

I'd forgotten. A week ago, Ma had gone to the movies with Joe Jr. on his day off like Jimmy sometimes did. Another new frontier for her, and she'd only had to breathe into the paper bag she carried once, she bragged.

The movie was okay, but that popcorn, my goodness, Louie, it was out of this world, she said at supper. *Everything's a damn wonder to you these days, ain't it, Dahlia?* he grumbled.

"He's not crazy," I said to Jane. "He's just . . . he's Joe Jr. is who he is."

"Now you sound like that asshole Jimmy. Anyways, I only came here cause I wanted to talk to you and I knew your ma and Agnes would be out."

I looked at her nervously. "Me?"

"If anyone can understand my predicament, it's you, Z."

Though I still wasn't sure what she was driving at, my mind flashed uncomfortably on the talk we'd had in the alley outside Rusty's Hideaway and that fateful little packet she'd handed me.

My eyes must have been round as soup plates. "Predicament?"

She stood up and open her arms. "Notice anything different?"

Poking out from her baggy clothes, her arms were as skinny as ever, but wiry with strength. Different? Her face was more angular, and in spite of her tears in the hallway, there was a new flintiness in her eyes.

"You cut your hair?" I asked weakly.

At that, she lifted up her shirt, revealing the hard round lump beneath it. "Most of the girls at the house are twice as big at five months. I carry small."

Girls? The house? Five months? I didn't know what to ask first. And why was she still holding her shirt up? Was she proud of that mortifying sight? Or did she just want to force me to look at it, the way she had pressed the Trojan on me in the alley?

"I made brownies yesterday," I finally said. "You want one?"

"Two. And a big glass of milk. We're supposed to drink—"

"So I've heard." Though she'd finally dropped her shirt, it was like she was still forcing me to see. Still making me hear those words: five months.

Meanwhile, where was Ma? Sitting at the Colonial, a bucket of the most amazing popcorn ever in her hands, entranced by some dumb movie. I practically ran for the kitchen.

When I emerged with a plate of brownies (adding a few Lorna Doones since she was eating for two), I found Jane leaning back on the couch. Her eyes were closed as if, weary from her adventure, she'd drifted off to sleep, the traitorous Flufferbell curled up on her lap. Now that she'd dumped her horrible story on me, she was smiling as serenely as the Madonna.

I cleared my throat and thumped the plate on the table in front of her as loudly as I could, but what woke her was the sound of the front door flapping open.

"Ma!" Agnes sang out. "I made my best time in the butterfly!"

"Ma's at the movies," Jane answered, blinking awake.

So now she was calling my mother Ma. She seemed to think she'd taken control of the house, too.

"Get yourself a glass of milk," she told Agnes. "I might as well tell yas both at the same time."

Agnes took a quick look at the ominous, giant duffel, dropped her swim bag beside it, and obeyed.

Of course, Jane couldn't resist pulling up her shirt and giving

Agnes a taste of the shock I got. It seemed like the thing had grown since she sprang it on me.

Agnes turned about as pale as a brown-skinned person can. "Shit. Sorry. I mean—congratulations?" she stammered. "When did you find out?"

"I started to have my suspicions right around the time your asshole brother decided to go out and beat the crap out of that guy. Now you know why I was so pissed." Her eyes flashed. "I couldn't friggin' believe it. I mean, we used a safe every time . . . Well, all but that night we were out late walking in the graveyard."

"The graveyard?" By then, Agnes looked as if she was the one with morning sickness.

"When the spirit hits, it hits, honey. Anyway, the dead don't mind; that's what Jimmy said." She almost smiled before she remembered how pissed she was. "My mother figured it out before I did. She came home with one of those tests."

"Does Jimmy know?"

"Why would I tell that asshole?" Jane said, but again I saw a watery glimmer in her eyes. "After the shit he pulled, he wouldn't see the kid till he was six—even if I was allowed to keep it."

Suddenly, it all made sense. "You said you were staying at an, um, a house?"

"Same place I went last time." Agnes moved in closer and I went for the paper towels, because by then, Jane was crying so hard Kleenex weren't going to cut it.

"At first, I refused. I'm twenty-one now so it's not like they could make me. And you know, I almost had my mom on my side, but between the first pregnancy and then my job at the Hideaway, and most of all Jimmy, my stepdad had already about had it with me.

"'Once was a mistake,' he yelled at my mom, making sure the whole house heard him. 'But twice? That's a pattern.' Even I couldn't deny he had a point.

"He started following me and my mom around the house, asking how I thought I would support a child on my waitress money. And where I planned to live. 'Not at this house, with my daughters,' he bellowed, making it clear I'd never been one—even in the beginning when he pretended. 'I can't have that here. I won't, Iris.'" Jane unfurled a few more towels from the roll and mopped her eyes.

"What could Mom say? She's been giving in for nineteen years. At this point, it's the only thing she knows how to do—and besides, deep down she knows everything in that house is his. Everything but me, that is. So one night she comes into my room. 'We can't be selfish, Janie,' she says. 'Think of what's best for the baby. And once it's all over, you'll still have your whole future ahead of you.' Same shit I heard the last time. The only difference was that this time my stepdad had agreed to pay my tuition if I wanted to go back to school. Once again, I saw my shiny ticket . . ."

She paused for another raucous blow of her nose. "That's not why I agreed, though."

Agnes and I stared at her.

"I did it because I wanted to get back at Jimmy for ruining everything when I needed him most. Someday I'd write him a letter and tell him I'd given his son away just like his mom and dad had done to him. The way I felt having to do this all over again? He'd feel it double." Staring at the floor, she nodded her head. "Yeah, that's what I thought."

My eyes pivoted, almost involuntarily, toward the duffel bag. "But then you changed your mind?"

"It was last night. I was in my room with the bitch of a roommate they give me. Anyways, I had just started to fall off to sleep when I feel this . . . this flutter. Course, I knew what it was, from . . . before. But I don't know, all a sudden it was like Jimmy was with me. Like he hadn't done what he done, hadn't been sent where he was sent. Nope. He was right there with me."

She paused, unconsciously putting a hand on her belly, as if she was back in that room. Just her and the flutter. "You know what he used to do sometimes?"

My sister and I shook our heads in unison, afraid she was going to tell us more about the graveyard. I was even more scared when she got up, closed her eyes, and took my face in her hands.

"This," she said, with the kind of solemnity Nonna talked about her Communion.

After a minute, she released me and returned to the hole. "Yeah. He'd put his two hands on my face and hold it like it was the most precious thing in the world. Then he'd tell me how friggin' beautiful I was. Me. Jane Miller. And you wanna know the crazy thing? He meant it. No one ever did that before, and let's face it—with the mug on me? It ain't gonna happen again.

"Anyways, I was so rattled up, I went and told my roommate about the flutter—and about Jimmy. Well, everything. 'This baby might be all I have left of him,' I told her. How could I give him away? But what else could I do? Where the hell would I go?"

"You mean the bitch? That's who you told?" Agnes asked. "What did she say?"

"Nothin'. Not a single damn word." Jane's eyes drifted to the duffel and ours followed. "She just dragged that out of the closet and helped me pack, the both of us bawlin' like idiots."

For a full five minutes, we sat there in stunned silence, our eyes fixed on the giant bag that almost seemed to be breathing in the middle of our parlor. No matter what we thought, how could we argue with the flutter?

"You said he," Agnes finally said. "What makes you so sure it's a boy?"

Jane looked at her with the same weary expression she'd given me that day in the alley when she taught me about Trojans. "It's what they call maternal instinct, honey. When you're older—a lot older if you know what's good for you—you'll find out."

"But there's one more thing I still don't understand," I interrupted. "Why'd you come here? You know Jimmy's not coming home in . . . a long time, and even if he was, you said you don't want him to know."

"It had nothing to do with that ass—" she began, but when Agnes and I winced, she spared us. "The only reason I came was . . ." She picked at her nails for a minute, as if considering the answer. Or as if she really didn't know. "Well, where else?" She finally shrugged. "Isn't this the place you go when you ain't got nowhere's else?"

Not knowing how to respond, we turned to the brownies and finished the whole plate, even though we were already full. Then Agnes and I got up and dragged the duffel bag up to Jimmy's room.

We were coming down the stairs when Ma pushed the front door open, all riled up over this new actor—Dustin Hoffman—and the movie she'd seen. "The best movie of all time," she said.

"Almost as good as the popcorn," Agnes whispered to me, and then we both giggled. The theater was more crowded than usual, so Ma had to use her paper bag twice, but after a while, she'd gotten so lost in Mrs. Robinson that she forgot the people around her. "And Joe Jr. only shouted out once in the whole two hours," she added proudly.

At that point, though, she must have caught something on our faces because she stopped where she was. "Everything all right around here?"

"You were only gone a couple hours, Ma. What could go wrong?" Agnes said. When Ma went to hang up her pocketbook on a hook, my sister caught my eye.

Agnes headed for the parlor first, and then I led Ma in.

"Look who stopped by," I said, like I was as surprised as she was to see Jane nesting in the center of the couch.

I was scared of how she might react. After their visit with Jimmy, she and Dad had a few harsh words for the girl who had broken his heart.

"We knew you wouldn't mind so we invited her to stay for supper," Agnes said.

"Hmph." Ma looked from my sister to me and back. Without so much as a greeting for the pregnant girl, she headed toward the kitchen.

Jane looked like she might need the paper towels again, so Agnes went and sat beside her. "Give her time," she said, taking Jane's long bony hand. "It took her a while before she knew I was supposed to be here, too."

And sure enough, after she reminded me it was my turn to set the table, Ma called from the kitchen. "If that . . . girl's staying, you better set her a plate."

CHAPTER NINETEEN

A Jade Elephant

AGNES

IT WAS JUST PAST FOUR A.M. WHEN I WENT TO THE CLOSET AND DUG out my treasure box. In the light of my room, the elephant was more a drab green than the vibrant jade I imagined in the fluorescent lighting at social services. More than anything, I wished I had never gone there that day, wished I'd never seen the collection on Julie's desk or the feather on her wall.

Sometimes all we can do is forget.

For so long, I couldn't remember who had told me that, but now I saw Ma's face hovering over me after I woke from another dream about my sister back when I first came.

It's the move, she said to Dad when he padded into the room. *A lot of times, it brings it all back. But don't worry. She'll settle down when she's been here awhile, won't you, Agnes?* Were those the exact words she said? I can't be sure, but the touch of her hand on my cheek, the tenderness she held back in the daytime, that was indelible.

BY THE TIME I went to see Julie, I'd already forgotten almost every-thing. I'd held tight to who my sister was for me—Mau Mau—and lost Maud-Marie. But after the case worker read from my records, I could no longer keep it back. Now, if I dreamed about her, I didn't see the girl in the waves at the beach or the one beside me in the car, our four legs striped by the same sun; I saw Maud-Marie thrashing wildly, shrieking, and in the background someone else—me—crying like I'd never done before or since. Crying because there was nothing I could do to help her. Nothing we could do to help each other. Was that when I had become the kid they described in the files, the one who moved from house to house, misery to misery, as if nothing could touch her?

I put on my clothes, determined to walk to Buskit's River and chuck Julie Rocher's elephant as far as I could the way Zaidie had done with Henry's tie tack after Jon left.

Zaidie rubbed at her eyes when I climbed into bed beside her. "What—Agnes? Don't you think you're a little old for . . ." But then she scooted over toward the wall. Though she had pulled the shades tight to keep out the early-morning light, I could sense her folding her hands behind her head, staring upward, the way she did when she was pondering something.

"Boy trouble?"

"I wish. That would be a lot easier." I found her hand in the dark and placed the elephant inside her palm. She fingered it like it was braille.

"Okay, I give. What is it?"

"Just hold on to it."

As she turned the elephant over and over in her hand, I told her about my meeting with Julie Rocher. About the file and the shifting labels they'd given Maud-Marie.

Before they settled on mentally retarded, they'd called her bipolar. Possibly schizophrenic. When Zaidie reached for my hand, the tiny elephant cut into my skin.

"Why didn't you tell me, Zaidie? All those years ago, when you read the file, why didn't you—"

It was a long time before she spoke into the dark. "Tell me something you remember about her," she said. "It doesn't have to be anything she did or even a specific memory. Just the first thing that comes to mind."

I stood up and switched on the light so she could see the truth of the river on my face before I spoke. "This is what I remember. No matter who she was or what they said was wrong with her, I loved her like she was . . . my own self, Zaidie. Does that make any sense?"

"More sense than anything you'll read in the file. If you want to know why I didn't tell you, that's why. You already knew the only thing that mattered."

After that, we cried for a while. At first about Mau Mau and then about all the other people we'd lost. When we washed our faces and turned out the light, it was as if they were all streaming past us in the dark. I held Zaidie's hand like I used to, the jade elephant between us like all our unanswerable questions, and we slept until the morning could no longer be kept back. A new day that demanded we get up and live it.

TWO DAYS LATER, at breakfast, Zaidie waited till Ma left the room, and then—real nonchalant, as if this was an everyday occurrence, she asked Dad if she could borrow the car. I wasn't sure who was more shocked—Dad or me.

Eyes wide, he set down his coffee cup. "My car? Today?"

"Yup. Agnes and I have to go somewhere."

"We do?" I said. "But Coach Lois . . ."

"You spend your life at the pool, Agnes. You can afford to miss one practice."

Dad mumbled a few words about talking to your mother before he moved on to *absolutely not*. And how the hell would he get to work? But then he looked across the table at the daughter who had never made such a request before and glanced up at the clock. He clambered to his feet. "Well, no dawdlin' then. You need to get me to the garage by eight sharp, and no hot-roddin' around, either."

Hot-rodding? Zaidie? The two of us tittered, and even Dad almost laughed.

After we dropped him off, we stopped at the N. P. to pick up a couple of colas. It was already so hot that the profusion of pink petunias Joe Jr. had planted out front wilted five minutes after he watered them.

Mr. O'Connor cocked his head in the direction of the Buick parked askew outside the window. "Since when did Louie let you kids use the car?"

Zaidie counted out the change from her purse. "His way of saying he's going to miss me, I guess. I'm leaving for California in two weeks, you know."

Joe Jr. seemed to appear from nowhere. "Eleven days," he said, consulting his watch, as if he was expecting it to tell him the exact number of hours. "Eleven days till Zaida gets on a plane for college, six till Agnes flies off to swim in the nationals. Mrs. Moscatelli told me yesterday. Imagine."

He even had Ma's inflection down.

"So you going to tell me where we're going?" I asked once we were back in the car.

Zaidie put on her sunglasses and smiled. "Nope."

She kept driving until we reached the edge of town, out past the Egg Auction where she'd been traumatized for life by a row of chickens on a conveyer belt headed for decapitation. She came to a jolting stop in front of the iron gates of a cemetery.

"Sorry. It came up on me faster than I expected."

"A graveyard? The first time in history Dad lets one of us use the car and this is where you take me?"

She was already on the sidewalk, opening the gate. Driven by something I couldn't see, she moved purposefully through the field of stones while I trailed behind, reading the markers. I recognized the family names of several classmates.

Despite the drought, it was lush and green, and tucked beneath a canopy of pines, noticeably cooler. "Nicest spot in town on a day like this. Too bad the, um, residents can't appreciate it," I said. When she stopped before a small flat stone in the back corner, however, we were reduced to hushed silence.

SYLVIE MENDELSON FINN
October 2, 1926–March 14, 1957

Now it was my turn to take her hand. "Oh, Zaidie . . ." And then a moment later, "How did you find her?"

"There's only one Jewish cemetery in town. And once I walked through the gate, I remembered so much—like you when you heard about Maud-Marie."

"But when? And why didn't you tell me?"

"It was after Jon left. That terrible time when—what did you say about watching your sister scream? You realized there was nothing you could do to help her anymore. Nothing you could do to help each other. I suppose it was true for all of us."

I stared down at the stone. "So you came here and told her."

"Sometimes, yeah, I did. And you know, there were days— ordinary afternoons like this one—when it really seemed like she heard me. But mostly, I just sat here and wrote to Jon. I tried different spots, but my best letters, my truest ones, always came from here. It was almost as if they were from both of us—our mother and me."

"Wait a minute. You've been writing—to Jon? My God, Zaidie, how long?"

She looked up from her mother's name. "Every day since he left. Never missed a one."

"And did he—"

A long moment passed before she answered my unfinished question with a quick shake of the head. "No, he never wrote back. For all

I know, he burns the letters soon as they arrive. Or Michael Finn just throws them away. But I keep writing—day after day and year after year. At this point, it isn't only for him. It's for me, too."

Wordlessly, we began to clean off the stone, to pull the dead leaves from a limp geranium that had been left there.

"You know, sometimes I try to imagine him at thirteen," I finally said. "But I keep picturing the little kid—that crooked run he had."

Though I was talking about Jon, I was also thinking of Maud-Marie.

"Someday you'll find her again," Zaidie said, responding like she often did, to words I hadn't said. "Then you'll learn the truth about what really happened to her."

"You really think so?"

She nodded. "And you know what else? Someday, when we're done with growing up, we'll get on a plane or a bus—or hell, we'll just walk to Colorado if that's what it takes. But we will be with Jon again."

She stood up and brushed the dirt from her clothes. Then, staring down at the finality of the dates on the stone, she said, "There's only one thing that could stop us."

CHAPTER TWENTY

Migration

DAHLIA

S O NOW WE'RE RUNNING SOME KINDA HOME FOR UNWED MOTHERS? Is that what we're doing here, Louie?"

We were lying in the dark, him on the edge of sleep, me stewing. Jane had been camped in Jimmy's room for more than a week, that hulking bag of hers resting deep in the closet—with no sign of leaving. *Ever*, I liked to emphasize when Louie and I argued about it.

"The kid'll be ten . . . twenty . . . dropping off his own pregnant girlfriend. For heaven's sake, Lou, where do we draw the line?" Louie walked away every time—except the once.

"Sometimes there is no line, Dahlia. Isn't that what you been telling me all these years?"

Dear God. There was nothing more aggravating than when he quoted me back to myself. I was about to say so when he sauntered off again.

In bed, however, there was no escape but into himself. He burrowed deep into the blankets.

"I don't mind helping out, but she's been here ten days now."

That didn't get a rise out of him, so I went on, speaking louder. "I'm sorry, Lou, but she's no relation to us. It's about time her own family—"

"And the rest of them are relations?" he said, seizing on one line and ignoring the heart of it.

"Jimmy and the girls were little when they came. And we decided to take them in; we asked for it. This one—"

"This one's carryin' Jimmy's kid. You think I'm gonna sit back and watch him end up with someone like the Deans or the one who left Agnes laying in her crib for a year?" Though it was dark, I could feel the energy of his hand slicing through the air. "Over my dead body."

In the past, I'd been the one to navigate Louie's grunts and growls as I argued to let a child stay, or to make room for just one more. I put my hand on his and listened to his breathing until it grew steady again.

"And you think I haven't considered all that? It's just . . . Jimmy's gonna be away so darn long. Once Jane gets her figure back . . . well, you know what's gonna happen."

"And the baby?"

"There's plenty of help available from the state if she applies."

"But the girl loves Jimmy. She says—"

"I know what she says, and right now she means it. But six years, Lou. Think of it. She'll be bringin' boyfriends here next—to Jimmy's room. I guess that's fine with you, though . . ."

Again, I butted up against his rocky silence. So he was going to make me confess everything, was he? Well, so be it.

"It was bad enough when they came for Jon, but after everything with Jimmy—I just don't have it in me, Lou. Getting attached only to . . ."

This time he was so quiet I was sure he was asleep. It wasn't till I turned away and started to drift off myself that he spoke.

"You know, Dahlia, every day I hear you braggin' about all the places you been. How nothin' stops you—not when someone slows a car to yell at you. Nothin'. Even when that kid pinged you in the back with his slingshot, you kept goin'. A fella would think you weren't scared of anything. But inside—" He took an audible inhalation. "—Inside, you're more chicken than ever."

I bolted up straight in bed. "Louis J. Moscatelli, are you calling me a coward?"

"You'll have to answer that one for yourself."

Again, he turned his back, and in less than a minute I heard the low rhythm of his snore.

If that wasn't just like him.

While he slept on, I spent half the night trying to figure out where Jane would go if we kicked her out, the other half worrying how Jimmy would take it all. Meanwhile, what in the world would happen to the poor creature growing inside her belly in the next room? The one she planned to name James. "Not Jimmy, either, I want my boy to be called by his proper name," she stipulated every time.

Sometimes, when she said it, I peered out the window, almost seeing the ghost of that two-year-old turning somersaults in the backyard.

"I don't have it in me, Lou," I repeated in the dark. "Do you understand? I don't have it in me." The same words he'd said to me the last time I'd taken to my bed. He snored louder.

And for all my thinking and analyzing and fretting, what did I come up with in the morning? Nothing but a thumping headache— same as always.

Louie shook his head when he saw me reaching for my Anacin. "Someday you'll learn. What's that thing Agnes's coach says? Don't anticipate; participate."

"So now you're quoting happy jargon from a coach? You of all people?" I stormed away, still nattering to myself. "What next, Louie? Norman Vincent Peale at the breakfast table?"

He almost smiled, but not quite. "Might not be a bad idea." Then he grabbed his lunch pail and left me in my stew.

If that wasn't just like him.

IT WAS WARM and breezy the night before Agnes flew out to Wisconsin for the nationals. Louie was trudging up to bed when she called us out to look at the sky. Jane claimed to be under the weather, which meant she planned to spend the next hour or two in her room bawling. And none too quietly, either.

But on this particular night, the rest of us felt as if we had to honor Agnes's wishes, however silly they felt. We filed out, even Louie, grumbling about the long day as he went.

"Have you ever seen it so bright?" Agnes said, opening her arms wide as if to pull the sky into herself. "I didn't want you to miss it."

"They're stars, Agnes," Louie sighed—sounding more like himself than he had in the last few days. "We've all seen 'em before." He started for the house.

"No, look—she's right, Lou." I put my hand on his arm. "It's almost like that puzzle I did a while ago. What was the fella's name?"

In the light of the moon, I saw Zaidie roll her eyes. "Van Gogh, Ma. Vincent van Gogh. You've done a few of his. I got you a book from the library about him and everything, remember?"

In the past, I might have taken offense at her tone, but not that night. She was eighteen and about to leave everything she knew, and mixed with the excitement, I could tell she was as scared as I was.

"When I was working on that puzzle, I thought he was crazy, but now . . . now I see what he saw."

I dragged Louie to the picnic table where we'd never once in all our years picnicked. "You know, we should pick up some hot dogs at the N. P. and have a cookout out here sometime, Lou. I could make up my Jell-O mold and a nice potato salad, maybe invite the neighbors over."

"Don't get crazy, Dahlia," he said. "No matter how far you walk, we'll never be that normal."

The girls would have sniggered, but their eyes were fixed on the sky. I noticed they were holding hands, almost unconsciously, the way they did when they were little.

"You know what it reminds me of?" Agnes asked. "The night Jimmy got out his bat and sent that ball flying over the Guarinos' fence and beyond. He wanted me to know how good it felt to win something—not just for yourself, but for everyone around you. And not just to know, but to feel it." On a night just like this one, I did.

"I tell Coach Lois that was the beginning of it all for me. And you know what she says?"

We all turned to her.

"She says that whenever I'm tired or the competition is too tough, or I just think I can't—especially then—all I have to do is close my eyes and go back to that night. See the ball Jimmy hit for me, soaring for the moon. Hear his yell, and then all of yours."

"Does it work?" Louie asked.

"Every time, Dad. Every single time. And not just when I'm in the pool."

THE NEXT MORNING, the house was more empty than it had ever been. I put on the magenta lipstick I'd bought at Apex Drugs to give me courage, and walked to the five-and-dime. With the money she'd earned at Hanley's, Zaidie had bought most everything she needed for college, but I wanted to give her something from Louie and me. After poking around for a good half hour, all I could find was a plain blue notebook and a nice Paper Mate pen to go with it. Same as I gave her on her eleventh birthday.

On the next block, I found myself peering in the window of Mather's Furniture, and then inexplicably wandering inside. I took in the fancy velvet couches (for heaven's sake, how would you ever get the stains out?) and the new geometric tables and chairs.

Mr. Mather came sidling up behind me like those salespeople types do. "Mod, they call it. Very popular these days."

"Hmph."

Hoping to shake him, I sauntered away till I found myself standing in front of a fine-looking baby crib. It was a lovely off-white color.

The salesman followed. "A real beauty, isn't it? And there's a bureau to match, if you're interested. Are you expecting, Mrs.——"

"Moscatelli—and heavens, no. I'm an old woman, sir. Forty-six last month."

"It wouldn't be the first time I've had a lady around that age shopping for her nursery," he began before the name registered.

By the look of him, he'd heard about me or my kids. But keeping his eye on a potential sale, he quickly brought his face back to neutral. "We have a layaway plan, Mrs. Moscatelli, if you're purchasing a gift for someone you know."

"Not someone I know, Mr. Mather. My grandchild." It was the first time I'd said the word out loud—heck, the first time I'd even thought it. The force of it almost knocked me over.

Apparently, it was visible, too, because poor Mr. Mather forgot about selling me anything as he took my elbow. "All right there, Mrs. Moscatelli? Can I . . . call someone for you? A drink of water, maybe?"

"The heat must've got to me," I said, though the air-conditioning made the place downright chilly. "If it's all right, I'll just have a little sit-down on one of your mod chairs up in the front."

Mr. Mather brought me a glass of water anyway, and since there were no other customers in the store, he took the lime-green chair opposite my screaming yellow one.

"So this is the new style, huh?" I asked when I regained myself. "Hideous, if you ask me."

"Uncomfortable as hell, too," he said, shifting in his seat. The man had a fine set of teeth when he smiled.

It wasn't till I was ready to go that the salesman in him returned. He handed me his card. "If you come back, ask for Artie. I'll give you a good price on that crib."

I stared at the card as if I was seeing much more than his phone number and the store's hours of operation. "I'll talk it over with my husband . . . and the mother . . ."

Then I looked up at him. "A grandchild. Imagine."

Again, he showed me those fine teeth.

On the way home, I turned my thoughts back to the notebook and pen I was carrying in my bag. You could hardly call it a present, but it was all Zaida ever wanted. I'd bought a bow and a card, too. But what could I, who didn't have her gift of words, possibly write inside it? Now that she was leaving, with Agnes to follow soon enough, what could I say to the girls who had come to me like Jimmy, in the fabulous migration of souls, and given me back a world that was dead to me?

AND YET, FOR all my newfound bravery, Louie was right. There was one place I still hadn't dared to go. I still hadn't climbed the precarious fourteen steps to the attic. I still hadn't faced the boxes stacked in the corner, particularly the one full of pictures of the late Dahlia Garrison. The hopeful, yearning fool who had died beneath the golden tree. And beside them, the only thing of Jon's I couldn't bring myself to part with: that damn train. One thing at a time, I told myself.

I went to the kitchen and made me a nice cup of tea while Flufferbell took the chair opposite me. Then I glanced at the clock above the stove: 1:03 p.m. By that time, Agnes would be in the air, flying to the nationals, where, win or lose, she would swim as if her life depended on it. And Zaidie, who had borrowed the car to drive Jane to the prison for the first time, would sit in the parking lot, nervously waiting to see how the visit went. Though they still weren't exactly back together, I was grateful when Charlie Putnam offered to go along for the ride. With any luck, he's taking her hand right about now. Meanwhile, that sniveling mess of a girl Jimmy thinks is the prettiest one on earth is setting her flinty eyes and walking inside to tell him the news about a child he'll hardly see till he's six. And over at Louie's Texaco, the good man who went out every day and did his part to repair what he could breathes in the fumes of his life, picks up his wrench, and continues.

What could I do but put on my shoes, start down the street, and see where the day might lead?

ACKNOWLEDGMENTS

FIFTEEN YEARS AGO, FORTUNE SHINED ON ME WHEN AN AGENT named Alice Tasman called to chat about a novel I'd submitted to her. That conversation, which continues to evolve, changed my life more than once; and sustained me throughout the writing of this book. I am forever grateful for her brilliant comments, honesty, fierce support in all stages of the process—and for coming up with the perfect title.

I felt a similar connection the first time I spoke to my editor, Sara Nelson. Her passion for this story, and especially for these characters, incisive suggestions and edits, and her steadiness have been an anchor in this tumultuous time. I'm immensely grateful to her and to the amazing team at HarperCollins and Harper Perennial who lent their enthusiasm and expertise to this novel, especially Jonathan Burnham, Mary Gaule, Amy Peterson, Lisa Erickson, and Kristin Cipolla.

Friends and family read sections while in progress and offered their support and suggestions. Many thanks to Nellie Kelsch, Jessica Keener, Susan Messer, Virginia Ryan, Stacey Francis, and especially to Lynne Hugo who provided critical encouragement and feedback when I wasn't sure this would ever become a real book.

Though the characters in this novel are fictional, the spirits of many who went before stealthily worked their way into these pages. To my parents and grandparents, Emma Francis, Pat Francis, Kaeli Conley, Joan Keiran, Susan Kianski, Nancy Larkin, and Jake Mysliwiec, your joy, your resilience, your deep love for others and for this world continues to inspire me.

And finally to my family, Gabe and Nicola, Josh and Stacey, Nellie and Steve, Jake, Lexi, Hank, Will, Jude, Sebastian, Cora, Hope, and especially to Ted, the husband who is both my first reader and my greatest supporter, all my love and gratitude.

ABOUT THE AUTHOR

PATRY FRANCIS is the author of *The Orphans of Race Point*, *The Liar's Diary*, and the blog "100 Days of Discipline for Writers." Her poetry and short stories have appeared in the *Tampa Review*, *Antioch Review*, *Colorado Review*, *Ontario Review*, and *American Poetry Review*, among other publications. She is a three-time nominee for the Pushcart Prize and has twice been the recipient of the Mass Cultural Council Grant. She lives in Massachusetts.